Sweeter Than Life

A NOVEL BY LAKEISHA LAKAY

Sweeter Than Life
© 2023 by LaKeisha LaKay
All rights reserved

ISBN: 978-1-7371723-0-7
ISBN: 978-1-7371723-1-4

Library of Congress Registration Number: 1-12662254831 [Case Number]

Printed in the United States of America

I GIVE THANKS...

To God for my many gifts. Without a doubt, my ability to create comes from the Almighty Creator;

To the host of family and friends who encouraged this project to its end, particularly my parents who are the first champions of my dreams; and my inspiring four siblings (Clayton, Evelyn, Janay, and Natalie). Thank you for always lending your ears to my stories—no matter how farfetched they are;

To my dedicated primary readers: Natalie Jones, Corin Winn, and Nadir Abdulhaqq. I greatly appreciate you for your time, patience, and assistance in the development of this manuscript;

To my wonderful editor, Celeste Gantt. You were and will forever be more than my high school English teacher. You truly are the epitome of an educator who invests tirelessly into the future; and

To you who have supported my endeavor with the purchase of this book.

None of this would be possible without the community of love that surrounds me.

I thank you; I love you...

DEDICATED

To all those who give until they are empty...

Revenge is sweeter than life itself. So thinks a fool.   ~Juvenal

PROLOGUE

The final plunge into her warmth filled her body with his seed. In an unhurried pace, he had given her all that he had and his body began to quake by the intensity of his orgasm.

"…I love you," he breathlessly panted on her lips.

"I love you, too," she responded in an equivalent whisper.

Though she fought hard to control her emotions, tears had formed in the corners of her eyes.

"…And…and I am going to miss you," she nervously added.

He huffed in disappointed frustration. It was his hope that their shared moment of unbridled passion would have mitigated her feelings of abandonment.

"Alex, please…Please don't do this," he beseeched.

Ignoring the water's journey to her hairline, Alexandre contritely professed, "I'm sorry…I'm…I'm just so afraid, Lance."

Lance slowly left his wife's body and dismounted her. He then gathered her in his arms in a genuine show of empathy. "I know you're afraid, Alex."

"I'm not just afraid, Lance. I'm pregnant...This time I am pregnant."

He lowered his hand to the slight swell of her womb and kissed her temple. "I know, Alex. You're not telling me anything I don't already know. But we've discussed this several times already. Everything is going to be fine—you're going to be fine, and you've got to believe that."

"It's hard to believe when-"

"Please try," Lance tersely beseeched as the hour did not allow them the opportunity to discuss again her many misgivings.

Caressing her firm protrusion, he delicately admonished, "Remember what the doctor said: 'Anxiety is not good for you or the baby.' So, please, Alex. Please try."

Alexandre deeply respired and conceded on that position. She then placed a warm hand on the one he rested on the life within her while she pondered her other trepidations. Carefully introducing into the conversation, Alexandre reminded Lance, "You're going to miss the final trimester."

"...I know," he uttered to first, respond to her observation and, second, acknowledge the various experiences of their first child that he was opting to forgo.

"And his birth."

Lance filled his lungs with air and breathed in reply, "...I know, Alex."

"And my graduation," she relentlessly stressed.

Vexed by all that she was steadfast in belaboring, Lance exhaled aloud in an effort to contain his irritation. "It's just a year, Alexandre."

"You say that, but-"

He placed his fingers below her chin and lifted her mouth to his. Touching her full lips, he repeated in a forceful murmur, "It's just a year."

Alexandre curtly moved his hand from her face, perturbed by his second interruption and the apathetic dismissal of her concerns. As she turned her back to him, she reminisced on their past three years as a newly wedded, military family. Truthfully, Alexandre did not regret her decision to marry into this life. She loved Lance and understood that love suffers long. However, she wholeheartedly believed that her myriad sacrifices and feelings of isolation were far more than she bargained for. All that she was expected to amiably tolerate was now becoming increasingly intolerable.

Struggling to suppress her discontentment, Alexandre wiped her eyes dry while she contemplated the culprit of her unhappiness. Without a doubt, she blamed her husband for each misrepresentation he proffered, but, indisputably, she faulted herself more for accepting each of those offerings.

After Alexandre adjusted the pillow beneath her head, she crossly retorted, "It's never just anything with the Marine Corps, Lance, and you know it."

In lieu of an immediate response, Lance gently stroked the almond-colored skin on her neck and back. He was determined not to have their final conversation prior to his deployment be an argument. He needed the assurance that everything was copacetic between them and, despite the fact that they spent more time apart than together, Lance knew Alexandre needed it too.

Alexandre slowly closed her eyes when his warm fingertips moved to the muscles in her shoulder. During their brief moments of togetherness that the years permitted them, Lance had quickly learned her body. She was a sensual woman who enjoyed immensely when he spoke her primary love language—physical touch.

Breathing deeply, she reveled in the loving caress of where she carried most of her stress. To reduce her tension more, Alexandre fingered and then gradually raced the diamond heart pendant along the silver chain around her neck. While she began to reflect on the wedding night in which Lance gifted her the symbol of his gratefulness, she engaged in the square breathing technique that her therapist taught her—inhale four seconds, hold four seconds, exhale four seconds, hold four seconds. Repeat.

Lance nudged her dark tresses to the side, kissed the nape of her neck and then her bare shoulder. "…Feel better?"

Alexandre provided no answer. Instead, she rotated to face him and pleaded, "Promise me that this deployment is the last one— that you won't volunteer for another."

Exasperated, Lance breathed audibly, threw back all that covered his nakedness, and began his descent from their bed. Prior to standing, he seized a moment to sit on the edge of the mattress and considered all that she had articulated.

With his back towards her, Lance organized his thoughts and then finally questioned, "...Are we really having this conversation again, Alexandre? Now, of all times?"

"Yes," Alexandre vehemently answered, refusing to be guilted into conceding on the matters that troubled her heart.

While she rose to a seated position, she held the sheet close to her breasts. Despite three years of marriage, she still remained bashful in the presence of the only man to see her nude.

"...I can't believe we are having this conversation again," Lance bemoaned into the palms of the hands that covered his face. He stated nothing more in hopes that his young wife would show him mercy.

"Yes, we are," Alexandre flippantly remarked as she watched while Lance attempted to, no avail, wipe the frustration from his visage.

In most circumstances, Alexandre's heart would be moved by his grief and she would relent for the sake of peace in their home as well as solidarity in their marriage. However, due to her self-proclamation as the victim in that moment, Alexandre possessed neither sympathy for his response to the anxiety she caused him nor remorse.

Obstinately, she expounded, "Because I am not convinced that you fully understand how your decisions impact me."

Lance abruptly looked over his shoulder at her. "Impact you?"

"Yes, impact me because *nothing* in our marriage can be decided without you first conferring with the Marine Corps."

"Alexan-"

"AND," she spoke over him, "every time you put that uniform on and walk out that door I am on pins and needles until you return. Not to mention, that, this time, I am now being left to assume everything on my own when we *both* planned to start a family after your last deployment—right before I took the California bar."

He pivoted more to glare into her light brown eyes and fervently reminded her, "That was your plan, Alex."

"It was a plan," she rejoined, refusing to concede. "A plan that you did not object to—might I add."

Disgusted by her use of his efforts to make her happy against him, Lance turned from her to stand from the mattress.

"Sorry," Alexandre hastily stated with a quick grip of his arm that brought him back to his seated position.

"Sorry. I'm so sorry," she contritely murmured, swiftly shifting her posture when she realized that she had pushed too hard.

Alexandre inhaled through her nostrils, exhaled through her pursed lips, and humbly implored, "Please, Lance…All I want—all that I am asking for is your word…Please…please just promise me."

Lance breathed deeply to first calm his rage and then tame his frustration. "…I can't make such a promise…You know that, Alexandre."

"You can if you agree not to re-enlist," she advised.

Alexandre released his arm and moved closer to his warmth. She rested her cheek on his smooth, chocolate back and assured, "Major is quite an accomplishment, Lance. You can forgo another promotion…Please, forgo it and just retire…for me, for us…"

Feeling Alexandre's heat radiating on his skin, Lance contemplated her petition and the sound logic from which it derived. Undeniably, she had forfeited much for the sake of their union as well as his military ambitions. Each compromise that Alexandre had made was always greater than the one prior to it. Lance had not only appreciated her cooperation but, more importantly, he loved her and the life they were forging together.

Unfortunately, however, Lance appreciated and loved his career also. It was one that Lance aspired to gain since his youth and, with tunnel-vision, he remained affixed to the pathway to his goal. Every decision he had made and each opportunity he had seized were strategic efforts to achieve his overarching objective— to become a 4-star general.

That was until his chance encounter with Alexandre redesigned the blueprint he meticulously prepared for his life. Their meeting occurred during the inception of his final year in graduate school. Although she was six years his junior, her intellect, confidence, and maturity were immediate attractions for him. To add, Alexandre's very essence heightened more his drive and determination. All that she believed in and stood for were the constant convictions Lance needed in his life and desired in a partner.

While he continued to meditate on their eight-year history, Lance's heart grew heavy. He had, once again, found himself torn asunder by his two greatest passions: the Marine Corps and his wife. Like competing adversaries, they both vied for his time, attention, and allegiance; and, more often than he would ever verbally acknowledge, there were multiple occurrences in which neither of them received his full commitment.

Nonetheless, despite the pull on each side of him, Lance had managed to achieve much in the Marine Corps while courting, loving, and marrying sooner than his life-plan dictated. While Alexandre worked to complete her undergraduate and law school studies, he doggedly sought occasions to advance his career and hasten his military accomplishments. Regrettably, all that he had completed pale in comparison to what he still yet wanted to achieve—no matter the cost.

It was in that moment of self-centered reflection did Lance shamefully realize his egotistical desire to obtain more accolades, even at the detriment of Alexandre's and his union.

With a broken spirit, Lance finally inquired, "…And do what, Alexandre?"

Silence lingered in the bedroom as he awaited her response. In his staying, Lance remembered his forthcomingness during his marriage proposal to her. It was presented at the conclusion of Alexandre's senior year in college. He had pledged his commitment to her, but also expressed his steadfast commitment to his dreams. With the ring he proffered, he had implored that she stood with him in his commitments.

"…I don't know," Alexandre at last murmured in defeat. Lance's question had befuddled her as it gradually unveiled the realization of her request—she was demanding that he relinquish his identity without suggesting a fitting alternative. "…Anything, I suppose… You're so talented, Lance, and you are so much more than a conveyor of intelligence…You can literally do anything…"

She allowed herself a moment to quash the growing feelings of selfishness before reiterating, "I'm just asking that you chose something that will allow you to be at home...with your family...Please..."

Lance respired out loud at Alexandre's misspoken statement concerning his capabilities. She had afforded far too much credit to the talents that only aligned with the sole career he ever desired. Unequivocally, Lance was a loyal Marine—a faithful member of the few and the proud. He had proved, and still yearned to prove, his career dedication. For this reason, Lance could not be the husband, or the father, or the family that Alexandre needed—he could not be the suitable persona she was entreating for.

Though it pained him to recognize that he was failing her, Lance reasoned that the long-term success was undoubtedly worth the short-term tradeoff. So, he stifled the emerging thoughts of failure and replied, "Being a Marine is all I ever wanted to be; all I have ever studied and trained for; and all I have ever done. I can't do anything else, Alex." He twisted his body to face her and affirmed, "And, truthfully, I don't want to."

At the sight of her devasting heartbreak, Lance lowered his lids over his eyes and began to marginally regret the words he uttered immediately after they escaped his lips. Despite the fact that he had honestly articulated all that he felt, Lance realized that his delivery could have been more delicate had he employed a different tone. Unfortunately, he was too prideful to admit his wrongdoing, too selfish to acknowledge the strain each deployment had on their marriage, and overly stubborn to apologize for the stress that a Marine Corps life caused his young wife.

More committed to the military oath of office than his marital vows, Lance rose from their bed to shower and dress prior to the arrival of his ride-share.

Alexandre subdued the urge to release a solemn cry as her fragmented heart ached at the resounding words of Lance's confession. In that moment of her despair, she began to recollect the many sacrifices she made to place him first among her priorities. Reflecting on her innumerable concessions pained Alexandre immensely because she now knew with absolute certainty what was first among Lance's priorities.

Her misty eyes watched as each stride of her muscular husband grew the distance between them. While his steps only took him to the next room, Alexandre felt in her spirit that they were leading him to a war that would take him from her forever. The unsettling feeling in her abdomen was caused by the belief that Lance's dedication to his true love tempted fate far too many times. Year after year, his leadership role in the Marine Corps and various displays of risky altruism had created an insurmountable debt with death. It was a debt in which Alexandre was certain that was due and payable.

"…Good-bye, Lance," Alexandre whispered. She then rested her head on his pillow and quietly wept herself to sleep.

*** *ONE* ***

Thirteen Years Later

"But, Your Honor-"

"My decision is final, counselor," Alexandre forcefully interjected no longer interested in anything he had to offer. "The child is to remain among the juvenile justice system and I will preside over the matter myself."

The attorney breathed in exasperation and defiantly continued in an effort to remind her, "Your Honor, the child has not been responsive to any of the programs afforded by the juvenile justice system. That is why the state is recommending-"

"I am aware of the state's recommendation, Mr. Jackson. But my decision is final and your petition is still denied."

"So what? We forever continue this game of catch-and-release?" He hotly inquired in a tone that implied that his ask was more of a statement than a question.

Alexandre abruptly removed her reading glasses from her face as she challenged the attorney to repeat his assertion, "Pardon?"

The fear of being cited for contempt of court compelled him to hold his peace. He kept her gaze as a show of respect and contrition, but loosened the tight knot of his silk necktie in an effort to display his discomfort and concession.

"...Counselor," Alexandre began as an introduction to her protracted castigation, "you may be of the opinion that law enforcement tirelessly catches criminals and court officials, like myself, recklessly releases them back into society. But I can assure you that that is not the case because I do not take for granted the decisions I make from this bench. I am aware of the varying impact my decisions have on multiple lives. However, the impact that I am most concerned about is that of the children that come before me every day." Narrowing her eyes, Alexandre finally spoke with conviction, "Therefore, the work that I do is far more involved than what you could ever fathom. In fact, I would venture to say that it is far more involved than the work that you do."

A pregnant silence grew in the courtroom as Alexandre allowed the stillness to calm her irritation. After watching the attorney lower his head, she respired deeply, returned the lenses to her face, and glanced at the document before her. She then shifted her glare to scrutinize the young, Hispanic male who was only a year older than her own son. Looking beyond the suit two sizes too large that engulfed him, she saw a child broken, dejected, and afraid. A child whose true crime was succumbing to the tragic social and economic circumstances in which he was born.

When their eyes met, Alexandre knew that allotting time for his hearing prior to her sabbatical was the right decision. More often than not, the best verdict is rendered when the judge and the judged meet in-person. Without a doubt, Julio Hernandez was a habitual miscreant—one who society expediently labeled a menace. However, his lawlessness was more farcical than criminal. For this reason, Alexandre was compelled to see him in the flesh. She needed to determine his truthfulness for herself and it could only be ascertained by peering through the windows to his soul.

As he contritely dropped his gaze, Alexandre considered the earlier guidance proffered by psychology experts. Based on their testimonies, the development of the prefrontal cortex will not be complete until the age 25. Until then, many adolescents will struggle with impulse control, resulting in the engagement in several reckless antisocial behaviors regardless of the repercussions.

Exhaling audibly, Alexandre concluded that the child before her was pleading for help. She removed her reading glasses from her face once more and closed the case file as she contemplated how best to react to the juvenile's petition. At that moment, Alexandre was not certain of how to adequately respond, but she was certain that whatever Julio Hernandez was in need of he was not going to receive among the adult justice system.

"Let's reconvene in two weeks," Alexandre finally spoke, ending the silence in the courtroom. She darted her eyes between the parties on both sides of the aisle and added, "That is more than enough time to obtain additional testimonies from the experts." She then extended the case file to her bailiff who then gifted it to the law clerk, and struck the block with her gavel. Following, the courtroom immediately filled with commotion.

"Judge Denton."

"Not now, Cynthia," Alexandre responded to the law clerk on her heels as she walked to her chambers. "I have a flight to Aruba to catch in a few hours."

"Yes, I know," Cynthia spoke. "…The wedding."

"Yes, the wedding—MY wedding."

Alexandre removed her black robe and hung it in her closet. As she walked to her desk, she noticed a beautiful assortment of tulips in a crystal vase.

"Wow!" Cynthia breathlessly uttered, tucking a lock of blond hair behind her ear.

"Wow, indeed," Alexandre lowly restated. Immediately, her heart raced at the same pace of her growing anxiety. In the prior weeks, she had received a number of unfavorable gestures. The thought of unveiling another spiteful threat—this time in the presence of her law clerk—compounded her worries.

Suppressing her angst and vexation, Alexandre carefully removed the folded card from the plastic floral pick in the center of the colorful arrangement. After she opened it, Alexandre silently read the inscription:

Congratulations on your nuptials. May you be blessed with all of the passion your hand can capture, love your heart can cage, and joy your soul can contain.

"Who are they from?" Asked Cynthia, interrupting the pregnant silence that grew with her suspense.

Alexandre shrugged, rotating the card in search of a name. "…I don't know; the card doesn't say."

"Well, whoever the sender is, they must know you well to send you tulips."

"I agree wholeheartedly," Alexandre murmured as she recalled the last time she received such a gift. They were given as a token of appreciation from-

A hard knock on her chambers' door interrupted her voyage down memory lane.

"It's open," Alexandre called out.

"Alexandre Kaniece Denton," a deep male voice greeted.

Alexandre's lips stretched in a wide grin when the man eleven years her junior entered the room. "You're early."

"Yes, to ensure you are on time," Jacob explained. He then acknowledged with a nod the slim law clerk who wore a white sheath dress and black blazer. Following, he saluted, "Ms. Sackie."

"Mr. Hall," Cynthia responded quickly, dropping her green eyes as her pale skin flushed. While she struggled to regain her composure, she hoped that he did not detect her admiration of his handsome, brown, 6'2 physique in his grey tailored suit. "Congratulations, again."

"Thank you," Jacob responded. He returned his eyes to his bride-to-be and held her soft gaze.

Feeling now out of place by the romance in the atmosphere, Cynthia cleared her throat and confirmed, "I will see you in two weeks, Your Honor." She then excused herself from the room and closed the door behind her.

Jacob walked to Alexandre and properly greeted her with a kiss. "Are you ready, Mrs. Denton-Hall?"

Alexandre reveled at the ring of the new surname that will honor both her late husband and future groom. She pecked his lips once more before answering, "almost," and walked behind her desk.

Taking notice of the floral display, Jacob fingered the expensive vase and spoke, "Nice flowers. A gift from Leah?"

Alexandre pondered the thoughtful character of her assistant and concluded that a gesture from her would never arrive unidentified.

"No," she merely responded with hopes that it satisfied his curiosity. A continuous probe would ultimately disclose the various acts of verbal abuse that she concealed from him.

"Cynthia?"

"No. The sender is nameless…Are you sure they're not from you?"

Jacob contorted his face. "Why would I send you tulips? They're not your favorite."

She chuckled and reminded him, "You know me well enough to know that I don't have a favorite anything, Jacob."

He grinned at her idiosyncrasy. It was one of many that he had learned as he became more acquainted with her during the past three years. Winking his eye, he conceded, "You're right."

Alexandre blushed at the adoration that compelled her to elucidate, "Buuuut, as ironic as it may appear to be, tulips are one of my few obsessions."

Jacob thought for a moment then merely replied, "okay," to acknowledge the new fact that he had just come to know of his betrothed. His horrific past experiences with gifting her anything that pollenated led him to believe that her allergies made her sensitive to all flowers, including those that were hypoallergenic.

Forsaking the thoughts of his prior blunders, he observed Alexandre while she retrieved her designer handbag and briefcase. After she placed them on her desk, she began to mutter inaudibly to herself as she commenced her frantic search for something.

"What are you looking for?" Jacob finally inquired.

"…What I am looking for…are…my…keys."

"Your keys," Jacob began, stepping closer to her desk, "are right here." He pulled them from under a stack of red expanding files and held them out to her.

Alexandre bashfully smirked and expressed her gratitude while she received the keys and placed them in her handbag.

"You really do have to stop losing your keys like this, Alex."

"I didn't lose them, Jacob. I merely misplaced them."

Jacob turned his eyes upward at her semantic reference. Just as much as he loved her, he loathed, to the same degree, her inclination to be cavalier. "Well, your misplaced keys are going to end up in the wrong hands one day."

"You mean hands like yours?" She quipped.

Desiring her to take his concern seriously, Jacob stifled his laughter at her jest. "Worse than mine."

With no interest in heeding his warning, Alexandre hastily shoved her laptop and files in her briefcase and diverted the conversation. "Jaamyas packed and ready to go?" She inquired of her soon-to-be thirteen-year-old son.

"Yes, and he is downstairs in the car, patiently awaiting Round 2 with the city of Charlotte's traffic," Jacob confirmed.

"...Perfect," she absentmindedly responded.

Jacob puffed at her comment and the way in which the packing of her briefcase distracted her.

"What are you doing, Alex?" He asked after he placed a hand on the leather bag.

Alexandre looked up from her task and replied, "Just a few things to-"

He shook his head in dissent. "You promised."

"Jacob, it's just a-"

"I do not want to start our union with a broken vow," he firmly protested.

Alexandre was taken aback by the heightened seriousness she saw in his eyes. He indeed was mature beyond his thirty years. "You're right."

"I don't want to be right, Alex—just heard."

"Okay." Alexandre gently rested her hand on his. "I hear you, Mr. Hall."

"Good." He grabbed her hand, led her from behind her desk, and pulled her into him. In her heels, she was four inches above the average height of a woman. "Now, let's go get married. I've been looking forward to our wedding night from the moment you accepted my proposal."

Alexandre smiled at the innuendo and wrapped her arms around his neck. "It's been thirteen years. Are you sure you are ready for me?" She spoke, first, to remind him of her chastity; then, to forewarn him of her enthusiastic yearnings.

Jacob impishly grinned as he hugged her slender waist. The firmness of her forty-one-year-old body never ceased to amaze him. "If I am not, then I will learn to be."

*** *** ***

"Good morning, Your Honor, and welcome back," Cynthia greeted, entering the chambers after a single knock on the door. "I have some bad-"

Without looking up from her desk, Alexandre held up her hand to halt the law clerk's impending barrage of distressing updates. "Not now, Cynthia. I am reviewing materials for a status call I have in 45 minutes."

"But, Your Honor, I prepared a memo for you concerning the Johnson matter so you would not have to do that."

"Yes, I know and I thank you." Alexandre looked up from the documents and spoke, "But, as I am sure Tynisha had informed you prior to her departure, your summaries do not preclude me from my own in-depth review."

Cynthia inhaled deeply and exhaled slowly as she stretched her lips into a bogus smile. Fairly new in her role as Alexandre's law clerk, she had much to learn concerning how the Honorable Judge Denton-Hall preferred to manage her cases and direct her courtroom.

"You're welcome," Cynthia finally spoke prior to exiting her chambers so that Alexandre could continue her preparation without interruption.

Twenty minutes later, the phone on her desk disrupted the silence in the room with its soft ring. Alexandre pushed her reading glasses to the top of her head, retrieved the headpiece, and announced, "Denton-Hall."

"Hey, Mom, it's me," Jaamyas greeted.

Alexandre glanced at her wristwatch. "Hey, son. You made it to the youth center?"

"No, not yet. Jacob is going to drop me off en route to the office. He is going in late today."

"Oh okay." She pulled her glasses back down to her face and began to flip through the pages of a police report. "Well, what is it, baby? Mommy has a meeting in few minutes."

"Can—MAY," he reflexively corrected, knowing his mother's penchant for proper English, "I go to Stephen's tonight for dinner?"

"No," she simply responded.

"Why not?" He whined in disappointment.

"Because it's during the week."

"Moooom, we are on summer break."

"I am aware of that, Jaamyas, but you still have camp."

"Mom, please. Jacob already said that I could, he just said to confirm with you."

Alexandre removed her glasses from her face and rolled her eyes. She loathed feeling like the villain when it came to raising her child—first with her parents and, now, with her new husband.

"Well, Jacob is not your parent—I am," Alexandre ardently clarified.

When the phone fell silent, Alexandre immediately regretted the words that slipped through her lips. She exhaled with remorse and spoke, "I'm so sorry, Jay. I...I didn't mean that. You know I didn't mean that."

"Whatever, Mom."

"...Look, there isn't much on the docket today. So, I plan to be home early; and, when I do, I want to see my son's handsome face." She paused for a moment to allow her request to resonate with him. "May I have that? May a mother, who has not spent any time with her son in ten days, have that?"

Jaamyas turned his eyes upward at her petition. Now that he was more knowledgeable of the inner-workings of her profession, Jaamyas was convinced that his mother was beyond the bounds of an overbearing parent. She was a low-hovering helicopter.

"I saw that," Alexandre admonished him.

"You always do," he mumbled, careful not to test the waters with another eye roll.

She smiled. "Have a good day at camp. I will see you when I get home. Love you."

"Love you, too," he begrudgingly recited.

Exhausted from the long day, Alexandre walked through the front door of her two-level house shortly after 9 P.M. "I'm home," she announced as she placed her keys in the glass dish on the cherry wood foyer stand.

"Guys?" She called out while she set her handbag on the stand and lowered her briefcase in the hall closet. "Hello?"

Alexandre walked further into the entryway and the sound of her heels bounced off the high ceilings. "Anyone ho-"

She turned to see Jacob sitting at the black, baby grand piano in the sitting room. Rather than playing, as he typically did to decompress, he was watching the sun make its finally descent behind the horizon.

"Jacob, didn't you hear me? Why didn't you say anything?" She quickly scanned the room for her son. "Where is Jaamyas?"

"In the study working on a report I assigned him," he answered without facing her.

"Oh…okay…How upset is he?"

"He's pretty peeved."

Alexandre breathed aloud. "Okay…And you?...How upset are you?"

"You could have called, Alex, especially since you kept him from dinner at Stephen's because you said you were going to be home early."

Alexandre recalled the prior conversation with her son and guilt overcame her. "So, Jaamyas told you what I had said?"

Jacob pivoted on the piano bench to finally face her. "He didn't have to. While he waited in the kitchen for me to finish prepare his breakfast, he had you on speaker."

"...Damn it," she muttered when she remembered the crass comment she made about his parental rights. "Jacob, I'm so sor-"

"Don't," Jacob interjected in anger.

"Please, Jacob," she beseeched, attempting to expound on her statement despite his request for her to cease speaking. "You have every right to be upset, just allow me the chance to explain why I said what I said."

"I don't care to know why, Alex," he hotly rejoined. "So, don't bother." He rose from the cushioned bench and grabbed the yellow legal envelope he had placed on the lid of the piano.

Alexandre's heart dropped and began to race at the same speed of her mind's thoughts. The endless possibilities of the envelope's contents increasingly distressed her. So, as she always did in moments of despair, she inhaled deeply and held her breath captive in an effort to maintain her composed disposition.

Jacob carefully ripped the seal of the envelope. "I was going to wait until after Jay's birthday, but your stunt today gave me cause to expedite this."

Alexandre avoided his eyes and bravely asked, "What is it?"

Jacob pulled out the stapled document, quickly revealed it to her, and then tossed it and the envelope back on the piano top. "...Adoption papers."

Alexandre exhaled in relief once she determined that Jacob's presentation was not one that was dire. She then met his gaze and confirmed by asking, "...Adoption papers?"

"Jaamyas *is* my son, Alex, and has been since the moment you introduced me to him three years ago." He held her eyes with intense conviction and ordered, "See to it that the state of North Carolina acknowledges him as such." With that, he left her to ponder his demand.

Her trembling hands collected the document and fingered through the pages. As she reviewed the language drafted by Jacob's attorney, Alexandre considered the requisites of a legal adoption. With certainty she knew that garnering Jaamyas's consent to be adopted would be no issue; he adored Jacob and had been longing for a father to call his own since coming to learn of the absence of one. Alexandre, however, had her own reservations and they were attributed to more than one cause—causes that would ultimately preclude her from consenting to a legal adoption.

As she walked to the foyer closet to place the document in the inside pocket of her briefcase, Alexandre made a mental note to discuss with her therapist the uneasiness and guilt she felt in the pit of her stomach. By her own convictions, Alexandre believed that she would be dishonoring her late husband by allowing another man to adopt his son. If for no other reason, the preserving of Lance's legacy warranted the need for professional aid. Alexandre needed help exploring the self-imposed obligation and coping with her deep-seated convictions.

Following the task of securing the document, she ascended the winding steps to the second level of her home and made a stop at Jaamyas's bedroom. Respecting his privacy, she knocked on the closed door.

"Go away, Mom," Jaamyas called out to the familiar rap on his door.

Alexandre defiantly opened his barricade and walked into the room. With the exception of his almond complexion that he inherited from her, Jaamyas resembled his deceased father in looks and stature more each day. "Hey, son…You're in bed early."

Reclined against his headboard, Jaamyas pulled his comforter closer to his chest and adjusted his book on his abdomen. "I have an early day tomorrow; going to the library for books on black architects."

Alexandre lowered herself into the sofa chair next to his bed, and, by habit, adjusted the framed photo on his nightstand. It was the lone picture of his father that remained displayed in their home following their familial transition. Though young, unlettered, and inexperienced, Lance appeared confident and mature in his basic training photo.

"…Oh okay," she finally uttered in response, diverting her eyes from the handsome man in dress blues. "…Is that something new you're interested in? Architecture?"

Jaamyas shrugged. "I don't know. Jacob seems to like it and he is doing really well at his firm."

"I understand, but do you like it? What do you like?"

Though he could feel her gaze burning into him, Jaamyas avoided her eyes. "...Gee, I don't know...Dinner with my mom," he snidely remarked.

The initial sting of his sarcastic comment had succumbed to the anger caused by his tone, but Alexandre released it understanding that he was hurting. She cleared her throat and confessed, "I deserved that." After leaning forward to gain his attention, she asked, "Can you forgive me?"

Jaamyas ignored the question and turned the page of his book. When Alexandre gently closed the paperback and removed it from his hands, he finally looked at her.

"Mooooooom," he groaned, agitated that she lost his position in the book. Worse than boredom of a bad book, he detested losing his place in a good one.

"Mooooooom," she mocked.

Jaamyas puffed hot air and then replied, "Of course I forgive you, Mom. Don't I always?" He reached to regain what belonged to him, but was unsuccessful. She had quickly maneuvered her hand.

Alexandre chuckled. "No, you don't."

"Yes, I do. I do because I am used to coming second to your job." He finally retrieved his book from her and began to shuffle through the pages to locate the familiar paragraph. "I just feel bad for Jacob," he muttered. "...He's the newest member of the family who now has to get used to it."

"Whoa...That was harsh."

He looked at her. "Sometimes reality is harsh."

Alexandre was taken aback by the familiar verse often recited to her in her youth. It was what her mother flippantly spoke to her each time Alexandre expressed her displeasure.

"...You know what? No Papa or Nana's this week; better yet, not until I've had a chance to talk to them about what they are teaching you. You understand me?"

Not awaiting his response, Alexandre continued, "You go to the center, you go to practice, and you come straight home. You got that?"

Jaamyas merely nodded in reply as he turned the page of his book. Now a decade and two years as her son, he was accustomed to the rants in which Alexandre spoke only to make her position known, never for a sincere response. So, he learned and then mastered the art of gesturing so that she believed she had his ear all the while his mind was occupied with another task.

"You're old enough now to be home alone until Jacob or I get in from work. But now that Jacob has moved in, you will not be alone long."

Jaamyas shrugged his shoulders and uttered, "Okay."

"We will teach you how to enable and disable the alarm. Each afternoon you get in, you will enable it, stay indoors, and answer the door for no one. Do I make myself clear?"

Jaamyas clandestinely rolled his eyes, ignored her question, and turned the page of his book. He desperately yearned for her to depart his sanctuary so that he could return to actively reading the contents of his book.

Infuriated by insolence, Alexandre yanked the book from his hands and repeated, "Do I make myself clear?"

He recoiled in astonishment and peered at her with rage—an emotion that he knew he had to quickly extinguish despite that fact that it was she who had not only failed him, but disappointed him again. "…Yes, ma'am," he grumbled in concession.

"Good. Now, good-night." Alexandre rose from her seat, walked to the exit, flipped the light switch, and slammed the door behind her after she left the room.

Alexandre stood outside the door to collect herself and fought the urge to reenter the room at the sound of her son's solemn cries. She knew that Jaamyas had been correct in his surmise of her priorities, but it was still a tough pill to swallow—especially when it was being shoved down her throat by her own child.

After walking down the long hall, Alexandre strode through and closed the double doors of their master bedroom. She immediately exhaled a sigh of relief when she found Jacob sitting in their bed reading a book. He had showered and changed into plaid pajama pants.

"…I thought you would have opted for one of the guest rooms tonight," she confessed, considering their heated exchange moments earlier.

Without looking up from his book, he shared, "I am upset, but not angry enough to leave our marriage bed."

"Want to talk about it?" She asked, walking to his bedside and placed Jaamyas's book on the nightstand.

"Not again tonight, Alex." He turned the page of his book. "Let's table it for another time."

"Fair enough," Alexandre conceded as she closed his book and removed it from his hands. She placed it on top of the other she had set on the nightstand.

"...So, tell me, Mr. Hall, how was your day?" She asked, attempting to assuage his anger as she stepped out of her heels and lifted her pencil skirt.

"Obviously not as long and stressful as yours, Mrs. Denton-Hall," he responded, making way and assisting her with the straddling of his lap.

Alexandre covered his full lips with hers. "That wasn't the question." She dipped her tongue in his mouth and tasted the peppermint of his toothpaste.

Jacob held her hips and sighed as he grew firm beneath her. His fury was no contest for her tantalizing kisses. "...Well, no matter the day I was having before, it is definitely better now."

"Oh really?" Alexandre grinned, dropping her mouth to kiss his neck. She inhaled the fresh scent of his body wash while she ran her hands up his bare, muscular chest.

"Yes, really," he responded when she met his eyes. Jacob kept them as she released him from the button enclosure of pajama pants, pulled her wet panties to the side, and guided him into the warm firmness of her body.

Alexandre smiled triumphantly when Jacob closed his eyes, moaned his pleasure, and gripped her hips tighter. She slowly moved in his lap as her body gradually opened for him.

"Alex," Jacob breathed, forgetting his anger altogether as he pulled her down further onto him then moved her hips to aid her grind. He growled in delight when an erotic chill enveloped his body and curled his toes.

Alexandre pulled him from his lean against the mounted headboard and held him tight against her body. She clawed his back and groaned in ecstasy when he raised his pelvis to thrust deeper into her world. He had penetrated her G-Spot and each stroke of it prompted her to dig her nails further into his flesh. As she nibbled at his shoulder, his neck, and lobe of his ear, Alexandre panted his name in whispers in rhythm with her movement.

Jacob gently tugged at her long and thick, chestnut hair to move her lips from his ear to his mouth—her seductive calls were tempting him to defy the *ladies' first* mantra that he lived by. He dipped his cool tongue in the warmth of her mouth and whined, "Please, Alex…I'm…I'm about to explode."

Alexandre wrapped her arms around his neck and began to ride faster his hard member. Feeling a strong release build in her lower abdomen, she held him tighter as she breathlessly panted. When he gripped her shoulders to pull her down onto his strong thrust, her body quaked with a strong orgasm and she cried out into the room's stillness. In exhaustive relief, Jacob relaxed his control and gave into his own climatic release.

She held her husband close as he lowered his hands to her firm buttocks and aided her movement until the last of him filled her. He then wrapped his arms around her waist and buried his face in her breasts, groaning his satisfaction.

Jacob fell back into the headboard and exhaled in exhaustion. He opened his eyes and looked up at his now glowing wife. "…Feel better?"

Alexandre grinned and nodded. "Thank you."

He sat up, pushed her hair back from her face, and kissed her lips. Jacob then lowered his mouth to her neck, kissed it, and recited his wedding vow, "I'm here to love you, Alex."

Alexandre yelped and then giggled when he flipped her on her back and carefully exited her body. She watched as he slipped his hand under skirt and removed her underwear. He taunted her with a trail of kisses down to her inner thighs before he finally stroked, with his tongue, the folds that made her a woman. Alexandre closed her eyes and sighed as he drank from her fountain until she cried out into the stillness of the room a second time.

*** *** ***

"Honestly, Alex, I don't see the problem," Seanna McCoy commented after serving herself a forkful of kale salad, chewing, and swallowing. "He loves you; you love him; and you both love Jay."

Alexandre rolled her eyes at her friend of thirty-five years and then glanced at her watch to confirm the time left of her lunch break. "Love has nothing to do with it, Sea."

Seanna rolled her eyes in return and huffed. "I'm going to need another drink for this," she announced as she politely lifted her hand at the level of her head to gain the attention of their suited attendant. When he acknowledged her with a nod, Seanna displayed her close to empty wine glass. After he nodded a second time, she returned her gaze to Alexandre and confirmed, "You're paying for all of this—by the way."

Alexandre chuckled and admonished in jest, "Then your sound advice better be worth the trouble."

"Isn't it always?"

Alexandre smiled and shrugged.

"Jacob is a good man, Alex. If he wants to be a father to your son then don't discourage him by not allowing him to adopt him."

"I don't know, Sea. This all seems too rushed to me."

Seanna chuckled at her nonsensical assessment. "It's been three years, Alexandre. I know you; you would not have married him if you didn't believe him to be a good fit as a husband *and* father."

"…Yeah, you're right," Alexandre acknowledged after she pondered what she knew to be true. "I still think it's too soon though," she vacillated. "I mean, the ink is not even dry on our marriage certificate…Anything could happen…"

"Anything like what, Alexandre?"

Alexandre raised her shoulders and responded, "I don't know—anything."

Seanna took a moment to assess the visage of her longtime friend. When she speculated that Alexandre was cleaving to a secret that held her emotionally hostage, she inquired, "…Alex, is everything okay?"

Taken aback by the question, Alexandre returned, "What? Why?"

"Because you're speaking as if you are expecting your marriage to fail."

"No, I'm not; and everything is fine…It's just that *anything* can happen between Jacob and me. So, I just think it prudent that we wait a while before discussing adoption proceedings—at the very least, a year."

Seanna rolled her eyes and groaned. "You and these insufferable timelines…A year, Alexandre? Seriously? Do you know how many women would kill for a man to step up and be a father to their kids?"

When Alexandre failed to respond to her barrage of questions, Seanna added, "Hell, he can adopt my mulatto three."

Alexandre struggled to ignore Seanna's snide epithet. She knew that it derived from a place of racial tension, anger, frustration, and pain. All of which were attributed to her in-laws who were not only Caucasians, but also among the mean-spirited confederates who still subsisted in North Carolina. Despite being a paradox to their Christian faith, their actions, verbal and non-verbal, were a constant reminder of the red stain on the white carpet of America.

After clearing her throat, Alexandre pulled the tail of her French braid from one shoulder to the other as she attempted to push from her mind her three innocent god-children. Like so many others with more melanin in their skin, they were the ones impacted the most by the animosity. With their light toffee hue; bronze loose coils; and deep amber eyes, it was difficult to discern how anyone would deny them to be anything other than beautiful, loveable creatures.

"Sea, I highly doubt that your husband would terminate his parental rights," Alexandre spoke to lighten the air.

Seanna put her glass to her lips and swallowed the last of her wine. "Oh, yeah, I forgot about him." She huffed and murmured with discontent, "So easy to do these days with all of his business travels."

Alexandre shook her head as she mentally noted the conversation that they needed to have another day. "…Look," Alexandre began, redirecting the conversation, "I just believe that Jacob can father Jaamyas without judicial intervention."

Seanna returned her wine glass to the table and fingered the stem. Remembering the primary reason of their lunch meeting, she inhaled deeply then responded, "Of course he can, Alex. But, evidently, that is not good enough for him." She met her companion's eyes and reinforced, "He wants Jay to be *his* son and wants all the rights that come with the responsibility of being his father...I find it hard to believe-"

Their attendant arrived to the table to fill Seanna's glass. When he completed the task, both the women thanked him and watched him step way.

"I find it hard to believe," Seanna continued, "that you cannot comprehend this. You are a brilliant woman and a kick-ass juvenile court judge...So, really, Alexandre, what is this really about?"

Alexandre retrieved the cloth napkin on her lap and placed it next to the plate of uneaten portion of her pasta primavera. She then briefly met Seanna's brown eyes, looked away, exhaled, and finally answered, "Lance." She returned to their gaze and confessed, "A part of me feels that an adoption will obliterate the last of his legacy."

"...I...I knew it...I...fucking...knew it," Seanna responded under her breath as she became torn by the emotional irony. In one facet, she was elated that she had finally coaxed the truth from Alexandre, but, in the other, she was enraged by what the disclosure revealed.

Slowly shaking her head in dismay, Seanna felt her cocoa skin grow red with fury. She had grown both exhausted and furious by the torch Alexandre continued to carry for her late husband. It was a torch that Seanna felt Lance was undeserving. However, to argue her point with Alexandre would be futile because, as the wife of the fallen Marine, she would only vehemently disagree.

While she side-swiped the long bang of her short haircut from her eye, Seanna carefully considered the secret Alexandre had just professed and judiciously contemplated her next words. She placed her own napkin next to her empty plate and finally warned, "Alexandre, you are my best friend and I love you, but I will be damned if I stand by and let you sabotage your future because you are hell-bent on cleaving to your past."

"Seanna-" Alexandre started.

"No, don't Seanna me, Alex. It's been, what?...Thirteen years?"

Alexandre proffered no response.

Seanna huffed at her silence and then continued, "Alex, Lance is gone and he is *not* coming back. I need you to comprehend that...You mourned him; I mourned him; hell, we all mourned him for years. We gave him the proper due owed to a husband, father, friend killed in the line of duty. So, now, do the same for your son by giving him the father he has always yearned for, but never had."

Alexandre watched her friend calm her irritation by downing her white wine as if it was a glass of water. When she placed the empty glass back on the linen covered table, Seanna asked, "What do your parents think?"

"I'm not talking to them right now."

Seanna exhaled loudly as she rolled her eyes. "What have Cheryl and Victor done now?"

Alexandre shrugged and responded, "What they always do—usurp my parental authority."

Seanna chuckled, seizing the opportunity to shift the conversation to a topic that was more lighthearted. "You are their *only* child that has given them *only* one grandchild; and they are retired with nothing else to do. You want to put an end to their unsolicited advice? Give them more grandchildren. They will be so exhausted that they won't be able to synthesize any insults let alone articulate them."

Alexandre laughed at her unsound logic then reminded, "I told you that Jacob and I agreed to wait at least a year. The three of us need time to get acclimated to our new family dynamic...So, we are sticking to the plan."

Seanna turned her eyes upward and sardonically corrected, "You mean *your* plan."

"It's a plan, Seanna."

Seanna disagreed, but, for the sake of peace and time, she relinquished the point. "...How are the two of you?"

"What do you mean?"

"You and Jacob. We haven't really talked since Aruba, and your wedding itinerary really didn't allow much time for just you and me."

Alexandre raised her shoulders, initially uncertain of how to appropriately answer the question. Avoiding Seanna's gaze, she finally responded, "I—we are adjusting…It's only been a few weeks. So, the growing pains that accompany two lives forging into one are to be expected…"

Seanna permitted a moment to pass before responding in hope that Alexandre would elaborate. When she failed to do so, Seanna assuaged the tension in the air with the compliment, "Well, you are glowing. So, even if you have not yet arrived at marital bliss, you are definitely having a lot of great sex."

After meeting her best friend's eyes, Alexandre blushed. "Geeez, Seanna."

"What? As long as you held out, you better be."

"You know that the Christian-"

Seanna rolled her eyes as she interjected, "Yes, I know that the Christian dogmas are important to you, Alex. That is why I am hoping that you are experiencing a torrential downpour now that the drought has been officially declared over—with our good Lord's blessing, of course."

Though Alexandre feebly smiled, she maintained her peace. So, Seanna finally relented on the matter. "Fine, don't answer." She snickered and then affirmed, "You really don't have to though; the answer is in the flush of your skin."

Alexandre turned her eyes upward and huffed at her perceptiveness. In the way that Seanna knew her so well, they could have been sisters from the same womb.

"…So, what about Dr. Shrink-Your-Head?" Seanna asked breaking the brief silence and changing the subject.

Alexandre rolled her eyes another time. What she despised more than the lack of seriousness that the naysayers possessed for mental health was the offensive mockery of it.

"What about her?"

"Have you talked to her about the concerns you just shared with me?"

After breathing through her disgruntlement, Alexandre confessed, "I have not spoken with Dr. Ahmed or anyone else about this—you are the first."

"Well, have you at least shared your concerns with Jacob?"

"And say what? You are free to be a father-figure to my son, but I reserve the right to maintain all parental rights?...He will never understand."

"You don't know that, Alexandre. You really don't...He is your husband now; so, he may just meet your reservations with compassion and understanding."

Alexandre did not respond. Instead, she retrieved her wallet from her tote.

"Just talk to him, Alex, and soon. The longer you wait the harder the conversation will be for you."

Alexandre gave Seanna her credit card. "I will get that back from you at the birthday party Saturday. You're still coming, right?"

Seanna suppressed her growing concerns at the dismissal of her counsel and simply answered, "With bells and whistles."

"Thank you and thank you for meeting me. I know it was short notice."

Seanna shrugged and jested, "You know me, as long as you are paying, every moment is a treasure."

Alexandre chuckled. She then rose from her seat, kissed her friend's cheek, and spoke, "I love you," before departing the restaurant.

That evening, Alexandre walked into her home to the smell of roasted chicken in the oven and Einaudi's *Nuvole Bianche* on the baby grand piano. Routinely, she placed her handbag on the foyer stand, keys in the glass dish, and briefcase in the hall closet. Afterwards, Alexandre stepped out of her heels and crept to the door of the sitting room. She rested her shoulder on and leaned her body into the door frame as she enjoyed the melodic performance.

Sensing a presence in the room, Jacob looked up from the ivory keys to discern his audience of one. He then smiled and winked at his wife as he completed the measure.

"Please, don't stop on my account," Alexandre beseeched, standing erect from her lean and walking to the piano. She retrieved his glass of red wine he had placed on the piano's lid and sipped from it.

"Prior to you," Jacob began as he gripped her waist and moved her between himself and the piano, "I never would have left a composition unfinished. But now…" He pushed his hands up her navy, high-waist skirt and tugged at the lace undergarment she wore until it fell to her ankles. "…Now, I have a more important use for my fingers."

Alexandre swallowed the last of his wine and placed the glass back on the piano lid. She slowly lowered her lids over her eyes as she enjoyed his tender stroke of her folds.

Jacob rose from his seat and finally greeted her with a kiss. "How was your day?" He asked, lifting her to sit on top of the piano.

Alexandre met his longing stare and answered, "No matter; it's definitely better now."

He smiled, pushed back the hairs that had fallen to her face from her French braid, and replied, "Glad to hear of it."

Jacob moved to lay her back when he slowly lifted her legs to rest her feet on the piano keys. He ignored the discord that resounded from the instrument and methodically pulled her skirt above her waist then gently pushed her knees apart. Jacob then lowered his mouth between her thighs and stroked her swollen member with his tongue.

Alexandre arched her back and clawed at the polished lid. She moaned her pleasure and breathed his name as the rapid intoxicating effect of the alcohol and his quick-talent caused a subtle quake in her legs. When Jacob moved her legs onto his shoulders and pulled her body closer to his lips, a ring of the bell and a knock at the door interrupted his feat.

Alexandre relaxed her back and huffed in disappointment. She pushed back the hair from her face and panted, "I've got to get that."

"Don't answer it," Jacob whispered on her.

She slowly sat up and gently nudged him from her. As a mother of a minority son who was not yet safely home, she could not allow the second ring and knock go ignored.

"I have to," she spoke more forcefully, peering deep into his eyes.

Jacob begrudgingly released her, watched her adjust her skirt and walk to the front door.

"Hi, Judge Denton," the husky, twelve-year-old greeted.

At the sight of the minor, Alexandre further adjusted her clothes, smoothed out her hair, and responded, "Hi, Elijah. How are you?" She felt Jacob stealthily sneak behind her and graze her inner legs with his fingertips.

"I'm fine—thanks."

Suppressing her arousal, she cleared her throat and spoke, "That's always good to hear…How may I help you?"

His stubby brown fingers held up a drone and accompanying control. "My birthday present from my grandmother came early. I was hoping that Jay and I can test it out. Is he home?"

"No, not yet. He has baseball practice today."

Elijah dropped his hands and head in disappointment.

Alexandre felt Jacob's fingers nudge her skirt up and she hastily pushed his hand away and pulled her skirt back down.

"Don't fret, Elijah," she encouraged. "He does not have practice on Friday and I will be sure to let him know that you stopped by with your new birthday gift."

Elijah shrugged his slumped shoulders and simply said, "Thank you," before walking away.

Alexandre quickly closed the door and turned to meet Jacob's fervent kisses with equally passionate ones. "How much time do we have?"

Jacob kissed her neck while he unbuttoned her blouse. "Plenty." He lifted a breast from the cup of her bra and covered the nipple with his mouth.

"I have to pick up Jaamyas," she whispered.

He kissed her lips and offered, "I will do it…You decompress from your day." He then freed himself from the pants he wore and lifted her on him to finish what he had started.

*** *** ***

"Your Honor," the law clerk called out again as she struggled to keep pace with Alexandre's stride down the long corridor.

"What is it, Cynthia?" Alexandre called back to her.

"Can you stop so that I can tell you?"

"No, I cannot."

"Well, can you at least slowdown?" Cynthia pleaded almost jogging to match Alexandre's steps.

Alexandre shook her head and responded, "I'm late for a meeting with counsel in the Hernandez matter."

"That is what I have to tell you. There is no meeting," Cynthia breathlessly rejoined.

Alexandre immediately halted her steps and turned to face Cynthia who had done the same. "What? Why?"

"Because Julio Hernandez is missing." Cynthia raised her shoulders cavalierly and added, "Maybe even dead if he has returned to his deviance."

Alexandre's heart dropped and stomach ached as she reflected on the young, Hispanic male that wore a suit two sizes too large the last she saw him.

"Since when?"

Cynthia shrugged a second time. "Since the last 24 hours. No one has seen him since breakfast yesterday."

Alexandre turned on her heels and continued en route to her chambers. "How is that even possible in a juvenile facility?"

Cynthia hurried after her while answering, "Your Honor, when he wasn't causing a ruckus, or inciting violence, or being disciplined, he was regularly isolating himself—refusing meals, declining group activities, forgoing time outdoors…So, to be frank, it wasn't difficult to not notice his absence."

Frustrated, Alexandre pushed opened her door, walked to her desk, and tossed her leather padfolio on it. She ignored the various family photos that fell over. "So, you're telling me checks are that infrequent that a child can go missing for an entire day before anyone notices it?!"

Cynthia closed the door behind her and, despite her trepidation, she daringly answered, "Your Honor, you of all people know that the system governing our youth is not only broken, but overwhelmed."

When Alexandre noticed Cynthia's hesitation to walk further into the room, she took a deep breath to suppress her anger and walked to the oversized bay window that overlooked the well-manicured courtyard. As Alexandre observed the ducks freely bathing in the large pond, she moved her tresses to one shoulder and began to race the diamond heart pendant along the silver chain around her neck. To alleviate more her stress, she permitted her mind to wander to her first wedding night in which Lance gifted her the jewelry.

The gentle call of her name brought Alexandre back to the confines of her chambers. Disregarding Cynthia's soft, quivering voice, Alexandre continued to watch, and now envy, the ducks' freedom. Their liberty forced her to acknowledge the sudden loss of her own—she no longer possessed the autonomy to judge the Hernandez matter. And, any unrelenting attempt to do so, would have the public at the courthouse doors with battering rams.

Vexed by everything that was contrary to her beliefs and all that she stood for, Alexandre begrudgingly yielded at last. As she did so, thoughts of decertifying Julio Hernandez haunted her and ultimately emerged feelings of defeat. Recalling the child that was broken, dejected, and afraid, she remembered his silent plea for help. Her heart began to ache and Alexandre contemplated, with guilt, on what she could have decided differently.

After her moment of reflection passed, Alexandre concluded that, despite her best efforts and protections, Julio Hernandez was indeed a menace to and a great strain on an already taxed system. All that was now needed to substantiate the claims that judges accurately predict liars only fifty-four percent of the time, thus contributing to the plight of the justice system, was another criminal act committed by the delinquent while he was absconded.

Deeply respiring, Alexandre recognized that the odds were no longer in her favor. She had to concede. As she turned to meet Cynthia's eyes and extended her hand for the materials she held, Alexandre accepted that there was no other choice but to finally grant the petition to transfer the case to the adult court system.

"What are the details? Who should we call first?"

Alexandre waited patiently in her black luxury sedan—a wedding gift from Jacob—for Jaamyas to notice her arrival at the youth center. In her staying, she observed in adoration her seed that was sprouting far too fast for her liking. In spite of her protest, her lone child was transitioning into a man, but not just any man—his father, a man who Jaamyas mirrored in every facet though they never met.

Returning the wave and smile she received from her son, Alexandre abruptly ended the thoughts of her deceased husband. She then watched as Jaamyas bid farewell to the adult male he was conversing with and begin his steps to the passenger door. Although he remained below the 50th percentile for his age height, Jaamyas was muscularly developed. So, his strong stride shortened the distance between them in little time.

"Where's Jacob? Why didn't he come get me?" Jaamyas asked as he climbed into the seat next to his mother and removed his bookbag from his shoulders.

Alexandre rolled her eyes and sucked her teeth in discontent. "Hello, Mom. How are you, Mom? In addition to giving me life, thanks for picking me up, Mom."

Jaamyas chuckled, leaned to kiss her cheek, and spoke, "Hi, Mom."

She smiled and greeted, "Hi, son." She nodded towards his seatbelt and finally answered, "Jacob is working late today—just you and me tonight. That's cool?"

Jaamyas nodded, placed his bag at his feet, and then secured his safety. Following, he replied, "That's cool."

As she placed her car in drive and navigated towards the main road, Alexandre asked, "Who was that stranger you were talking to?"

"He's not a stranger, Mom."

"Well, I don't know him and you know I don't want you conversing with people I don't know. We have talked about this a million times, Jay."

Jaamyas clandestinely turned his eyes upwards in annoyance with his low-hovering helicopter mom. As he ignored her subliminal message that sinister happenings can, too, occur in their seemingly safe, gated corner of suburbia, he stifled the inclination to correct her exaggerated count of their conversations. Instead, Jaamyas elucidated, "He's Coach Carter, our new volunteer."

Alexandre ignored his insolence to allow herself a moment to contemplate his response. "…I wasn't aware that the center had brought on a new volunteer."

"Well, they did and he's nice. He's actually been here for a few weeks now. You should meet him—Jacob already did."

"Did he now?" She asked rhetorically as her mind slipped to thoughts about dinner.

"Yeah—YES," he quickly corrected, "and we both like him…May I invite him to my birthday party on Saturday?"

"I don't think so, son. The guest list has been solidified."

"What's one more person going to hurt?" He bemoaned. "…I can always disinvite Rebecca if it's a problem. I don't want her to come anyway."

Suppressing her aggravation with the ingrate she was raising, Alexandre offered, "Or, I can disinvite everyone and use the money I will save to buy *myself* a present for having given birth to you."

Jaamyas crossed his arms at his chest and relented, "Fine."

"Thaaaaank yooooouu," Alexandre sang.

Disregarding her poor attempt at humor, Jaamyas asked, "…What about dinner? Can we invite Coach Carter over for dinner the same way we did Coach Daniel when he first volunteered?"

Alexandre nodded. "Yes, after your party, you can invite him to dinner."

Jaamyas looked at her and beamed. "Thanks, Mom…I'm sure he will appreciate it, too. He is new to town and has no local family. He said he is from…"

Though her son's voice enunciated over the jazz pulsating through the speakers, Alexandre could not comprehend what he was saying. Her thoughts again drifted to the tasks that awaited her at home, one of which being the Julio Hernandez matter. Before her mind delved deep into the missing child, she made a mental note to meet Coach Carter before her son invited him to dinner.

At light tap on her home office door interrupted her trance. She turned from the laptop screen that she blankly stared at and saw that it was Jacob standing at the threshold.

"It's after midnight. What are you still doing up?" He asked, widening the door she kept ajar.

Alexandre wiped her cheeks dry and then took another swallow from her wine glass. "I couldn't sleep."

Noticing the business attire he still wore, she inquired, "Just getting in from the office?"

"Drinks with a new client."

She nodded in acknowledgement.

Jacob walked further into the dimly lit room and took a seat on her wooden, L-shaped, executive desk. He gently nudged her chair so that she could face him and asked, "What's wrong, Alex?"

She turned from his eyes, finished her glass, and placed it on the coaster. "Nothing," she dismissed.

"It doesn't look like nothing."

Alexandre cleared her throat then quick-wittedly stated, "Probably just the adverse effects of the birth control."

Though he suspected that she was not being truthful, Jacob entertained the lie, "Well, I don't want you to develop an iatrogenic illness because of a prescription. We-"

"Jacob," she spoke in an attempt to quiet him. She did not want to hear again his concerns with synthetic hormones and their disruption of her natural balance.

"Can use another form of contraception," he stated over her determined to complete his thought as she had a habit of disrupting any consideration that countered hers.

Alexandre sat motionless in her seat while she continued to avoid his gaze. The blanket of silence that covered the room allowed her the opportunity to reflect on Jacob's comment. In addition to reasons related to illness and disease, his lack of support of her taking an oral contraception was also attributed to his longing to immediately expand their family.

"It's just a year, Jacob," she finally uttered. "I will be off it in a year before any harmful impact that you believe can happen, will occur."

She paused a moment, anticipating his rebuttal. When he did not speak, she turned to him and reminded, "I have never been on the pill. So, I just need to give it a little more time to even keel."

Suppressing his apprehension and the point he wanted to press, Jacob nodded reluctantly in deference to her. Marriage may have sealed their belongingness to each other, but decisions concerning her body were hers to make solely and he, as her husband, had no right to impose his will.

"Okay," he replied.

Astonished by his concession, Alexandre repeated, "Okay?"

Jacob shrugged at the contest she was expecting and repeated once more, "Okay." He then transitioned the conversation to get to the crux of her anguish. "Now that that has been resolved, how about the truth this time."

Alexandre dropped her eyes then lowered her head.

"What's really wrong, Alex?"

"…I lost a child today."

His heart dropped and instantaneously ached for her. Alexandre was a woman who gave all that she had to offer to everything she did, and her career was no exception. However, it was not her passion for the law that was her driving force, but her incessant love for children.

"Who?...Who was it?"

"Julio Hernandez." She looked at him and shared, "Not much older than Jaamyas."

Jacob watched her used her left thumb to vigorously massage the palmar creases of her right hand—one of the two stress habits that she possessed.

"…He could just be missing or very much dead—I don't know. But, what I do know is that I failed him."

"You didn't fail him, Alex."

"No, I did," she dissented. "…I failed him and now, whenever he is recovered, the adult system will render justice as they see fit."

Jacob inhaled deeply and exhaled loudly. "Alex, please…Please don't do this to yourself. You can't save them all."

She met his eyes and questioned, "But can't I though? I mean that is what I set out to do when I became a public defender and then sought this opportunity on the bench."

"Alexandre-"

"Almost two years on the bench and never had I ever had to decertify a juvenile offender—NEVER…And you want to know why?"

Refusing to be baited, Jacob did not respond. To be tangled in her net of self-pity would plunge them both into the deep, dark abyss.

"And you want to know why?" She repeated.

"Alexandre-"

"Because I believe every child is capable of being rehabilitated—Every. Single. One of them."

"Alexandre, stop."

Tears fell from her eyes as she finally conveyed the inevitable, "The adult system will destroy him and, when it does, he will reenter society and destroy us…"

Alexandre peered at her empty wine glass and fought the overwhelming urge to refill it. As one who was no stranger to loss, grief, and disappointment, she knew that she had to manage her emotions and not douse them. So, in effort to achieve the first and second steps of coping, Alexandre confessed and accepted, "…We ultimately create the monsters that children become…So, we only have ourselves to blame…"

Following Alexandre's final statement, Jacob allowed the office to fall silent as he contemplated the appropriate words to comfort her. They had met at this precipice several times before, but were never forced to leap. However, her growing attachment to the children she served and the increased demands of the judicial system intensified the challenge of talking her from the ledge.

Finding no words to conjure an adequate response, Jacob finally beseeched, "Please speak with Dr. Ahmed…For you, for Jaamyas, for us—please, make an appointment to speak with her." With that he leaned forward to gently kiss her forehead, rose from his seat, and exited the room.

*** *** ***

"Yes, I understand that, Senator," Alexandre spoke into the headset, "but you are not grasping the critical issue here."

Alexandre clinched her fist in exasperation as she listened to the typical rhetoric on the opposite end of the phone. To dissipate her agitation, she began to pace the floor of her chambers while she lent her ear to the poorly rehearsed statistics.

"Okay, Senator. Even if all that were true—and I am not saying that it is—our recidivism rates among juveniles in the state of North Carolina are not improving. Therefore, contrary to popular belief, juvenile waiver is not an effective practice—particularly among non-violent delinquents. So-"

He interrupted her with additional propaganda that she was certain that an inexperienced intern had gleaned from a simple internet search.

"That is not true, Senator. In fact, all that you have done with your support of the ineffective policy of waiver is thrust juveniles into criminal adulthood."

Alexandre ceased pacing the floor and stood in front of her desk. While she held her peace as he offered his response, she fought the urge to disconnect the teleconference she waited weeks to confirm.

"Well, I disagree," she candidly responded. "…Why? Because I know that-"

There was a light tap on the door just as the Senator interjected.

"Come in," Alexandre called out over the Senator's monologue.

Cynthia opened the door and crossed the threshold, but stood near the entrance when she realized she was interrupting a call.

"…Yes, I have spoken with the Governor. I've spoken to the Governor, the Mayor, the City Council, the-"

He had disrupted her again.

"Well, with all due respect, Senator, you don't know because you don't see it. I, on the other hand, do know because I see it every single day. I have been on the ground for over a decade working these cases. I have literally been busting my ass for these children for years while you congressional neophytes create knee-jerk policies that not only fail to get to the core of the problem, but make the problem worse."

Alexandre listened to his halfhearted response and finally offered, "Yeah, well, I'm sorry you feel that way, too. Don't count on my vote in the next election." With that she slammed the head piece into the base and growled her frustration.

Once the exchange had ended, Cynthia walked further into the room. "Your call with the Senator?"

Alexandre returned behind her desk, dropped into her seat, and answered, "My call with the Senator."

Cynthia placed an accordion file of documents in front of her and inquired, "Dare I ask how it went?"

Alexandre eased the documents out of the file and quickly thumbed through them. "Nothing worth repeating. Just plan to vote a straight democratic ticket in the next election…Believe you me, at this point, we are not voting *for* the opponent, but *against* who is currently in office."

Cynthia snickered. "Aren't we always voting for the lesser of two evils in this country?"

Alexandre smiled and looked up at the twenty-something year old—fresh out of law school and recently passed the bar exam. "You are far too young to be this cynical."

She shook her head in dissent. "I am from a pedigree of politicians and lawyers. We bleed cynicism."

Tickled by the law clerk's statement, Alexandre burst into an unexpected laughter. "…Thank you," she uttered to Cynthia in appreciation for the light humor. Alexandre was in desperate need of the endorphins that the jest prompted her brain to release.

Once she regained her bearings, Alexandre spoke with a serious intonation, "Promise me your stay here won't be long—a year, two tops. The world needs you to go on and do greater things."

Cynthia nodded, "I intend to, Your Honor." She extended to her an unsealed envelope.

"What's this?" Alexandre asked, receiving the envelope.

"A little bit of good news."

Alexandre removed the tri-folded sheet and opened it to read its content. She leaned back into her chair and smiled.

"She did it," Alexandre spoke in pleased adoration.

Cynthia smiled as well and confirmed, "She did. She successfully completed the diversion program and will be starting her final year of high school in a few weeks."

Alexandre reminisced on the truant runaway that the community surrounding her had forsaken like a hopeless cause. From her bench, Alexandre looked beyond the hard exterior and found a delicate soul in need of restoration. So, she infused the adolescent with what she needed most to thrive—love, unabated and sometimes tough.

Refolding the document and replacing it in the envelope, Alexandre commented, "This is wonderful news." She then tossed the item in her inbox and requested, "Please arrange a status call for me. I want to encourage her endeavors."

"Of course."

After inhaling deeply and exhaling loudly, Alexandre prepared herself for discouraging news as she asked, "So, any updates on Hernandez?"

"No, not yet, Your Honor," Cynthia despondently responded and then immediately encouraged, "but law enforcement has been in touch with his family and friends, and all have been cooperative thus far."

Alexandre respired in disappointment and murmured, "Where could he have gone?"

"With respect, Your Honor, I believe the more important question to be: 'Why is he running?'"

Alexandre met her green eyes and answered, "Who wouldn't run from the possibility of sharing space with adult convicts?"

"You don't think that…" Cynthia voice trailed off while she pondered the unfathomable possibility of youth and adult criminals in similar domiciles.

"Yes, I do. In fact, it's what I know to be true," Alexandre stated, completing the thought that Cynthia could not bring herself to verbalize. "Several adult facilities across the country do not have the capacity or capabilities to keep juvenile offenders separate from the adult ones…It's grossly tragic and many children take their own lives just to escape the torturous hell."

"…That is awful…" Pondering the gruesome thought more, Cynthia spoke under her breath, "…No wonder Hernandez is running…"

As the law clerk's words dissipated into the air, Alexandre's imagination recklessly navigated in a sea of unknowns. The world was no place for a parentless adolescent. Lurking in every corner was destruction as well as death.

"At this point, how likely is Hernandez still alive?" Cynthia asked, ushering into the conversation that the runaway may no longer be among the living.

Alexandre held her breath at the thought. It was one that was mentioned several times before, but each time she refused to give it serious consideration. "…It is my desperate prayer that he is still among the living…For the sake of his family, I really do hope that he is…There is no greater pain than that of having to out-live the life of your child…"

An uncomfortable knot swelled Cynthia's throat and she struggled to swallow it. When she finally did, she simply nodded to acknowledge Alexandre's appeal and garnered the courage needed to manage Alexandre's expectations.

"Your Honor," Cynthia began, "we both know that time is of the essence when it pertains to missing persons. The more time lapses the less likely the missing person is to be discovered…that is discovered alive, at least…"

In lieu of a response, Alexandre inhaled and exhaled deeply through her nostrils. She then observed the stoic look of resignation on her law clerk's face and, before the silence settled to long in her chambers, she merely offered, "I'm so sorry that your first case may have a ghastly ending."

Cynthia shrugged in a nonchalant manner and replied, "We can't save them all, right? I mean, we can try, but we truly can't—the system is not designed for us to…"

Alexandre winced at the law clerk's cynicism, but immediately recovered when she remembered that it derived from her pedigree. Without a doubt, Cynthia was conditioned to reason in the way that she did. And, having been also surrounded by her share of politicians and legal practitioners, Alexandre knew all too well the hefty effect of indoctrination. If one failed to commit to anything, one was at risk of being distracted by everything.

Because she believed that Cynthia's propensity to subscribe to a contemptuous school of thought was no fault of her own, Alexandre made the silent vow to do just as her mentors had done for her—invest in her change. Unequivocally, Alexandre knew that to abate the impact of Cynthia's cultivation, she would have to challenge and reshape the way she thought.

"…Besides," Cynthia added to end the awkward silence, "I'm only a couple months in. So, I am still riding the coattails of Tynisha's successes."

Alexandre smiled at the thought of her former law clerk who resigned to pursue a career as a legal political analyst in Washington, D.C.

"Not long I am sure," Alexandre encouraged. "You will have your own docket of successes in no time."

"I'm certain of it, Your Honor." Cynthia turned to leave after reciting, "Enjoy your evening."

"Thank you and I expect you to do the same. Actually, take the day off tomorrow. There is nothing on the docket. So, get a head start on your weekend," Alexandre called out to the tenacious worker before she closed the door.

*** *** ***

"What are you doing?" Jacob inquired as he exited the bathroom, pulled his cotton t-shirt over his muscular torso, and adjusted his plaid pajama pants.

Alexandre reluctantly flashed her black compact at him. "Taking my pill," she answered, hoping that her reply would not invite a squabble she was too exhausted to entertain.

Jacob watched her place the small tablet on her tongue and swallow it. He then huffed and rolled his eyes at her deflection. "Not that—that." He nodded toward the manila folder placed on their bed in front of her.

Alexandre replaced the compact near her lamp so that she would remember the contraception the next day. She then leaned against the mounted headboard and smoothed out the comforter that covered her. "Just a few things I wanted to-"

"Alexandre, no. We both agreed that this would be a no-work-all-play zone."

She grinned at the pact made prior to their wedding. "Are you kidding me?"

"No, I'm not." Jacob retrieved the folder and placed it in the nightstand drawer nearest to her. He then kissed her lips and peered into her eyes. "Please take this seriously."

"Okay."

"Besides," he began as he climbed over her to the empty space, "there is something important I want to talk to you about."

Alexandre impishly chuckled and lowered herself into the bedding. "Oh, really?"

"Yes, I think I want to forgo selling the penthouse."

"Oh, you were serious about talking?"

Jacob laughed. "Yes, I was serious about talking."

"I'm sorry." She rose back to her seated position and encouraged, "Continue—why do you want to hold on to the property?"

"For Jay."

Astonished by his response, she captured his gaze and held it for a moment before asking, "Really?"

"Yes, I want to gift it to him."

Alexandre turned from his eyes and exhaled in disbelief. "Wow…Wow…Babe, he is only 12—well, thirteen—almost."

"It won't be now, but maybe when he graduates high school or college. I want to help him build generational wealth…I mean it is a great property in a prime real estate location. He will do really well."

"…I'll say…" Alexandre considered the gesture and was absent words as the benevolence flabbergasted her. When she contemplated more his generosity, she taunted, "Wait, are you sure this is not a ploy for you to keep your bachelor-pad for nefarious reasons?"

Jacob snickered at the jest then winked at her. "Only if those reasons include you."

Alexandre giggled and then leaned into his warmth to kiss him. "Thank you, Jacob…Jaamyas won't understand the value now, but he will come to appreciate the gesture in ten years."

"No thanks needed. I'm only doing what rich dads do."

Alexandre grinned and gently smoothed down the waves on the top of his head. "So, you're a rich dad now?"

"I'm working on it."

"Oh, I know you are," she concurred with no reservations. Jacob was a man that possessed an unwavering tenacity to achieve his ambitions—including marrying her.

"I'm actually not too far from it with a promotion in my immediate future."

She proudly beamed at the successes he worked diligently for and stated, "A well-deserved promotion at that."

Silence fell among them and Alexandre's smile gradually faded. Her thoughts wandered to each advancement that pulled Lance further away from her. The possibility of enduring the same plight with Jacob saddened her heart.

Noticing her disenchantment, Jacob inquired, "What's wrong, Alex?"

She shook head and replied, "Nothing," then quick-wittedly added, "just thinking of how blessed we are and how things would have been different for Julio Hernandez and his family if they were equally blessed."

"Still no movement on the missing person case?"

She shook her head a second time. "Still no movement…If nothing breaks soon, the city could be looking at a lawsuit."

"Really? A lawsuit?"

Alexandre nodded and replied, "Yeah."

"For what?"

After exhaling loudly, she answered, "For a whole host of reasons—negligence, child-endangerment…"

"But what if he isn't a runaway?"

"What do you mean?"

"What if he was abducted?"

Deliberating the possibility that she had not considered before, Alexandre probed, "By whom?"

Jacob shrugged. "I don't know, Alex. You yourself said that in the times you volunteered to teach at the detention center that it has been understaffed. So, my thought is that anyone can sign in as a visitor and walk out with a child."

Alexandre contemplated his supposition and disagreed, "Staffing is a cause for concern, but not that dire."

Jacob shrugged once more. "Well, I guess it's all just my poor attempt to be Dr. Watson to your Sherlock Holmes. But I see now that I am only aiding and abetting your violation of our no-work-in-our-play-room policy."

Alexandre stretched her lips into a bogus grin as her mind still pondered all that Jacob had suggested.

"Get some rest, babe," Jacob suggested. "We have a long day ahead of us tomorrow with rambunctious and hormonal pre-teens." He kissed her cheek, turned on his side, switched off the lamp on the nightstand nearest to him, and closed his eyes.

*** *** ***

"HEY!" Alexandre hollered at a group of rowdy boys in the foyer. "No running in the house. Jaamyas, you know better."

"Mom, I wasn't running," Jaamyas contested.

Alexandre snapped her fingers and pointed towards the backdoor. "Outside—now!"

Jaamyas slump his shoulders, turned on his heels, and led his friends to the backyard.

"What was that all about?" Jacob asked, meeting her at her side and kissing her temple.

"Just your typical standoff with a group of adolescent boys." She turned to meet his eyes. "I really do hope that you are a producer of only X-chromosomes."

Jacob laughed at her wit. "I'm going to let you take that up with God."

"And I will." She touched his lips with hers and then asked, "Did you get the ice cream cake from the deep-freezer in the garage?"

"I did, and it's in the kitchen waiting for you."

"Good. The quicker we cut it and do the gifts, the quicker this shindig can be over," she exhaustedly breathed.

"Aaaaaw. It's not that bad," he spoke, walking to answer the ring at the front door.

"Ha! This is your first birthday. I've got 12 on you. We will see if you are singing that same tune by birthday 16."

Jacob laughed and swung the door open.

"Seanna," he greeted with sarcasm. "How nice of you to finally join us, and right before the cutting of the cake."

She embraced him and implored, "Please show me some grace, Jacob…It's not easy getting three kids ready and out the house before noon with my spouse out of town on business."

Jacob smiled with compassion and then kissed her cheek. "Well, I am glad you were able to make it—even if for the last hour."

Seanna swatted his arm and pushed past him to greet Alexandre. Afterwards, she instructed her children to salute their god-mother and then rushed them outside with Jaamyas's gift in tow.

"Well," Jacob began, "I will leave you two to it while I prepare everyone for cake and ice cream."

Seanna tugged the tail of Alexandre's orange, fit and flare dress as they walked to the open kitchen. She lauded, "Cute dress."

"Thank you."

"Was the family color your idea?" Seanna inquired, taking a carrot from the vegetable tray and biting into it.

"No, actually it was your god-son's. He picked out my dress and the plaid shirts and khaki pants that he and Jacob are wearing."

"I like it, but why orange?"

Alexandre rolled her eyes. "Because it's his favorite color."

Guilt overcame Seanna. "Oh…Was I supposed to be wearing it, too?"

Alexandre snatched the uneaten carrot from her fingers, slammed it on the marble island, and shoved utensils in her hand. "Yes, you were," she answered, "along with his god-brother and god-sisters."

Seanna looked down at her black wedges, denim skinny jeans, and off-the-shoulder, white shirt. "I'm so sorry, Alex. I really am…You know that I am having the hardest time managing on my own with Brent gone."

"It's fine, Sea. You just have better gotten him a damn good gift."

Seanna grinned. "Of course, I did…And speaking of gifts," she began, placing the utensils on the marble island and a hand at her waist, "did you talk to Jay about the adoption?"

"No, I did not."

Seanna exhaled in disappointed frustration. "And why not?"

"Because I'm seriously considering the year wait, Seanna," Alexandre retorted. "I don't want to present Jaamyas with something that I am not even sure about."

"Soooo, he and Jacob suffer because you have somehow managed to make this act of love and commitment about you," Seanna surmised.

"No, that's not my-"

"Babe, we're ready," Jacob announced after opening and appearing at the kitchen backdoor that led to the festivities in the backyard.

Alexandre simply nodded, feeling Seanna's eyes on her. When her own eyes finally met them, she knowingly answered, "We'll continue this conversation another time. Right now, it's time for cake and ice cream."

Once she strategically placed and lit the final candle, Alexandre carefully gripped the tray and walked one of Jaamyas's favorite desserts outside while singing the traditional birthday song. Seanna rolled her eyes at her best friend's obstinacy, yanked the utensils from where she placed them, and joined the group outside.

While the guests enjoyed their sweet treats, Alexandre encouraged Jaamyas to open his gifts. As he obliged, the crowd exclaimed their excitement of the video games, clothes, shoes, money, and…

"Who is it from?" Jaamyas asked, retrieving the stamped envelope from his mother's hand.

"I don't know, son. It doesn't have a return address on it. Just open it and see."

Jaamyas carefully broke the seal of the envelope and removed the card. He read aloud, "A special gift for a special kid and..." He opened the card and ignored the inserts until he completed reading, "the best player in the game. All the best, Coach Carter."

When he flipped the inserts, Jaamyas discovered they were two 50-yard line seats to a Carolina Panthers game.

"Wooooooooow!" He exclaimed. "Mom, look at what coach got me!"

Alexandre was taken aback by the gesture and the exorbitant cost of the gift. "I see, son." She looked at Jacob who only shrugged his shoulders. "Let me hold on to those for you," she offered with the intention to return the gift on Monday.

Without question, Jaamyas extended the card to his mother along with the others that included cash and gift cards.

"Well, I don't think I can beat Panther tickets, but you do have one more gift from me," Jacob announced.

Alexandre turned her eyes upward as she shook her head. "Babe, you are spoiling him."

"Hardly," Jacob rejoined before he went into the kitchen and return with a pristinely wrapped box. "Happy birthday, Jay."

"Thanks, Jacob," Jaamyas replied as he moved to open the gift. When he uncovered the drone, he yelped, wrapped his arms tightly around Jacob's torso, and thanked him profusely.

Rage grew in Alexandre at the sight of the gift and she did not conceal it when her eyes met Jacob's. She pardoned herself with the cards in hand so not to make a commotion in the presence of their guests.

Sensing the newfound tension between his wife and him, Jacob removed his arms from around Jaamyas and instructed, "Why don't you un-box it and I will be right back to help you get that in the air." He then took off behind Alexandre in the kitchen.

"Alex, look-"

Alexandre shoved the cards into a kitchen drawer and slammed it shut. After pivoting to face him, she hotly questioned, "What the hell was that?"

"I'm sor-"

"We agreed to wait until Christmas."

"I know, but his friend came over the other day with his and I thought it would be something fun they could both enjoy together."

"I don't care about his friend, Jacob! I care about teaching my son about delayed gratification—that he cannot have what he wants whenever he wants it or because someone else has it!"

"Well, for one, he is *our* son and-"

"DON'T! Don't you dare go there with that *our son* bullshit, Jacob."

Temporarily conceding on that point in an attempt to diffuse the heated exchange, Jacob calmly spoke, "Look, Alexandre, all that I am trying to convey is that your rules-"

"Are in place for a reason."

"For a kid like Jay, what is the reason?" Jacob asked, befuddled by her interjection.

"They provide boundaries and afford structure. Without them chaos ensues."

Laughing lightheartedly at her dramatic explanation, he replied, "And you would know?"

"Yes, Jacob, I would know," Alexandre responded to his insolent sarcasm. "Because every day I witness the horrid outcome of children having no guidance."

"Alex, our home is not your courtroom and Jay is not one of the children who has gone before your bench."

"I know that, Jacob," Alexandre vehemently spat, offended by his callous reminder.

"Well, know this, too, Alex, some of your rules are excessive. Jaamyas is a good kid so he does not need-"

"Yes, Jaamyas is a good kid because I am raising him to be a good kid! So, I don't need you in your first few weeks as a stepfather imparting your haphazard parenting style on *my* son!"

Insulted by the comment that grossly minimized his efforts and his parental desires, Jacob inquired, "How dare you? How DARE you?! From the moment-"

Jaamyas placed the drone and its accompanying control on the breakfast nook that extended from the marble island and spoke, "I can wait until Christmas." He then left the kitchen in the direction of his room with no intentions of returning to his party.

"Great," Alexandre murmured, frustrated that their volatile exchange overlooked Jaamyas's stealthy entrance into the kitchen. "Just fucking great."

Jacob caught her eyes. "Are you happy now? Once again, you got what you wanted, but you ruined our son's birthday in the process." He left to retrieve his car keys from the foyer table and went for a drive.

When Alexandre turned in the direction of the kitchen backdoor, she saw her gracefully-aged reflection disappointingly glaring at her. Alexandre fought back her tears and pleaded, "Not now, Mother," before making the journey to her own bedroom.

Following a light tap, the double doors to the master bedroom slowly opened. Alexandre broke her gaze out the window and saw Jaamyas standing at the threshold. She placed her feet on the floor and sat erect in the cushioned chair.

"Hey, son," she softly spoke.

"Hey."

She patted the seat of the cushioned chair next to her and invited, "Come sit next to me."

Jaamyas shook his head. "I just wanted to say good night…You know, so the sun doesn't set on my anger."

Alexandre feebly smiled at his regurgitation of Paul's Biblical instruction to the people of Ephesus. "…I'm really sorry about your party, baby."

Jaamyas shrugged. "…Maybe next year will be better."

Alexandre knew her son well enough to know that his inherited optimism could conceal neither his despondency nor his pain. He had long awaited his transition into his teenage years and the party was to serve as a rite of passage. So, to have his celebration abruptly end on her account was another grave disappointment.

After clearly her throat, Alexandre reported, "Nana told me that she put all your gifts in the hall closet downstairs."

Jaamyas nodded in acknowledgment, but with little care.

Forsaking all that she strove to teach him about covetousness, hard-work, and patience, Alexandre exhaled audibly and conceded, "…You can have your drone."

Jaamyas beamed. "Really?"

Alexandre nodded. "Really."

Jaamyas rushed to throw himself into her arms. "Thanks, Mom."

She held him tightly and replied, "You're welcome, son."

When he released her, he met her eyes and asked, "And the tickets?"

Once more, Alexandre exhaled loudly. Just as well as she knew him, he knew her also. "I don't know, Jay. That's quite an extravagant gift from a coach; especially one you met only weeks ago…And I don't even know this Coach Carter well enough for him to take you."

"But, Mom, they're lower level, 50 yard-line tickets," Jaamyas emphatically explained.

Alexandre shook her head and, against her better judgment, offered, "I tell you what, I will speak to Coach Carter next week, offer him the money for the tickets, and you and Jacob can go together instead…Deal?"

Jaamyas's lips stretched into a wide grin as he replied, "Deal. I will-"

His thought was interrupted when Jacob walked into the bedroom.

"Hey, Jacob," Jaamyas greeted.

"Hey, Jay…May I have a moment alone with your mother?"

Jaamyas nodded, kissed Alexandre on the cheek, and whispered, "Good night." He then walked to Jacob, gave him a hug, and spoke, "Thanks, again, for my gifts."

Jacob held him firmly, kissed the top of his head, and replied, "You're welcome. Happy birthday, son."

After Jaamyas exited the room, Jacob closed the double doors and walked towards Alexandre. He pulled the cushioned chair that was next to her in front of her and lowered himself in it so that she could see the seriousness in his eyes.

"Why did you marry me, Alex?"

Alexandre contorted her face in bewilderment. "What?"

"Tell me why did you marry me, and I don't want to hear the typical 'I love you and want to spend the rest of my life with you' response...There has to be more to it. There just has to be...and...and I am racking my brain to figure out what it is."

Alexandre parted her lips to speak, but, to no avail, as no words surfaced. And it was not because she lacked anything to say, but rather she lacked the confidence that what she had to say would give him comfort.

Jacob watched her take the diamond heart pendant in between her thumb and forefinger and begin to race it along the silver chain around her neck. As the primary quirk of her two stress habits, he understood the meaning of it, and it would not be long before her mind wandered to the life she enjoyed prior to him.

Lowering his head in disappointment, Jacob attempted with little success to wipe the frustration from his face. When his eyes met Alexandre's again, he confessed, "When I met you three years ago it was painfully obvious that you didn't need me—you don't need anyone, Alex...But at the very least, I thought you wanted me...Wanted me as your lover, your partner, your companion...a father to your son...Was I wrong? Am I wrong?"

Alexandre released the pendant, lowered her hand, and shook her head. "No," she whispered.

"Then why not let me be these things? Why do you have this incessant need to be in control?"

Tears fell from Alexandre's eyes as she contemplated Jacob's questions and the varying ways in which she could respond to them. She parted her lips once more in an attempt to disclose the truth—that the lack of control made her vulnerable, and yielding control made her weak. Furthermore, and most importantly, that her past experiences with acquiescing changed the entire trajectory of her life.

Jacob anxiously awaited her response as the deafening silence enveloped the room. He struggled to suppress the urge to encourage her to speak, recognizing that his well-intended efforts could incite another argument.

Alexandre's mouth remained opened, but she did not utter a sound. Though she desperately wanted to vocalize all that her heart wanted to communicate, the words would not emerge. At last forsaking the search for language that would amply articulate her concerns to the man before her, Alexandre merely stated, "I always had to be, so I always am."

Jacob turned from her teary eyes and puffed hot air at her cavalier response. Looking out the window at the rust color sky, he allowed again the stillness to settle in the room so that he could calm his vexation.

In their quietness, Jacob reflected on the many things that he had considered prior to committing himself to Alexandre. Of these many things, her unwavering obstinacy was not among them.

"Do not speak to me in the way that you did today ever again," Jacob admonished finally breaking his silence. He then met her eyes and enforced his demand by saying, "I mean it, Alex."

He rose from his seat to gather a few items to shower and sleep in the guest bedroom.

*** *** ***

"Soooooo, no one was going to tell me that we are playing hooky from church today?" Jaamyas asked, walking into the kitchen the next morning with his Bible in his hand.

Alexandre looked up from her political subscription that she read in her seat at the island's breakfast nook. "You're not playing," she disabused after giving him a glance over. In his tailored black suit, tie, and white shirt, he uncannily mirrored his father's image.

"It's your Sunday to usher," she reminded him. "Give me a moment and I will take you." Alexandre then sipped green tea from her Mother's Day mug and motioned for him to grab a freshly baked muffin and fruit for breakfast.

"I can take him," Jacob offered from his seat at the table in the morning room. He folded his newspaper, placed it on the table, and stood.

Alexandre stood and contested, "No, I can take him. I have errands to run anyway."

"What errands, Alex? You never run errands on the Sabbath." He glanced at her silk robe that hid her short gown and added, "Besides you are not even dressed."

Alexandre met his eyes for the first time that morning and responded, "Does it matter what errands and what I do on the Sabbath? You're not speaking to me anyway, remember?"

"Not now, Alex," Jacob abruptly spoke in hopes of ending what could morph into a squabble. He turned his gaze to Jaamyas and instructed, "Jay, go grab your gloves and your pin then meet-"

"I said I would take him, Jacob!"

"Alex, please-"

"Why are the two of you still fighting?!" Jaamyas questioned in anger and frustration.

When they both looked at him, but neither responded, Jaamyas placed his apple back in the fruit bowl and conveyed, "I will call Papa and have him come get me." With that, he exited the kitchen and entered the sitting room to make the call and await his grandparents' arrival.

Jacob met Alexandre's eyes, shook his head, and spoke, "True to form."

"I am not the only one to blame here, Jacob," she retorted under her breath so that Jaamyas could not hear their continued spat. "You barely spoke two words to me this morning and now you want to be Mr. Helpful."

Jacob huffed in disbelief. "I don't have time for this." He turned and began his walk towards the winding staircase.

"Where are you going?" Alexandre inquired, following him at his heels.

"DON'T," Jacob commanded, turning to face her. "Don't follow me."

Recognizing by his tone that she was testing the bounds of his patience, Alexandre relented. She inhaled deeply and exhaled loudly. "Will you be back before Sunday dinner at my parents'?"

"Not likely."

Alexandre glared at him. "And why not? What do you expect me to tell the family?"

"Because I need to get away from here; I need to be away from you…Whatever you decide to tell the family, Alex, I am sure you have a firm handle on it."

Jacob continued en route to the master bedroom to change for the place he dreaded and avoided most on Sundays—the office.

⁂ *TWO* ⁂

"That is a valid point, but do consider that-" Alexandre was interrupted when her predecessor burst through her chambers' door without invitation or greeting.

"Judge Leigh," she spoke, standing to her feet in deference to him. Those seated in the room did the same.

"I'm so sorry, Your Honor. He was insistent," her assistant spoke, trailing the seasoned, appointed official that retired a few years prior.

"It's fine, Leah," Alexandre assured without breaking the gaze with her mentor who was dressed in light blue suit. "Counselors, let's reconvene this afternoon; synchronize your calendars with my assistant."

When the last of the attendees exited the room and the door was closed, he dropped the newspaper on her desk. "What the hell is that?"

She nervously unfolded the paper and read the headline, *Tragic Outcome for Child Offender*. "...I...I don't know...I haven't read this morning's paper yet.

Alexandre took a moment to scan the first few sentences. "What? What is this? When did this go public?...I wasn't even aware that information pertaining to the Hernandez matter had gone public."

The seventy-six-year-old glared down at the woman he thought of as a daughter—one that could have been had he remarried after the painstaking loss of the love of his youth.

He scoffed and then mocked, "You weren't aware it had gone public. You're weren't aware...Damn it, Alex. Have I taught you nothing?"

"What? No—I mean, yes. Of course, you have...Everything I know, everything I am is attributed to your tutelage; even this very position."

He met her eyes and shook his head in dismay. "Then how could you let such shame befall this bench?"

Alexandre pivoted her head from the gaze of the gracefully aged man that resembled the good health and fitness of her father.

"I am but one person. I cannot save them all," she lowly uttered.

He huffed at the concession. "Spoken like a true coward—something my brother did not raise you to be."

She met his gaze again and pleaded, "Uncle Charles-"

"Don't! Don't you dare Uncle Charles me, Alexandre! A child is dead—presumed to have committed suicide. Hung himself to his death."

Alexandre's knees grew weak at the news, forcing her to lower herself to her seat before they buckled.

"It's all there in the paper, Alex. Read it."

When she remained stoic in her chair, he elevated his tone and commanded more forcefully, "READ IT."

Alexandre folded the paper closed and eased it to the corner of her desk. "I can't read it, uncle," she breathlessly replied. "I-I...just can't...I just can't read it."

Charles forced warm air from his nostrils. Had she been any other protégé, he would have yielded. But he was her kinsman; therefore, more was at stake than his reputation and name—he literally had flesh and blood to lose. For this reason and others related to her race, age, and gender, Charles felt obligated to caution his inexperienced sheep for the advent of wolves.

"The media disclosed that the event was a death by asphyxiation due to acute stress. Stress presumed to be attributed to your decision to transfer him, a non-violent offender, from the protections of this court."

"Whaaat?...How can they know that? They don't know that," she contested vehemently.

"Of course, they don't know that, Alex. If fact, they don't know shit. What's in black-and-white is all conjecture."

"So, if that is the case, then what's the issue here?"

In astonished disbelief at her question, he contorted his visage and repeated, "What's the issue here?"

"Yes, uncle, what is the issue here? Because the media prints half-truths and lies incessantly."

"The issue here, Alexandre, is that I know it to be true," he heatedly confirmed. "Three decades on this bench and the things I have heard and seen—believe you me, I know it to be true—all of it."

Silenced by the bulge that formed in her throat, Alexandre struggled to swallow it in lieu of attempting to respond.

Breathing through his aggravation, he walked to the oversized bay window and peered beyond the courtyard. Reminiscing on the thirty-plus years of gazing out that very window, Charles recalled the many times in which he sought to give hope in a world of naysayers. Like Alexandre, he, too, believed that even the greatest of menaces could be successfully rehabilitated with adequate support.

"…What would make a 14-year-old child commit suicide?…To lose all hope and not want to live anymore?" Charles asked, expecting no response.

The silence in the chambers afforded him the opportunity to consider the various mental, emotional, and physical tribulations that a child would have to encounter to be devoid of faith. Because he lived a blessed childhood and possessed no children of his own, Charles could not comprehend the level of bleakness necessary for self-annihilation. The concept always puzzled him.

Despite knowing the questions were rhetorical, Alexandre felt compelled to dismiss the quietness by offering, "I don't know. I suppose any number of things."

Charles huffed at the obscured response. "…Then what does that say about us, about our community, about our society?" He shifted his gaze from the window to Alexandre and then assured her, "Had not Hernandez taken his life before the transfer to the adult system, he would have certainly done it in prison—hopeless children like him often do."

Alexandre shook her head as she stubbornly dissented and recited again, "You don't know that."

He walked towards her and confirmed, "I do know that and you know it, too, Alexandre. We have studied it, reported out on it, and, now, we are living it."

She sneered at the notion of truth. In Alexandre's opinion, the truth most often lingered within various shades of grey. Due to the reasons that eyes are deceiving and mouths are misleading, the truth could never be black or white unless it was in print; and even then, the truth was someone else's manipulative version of it.

Rubbing her forehead in frustration, Alexandre reflected on her perceived missteps. After considering them for a short time, she concluded that any fault that her relative found in her was indeed a reflection of him. Undoubtedly, he was who she closely followed.

Exhausted by their conversation, Alexandre replied at last, "Okay, so, what is it that I am supposed to do," with hope to bring it to an end. "Because you are speaking to me as if your tenure was without any transfers?"

"No, I am not, Alexandre," Charles refuted. "It could just be the opinion that you have of yourself that is attributing to why that is all you hear."

She stated nothing in response, so he continued, "But be that as it may, my transfers were violent youth offenders that committed heinous crimes. Those crimes justified waivers."

Charles glared at her as he recalled the facts provided in that morning's newspaper. "They weren't wayward children that exercised poor judgment and went joy riding in a hundred-thousand-dollar car."

"The car was stolen, Uncle Charles," she elucidated. "And, for the record, which I'm sure the media failed to mention, Julio Hernandez was a chronic repeat offender."

Charles shook his head in dismay. "Do you hear yourself?...It is almost as if you have given up hope."

"I haven't given up hope. I am just giving consideration to the safety of the public."

"Public safety from a child committing petty, non-violent crimes," he spoke with skepticism. "Have we truly become a society that is afraid of our children?"

Alexandre looked up at him and challenged, "I don't know, uncle. You have done this far longer than I have. Why don't you tell me."

He suppressed his chuckle to her boldness and rejoined, "Yes, as a matter-of-fact, we have. But what matters most above that fear is the safety of these children of whom you are parens patriae."

Charles retrieved the newspaper, tossed it in her inbox, and took its place by lowering himself on the corner of her desk. He then leaned forward to be face-to-face with his niece and honestly asked, "As their legal protector, does it truly sit well with you to know that a lot of these children will not be separated from adult criminals?"

When she turned her head and failed to respond, Charles cupped her chin and brought her face back to his. "What if it were Jay?" He pressed.

In seething abhorrence, Alexandre retorted in the most respectful manner that she could conjure, "Not only is that question inappropriate, it is unfair and you know it."

Charles released her and then stood. As he adjusted his suit over his muscular lean body, he responded, "No. What I do know is that since your clerkship with me, I have told you time and time again that you cannot make knee-jerk decisions based on public outcries—that your first and only commitment is to the child."

Perplexed, Alexandre disputed, "In what way have I failed? I have never made a decision or determined what is right by some Gallup Poll. I don't follow trends—you know that, Uncle Charles."

After shrugging off her defense, he commented, "So what."

"What do you mean, so what?"

"I mean that you are of a generation that tends to misconstrue the concept of power. Despite popular belief, Alexandre, it is not the ability to flex muscles. It is the ability to influence—encourage change. So, once again, so what…You have this incredible strength to swim against the tide, but at the end of your tenure, what does all that might means?"

Believing the question to be rhetorical, Alexandre made no attempt to respond.

"Nothing," Charles spoke in absence of her answer. "Because what matters are the perceptions you have changed. You may not have searched for the consensus prior to the decisions you have made, but you have done nothing to mold it either, Alex. And that ultimately is what genuine leadership is—it is the shaping of public opinion because those opinions change policy."

Alexandre swallowed the rebuttal that formed in her belly then rose in her esophagus. Despite her subtle efforts to invoke change, she recognized his argument to be sound and had no choice but to relent.

She met his eyes and inquired in concession, "So, what now?"

Charles affectionately smiled at her and answered, "I've retired my gavel, Your Honor…I cannot figure this out for you."

Alexandre growled in agitation and hotly clarified, "I'm not seeking your resolve. I am asking for your guidance." She stood and beseeched, "Do I issue a formal statement? Do I resign? What?"

"We are forever in the throes of legal chaos in this country, Alexandre. Your job is to sift through all of the bullshit and forge order. And you do it while making no more mistakes and making a difference. That's what you do."

He leaned in to kiss her cheek, whispered, "See you Sunday," and then exited her chambers.

"Hey, Mom," Jaamyas greeted after he removed his shoes in the mudroom and washed his hands in the half-bathroom. He walked to the refrigerator and searched for a snack.

"Hey, son," Alexandre responded, looking up from the squash she sliced on the cutting board. "How was your day?"

Jaamyas retrieved a spoon from the drawer and took a seat in front of her on the opposite side of the island. "It was okay."

"Just okay?"

Jaamyas shrugged while he indulged in his yogurt. "Nothing to write home about."

Alexandre chuckled. "When have you ever written home?"

"Ha ha ha," he laughed with his sarcasm at his mother's jest. After swallowing a spoonful of the dairy snack, Jaamyas informed her, "Coach Carter said that Wednesday night works for him?"

"Works for him for what, son?" Alexandre inquired as she carried the cutting board of vegetables to the gas range. She slowly raked them into the cast iron wok.

Jaamyas stealthily rolled his eyes in annoyance with her absentmindedness. Unless she recorded it in her daily record, an event was good as forgotten. "For dinner, Mom. Remember?"

"What?" Alexandre quickly reflected on the conversation they had the week prior. "...I never committed to a date, Jay."

She pivoted to look at Jaamyas and then Jacob who had just entered the kitchen with a brown paper grocery bag and his briefcase. "Did you know anything about this? And why Wednesday?"

Jacob shrugged. He placed his briefcase in a corner and the groceries on the island. Ignoring her greeting that only barraged him with questions, Jacob exited the kitchen to remove his shoes and wash his hands.

"Because you said after my birthday," Jaamyas finally responded. "Thursday and Friday won't work because Thursday is the open-house for school, and Friday is my final summer game."

Vexed by the fact that he had committed her to the event before she had an opportunity to wholly consider it, Alexandre respired then spoke, "I really wish you had given me a moment to consider everything, Jay...My week is full as it is and I haven't even discussed the tickets with Coach Carter yet."

"Jacob already did," Jaamyas informed her in hopes that the one less task on her to-do list would prevent the cancellation of dinner. "They agreed to trade the tickets in for three less expensive ones and split the cost down the middle."

Alexandre caught Jacob's eyes and held them when he reentered the kitchen. She questioned sardonically, "Did they now?"

"Yup," Jaamyas gleefully affirmed. "And it's a win-win for me, Mom. My new dad and my new coach at a Panthers game to celebrate me!"

Alexandre broke the gaze she held with Jacob just in time to witness the smile her son beamed at her. Because it had only marginally extinguished her fury and frustration, she offered a halfhearted smile in return.

"Are you done?" Alexandre asked Jaamyas, nodding at his yogurt cup.

"Yes."

"Okay. Reading time," she directed.

Jaamyas sulked. "Yes, ma'am." He rose from his seat to wash the spoon and the yogurt cup. After placing the former in the dishwasher and the latter in the recycling, he ascended the stairs to the study.

"I wish you would have conferred with me before you made your decision about the tickets," Alexandre spoke to Jacob as she moved the squash around in the wok with a spatula.

"Hello, dear, my day was fair. How was yours?" Jacob deflected as he began to unpack and store the groceries.

Alexandre ignored his deflection and returned the conversation back to her point. "I had planned to pay for the tickets so that you and Jaamyas could go together."

Infuriated with her insolence and need to belabor her futile point, Jacob slammed closed the second of the two doors of the stainless-steel refrigerator. "And how was I supposed to know that, Alex?!...Since our spat yesterday, the only words that you actually spoke to me where that you couldn't get Jay from practice and you didn't want him walking or biking home in the rain."

As he awaited a reply, Jacob observed Alexandre reduce the fire of the brown rice and covered it. When she failed to speak, he construed her stiff silence to mean that she possessed no desire to respond to him.

Jacob breathed through his anger and explained, "Listen, Alex, Jay had already thanked Coach Carter for the tickets and shared with him your intentions to discuss an alternative arrangement. What else was I supposed to do?...Better yet, what would you have liked me to do?"

She burned her eyes into him and responded without hesitation, "You could have called me."

"I could have called you?..." Jacob scoffed in incredulity. "And you could have picked up our son like you said that you would as well as retrieve all the damn things that you forgot in haste during your grocery run." After deeply inhaling to calm himself, he tossed on the counter next to her the carrot bunch—one of the many items on the list she callously texted him.

"You can cancel the dinner if you want," Jacob finally suggested. "But know that I am not altering my decision about the tickets...I am going back to the office."

"You're going back into the city? At this hour? In the rain?" She questioned in disbelief.

"Don't wait up."

Alexandre watched him leave the remaining grocery items on the island, grab his briefcase from the corner, and walk toward the mudroom to exit the garage.

"I thought I told you not to wait up," Jacob spoke after quietly opening a single of their double bedroom doors.

Alexandre looked up from the book that she was reading and removed her glasses. "Well, if I didn't, then I wouldn't be able to tell you what I have to say."

He closed the door behind him and began to loosen the buttons of his business shirt in preparation for a hot shower. "It's after midnight, Alex. I don't want to hear whatever it is you have to say."

"...Not even an apology?"

Taken aback by her contrition, Jacob ceased his disrobing efforts. "...An apology for what?"

Alexandre pushed back the down comforter and sheet that covered her and stepped out of their bed. Wearing a satin nightie, she slowly walked to him. "For today…yesterday…Saturday." She took a moment to process her emotions. "I just have a lot on my plate and am having the hardest time managing and transitioning and…and I am taking it all out on you, and for that I'm sorry. I truly am sorry, Jacob."

Jacob searched her weary eyes and detected the stress she alluded to. "…Tell me what's going on, Alex."

She kissed his mouth.

"Please," he urged between their kisses. "Talk to me…I'm…I'm here for you..."

"…I know…"

"Then talk to me, Alex. Whatever it is, we will get through it together…I won't leave you—I will never abandon you."

Alexandre lowered her lids over her eyes as his assuring words resonated with her. The level of security she found in Jacob surpassed that of her first husband, but, still yet, she felt a need to yield unhurriedly and cautiously.

"…Please," Jacob implored another time, assuming that her silence was an indication of her imminent concession.

"I will, Jacob, but not tonight." She placed her mouth on his and attempted to enticingly peck away his appeal.

He pulled away from the softness of her lips and met her eyes. Despite the rise her affection had on his body, Jacob could not allow her to deflect in this moment. He knew that she was enduring in secret a hardship that was not only impacting her, but their home as well.

Pushing back her hair, he pressed his forehead on to hers, and entreated on her lips, "Don't shut me out, Alexandre. Please…Please, let me in."

Her lips stretched into an impish grin. "I plan to, but, first," she gently nudged him into the wall behind him, "let me return the many favors."

Jacob chuckled at the innuendo and, finally, relinquished his request. He then watched as she loosened his belt, then pants, and, at last, lower herself to her knees.

*** *** ***

"Well, I can't deny that I am surprised by this impromptu visit," the psychiatrist admitted as she secured her office door and took the cushioned sofa seat in front of Alexandre. She then crossed her right leg over the knee of her left, adjusted her ivory blouse, and folded her hands in the crotch of her camel-colored slacks. "You are typically my schedule-several-sessions-in-advance patient."

Alexandre peered beyond the beautiful Indian woman and gawked at her family photo mounted on the wall. It was a picture of Dr. Ahmed's husband and four children that Alexandre had seen several times before, but only this time did the smiles resonate with her.

"I had two people within one week suggest that I check-in. So, I figured it behooved me to do so before the third person to suggest it became a victim of my insanity," Alexandre finally responded.

Dr. Ahmed unwrapped and then removed her loosely worn hijab. "I seriously doubt that, Alex. Your incessant need to be in control won't permit you to lose it in an act of violence."

Alexandre puffed at the assessment. "Don't be too quick to discount it. I've been known to even surprise myself."

Unsure of how to receive Alexandre's statement, Dr. Ahmed inquired, "So, what brings you here today? Is there something specific you want to talk about?"

Alexandre met her amber eyes and answered, "My marriage is in trouble?"

"You have only been married for about a month or so, Alex. Why do you believe this already?"

Alexandre did not reply.

"Did something happen?"

After considering the question, Alexandre finally responded, "…Lance."

"Lance?"

"…Yes, Lance." Alexandre inhaled deeply and exhaled slowly. She contemplated all that she wanted to disclose and all that she wanted to remain hidden. "…Since the wedding I have been having more frequent thoughts of him."

"That's not uncommon. You encountered a life changing event. It was bound to unearth old memories of your former husband as you create new memories with your current husband."

Alexandre reached for her diamond pendant. When it was not immediately located at the touch, she lowered her eyes to discover that it was not around her neck. Recalling her late night and early morning, she assumed that, in her haste, she forgotten to wear it—something she rarely did.

"…I suppose…" Alexandre uttered as she dropped her hand so that the thumb of her left hand could massage the palmar creases of her right.

Dr. Ahmed looked upon her decade-long client. Despite the polished look of her heather grey pants-suit and soft pink shirt, Alexandre appeared disheveled. "Is there something more?"

"…Jaamyas is looking more like him every day," Alexandre whispered. "I mean he always has, but now that he has become a teenager and is transitioning into a man, he is the exact spitting image of his father—it's uncanny."

Dr. Ahmed contorted her face in confusion. It was not Alexandre's nature to return to conquered demons. "We have been here before, Alexandre, and prepared for this. So, none of this is new."

She awaited a response for Alexandre. When none came, Dr. Ahmed questioned, "What is this really about?"

Alexandre ceased massaging her hand and met her physician's eyes, "Jacob wants to adopt our son—Lance's and my son."

"Okay," Dr. Ahmed acknowledged and nodded in reply. "Is this a problem for you because of the love you still have for Lance?"

"No, not because I still love Lance, but because of his legacy."

"So, his legacy is the problem because you still love Lance."

"No, not because I still love Lance, but because I don't want the memory of him to die."

"So, his memory is the problem because you still-"

"Love Lance," Alexandre finished for her when she finally recognized Dr. Ahmed's slant.

Dr. Ahmed smiled at Alexandre's concession and confession. She then pulled her long, dark tresses to one shoulder and reclined her lean body into the pillows behind her. She now felt that their therapy session could begin at last.

"The thing about the truth, Alexandre, is that it needs no repeating. It is the lie that has to be stated multiple times for it to be believed."

"I'm not lying, I'm just…confounded."

"And that's okay. What you are feeling is okay. You don't love Jacob less because you still love Lance, Alex. Lance was the first of many experiences for you and you possess several fond memories of him. Because of that, you will always love him and his legacy and his memory will never die."

Alexandre shrugged as she swallowed the knot in her throat. "I don't know, I just think that…" Her voice trailed off.

"It will be difficult for you to share guardianship?" Dr. Ahmed completed for her. "That you never had to share custody before and with an adoption you would have to?"

"No," Alexandre denied. "This isn't about me."

"Well, it's certainly not about Lance because he is not with us to contest the adoption proceedings and can't be about Jaamyas— he adores Jacob."

Alexandre did not speak a word in response. As a result, the room fell silent for a brief moment.

"…I read the paper, too, Alexandre."

Alexandre exhaled audibly as she rolled her eyes and dissented, "This isn't about work."

"I think it is and just about every facet of your life that you are accustomed to controlling, but no longer can," Dr. Ahmed deduced before the office momentarily fell silent another time.

"…Do you believe everything happens for a reason?" Alexandre asked, interrupting the quietness in the room and diverting the conversation. "I mean, I know we are of different faiths, but do you believe that, by God's design, small occurrences happen to us so that we are prepared for a much larger event?"

Perplexed by the derivation of her questions, Dr. Ahmed merely responded, "Yes, I do believe that Allah is the supreme power and the cause of all causes."

Alexandre nodded in acknowledgment of her response. She then carefully considered her own reply and elucidated, "Well, I believe that I am in a season of preparation."

"Preparation for what?"

"A meeting with Lance."

Confused once more, Dr. Ahmed inquired of her morbid comment, "In death?"

Alexandre cavalierly raised her shoulders as there was no other explanation to her heightened sensitivity to her first husband. "…I don't know. Maybe."

"You're starting a new life with an amazing man, Alex. Why are you contemplating death already?"

"If not for death, then for what else? What else could possibly explain all these incidents—they are so real, so intense?"

"Fear."

"Fear?"

"Yes, fear," Dr. Ahmed repeated. "You are afraid to move on because you believe it means death to what you had."

Alexandre spoke nothing so not to confirm or deny what Dr. Ahmed had surmised. For a moment, she sat in silence to allow all that the psychiatrist had observed resonate with her.

"…Are you reciting your incantations?" Dr. Ahmed asked.

"When I remember to," Alexandre merely answered.

Dr. Ahmed allowed herself time to slowly breathe through her disappointment and aggravation. The joint-decision to employ talk therapy, in lieu of medication, to treat Alexandre's anxiety and depression was decided based on Alexandre's assured commitment to the psychiatric recommendations. To know that Alexandre reneged on their verbal agreement prompted Dr. Ahmed's regret. The therapist now wished that she had been more forceful of a prescription treatment.

"…Well, when you do remember," Dr. Ahmed began, suppressing her ill-feelings in attempt to make the most of the hour they had together, "do you find them helpful?"

"They calm me," Alexandre confirmed, "but they do nothing for the thoughts or...or dreams, or apparitions."

"And they won't. Those experiences are normal, Alex...Once again, the purpose of the incantations is to bring you back to your center when you are experiencing bouts of chaos...They only work if you work them."

Alexandre glanced at her watch. "Let's end the session early. You can still bill me for the entire hour."

Dr. Ahmed simply nodded, feeling no urge to impede her. "Okay. Should we schedule the next visit or will you make a point to drop-in within a week."

After standing, Alexandre responded, "I don't know, but thank you for accommodating me today."

"Enjoy the remainder of your day, Alexandre."

"Here the both of you are," Jacob spoke, standing at the threshold of Alexandre's home office. He found her sitting behind her desk and Jaamyas sitting in front of it, comfortably reclined in one leather chair with his feet propped on the slanted other.

Alexandre looked up from her laptop and removed her reading glasses. "Hey, babe. I didn't hear you come in...How was your day?"

Jacob raised his shoulders in indifference and responded, "It was fair." He walked further into the room, kissed her, and asked, "How was yours?" as he extended his fist toward Jaamyas to bump.

Alexandre quickly reflected on her day and recalled her impromptu visit with her psychiatrist. Not willing to disclose the details of the session in the company of her son, she simply replied, "It was fair."

Jacob sat on the corner of her desk. After pushing back her hair, he replied. "That's not good." He winked, lowered his voice, and offered, "Perhaps I can help change that later tonight."

"Eeeew—gross," Jaamyas interrupted, reminding them of his presence.

Jacob grinned and rose from his seat. "I didn't think you would hear that."

Jaamyas turned the page of his book. "Well, I did and it's gross."

Jacob chuckled and disregarded the youth's ignorance to the beautiful pleasures God created for husband and wife. "What are you reading?"

"Stowe's *Uncle Tom's Cabin.*"

"Really?"

Jaamyas nodded. "It's one of the last books on my summer reading list. Last school year, I was told that my new history teacher will use classic literature as an approach to examine the impact of slavery on America. He also has Harper Lee's *To Kill a Mockingbird* on the list."

Astounded by the Christian private school's commitment to incorporate critical race theory into their curriculum, Jacob could only respond, "Okay. Let me know if you need help. Those both happen to be my favorites."

Jaamyas nodded in acknowledgment.

Jacob returned his gaze to Alexandre. "Before I forget again or the time lapses, I need to add the two of you to my health benefits. What coverage do you currently have? I want to at least mirror it."

Alexandre thought for a moment and then answered, "Uuuummm. That is a really good question and I have no clue." After pondering a short while longer, she finally conceded, "Check the cards in my wallet. It's in my handbag—no, wait, my briefcase. Check my briefcase in the foyer closet."

Jacob nodded, thanked her, and exited the room to follow her directives. Holding her designer briefcase in one hand, he shuffled through a host of folders and papers with the other. No wallet was found. He unzipped the hidden sleeve and felt around to discover only an envelope. Recognizing the color of it, Jacob pulled the envelope from the discrete compartment and placed the leather briefcase on the foyer table.

To confirm what he suspected to be true, Jacob opened the envelope and removed the document. It was the adoption papers—unsigned and never filed. Feelings of disappointment and pain were quickly replaced with frustration and rage. He angrily strode back to the office with the document in hand.

"Care to explain this?" He tossed the stapled papers on her desk in front of her.

Alexandre looked away from her screen and down at the document. After recognizing it, she stammered, "Jacob, I-I-"

Jaamyas lowered his book and inquired, "What is that?"

"Adoption papers," Jacob responded at the exact moment Alexandre replied, "Nothing."

Jaamyas rose from his seat to retrieve the pages to determine the truth for himself.

Furious, Jacob retorted, "A legal petition to adopt my stepson is not nothing, Alex."

She extended her hand to Jaamyas and demanded, "Jay, give me those." She then looked at Jacob and confirmed, "I didn't mean it that way, Jacob."

"I don't know what you mean anymore, Alex. You continue to say things and don't follow through. You told me you were going to file them."

"No," she began as she fought to recall the most recent conversation regarding the petition, "what I said was that we would talk about it as a family—that this was not a decision to make lightly." She stood to her feet and ordered more forcefully, "Jaamyas, now."

Jaamyas stepped from her reach as he flipped the page of the petition and continued to read.

Jacob clarified, "You mean that this is not a decision to be made by anyone, but you."

Alexandre removed her glasses and placed them in the center of the law book she had opened. "Jacob, please, not now. We can have a serious conversation about this at a later time if you want, but-"

"We are having one now, or does this not qualify under Rule A.K.D.H. Section 24 point 7?"

Alexandre rolled her eyes at the allusion that she alone dictated the rules that governed their household all day, every day. "Don't be petulant, Jacob. It doesn't become you."

Jacob huffed at her slight and fought hard against the vulgar response he wanted to rejoin. "I ask so little from you, Alex...But this one thing—just this one thing that I ask you to push through with your judicial clout-"

"Geeeez, Jacob, it will get done."

"When, Alexandre?"

"When…" Alexandre contemplated a date in the distant future, but realized she was only validating his point of her monarchy rule. Undoubtedly, she did tend to operate by the terms that were most advantageous to her in the time that was most convenient to her. "…When all parties involved have decided."

Jacob shook his head in dismay. "…You're unbelievable, Alex. You know that, right?" When she did not respond, he continued, "You always seem to have an answer for me, but it's never the right one."

Alexandre exhaled audibly with vexation. "Jacob, I-"

Jaamyas searched his mother's mesh supply cup for a blue pen. Per her earlier guidance, signatures in blue ink differentiated an original document from an indistinguishable copy.

Upon retrieving the writing implement, he placed the document on the corner of her desk, and signed where indicated. Jaamyas then returned the pen to the cup and placed the document in her extended hand. "The only person left now to decide is you, Mom."

Alexandre accepted the document, watched him collect his book, and walk out of the office.

When her eyes met Jacob's, he spoke with discontentment, "Thank you for, once again, ruining a Hallmark-moment for our son."

Alexandre spoke no words in return. Instead, she watched the second male in her household walk out on her.

"I'm stepping out," Alexandre announced later that evening, standing at the entrance of the family room. She found both Jacob and Jaamyas reclined in the plush cushions of the sofa; they were reading as piano music softly played through the surround sound speakers.

Jacob lowered his architecture magazine and glanced at his watch. It was approaching 9 P.M. "It's late." He met her eyes and inquired, "Where are you going?"

"To my chambers."

He returned his gaze to his subscription and merely responded, "Okay." Jacob had learned years prior to never intervene or discourage her obsessive work ethic.

"It's an order that I have to sign so that it can be filed first thing in the morning…With the press conference tomorrow, I have no choice."

Jacob turned the page of his magazine as he replied, "Okay."

Alexandre turned on her heels to exit, but turned back to the face them. "I'm sorry."

Both Jacob and Jaamyas looked up from their reading materials and fixed their eyes on her.

"My thoughts and actions surrounding the petition for adoption were narrow- and single-minded, and that is not how I want decisions to be made in our family."

Jacob shrugged. "I'm sure you had your reasons. I just wish you would have shared them with us."

She shook her head in opposition as she suppressed thoughts of Lance. "They were all immaterial and selfish. So, it was best that I kept them to myself." After inhaling deeply and exhaling loudly, she offered, "I will review and sign everything and see to it that the papers are filed with the clerk. I will ask that it be made a priority on the docket."

Jaamyas beamed a wide smile at her. "Thanks, Mom."

"You're welcome, son…Hopefully, the two of you will forgive me for my selfishness."

"Don't we always," they both responded in unison.

Alexandre chuckled. "Don't wait up." With that she turned on her heels another time to exit the garage and make the drive back into the city.

*** *** ***

"So, what is this I hear about you issuing a scathing public statement during a press conference today?" Jacob inquired. He then stepped around Alexandre as they worked together in the kitchen to prepare for their dinner guest. "You didn't share this with me."

Alexandre huffed at the memory of the hand she was forced to proffer. Each day, the judicial role she recently embarked created more a life of compromise for her. All of which she was not accustomed to, particularly since it compelled her to do things she would not ordinarily do.

Before she trod too long in the vast sea of her silence, Jacob probed, "What was that all about? You typically don't speak to the press."

"You mean the P.R. move that my uncle *strongly encouraged* me to make?"

"Charles?"

"Who else?" She rhetorically asked, removing the garlic butter salmon from the oven.

Jacob transferred the roasted carrots and broccoli from the baking sheet to the China serving dish. "When did you speak to him?"

"He dropped in for a visit at my chambers on Monday."

"Really? For what?"

After exhaling the resurfaced dejection, Alexandre responded, "To remind me of how I have abysmally failed in maintaining my judicial obligation to his former bench."

Jacob merely rolled his eyes and shook his head to avoid speaking ill of his in-law. "Honestly, Alex, I don't know why you subject yourself to his scorn. He is retired after all."

She contemplated her husband's observation for a moment and, when no adequate explanation unveiled, Alexandre shrugged and defended, "…He is my uncle—I am his legacy."

"No, Alex, you are your parents' legacy," Jacob corrected.

She exhaled audibly at the thought of her parents and the demands that accompanied them. "Yeah, like that's any consolation. Remember, I am the constant reminder of the son they always desired, but never had. Hence the name Alexandre…Truthfully, I feel that I am merely the prodigal daughter of the pilot and the microbiologist."

Jacob smiled and winked. "But you did return. So, dwell on that and the additional honor you brought to your family name."

She sneered and recalled, "Circumstances brought me back—not desire."

He met her eyes. "Well, I in no way celebrate your loss, but I am elated that the circumstance brought you to me."

Alexandre smiled. "I am truly blessed."

"Indeed *we* are." He leaned forward to kiss-

"He's here, he's here!" Jaamyas exclaimed, rushing into the kitchen.

"Okay, okay. No need to ring the alarm. We have had dinner guests before," Alexandre reminded in an effort to pacify him.

"Yes, but never Coach Carter," Jaamyas reminded in return in an effort to galvanize her.

Alexandre turned her eyes upward and extended to him the bread basket and China dish. "Take these to the formal dining room and DON'T drop them."

Jaamyas received the warm honey yeast rolls and steaming vegetables and did as he was instructed.

"I will get the salmon and the wine," Jacob offered. When the doorbell rang, he added, "And the door."

"Thanks, babe. I will check dessert in the oven and will be right out."

"Don't forget the glasses," he called out behind himself.

"Don't forget the glasses," she repeated to herself.

Alexandre carefully removed the homemade apple pie—another one of Jaamyas's favorites that he insisted on having with vanilla ice cream. At the sight of the bubbling goodness, she placed the dessert on a silicone cooling mat and then returned to the wall to turn off both ovens.

"Any day, Mom," Jaamyas called out to her.

"Okay, okay. I'm coming." She untied her half apron, placed it on the island, and started out the kitchen. Midpoint to the dining room, Alexandre remembered the wine glasses. She turned on her heels to retrieve them.

"I'm so sorry," Alexandre apologized, entering the room. "I almost forgot the wine gla..." Her voice gradually quieted when their guest, engaged in conversation with Jacob, pivoted to meet her.

The familiarity of his smile caused the three crystal glasses to slip through her fingers and crash to the floor.

"Mom!" Jaamyas exclaimed, rushing to her aid. "Are you okay?"

"…Yes…Yes, I'm…I'm fine, son," Alexandre assured, breaking her daze and returning his embrace. She directed him to fetch the broom and then slowly knelt in her skirt to collect the larger pieces.

"I got it, Alex," Jacob said, pulling her to her feet. He caught her eyes and asked, "Are you sure you're okay?"

Alexandre nodded and whispered, "Yeah. Yeah, I'm fine…I'm so sorry…Please…Please give me a minute. Start without me." She exited the room, raced to the foyer, and up the winding stairs.

In her master bathroom, she pressed cold water on her face and neck. After gently blotting her skin dry with a hand towel, Alexandre gazed at her reflection in the mirror above her sink. She began to recite one of her many incantations, "I can't move forward if I keep looking back. I must learn to let go; I can't move forward if I keep looking back. I must learn to let go; I can't move forward if I keep looking back. I must learn to let go…"

After a few deep breaths, Alexandre refreshed her makeup and made her way back to the formal dining room.

"I apologize again for the mishap."

Jacob rose to help her to the seat next to him in front of a plate he had prepared for her. After he took his own again, he asked, "Are you okay?"

Shamefully avoiding Jacob's eyes, Alexandre nodded. She then met Coach Carter's brown eyes aslant to her. His smooth, chocolate face was partially covered with a low cut, salt and pepper beard. "I hope I didn't startle you," she spoke to him.

"A little," Coach Carter honestly confessed, "but I'm at ease now that I know that you are okay."

Alexandre feebly smiled and then looked at Jaamyas's plate. He had opted to sit in front of her and next to his coach. "More vegetables, Jay," she directed her child who was finicky about the vegetables he consumed. She then placed a forkful of carrots in her mouth.

"But, Mom," he whined.

"More vegetables or no apple pie," she simply admonished after swallowing, refusing to entertain a squabble with him.

"Apple pie? That's my favorite," Coach Carter acknowledged.

"Mine, too," Jaamyas spoke as he begrudgingly added more carrots and broccoli to his plate.

Jacob snickered. "Jay actually has many favorites."

"…And Mom has none," Jaamyas mumbled.

Alexandre chewed and swallowed the morsel of fish in her mouth, then explained, "Well, it's hard for a girl to choose when she is presented with so many options…But, I do obsess over a few things."

"Like home décor," Jacob slipped in. "Can you believe she designed the interior of this whole house?"

Coach Carter met Alexandre's eyes and remarked, "Amazing. I would love to see the rest of your work after dinner— if I may."

Alexandre politely nodded. "Of course."

"Maybe Mom can decorate your house, coach," Jaamyas offered, "…Whenever you buy yours, of course?"

"I don't think I can afford your mother's rates, Jay."

"She is a judge, not an interior decorator. Decorating is how she unwinds; it's her hobby."

"It's interesting how you have managed to regurgitate all that I have said, but still can't remember to put the trash out for pick-up on Tuesdays and Fridays."

The table, with the exception of Jaamyas, erupted with laughter.

"So, now that you are retired, is volunteering at the center all that you plan to do? Or do you plan to do anything more, like work with any of the local schools?" Jacob asked.

Alexandre lowered her wine glass. "Retired? From what? You look so young."

Coach Carter smiled. "I appreciate the compliment, but I am a few years shy of fifty."

"And no family?"

"Geeeeez, Mom, let coach enjoy his meal without an interrogation…You always do this," Jaamyas groaned.

"Well, you wanted us to get to know him, right? Isn't that why you proposed dinner?"

"No—yes—but to discuss sports, and hobbies, and NFL stats."

"Oh, I see. So, in other words, to engage you," Alexandre surmised.

"Yes!" Jaamyas exclaimed, excited that his mother finally comprehended his intentions.

Alexandre rolled her eyes at her son's lack of selflessness while she simultaneously laughed at his enthusiasm. Understanding that Jaamyas had now transitioned into a period in life in which male attention and bonding was critical to his development, Alexandre allowed her him to carry the dinner conversation as they ate. When there was finally a break in the discussion, she took notice of the empty dinner plates.

"Well," she spoke, breaking the brief silence as she rose to her feet. "I will clear these and bring out dessert."

Jacob stood to assist her.

"Please let me help," Coach Carter offered, standing as well.

"Not at all. You're our guest." She took the plates from each of them. "You boys stay and continue to talk football. I've got this."

Following dessert, Alexandre provided a brief tour of their home while Jacob and Jaamyas washed the dishes.

She blushed at Coach Carter's accolades and responded, "I am not sure about that, but I do try."

"Don't be modest. Your mastery of work-life balance alludes to the proverbial S on your chest."

Alexandre chuckled. "You're far too kind."

"Trust me, I'm really not." He tried to catch her gaze, but she carefully avoided his eyes. "So," he started as he followed her into her dimly lit office. "I happened to notice that I caught your eyes on me a few times during dinner."

Alexandre stopped at her desk. "Please do not misconstrue my affections, Coach Carter. You are my son's coach and I am merely trying to get to know you." She turned to face him. "Besides, I am a happily married woman."

He grinned. "Of course. I didn't mean anything by it…It's just that-"

"You remind me of someone," Alexandre interrupted with the intent to disabuse him of any romantic hope.

"In your past?"

She nodded. "Yes."

"Your first husband?"

"Jay has told you about him?"

Coach Carter nodded.

"Wow," she uttered in astonishment. "…I…I didn't know that Jay still spoke of him…especially since…"

Though her voice trailed off, Coach Carter waited for her to complete her thought. When it never transpired, he merely shrugged and commented, "We all have someone anchoring us to the past."

Alexandre scoffed at the supposition. She then peered deep into his eyes as she inquired, "If that truly is the case, then who is yours?"

"Excuse me?"

"Your anchor?"

Taken aback by her inquiry, Coach Carter cleared his throat and began, "…Well, if I had to choose one, it would be-"

"Mom," Jaamyas greeted, pushing wider the opened door. "The dishes are all done and the kitchen is all clean." He walked in without invitation and hugged her torso.

She returned his embrace, kissed his forehead, and spoke, "I appreciate it."

Jaamyas looked up at her and smiled. "Another slice of pie will show me just how much."

She chuckled. "Nice try, kiddo. But you know the rules and they are not to be broken."

"Well, if that were true, then there would be no consequences," Jaamyas remarked.

Alexandre shook her head at the child replica of herself and retorted, "Or judges to punish the rule breakers."

Jaamyas groaned at his defeat; and, to annoy him, Alexandre groaned along with him.

She released him and instructed, "Say good night to your coach and go get ready for bed."

Jaamyas grumbled best wishes to his coach and then exited the room to do as his mother commanded. Alexandre moved to follow, but was stopped by the clasp of her hand.

"You," he finally responded.

Alexandre looked down at the hand that held hers and then up at the face that peered down at her. "Excuse me?"

"If I had to choose one," Coach Carter began again in a whisper, "it would be you."

Alexandre intensely looked past the low cut, salt and pepper beard and saw a visage that was now more all too familiar to her. "Lance?"

"…Alex."

She gasped and abruptly yanked her hand from his hold. "Is this some sort of sick joke?"

"When have you ever known me to be a jokester?"

Perplexed by what to believe, what to say, and what to do, Alexandre finally requested, "Please leave."

"Alex-"

"Now."

"Alex-"

"NOW!"

He took a moment to allow silence to calm the room. "I will be at the center. Please meet me at the stadium in an hour."

"Everything okay?" Jacob asked, arriving at the threshold.

Alexandre met Jacob's eyes and quickly recovered. "Fine. Just a slight disagreement over Jay's practice schedule once classes start." She turned to their guest and bid, "Have a good night, Coach Carter. My husband will walk you out."

He rose to greet her when she ascended the last step to the bleachers and walked toward him. "Alex, I am so glad that you made it. I didn't think you would-"

She struck his face with an open hand and fought the urge to do it a second time when he turned his head back to her. Though it was dark, Alexandre kept his gaze with the help of the stadium lights.

Lance ignored the taste of blood in his mouth as he massaged his sore cheek. "I guess I deserve that."

"...Is it really you?"

He contemplated the question and an adequate response to it.

"Lance Carter Denton. Is it really you?"

He stepped to close the space between them and gently stroke her cheek. "On our wedding night, you were so bashful that you would not let me touch you until all the lights were out in our suite."

At the memory of that night over sixteen years ago, Alexandre lowered her lids over her eyes and released a solemn cry. "...They...they told me that you were dead...They told me that you were dead," she murmured in his chest after he enveloped her waist and held her firmly against his body.

Lance stroked her hair and kissed her temple as her body trembled in distress.

A moment passed before she stepped out of his embrace. "I'm so sorry. I guess...I guess I'm just overwhelmed with so many emotions."

"Don't apologize for the way you feel."

She met his eyes and confessed, "You're supposed to be dead."

"But, by the grace of God, I'm not."

"...How? Why?...How?" She shook her head. "Never mind...D-don't bother. I...I can't stay...Jacob believes I am out buying aspirin."

Lance face contorted at the lie. "But you're allergic to aspirin."

"Jay isn't," she responded, impressed by his memory.

"Alex, please," he pleaded, gripping her hand as she turned to leave. "Please, stay a while. I have so much to tell you, so much to explain."

"I need time."

"How much?"

Alexandre shrugged her shoulders and retorted, "I don't know—thirteen years."

Lance released her hand and forced both of his into his pants pockets. He turned his face toward the track and field. "That was a cheap shot below the belt, Alex." Looking again into her eyes, he asked, "When did you stop playing fair?"

She inhaled deeply and exhaled slowly. Evading the question, Alexandre requested, "Please do not unveil yourself to Jaamyas until I've had time to process all of this."

He respired and contested, "He's my son, Alexandre."

"Yes, so think about your son, Lance. Think about how all of this is going to affect him...Hell, I just got married a month ago and he is still adjusting to that."

"...I know...You're right, you're right."

Alexandre's heart softened at his concession. "...Meet me at the French bistro a few blocks north of the Mecklenburg County Courthouse tomorrow at noon."

Lance nodded. "Thank you, Alex."

"Good night, Lance."

*** *** ***

Alexandre's attention dropped to the blinking lines on her phone immediately after the attorney vacated her chambers. Stressed, she lowered herself to her chair and began to engage in square breathing—inhale four seconds, hold four seconds, exhale four seconds, hold four seconds. She repeated the technique a second time before retrieving the headpiece, selecting a line, and announcing, "Denton-Hall."

"Alexandre," he calmly, but firmly spoke in irritation.

"Jacob?...I'm so sorry. I forgot you were holding."

"Apparently so." He paused to suppress his ill feelings and then asked, "Are you okay, Alex?...You were out late last night and then you left early this morning."

"Yeah, of course. Just a little stretched thin—that's all."

Jacob contemplated her response then cautiously asked, "Are *we* okay?"

Taken aback by his question, Alexandre stammered, "W-what? Why, why would ask that?...Of course we are."

Recalling their various marital discords, Jacob doubted her response. However, he was reluctant to press her with probing questions. Instead, he offered, "Let me take you to lunch. I can come to you and we can dine at your beloved French bistro."

"Not today, Jacob. I have a conflict."

"How about dinner after the school's open house? I can check your parents' availability, or even Seanna's."

When she did not immediately respond, he further coaxed, "I can ask my brother as well."

Alexandre pondered his older brother, Raymond, and his family. Though she possessed the desire for Jaamyas to develop a relationship with his new cousins, she was weary of what her young impressionable son would learn from four high school boys.

"I really don't want another late night, Jacob," Alexandre replied in a half-truth. "I have a status call at eight in the morning...Maybe tomorrow after Jay's game? The three of us can do something as a family."

Jacob exhaled loudly. "I was really hoping that just the two of us cou-"

"Hold that thought...COME IN."

The door crept open and her assistant peered in. "Judge Rollins still holding on line one."

Alexandre nodded. "Babe, I have to go. Let's plan to talk tonight. We can plan something for the weekend."

Jacob rolled his eyes and remarked sarcastically, "Another plan to make plans."

Her heart ached at the revelation of her neglect. The pain seemed to have exacerbated now that she was neglecting a husband in addition to her son. "Jacob, I'm sorry. I really am doing the best tha-"

"Good-bye, Alexandre," Jacob interrupted before abruptly ending the call.

She thought to dial his office number, but the now lone blinking light on line three forced her to postpone the conversation with Jacob.

"Denton-Hall," Alexandre greeted after connecting the line.

"Alex, are we still meeting for lunch?"

"Lance?"

"Yes. You said noon, right?"

"I did. Is it noon already?"

"A quarter after now."

Alexandre exhaled audibly and then assured, "Okay, give me twenty minutes. I will be there in twenty minutes."

"Okay. See you in twenty minutes."

Alexandre used her linen napkin to gently press her face dry of the tears that fell from her eyes. Lance had relived the past thirteen years of his life as a prisoner of war that began with the enemy's infiltration and seizure of his platoon. When his days were not filled with torture and humiliation, they were subjected to forced servitude. Relief finally came with the recent change in regime that found no beneficial use of the surviving Marines. Their release among the lowest of the caste was considered a generous favor when considering the alternative—death.

"It's a wonder how you survived thirteen years in those conditions."

He met her eyes across the table and corrected, "No wonder—all God and loving thoughts of you and our beautiful son."

Alexandre turned from his gaze. She found it difficult to believe that thoughts of Jaamyas or her occupied his mind when he was grossly consumed with a military mission.

"Does your family know of your return?" She asked diverting the conversation. "Your father passed away a few years ago, but your mother is doing well. I call and visit as often as I can, when life allows it."

"They know and they've seen me…It was my mother who informed me of your whereabouts…Actually…" Lance voice trailed off for a moment as he contemplated the delivery of his confession.

"…It was my mother who informed me of everything about you—both you and Jaamyas…She spared no picture, no story, no detail, Alex."

Alexandre lowered her head and began to recall all that she shared with her mother-in-law. In the last thirteen years, she had divulged much concerning her loneliness, anguish, and fears, trusting that the secrets shared would not be repeated.

An uncomfortable pregnant silence grew between them while they both remained stoic in their seats. Swallowing the knot in his throat, Lance observed Alexandre vigorously rub the palmar creases in her right hand with the thumb of her left. Undoubtedly, she was distressed. His appearance was not only unexpected, but ill-timed—the two elements of events that Alexandre despised the most.

Sensing the question that she was reticent to ask, Lance cleared his throat in preparation to answer. "I asked to be the one to tell you." He stretched his arm across the white linen covered table for her hand to ease her discomfort and explained, "Once I found out where you were, I wanted to be the one to tell you and…and I wanted it to be in-person and at the right time."

She rose her eyes to peer blankly at him as she slowly withdrew her hand from his. Though she spoke no verbal response to his perception of the "right time," her nonverbal reply communicated intense disdain with his wonted selfishness.

"…So, you chose a long way from San Diego," Lance observed, breaking the awkward quietness. "I never would have thought you would return home. Coming back couldn't have been easy for you."

"What was the alternative, Lance?" Alexandre shrugged her shoulders and inquired further, "Stay in California and struggle on my own with a newborn?"

He parted his lips to reply, but she halted him, "I gave birth to our son and weeks went by before I could personally deliver the news to you. Then it was another several weeks before we would video chat again—and that turned out to be our last…"

Alexandre took a few deep breaths to calm her enraged nerves and quickly wiped away the tears that wet her cheeks. "…Your death altered the entire trajectory of my life."

Lance considered her many sacrifices and exhaled loudly with regret. "I'm so sorry, Alex. I really am, but you know my family would have helped you."

Alexandre shook her head in opposition. "No, I had to leave California. No amount of familial help or your survivor benefits could sustain us there, and no law firm was in a rush to hire a new lactating mother."

"Be that as it may, Alex," he began in contest, "you did not have to come crawling back here. Coming back was the last thing I wanted for you, especially with your parents."

"And starting all over with your family in Texas was?" Alexandre retorted, frustrated with his disregard of her fears: she was a new mother expected to start a new career in a new area with people she knew little about. "At least here I had family *and* friends to help me with Jaamyas while I studied for the bar and worked to build a solid legal career."

Lance respired lowly and rubbed his brow in grief. Finally, the importance of a trustworthy and reliable support system that Alexandre not only needed, but was content with, was resonating with him.

After apologizing once more, Lance explained, "I just know how your parents are, Alex, and how they were when we met at North Carolina A&T." Recalling past interactions with his in-laws, he shook his head and sneered. "They never approved of me, or us; and they loathed the day we married, and hated more the hour I took you from here."

Alexandre, too, reflected on the memories. "I am their baby girl, Lance—their only child. What did you expect?"

He chuckled at the truth she stated and responded lightheartedly, "Yes, I know. And they reiterated all of those facts multiple times on our wedding day."

Alexandre did not find his banter humorous. To the contrary, his conversation was beginning to increase her anxiety.

"What is it that you want, Lance?" She pejoratively asked. It was her hope to end their meeting before she grew more anxious.

Taken aback by her abrupt forwardness, Lance carefully contemplated her question and an appropriate response. Their history has taught him that unfavorable responses were equally matched with unfavorable reactions. "…I know that you are married now, Alex…In fact, I knew of your engagement prior to coming out here."

She pondered his statement along with a series of unexplained events and deduced, "Your sister told you, didn't she?"

Lance nodded.

"…And the tulips?"

"They've always been one of your obsessions."

"…So, it was you who sent them to my chambers?" Alexandre spoke more as a declaration than an ask.

In lieu of a simple response, Lance recited the inscription noted on the card that accompanied the floral arrangement, "May you be blessed with all of the passion your hand can capture, love your heart can cage, and joy your soul can contain."

Alexandre shook her head in dismay at the poetic regurgitation. Had she not been convinced that he was deceased, she would have assumed that the tulips were a gift from him. Afterall, it was he who enlightened her of their symbolic meaning of enduring love and devotion. And, it was he who was the first to present her with the perennial.

"…The infamous Lance Carter Denton," she mumbled under her breath, realizing that he was also the last person to fuel her floral obsession.

Uncertain of what her sardonic statement meant, Lance cleared his throat and deflected by professing, "…Look, I just want to forge a relationship with my son, Alex. To be his father, to be a part of his life, to be his family…I know it is too late for us, but not for him—not for my son."

Thoughts of their tumultuous past would not permit her to be moved by his sincerity in his voice. Despite their abiding love and unbridled passion, their marriage lacked certainty, stability, and, more importantly, commitment. For these reasons she could not be immediately supportive of a father-son relationship between Lance and Jaamyas. It was one matter for him to abandon his wife, but for Lance to abandon his son was another, and one that Alexandre could prevent.

The reflection on their younger years compelled Alexandre to remind him, "Thirteen years ago I begged you to choose us—your family. But you didn't, Lance. Instead, you chose the Marine Corps—your true family."

"Alex-" he began, vexed by the familiarity of her monologue.

"No, Lance," Alexandre forcefully interjected. "You don't get to reappear, literally out of nowhere, and ask me to choose you to be his family, to subject him to the same mental anguish and emotional torment caused by your absence."

"Alex-"

"Why?"

"I-"

"Why should I, Lance?"

"Because-"

"You left before. How do I know that you won't leave again? Because that is what you do—you leave."

"Because I am his father damnit!" He finally exclaimed, leaning as far into her face as the table would allow. "You of all people know that I don't need any other reason than that...I am his father."

"And I am his mother," Alexandre rejoined, unmoved by his passion. "And I will shield him to the best of my ability from any unnecessary heartbreak."

"Be that as it may, Alexandre, that changes nothing. I am who I am, and that is Jaamyas's father."

Ignoring the truth in his statement and the few glares that his elevated voice shifted to them, Alexandre shook her head and dissented, "...No, you're not. Jacob is."

Taken aback by the revelation, Lance reclined again into the back of his chair and struggled to swallow the swell in his throat. When he finally did, he hesitantly asked, "You allowed him to adopt my son?"

Observing the pain in his eyes, Alexandre placated her fury and gingerly responded, "No, not yet. But Jacob has been adamant in his request and...and I am seriously contemplating it."

Lance lowered his head and carefully considered the delivery of the message he wanted to convey. "Alexandre," he began, bringing his stare back to hers. "I'm trying to do this the right way. The honorable way. The RESPECTFUL way." He swallowed hard and then admonished, "But, please, don't push me on this issue. I will fight this matter to the end if I have to and you know that I will."

Alexandre kept his gaze as several emotions ambushed her. Her fastidiously constructed world was quickly crumbling, prompting her to frantically scan her mind for feasible workarounds. When the realization set in that no court would execute an adoption order without the living parent terminating their rights, she humbly implored, "Just…Just give me so more time, Lance. Please?"

He shook his head. "No, Alex. I've already lost so much time. I-"

"Please," she pressed. "In the interim, you can continue to be Coach Carter and see Jaamyas whenever you want—every day if you want. He already adores you, Lance; since meeting you, you are all he talks about. So, it won't be difficult to include you in the intricacies of his life."

"It's not the same, Alexandre."

She reached for his hand, held it, and then appealed to the soft spot she hoped she still held in his heart. "I know. And, I know that I am requesting a lot from you. But…But, I really need you to understand that I need time—time to absorb all of this and make sense of it all, time to plan an unveiling, time for all of us to transition-"

"You mean time to fix this?" He clarified, sliding his hand from beneath hers. When she dropped her eyes and turned her head away, the place in his heart where he carried her softened him. "How much time, Alexandre?"

She faced him and shrugged. "I don't know. A few weeks?"

Lance puffed hot air, shook his head, and simply spoke, "No."

Alexandre exhaled loudly in distressed frustration. Lost for words with little left to bargain, she offered in a final attempt to coax him, "Before anything else, we were the best of friends. Let's use those weeks to rebuild that friendship."

Lance considered her offer. Since learning of her engagement, he had no hope of rekindling what they once had. His lone aspiration was to develop a bond with his only child. If a renewed friendship with Alexandre brought him closer to that end, then he was inclined to oblige.

"…Okay," he finally conceded. "I suppose a renewed friendship would be paramount to our co-parenting journey."

She nodded and feebly smiled. "Thank you." Afterwards, she searched her tote for her wallet and retrieved her credit card.

"Don't," Lance intercepted. "I've got this."

"Are you sure?"

He nodded then retrieved and placed his credit card on the table. "Of the many things I've lost while in the Middle East, chivalry was not one of them."

Alexandre secured her card in her wallet and then her wallet in her tote. "I understand, but I've got the next one."

"And when is the next one?"

She respired aloud and contemplated her response. "…I don't know. Jay's game is tomorrow; we've got last minute school shopping to do on Saturday; and, Sunday is church and dinner at my parents." When she caught his blank stare, she ceased rambling. "How about Sunday brunch? I will forego church and dinner at my parents and we can do brunch."

"Sunday brunch it is."

She retrieved a pen and an old receipt from her tote. After scribbling her cell phone number on it, Alexandre slid the receipt to him. "Call me with the specifics."

Taking the paper in hand, Lance smiled and assured, "I will." He then stood and helped her from her seat as she rose from the table. "See you at the game."

Alexandre nodded and confirmed, "See you at the game," before turning to exit the restaurant.

*** *** ***

"Babe, you are missing the game," Jacob alerted, returning with her salted pretzel.

"I'm not," Alexandre contested, looking up from her phone. "Jaamyas is up to bat."

Jacob shook his head in discontent, reclaimed his seat next to her, and extended her the hot snack. "He is pitching."

Ashamed by the moments she allowed to escape her, Alexandre bit into the only meal she had had all day and chewed it along with her guilt. She then watched her son strike out the first batter, struggle with a couple of balls, but eventually strike out the second batter. As the third player walked to the batting box, Alexandre realized just how much Jaamyas's skills had improved. She smiled at Jacob's display of excitement—he was elated that his hours of practice with Jaamyas had resulted in a positive end.

The vibration in her lap once again took her attention from the game. "Denton-Hall," she greeted. "...No, it's fine. I was expecting your call...Okay...Sure. I will take a look at it now...Okay. Thanks. Bye."

Perturbed by the diversion, Jacob inquired with sarcasm, "How is your pretzel?"

"Salty," she simply responded as she read through the document emailed to her.

Jacob glanced at Alexandre then returned his eyes to the field. Despite his agitation with her, the sweltering late August heat, and suffocating humidity, he offered, "Would you like me to get you another? Perhaps one that is unsalted?"

Without looking up, she shook her head and answered. "No, this one is salted enough."

Confused by her response, Jacob returned his gaze to her. "What?"

Alexandre silently cursed at herself after realizing what she had said—proof again that she was not present in the moment. She met his eyes. "I'm so sorry, babe...I...I just received this petition for transfer and-"

"And you've got to make your uncle proud. I get it." He rose to console their son who had thrown his mitt to the ground. Despite his best efforts, his team had just lost their final game of the season.

"Hey, kiddo," Jacob greeted after navigating his way through the crowd. He collected Jaamyas's mitt from the ground and hugged him. "Great game."

"Yeah, right. We lost," he sulked.

"But, you were great. You struck out a lot of their batters AND you placed a couple points on the scoreboard yourself."

Jaamyas shrugged in nonchalance.

Jacob wrapped an arm around his shoulder and ushered him toward the field's exit, where Alexandre was waiting.

"Baseball is a team sport, Jay, and you gave your team your best. So, be proud of that."

"I'm sorry about your loss, son," Alexandre expressed, removing his cap and kissing his damp forehead.

"Thanks, Mom," he murmured.

She playfully nudged his shoulder. "You still want that pizza? I'm sure that loser pizza tastes just as good as winner pizza."

Despite how he felt, Jaamyas laughed at his mother's wit. "You're such a cornball, Mom."

"I know," Alexandre sang, taking him from Jacob's arm and into hers. She kissed his forehead again and then began the walk to the vehicle. "So, what type of toppings do you want on your-"

"Mrs. Denton-Hall," a male voice called out from behind her.

The three of them halted their step and turned in the direction of the familiar voice.

"Coach Carter," Alexandre greeted. "Please, call me Alexandre—Alex."

He nodded in deference to her then dropped his eyes to Jaamyas. "Great game, kid. I see that our practices have really paid off; you did great out there."

As if his coach's opinion was the only one that mattered, Jaamyas beamed at the compliment and exclaimed, "Thanks!...We were just about to go for loser pizza. Do you want to join us?"

Coach Carter laughed at the comedic phrase and then regretfully declined, "I'm so sorry. Not tonight, Jay, but I will take a rain-check though."

Jaamyas nodded.

"Alex, a word please?"

Alexandre nodded. "Sure." She turned to Jacob and spoke, "I will catch up," before she stepped away.

"So, I've given a lot of thought about Sunday," Lance confessed.

The rays from the setting sun made it difficult for her to meet his eyes, but she faced him anyway and inquired, "It's just brunch; what is there to think about?"

"Let's have it at our old stomping ground."

"Pardon?"

"At A&T."

Alexandre snickered at the suggestion. "You can't be serious. Are you serious?"

"When have you ever known me to be a jokester?"

Alexandre considered the request and then shook her head in dismay. "No...No way...Absolutely not."

"Come on," he urged. "At most it's a two-hour drive to Greensboro."

"You're insane," she chuckled.

"And you love it," he instinctively laughed back.

She met his gaze and recited the next verse of their pact, "Always did."

"And always will," they spoke in unison.

The smile left her face upon realizing the historical moment they just shared. "...I don't think a road trip with you is a good idea."

He nodded. "I understand."

"Thank you...Good night, Coach Carter." She turned to walk away, but pivoted back to face him after quickly reconsidering his invitation. "You know what? Let's do it."

"Really?"

Alexandre nodded. "Yeah, it's been a while since I've been to our alma mater. I'm due for a visit."

His lips stretched into a wide grin. "See you Sunday."

Alexandre nodded once more and confirmed, "See you Sunday."

Jacob waited until she was secure in his sport utility vehicle before asking, "What was that all about?"

"Jaamyas." She turned to look at him to make the lie more believable—a skill she honed practicing law. "He wants him to play in a more advanced league."

"Oh wow. That's great!" Jacob glanced and smiled at Jaamyas in the backseat who beamed at him as well, then returned his eyes to her. "Are you okay with that?...I mean, what are you thinking? How do you feel?"

Alexandre raised her shoulders and peered beyond him to look out the driver window. She observed Lance engage other players and their parents as the crowd slowly dispersed. "I'm not sure yet...The jury is still out."

Jacob started the vehicle and began to maneuver out of the parking lot. "Well, you don't have to decide today. Take some time and think it over. I will ultimately support whatever it is you decide—no pressure."

Alexandre nervously chuckled at his comment and anxiously contemplated the web of deception she just weaved. "...Yeah, no pressure..."

*** *** ***

"I won!" Alexandre exclaimed, tapping the trunk of the large oak tree.

Lance rushed in behind her to where they often met in their youth. "Of course, you did," he panted. "You had a two-hour nap and are well rested."

She laughed. "Sounds like a bunch of excuses to me."

He returned the laughter and responded, "No excuses, just an explanation."

Alexandre patted his muscular abdomen and teased, "How about, in lieu of an explanation, you just spend more time at the gym and less time at the center."

Grinning at her nonsensical recommendation, Lance placed his hand on hers and moved it to his racing heart. "Or, I can spend more time with my son and less time with other people's children."

Alexandre slipped her hand from underneath his, turned from his gaze, and spoke in objection, "Lance."

He watched her step out of his personal space. "Alex, I know this can't be easy for you, but you have to know that this is not easy for me, too. I-"

"Can we not do this now?" She met his face and reminded him, "I agreed to this trip so that *you and I* can rebuild the wonderful friendship that we once had."

Lance smoothed the wrinkle in his white t-shirt and then shoved his hands in the pockets of his khaki shorts. "You want to walk the campus and then go for brunch?"

Alexandre smiled and replied, "Yes." She extended her hand for him to hold and affirmed, "I would like that very much."

"And this is where it all began," Lance reminisced as they stood outside Alexandre's freshman dorm.

Alexandre shook her head and rolled her eyes. "You mean the onset of your badgering."

"I did not badger. I was persistent...and maybe perhaps overly optimistic." He gave her hand a slight squeeze and reminded, "I knew you were special the moment we met during your freshman orientation."

She snickered. "Yeah, my parents knew it, too, and no longer wanted you as my team lead."

"Ugh—don't remind me. They had it in for me the moment I butchered your name at roll call and mistook you for a male."

"Nooooo, I think it was more of the fact that you were a graduate student, Greek, and very popular with the ladies." She turned her eyes upward and snidely remarked, "I still remember all those batting eyes that passed us when you conducted our group tour of the campus."

Lance grinned at the memories. "They were them, Alexandre; and then, there was you."

She huffed at the dismissal of his years as a satyromaniac and then replied, "Yes, just as you have always explained...In fact, as memory serves, you had your pledges stomp and chant something to the like outside this very dorm to prove it to me."

He erupted into a laughter that released her hand. Time had made him forget many of the details surrounding his pursuit of her.

"Well, it worked, didn't it?"

Alexandre rolled her eyes another time. "No, it didn't. And truth be told, that particular advance was an infuriating and embarrassing experience for me, to say the least."

"Really?"

"Yes, really."

"Well, I don't remember it that way."

"That is because you were not on the receiving end of the victimization."

Lance snickered at her exaggerated depiction. "Well, if that was not what did it for you, then what did?"

"It was your persistence. Despite what you may believe or what may have worked for other women, it was your tenacious pursuit of me."

"Really?"

Alexandre nodded. "Yes, it was never what you did as much as that you did not falter in what you did…I always admired that about you, Lance—you are persistent to a fault…"

She reflected on the son they shared and disclosed, "Jaamyas is the same—very persistent and overly optimistic, just like his father."

Lance blushed at the compliment that made him proud as a parent. "…Do you think he will matriculate here?"

Alexandre exhaled loudly as she considered the question. "…I don't know. I mean, I would love for him to, or attend any HBCU. It would be a great transition for him considering that I have admittedly coddled him."

Though he reveled in her admission of fault, Lance spoke nothing in response. Alexandre seldomly acknowledged her wrong-doings in their youth, and he did not want to highlight her growth with a snide remark.

"But, thanks to Jacob," Alexandre continued, "Jaamyas has taken an interest in architecture. So, that ambition entails universities further up north or further out west."

"Well, at least you are giving him freedom to explore and choose."

"Yeah, that's definitely more than what my parents afforded me." She reminisced on the countless spats with her parents regarding the freedom to navigate the trajectory of her own life. "…I still recall the night I threatened to leave the country and never return if they did not entertain the idea of me applying to an HBCU."

Recalling the experience she shared during one of their intimate conversations, Lance attempted to lighten the ambiance by reasoning, "They just wanted the best for you, Alex."

"No," Alexandre dissented. She remembered all too well the fiery debates in which her parents expressed the plans they devised for her life and their expectation for her to follow them. "…They wanted me close so that they could continue to control me."

"I mean, could you blame them?" He inquired in support of her parents' position. Now that he was a parent himself, Lance understood the parental desire to tightly cleave to a child and wanting what is best for it. "You are their pride and joy."

When she spoke nothing in response, he caught her eyes and added, "…You definitely are—were mine."

"Lance, please don't."

"Don't what?"

"Say those things to make me feel something again."

"Is that what you think I am doing?"

"I know that that is what you are doing, Lance. I know you and I see right through you."

Alexandre ignored his slight grin, the one he always displayed when she read him well, and assured, "But it's too late—you're too late…Yes, admittedly, I held on to you for a really long time, some believe too long. But, a long time ago, I finally put away those feelings so that I could open myself to romantic love again…And I…I finally buried those feelings when I married Jacob."

Lance pondered all that she stated and then inhaled deeply, exhaled loudly, and confessed, "Alexandre, I am not going to lie and say that there haven't been other women, because there were…Thirteen years in the Middle East is a long time. But you should know that each of those women was just a means of passing the time until I got back to you…I always held out hope for us—I never lost it…Well, not until the day I learned of your engagement."

Taken aback by his confession, Alexandre took a moment to regain her bearings. It was not within reason to have expected him to remain faithful to her or committed to their vows for the past thirteen years, especially when there was little hope of survival—let alone hope of returning to her.

When she collected herself, she peered deep into his eyes and responded, "I…I can't say the same, Lance. It's been you—only you, until Jacob. So, he is more to me than a mere means of passing the time."

"Alex," Lance breathed, breaking their stare. "I did not come to destroy what you're building with him." He met her eyes again. "I just want my son. But, make no mistake about it—the moment I hear that Jacob steps out of line, I'm coming for you, too…And, to be more transparent, I am praying to God that he steps out of line."

"…He is a good man, Lance."

"I believe it. You are not the type of woman to marry a man who isn't. I just know that marriage is not easy—hell, ours wasn't…And he is young, Alex. Being a generation apart must complicate things in your marriage."

Alexandre did not dignify his assumption with a response. Instead, she demanded, "Don't do that either."

"Do what?"

"Feel the need to rescue me. You always do that…I'm happy, Lance," she vehemently spoke to convince herself more than him. His conversation was gradually prompting her to question the decisions she made throughout the past three years.

"I know you are, Alex, and I want you to remain happy."

She questioned the sincerity of his well wishes because the coldness of his tone did not match the warmth in his eyes. "…Maybe we should head back to Charlotte and grab something to eat along the way."

"If that's what you want."

"It is…It is what I want."

"There she is," Jacob acknowledged when Alexandre walked into the kitchen. "I haven't seen or heard from you all day."

She briefly touched his lips with hers and then watched him season steaks. "I know. It's been one of those days."

"Are you okay? It's not like you to miss Sunday service and cancel dinner with your parents."

Alexandre nodded. "I'm fine. Just a lot on my mind, a lot going on." In an effort to change the subject she offered, "I'm going to change my clothes and help with that."

"No, I've got it. You sit and relax."

Jacob watched her take a seat across from him and fidget with her fingers before declaring, "I tried reaching you in your chambers when I couldn't get through to you on your cell."

"Really?" She carelessly inquired.

"Yes, really."

"Hmm." She simply responded then rose from her seat. "Where's Jay?"

"Out back with Elijah flying drones."

"I'll go check on them," she announced, turning toward the backdoor.

"They're fine, Alex," Jacob forcefully assured while he grappled to manage his annoyance with her deflection.

She turned to face him with a knowing look. "Okay, then I will go say hello."

Perturbed by her cavalier and dismissive disposition, Jacob commanded, "No, how about you tell me where you were all day?"

"Excuse you?"

"Excuse me? No, excuse yo-"

"I don't recall making the vow to tell you where I am every minute, in each hour, of every day."

"Are you kidding me?!"

Alexandre raised her shoulders. "About what?"

"About what," Jacob mocked sardonically and in disbelief. He rubbed with the back of his hand the tension developing in his brow and allowed a brief moment to pass so that he could tame is fury.

Meeting her glare, he asked, "Do you seriously think that it is okay for you slip out of our bed at four o'clock in the morning to go do I don't know what with I don't know who and not say anything to me?"

When Alexandre did not reply, Jacob recounted the events that transpired that day, "...You don't call, you don't text, and I am left wondering what the hell you've up to the last fourteen hours."

"I don't have to take this," Alexandre finally replied. She headed toward the foyer to leave the house. Space was needed between them before guilt had the opportunity to overcome her and made her divulged all that she had not had to time to fully process.

Jacob grabbed her wrist with his soiled hand. "I am your husband, Alexandre."

She yanked out of his firm grip. "And I am your wife, not your child, Jacob."

After he heard her exit the front door, Jacob shoved the meat into the preheated oven and slammed the door closed.

"Is everything okay?" Jaamyas asked, entering through the backdoor with his friend at his heels.

"Yeah, son, everything is fine. Why don't you and Elijah go put up the drones and wash-up. Dinner will be ready in about thirty minutes."

"Yes, sir." Jaamyas led his friend into the mudroom and they removed their shoes and placed their gadgets on the cubed shelf. After washing their hands in the half-bathroom, Jaamyas reentered the kitchen asking, "Jacob, is Mom, okay?"

"Yeah, why? Why do you ask?"

"Because she seems so unhappy ever since she came back from Aruba."

Although Jacob felt the same way, the truth pained him immensely now that it had been uttered from the lips of a thirteen-year-old child. Thinking that he could be the source of Alexandre's unhappiness, ached Jacob even more.

"She's fine, Jay," Jacob finally responded to the innocent eyes that peered at him. "She just has a lot on her plate right now— new cases, new husband," he winked at him and added, "a new teenager…It's a lot for her to deal with all at once. We just have to continue to love her and show her that we support her. Okay?"

Jaamyas nodded. "Okay."

"Good. Now, you guys go play in the game room until dinner is ready."

"I'm safe, Jacob. You didn't have to wait up for me," Alexandre spoke, entering the master bedroom and closing the door behind her.

Seated at the widow, he turned from staring at the full moon. "Yes, Seanna told me that much when I called her."

"So, what? You waited up so that I can watch you walk out again?"

"I'm not going anywhere, Alexandre." He rose from his seat by the window and closed the space between them. "I'm going to stay right here and we are going to talk. We are going to talk about whatever it is that is going on with you."

"Jacob," she muttered, turning to walk away. In addition to a shower and sleep, she wanted to avoid a protracted argument with her disgruntled husband.

He side-stepped to halt her departure. "I know that I am a lot younger and I have a lot to learn. I also I know that this is my first marriage, but damn it, Alex, I want this to be my only marriage. So, I got to get this right and…and, if I can't, then I have not only failed as head of this family, but I have failed as your spouse…I…I just can't live with that. I'd rather die than to live with the fact that I have failed you."

The words he spoke struck a chord and Alexandre buried her face in her hands and cried. "…I'm so sorry, Jacob…I really am. I'm sorry."

"Sshhh," he soothed her, taking her in his arms and rubbing her back. "It's okay."

"No, it's not okay…I'm drowning and I am taking you down with me."

He shook his head in dissent. "Impossible."

"What?"

"It's impossible for you to drown with me. I'm a strong swimmer."

Alexandre snickered at his wit, uncertain of the truth in it. She then kissed his lips to express her appreciation and whispered, "I love you."

"And I love you."

"…I went to Greensboro," she finally confessed.

He dropped his hands from her back. "Greensboro?"

"To A&T. I needed to get away," she responded in a half-truth, "and…and I didn't tell you because I did not want you to accompany me."

He exhaled loudly, allowing a brief moment for his immediate agitation to yield to compassion. "…I understand that, Alex, but you can't just take off without my knowing it." He cupped her faced. "I worry."

"I will work on it." She kissed his lips. "I promise."

He placed his hands on her waist and pulled her into him. "You know what we need?"

"What?"

"A nice hot, bubble bath. We both need it after the long day we just had."

Alexandre grinned. "You run the bath and I get the wine and the candles?"

"Deal."

THREE

"I mean this in the most respectful way possible, Your Honor, but I really do hope that you don't plan to run for a political office," Cynthia stated Monday morning as she walked through the chambers' door. She placed several expanding files on Alexandre's desk, and then held a legal pad in one hand and a pen in the other in preparation for dictation.

Alexandre laughed halfheartedly, refusing to be offended by the statement. She then invitingly gestured for Cynthia to sit and encouraged her to expound on her position, "And why is that?"

After lowering herself to one of the seats in front of Alexandre's desk, Cynthia answered, "Because you would appear soft on crime."

The unexpected slight faded the smile on Alexandre's face. She took a moment to regain her bearings and inquired, "Soft on crime?"

"Another transfer denial?" Cynthia answered her question with her own inquiry.

Alexandre exhaled in aggravation. The constant need to defend her view on rehabilitation over punishment was a never-ending exhausting feat.

"Contrary to what many believe, Ms. Sackie," Alexandre started as she removed a folder from an according file and fingered through its contents, "the premise of the juvenile justice system is treatment, not retribution."

"Until treatment fails," Cynthia offered in dissent, gripping firmly the legal pad she held in her hands. "I don't know if you have noticed, Your Honor, but the youth of today have become more criminally violent. And regardless of the juvenile's age, their victims suffer the same level injury as if the offense was committed by an adult."

Alexandre looked up from her review of the documents. She smirked at her law clerk as she raised her reading glasses to the top of her head. "Well, argued, counselor."

"...I...I-I just think that..." Cynthia blushed, her voice trailing off while she lowered the yellow notebook to the fullness of her thighs.

"Don't back-peddle now. You presented your argument, now stand firmly by it."

Cynthia held her peace. In spite of Alexandre's encouragement to engage in a contest, she was intimated by Alexandre's knowledge, experience, and power.

Discerning Cynthia's reticence, Alexandre grinned and then winked at the law clerk to ease her trepidation.

"I appreciate your opinion and respect it, Ms. Sackie," Alexandre spoke. "You will make a fine prosecutor one day."

"Thank you, Your Honor," Cynthia murmured, uncertain of how she was to feel concerning the accolade.

"You're welcome," Alexandre responded. She then leaned forward to peer deep into her green eyes. "But, please understand that, until one day comes, you will unwaveringly support and vehemently defend the beliefs of this court."

Cynthia swallowed the swell in her throat, then nodded and stammered, "Of-of-f course."

"Good." Alexandre pulled her reading glasses back down to her face. "Now that we are back on one accord, share with me what you discovered during your due diligence."

Cynthia cleared her throat, nervously flipped through the pages of her legal pad, and then provided, "Reverse waiver is not uncommon among the judicial system. However, it is disproportionately awarded to Caucasian-American youth, particularly males."

Alexandre nodded at the information that she already knew to be true. "Not a shocking find."

Ignoring the remark, Cynthia continued, "So, even if you grant the waiver petition to appease the public, it is not logically sound to hold out for hope that these cases will be transferred back to the juvenile justice system—at least not for minority offenders."

"Another un-shocking find."

Cynthia exhale audibly, dropping her notebook in irritation. "If all of this is immaterial, then why make me do this?"

"To prove a point," Alexandre merely replied.

Cynthia huffed. "And what point is that?"

"That the last second chance a lot of these children will ever receive is in my courtroom."

Cynthia diverted her eyes from Alexandre's stare and tucked a lock of hair behind her ear. After taking a moment to contemplate Alexandre's statement, Cynthia returned to her gaze and spoke, "I respectively disagree…Several of these children are a menace and they do not deserve a second chance. They deserve—no, they need—to be punished. Not rehabilitated, but locked away and punished."

Alexandre blankly gawked at her law clerk and absorbed all of the passion with which she spoke. She watched as her words glistened her eyes and reddened her face. There was much anger, resentment, and distrust harbored in her heart. Unfortunately, the caseload before her would not permit the time to inquire about the root of it all. So, Alexandre simply remarked, "Well, let us be grateful that I am the judge and you are the law clerk. Prayerfully, your time with me will-"

A knock on the door interrupted her.

"Come in," Alexandre instructed.

"A guest to see you, Your Honor," Leah announced.

"Please show them in."

When the familiar face entered her chambers, Alexandre quickly rose to her feet. "La—Coach Carter. What are you doing here?"

"I wanted to…" he began but stopped when the additional ears in the room reminded him of their lack of privacy.

"Ladies, please give us the room," Alexandre requested.

Following their departure and the door closure, Lance continued, "We left things strained yesterday."

"You can't just drop-in on me like this, Lance. I have no way of justifying your court visit."

"You mean you haven't quite figured out how to explain away the predicament you find yourself in."

"Lance, please."

"I want Jay this weekend," he spoke, swiftly getting to the point of his visit.

"Whaaat?!"

"There is a flight exhibition this weekend in Raleigh and I would really like to take him and make a weekend of it."

Alexandre shook her head in dismay. "No, absolutely not."

Lance breathed in frustration. "Why not, Alex?"

"Because he does not know you. Hell, I'm not sure if I even know you."

"You do know me, Alex."

"Yeah, the you thirteen years ago. I don't-"

"I didn't come here for a fight. I just came to ask for time with my son—our son."

Alexandre inhaled deeply and exhaled loudly. His sensible ask reminded her that she was no longer the sole guardian that governed every aspect of Jaamyas's life.

"Let me think it over," she finally compromised after her heart softened.

Lance lips stretched into a wide grin.

"It won't be Raleigh or an extended visit over the weekend, but you can possibly have a few hours Saturday."

"Thank you."

She nodded and returned the smile. "You're welcome. Now, please leave before any-"

"JUDGE DENTON!" A shout from the hallway interrupted her.

"Young lady, you do not have authorization to be here. You must leave."

"No. NO. NOOO."

"Young lady."

"GET OFF ME!...JUDGE DENTON!"

"What the hell is going on out there?" Alexandre inquired, stepping past Lance.

She opened the door of her chambers and walked into the hallway to see an African-American, adolescent female tussling with the male security officer.

"Excuse me," Alexandre spoke, walking towards them. "What's going on here?"

The juvenile continued her efforts to free herself of the officer's grip as she inquired, "Judge Denton?"

"Yes," Alexandre responded, growing agitated by the way the officer was aggressively strong-arming the child. "Excuse me. Could you please release her?"

When the officer failed to oblige, Alexandre moved to separate the two of them. The unexpected force of their struggle caused Alexandre's stiletto to slip on the pale terrazzo tile. She lost her footing and fell to the cold floor.

Lance rushed to her aid. "Are you okay?"

Alexandre concealed the sharp pain in her impacted hip and twisted ankle and lied, "Yes," as she accepted his strength back to her feet. When she fixed her eyes on the scuffle once more, she witnessed the teenager strike the officer's face and he, in return, thrust her feeble body into the wall behind her with his forearm at her throat.

"HAVE YOU LOST OUR MIND?!" Alexandre hotly exclaimed. "SHE IS A CHILD!"

A fellow officer stepped from the growing crowd and pulled the officer from the adolescent. The youth coughed profusely, sobbed, and collapsed to the floor.

Alexandre knelt next to the teenager that appeared to be no more than fifteen years of age and appealed to the crowd, "Someone please call for a medic."

"Judge Denton?"

"Yes, sweetie," she responded, taking hold of her hand. "Please..." She coughed. "Please...d-don't...don't send my little brother away."

Alexandre gently wiped the tears that fell from the child's eyes and then stroked her braids with her free hand. "Who's your brother, sweetie?"

The adolescent turned her head away from Alexandre and coughed with a force that quaked her body. When she returned their gaze, she assured Alexandre in a whisper, "He's...he's a good kid...Just...He just made a bunch of poor decisions out of desperation...Please...please..."

"Excuse us," an officer pardoned himself with the nurse on duty at his side.

When Alexandre made no effort to move, Lance lifted her to her feet and maneuvered her from being the obstruction she was to the care provider.

"Wait. WAIT!" Alexandre pleaded.

"You've got to let them do their jobs, Alex," Lance whispered in her ear. "It's going to be okay. Just let them do their jobs."

Alexandre turned in anger and frustration, and limped back to her chambers. En route, she caught the eyes of her law clerk and the offending officer. To the former she spoke, "Find out who she is," and to the latter she ordered, "I want your badge," before entering her office and slamming the door.

Alexandre placed her red wine glass on the bar and fingered the stem. "If I didn't know any better, I would think that someone was trying to sabotage all of my conscionable efforts."

Lance sipped from his glass of rum and coke, then inquired, "Now who would want to do that to the most caring, adoring, and loving juvenile court judge in all of North Carolina?"

Alexandre scoffed. "How much time do you have?"

He placed his hand under her chin, gently turned her face to his, and responded, "For you, all the time in the world."

With disbelief, Alexandre feebly smiled at what he proffered and simply thanked him. She then nudged his hand from her head and lifted her glass to lips. As she slowly drank from it, Alexandre pondered the day's earlier events.

Observing her disposition, Lance intuitively gleaned that Alexandre's reservations concerning his support derived from the mistakes of his youth. Undoubtedly, during those years of his myopic thinking, he was arrogant, selfish, and inconsiderate. All of which contributed to his inability to make her a priority and him a confidante she could rely on.

Guilt-ridden, he lowered his hand to the fullness of her thigh and assured, "I mean it, Alex. I'm here for you."

The intoxicating effect of her alcoholic beverage retarded Alexandre's reaction to Lance's gesture. In that moment, she was not quite uncomfortable or at ease with the position of his fingers. So, Alexandre merely glanced at and ignored the hand that he had placed on top of her black skirt. That was until his firm but gentle squeeze conjured flashbacks of their intense, passionate past, and chills traveled up her spine and shortened her breath. Instantly, her drunken spirit yearned to relive those unbridled moments; but promptly, her sober mind virtuously suppressed her longings.

Distressed that her familiar desires were not extinguished by Lance's thirteen-year absence, Alexandre retrieved the diamond pendant hidden underneath her blouse and began to unhurriedly race it on the silver chain around her neck. As she did so, her thoughts wandered to the usual memorable time.

"…You still have my heart," Lance acknowledged.

Alexandre returned to the current moment and explored his eyes for the truthfulness of the confession. "…Do I?" She inquired with skepticism.

He smiled at the way she misconstrued his statement and clarified, "You're holding it in your hand."

Remembering the wedding gift he had bestowed her, Alexandre quickly released the pendant and hid it again behind her blouse.

"Why are you here, Lance," she abruptly inquired before she drank from her glass.

"Pardon?"

"You heard me," she rejoined, lowering her glass. "Why are you here? Back in North Carolina? Back in my life?"

Taken aback as well as perplexed by the untimely questions, Lance merely responded, "You know why I'm here, Alex. I've told you why I'm here."

"Yes, you force-fed me some bullshit about Jaamyas, but I don't believe you."

Lance sneered. "And why is that, Alexandre? What reason have I given you to not believe me?"

Her thoughts now incoherent because of the level of alcohol in her blood, she admitted, "I…I—I don't know…My head is not clear right now; truthfully, it has not been for a while…"

She seized her glass for a swallow of wine and then rambled, "…I…I just find it uncanny that your resurgence occurred at the exact moment I was preparing to wed someone else…I don't know—it's just all too timely in your favor…Just as luck would have it…"

Declining her subtle invitation to squabble over what she believed to be his calculated intentions, Lance cavalierly murmured, "Damn that fortuitous lady named Luck."

Alexandre huffed at his quip and replied, "No, damn you, Lance," before sipping from her wine glass. She returned her beverage to the table and speculated, "I know that you are withholding much from me. I don't know what exactly, but I do know that there is so much more to this situation that you are not telling me."

"That is not true, Alex. I-"

"It is true, Lance, or else you wouldn't have returned when you did and in the way that you did. Jay's coach? Really?" Now, with liquid courage, she confessed her heart, "My life—our life, Jay's and mine—was just fine, and it was en route to becoming better after we blended it with Jacob's…We were—are—happy."

She sipped for her glass and returned to the table. After exhaling audibly, Alexandre murmured, "…Damn it, Lance. Why couldn't you just stay g…" Her voice trailed off at the realization of her insensitivity. "…I'm…I'm sorry. I didn't mean that…I didn't mean any of it."

Lance swallowed the bulge that formed his throat as he listened to her monologue. He was doubtful of Alexandre's sincerity in all that she spoke, but her state of inebriation did not afford him the opportunity to press for an elaboration of the truth.

After clearing his throat and swallowing another time, Lance responded, "I have shared with you everything I am at liberty to disclose at this time, Alex. And…and if you feel differently, then just ask me for what you want to know and I will try my best to answer."

When her response to his petition was not immediate, he reminded, "I know that it has been some time, but you lived the life of a Marine Corps wife. So, you know the obligations, sacrifices, and confidences it entails."

"Trust me, I have not forgotten," Alexandre bitterly retorted, recalling his role as an intelligence officer and how it gradually wedged them apart.

"…Please, Alex," Lance lowly uttered. By her intonation he deciphered the pain, disappointment, frustration, and anger that remained harbored in her heart. "…I really am trying here."

Peering into his eyes, Alexandre considered his request and the subtle demand to quash the skepticism that formed from the decisions of his younger years. As she searched for his genuine feelings, her heart softened and she unexpectedly discovered not what he felt, but what she was now feeling—feelings of forgiveness, compassion, and love.

When the newfound emotions heated her skin, Alexandre rapidly dropped her gaze. "…I-I've…ugh…" She cleared her throat. "…I've got to go."

"But you haven't finished your drink," Lance commented in protest, squeezing her thigh in a pulsating rhythm.

Blushing at the effect of the half-drunken glass, Alexandre merely chuckled. She then awaited the passing of the brief vertigo, triggered by the red wine, and responded, "…Trust me, I'm finished."

She placed her cool hand on top of the warm one that he rested on her thigh. Following, Alexandre slowly pushed it down to the hem of skirt until it touched her soft skin, stroked her smooth knee, and, finally, fell to the air.

"Kenneth," she called out to the suited bartender.

"Yes, Your Honor," he responded, walking to shorten the distance between them.

"Please add these to my tab. I will close it out on Friday, as per usual."

"Of course, Your Honor. Should I phone reception for your suite?"

She smiled and shook her head. "I'm a married woman now, Kenneth. No more drunken overnights for me."

He snickered at her jest as he has never known her to experience a drunken overnight. "Of course, Your Honor...I will ring valet for a sedan for you."

"Thank you, Kenneth."

"I could take you home, you know," Lance offered. He then nodded toward her sole drink of the evening and stated, "Clearly, my alcohol tolerance is a lot higher than yours."

Alexandre smiled at the innuendo despite not knowing if he had spoken of her home or his. Nonetheless, she shook her head once more, slowly stood to her feet, and whispered, "Good night, Lance," before walking to the grand hotel's entrance where she would await the arrival of her luxury sedan.

*** *** ***

"Soraya Thomas," Cynthia spoke the next morning, placing the file on her supervisor's desk in front of her.

Alexandre looked away from her monitor and lowered her reading glasses from her head to her face. She pointed to a chair, offering Cynthia a seat, as she opened the folder, scanned a few pages, then inquired, "And this is?"

Cynthia lowered herself into a chair and answered, "The eldest, half-sister of Tobias Johnson?"

"Johnson…Johnson…Sounds familiar, but…" Her voice trailed off.

"He is the fourteen-year-old brought before you last week for burglary, and you denied the petition to transfer," Cynthia recalled for her.

Alexandre contemplated the information for a moment and then spoke, "…Yes, I remember now. He was the one who entered the local market after hours for necessities for his family."

Cynthia fought to suppress her exasperation. She loathed Alexandre's inclination to mitigate the facts, particularly those of non-violent matters.

"Yes," Cynthia confirmed then restated, "he stole approximately two hundred dollars-worth of food and diapers."

Alexandre removed her glasses, placed them on her desk, and shrugged. "Less than a thousand dollars. He would have served at most a 120-day sentence in prison if waived to the adult court." She reached for the mail that flooded her inbox. "That was not worth the transfer and decertification of a child."

She began to sift through envelopes and assuredly reiterated, "So, I stand by decision and the community service hours Johnson must expend to pay off his debt."

"Your Honor, there is a frail balance when it comes to restorative justice. Research shows it is only seven percent effective in reducing recidivism."

Alexandre chuckled at her law clerk's cynicism. Despite her youth that falsely portrayed her innocence, Cynthia possessed little hope, faith, and trust in the goodness of people. In that moment, Alexandre recognized that she had much to teach her during the clerkship.

Following the clearing of her throat, Alexandre affirmed, "Yes, that is true when you consider the aggregate of high and low-risk offenders."

Cynthia shook her head in opposition and clandestinely rolled her eyes.

Alexandre ignored her show of insolence, understanding that it derived from a place of irritation, confusion, and ignorance. "However," she began contrarily in an effort to disabuse Cynthia of the information perceptibly obtained from a rudimentary internet search, "when you consider low-risk offenders separately, restorative justice is highly effective in the reduction of recidivism."

Cynthia vigorously rubbed her forehead and exhaled in confounded annoyance. She possessed faith in what she believed and confidence in what she felt, but she was no longer was self-assured in what she knew. Everything she learned both formally and informally was now being challenged under Alexandre's tutelage.

"'What?" Alexandre inquired, encouraging her to end her silence. "You don't support my decision?"

Cynthia shrugged. "...I've learned some time ago that I am here to learn and not to advise."

Alexandre grinned at the understanding she presumed Cynthia gleaned from one, or two, of their not-so-best moments together. "I would like to think that I hired you for both," she offered as a subtle apology and an attempt to calm the rough waters. "Please, speak your mind—candidly."

Not trusting the olive branch that Alexandre extended, Cynthia held her peace.

"You believe Mr. Johnson deserved a more stringent punishment?" Alexandre inquisitively deduced.

Cynthia shrugged her shoulders once more and finally answered, "I don't know...What's the going rate for marauding a convenient store?"

Alexandre ignored Cynthia's elusive invitation to squabble. Instead, she met her sarcasm with a question in return. "Are we considering mitigating factors or just the facts of the crime alone?"

Feeling her skin flush under her dark pants suit, Cynthia shifted her weight in her seat but did not answer.

"Because if we are only considering the facts of the crime then our justice system should revert to trial by water."

Perplexed by the concept, Cynthia requested, "Come again?"

"Trial by water. It was how the courts of Ancient East determined guilt or innocence. The accused was simply thrown into the river. If he drowned, then he was guilty. If he didn't, then he was innocent."

"That is absurd," the law clerk spoke in honest disgust.

"So is a justice system that does not consider mitigating factors."

Realizing Alexandre's point and another lesson she had elucidated, Cynthia sat in silence for a brief moment then finally stammered, "I-I…just…just think-"

Her statement was interrupted by the telephone's ring.

Alexandre raised her index finger and spoke, "Hold that thought." She then retrieved the handset and announced, "Denton-Hall."

"Hey, Alex, it's me."

She quickly glanced at the hands of her wristwatch and read that it was a few minutes shy of noon. She prayed that she did not forget another commitment with her husband. "Hey, Jacob. How are you?"

"I'm good—great—actually."

Alexandre nervously chuckled in relief. "Really? Why is that?"

Cynthia stood and whispered, "I will swing back by later."

Alexandre nodded, watched Cynthia exit her chambers, and then continued to separate her mail.

"It has finally happened," Jacob merely spoke, battling to contain his enthusiasm.

Alexandre reflected on the many possibilities that could have occurred at the architectural firm in which he invested so much of himself. When she completed the scour of her brain, Alexandre inquired, "You go the promotion?"

"I got the promotion," he confirmed.

"What?!"

"Yeah, the senior partner just told me—I made partner. They are not going to make the formal announcement until the firm's meeting tomorrow, but I had to call and share the news with you."

"Oh, wow. Congratulations, Jacob. You worked really hard for this and you deserve it."

"Thank you so much, Alex. No doubt I couldn't have done this without you. So, to celebrate I was thinking…"

Alexandre's attention wandered to the large business envelope with her name penned on it. She fingered the unusual bulk, ripped the seal of the package, and tilted it so that its contents would fall into her hand. What collapsed was a law enforcement badge, a name plate that read *Ross*, and a handwritten note inscribed, "*To protect and serve was not always easy, but indeed a pleasure.*"

Instantaneously, Alexandre lost her bearings at the recollection of her earlier demand. "…Listen, Jacob, I-I…I have to go. Something just came up and I have to go—but, yes, let's plan to celebrate later."

"Okay, sure. We can-"

Alexandre dropped the handset back into the base without politely terminating the call. She then rose to her feet in hopes to find someone who could undo what she had callously done in her anger.

*** *** ***

Jacob raised his head at the light tap at his opened door.

"Another late night?" Inquired the woman standing at his threshold. She was the senior paralegal of the architectural firm's in-house legal team.

True to her voguish reputation, the stunning, young beauty wore a fitted, navy sheath dress that left little to the imagination concerning her toned and voluptuous form; her taupe stilettoes that complimented her outfit, exuded the strengths of her calves; and, though the hour approached midnight, her makeup remained flawless and her hair fell in perfect layers to her bare, dark chocolate shoulders.

Jacob shrugged. "Isn't it always?"

"Not always," she dissented, inviting herself into his new corner office. "At least not on Fridays."

"Well, such is the life of a novel partner—I suppose."

She stood behind him and placed a hand on each of his shoulders. "It doesn't have to be…You've just completed your first week as a partner. You should be out celebrating."

Jacob closed his eyes and surreptitiously reveled in the fingers that methodically massaged away his tension. He did not realize how stressed he was until her fingers worked deep into his tight muscles. When they crept down to his firm chest, he gripped her hands and removed them from his body.

"I have too much work to do, Taylor."

She swiveled his chair to face her and admonished, "Don't become one of those, Jacob."

"One of what?"

"A partner with a stick up his ass whose idea of a good time is the bottom of a whiskey bottle stored in the credenza."

Jacob chuckled at the insinuation and the undeniable truth in it. "You've been working here far too long, Taylor."

"And so have you, Jacob—because I know it, you know it, we all know it..."

When her voice trailed off prior to completing her thought, he asked, "Know what exactly?"

"Where to find the best goddamn liquor this side of the Mississippi River."

Assuming the answer was in the office of their managing partner, he snickered once more and repeated, "Yeah, far too long."

After rolling her eyes at his dismissive comment, she reasoned, "Which is all the more reason why we should celebrate now...You're bound to become one of them, Jacob—it's inevitable."

"No, it isn't," he dissented despite the fact that the firm was his sole employer following his college graduation, and the partners that she spoke ill of were his only mentors. "...And I will celebrate—with my family."

She huffed in disbelief and probed, "Tonight?"

"Whenever our schedules permit," Jacob merely responded to quickly quash her malevolent intentions.

Taylor rolled her eyes a second time and questioned in a harsh tone, "And where is the Honorable Alexandre Denton anyway?"

"Denton-Hall," Jacob corrected. He pivoted his chair back to his desk to continue the work on his blueprints. "I presume in her chambers working late as well."

She stepped to ease her slim body between the desk and him then offered, "Well, I'm free and available to help you commemorate the occasion—tonight...It will be like old times—just like we used to."

Jacob shook his head at her audacity as he leaned her body to the side to remove his prints from underneath her. He then placed the plans on his other desk and rolled his chair several inches away from her personal space.

"What used to be was drunken, playful banter during happy hour, Taylor," Jacob reminded her. "There was never a *we* and you know that."

She shrugged off his emendation and responded knowingly, "We, us, them, they, the gang—same difference. But what is undisputedly dissimilar is the present opportunity...You and I are the only ones here tonight. So, let's make the most of who is currently in attendance."

Taylor leaned forward and placed her palms on his upper thighs. She gripped the solid muscles and encouraged, "I'm leaving in a couple of weeks. So, we can make this our farewell...No one has to know. No one will ever know..."

Jacob huffed. "You're unbelievable."

She licked her bottom lip. "And you are-"

"Married," he reminded her. Again, he pushed her hands from him. "Very married."

"I'm okay with that." She rose from her seat on the desk, inched the tail of her dress up her thighs, and closed the space between them.

Jacob abruptly stood and conveyed, "Well, I'm not and you need to leave."

"Why?"

"Because I can tell that you have been drinking."

Taylor chuckled and confirmed, "Just a couple glasses of wine at happy hour."

"Either way," Jacob explained, "this is grossly inappropriate. So, please leave now, Taylor. Leave before I escalate this to H.R."

Taylor snickered at the warning then pressed her body into his. "You can't be serious, Jacob...I've seen the way you've looked at me. They way all of you around here look at me."

"Well, you do leave little to the imagination," he defended.

She smiled at the slight and moved her hands down his strong torso. Of the many men that pursued her, Taylor believed Jacob to be the only one worthy of her reciprocity. Unfortunately, to her frustrated disappointment, he never made his affections known or made any advancements towards her. Jacob truly was a man that refused to play where he worked.

In her final effort to tempt the character that many found above reproach, Taylor uttered, "Well, let me transition that lingering imagination into something more pragmatic."

"Taylor, stop." He took steps back from her as she took steps towards him. When he was finally backed into the large ceiling-to-floor window, Jacob gripped her wrists firmly and warned again, "Taylor, you need to leave now."

She widened her legs and pressed her pelvis into the seat of his pants as she replied, "But, I-"

Alexandre cleared her throat as she crossed the threshold to Jacob's office.

Taylor immediately flinched and snatched her wrists from Jacob's grip. She then quickly adjusted the hem of her dress and smoothed down her hair. "...J-Judge D-D-Denton," she stammered.

"Denton-Hall," Alexandre corrected. She fixated her stare on Taylor despite her avoiding her eyes. "But, you may acknowledge me as Your Honor."

Boldness now giving way to timidity, Taylor met her eyes and nodded. "Yes, Your Honor...I...I was j-just-"

"Leaving as my husband instructed?"

"Yes...yes, I-I was just on my way out." She lowered her eyes then her head and attempted to hurry past Alexandre.

Alexandre side-stepped to block her path.

"Alex-" Jacob pleaded.

She temporarily raised her palm to silence his intervention and questioned of Taylor, "Aren't you to start law school in a couple of weeks?"

With her head still lowered, Taylor nodded and hesitantly responded, "...Y-yes, ma'am."

"Don't be ashamed now. If you had kept your legs closed the way your mouth is now, you would not be in this predicament."

Taylor spoke nothing in response.

"Look at me when I am speaking to you," Alexandre commanded.

Taylor did as she was ordered and repeated, "Yes, ma'am."

"Duke University, correct?"

"Yes, Your Honor."

Alexandre nodded. "If my memory serves me correctly, it was my letter of recommendation that transferred your name from the waiting list to that of acceptance. Is that not accurate, also?"

In that moment, the retarded affect that several glasses of wine had on Taylor's heartrate gave way to the racing impact of anxiety and fear.

"...It was, Your Honor, and, again, I am eternally grateful," Taylor answered as she became increasingly apprehensive of the conversation's end.

Alexandre scoffed. "You have a very peculiar way of displaying your gratitude."

Taylor closed her eyes as water filled them. "Your Honor...I don't know what came over me...I...I-I just had way too many drinks tonight...I'm...I'm so very sorry."

"Don't be," Alexandre encouraged. "My call to the dean on Monday rescinding my recommendation, due to your newfound questionable character and unethical practices, will more than suffice."

Jacob sucked in air through his teeth, inhaling the sting of the repercussions. Though he was offended by Taylor's actions, he extended his heart to her. She was without a doubt a benevolent person; always a team player willing to assist in any capacity to complete the mission. For these reasons and others, Taylor was regarded as one who worked hard.

Unfortunately, however, Taylor had a reputation of playing just as hard as she worked—even harder when alcohol was involved. Nonetheless, despite her one character-flaw, Taylor possessed a solid reputation at the firm. She was the ace that everyone desired in their card deck.

"Alex, please," Jacob beseeched on Taylor's behalf, recalling how strenuously and tirelessly she worked, both economically and academically, to gain acceptance into her first choice of law schools. To know that she could possibly lose it because of a drunken misstep, pained him. "She just had too much to drin-"

"Stay out of this, Jacob," Alexandre tersely admonished.

When Taylor opened her eyes, the tears immediately fell to her face. "Your Honor, please..." She met Alexandre's eyes and pleaded on her own behalf, "Please."

Alexandre closed the space between them until the toe of her stilettos met the toe of Taylor's. She peered deep into her eyes and admonished, "Don't you *ever* cross me again."

Taylor swallowed the knot in her throat then simply nodded.

Smiling, Alexandre wished, "Have a good evening," and side-stepped once more to allow Taylor to exit the office.

Jacob exhaled loudly with relief and watched his wife close his office door. He then grinned at her and shook his head. "You are something else...Remind me of this moment if I even consider dreaming of crossing you." He laughed halfheartedly and assured, "You know I had that under control, right?"

Alexandre returned the smile as she shrugged. "I know, but I didn't want to take the chance of you getting too far cornered...It was getting dangerously close to a potential sexual harassment suit...So, it was only fitting that I tagged myself in."

He held her waist and grazed her lips with his, whispering, "Well played, partner."

"Thank you...Now, for more pressing matters, I recall that congratulations are in order." She placed the large designer, leather tote on his desk and carefully retrieved the bottle of champagne and two crystal flutes.

Jacob lovingly looked on as Alexandre uncorked the bottle and filled their glasses. "Thank you," he spoke as he accepted his glass.

"You're welcome." She rose her glass in a salute and lauded, "Congratulations, baby. You did it." She took a long sip from her glass.

"*We* did it, Alex," Jacob corrected. "I could not have achieved this without your love and support." He rose his glass in a toast to her before swallowing from the crystal.

Alexandre humbly smiled, nodded at his acknowledgment, and drunk the remainder of her beverage in her own honor. Afterwards, she placed the glass on his desk then took his and did the same.

"So, I was thinking," she began as she unhurriedly untied the belt of her lightweight, trench jacket, "that your new corner office is need of some new memories." She seductively pulled opened the layers that covered her to reveal the black, lace corset and matching panties.

Jacob held his breath in astonishment. "You drove here in that?"

She smiled at his disbelief and shrugged. "Took a cab."

"And went through building security?"

Alexandre snickered and removed her jacket. "Will you stop talking already and open your gift?"

He closed the space between them, eased her to his desk, hurriedly shoved the blueprints to the floor, and comfortably seated Alexandre on the cool wood. He dipped his tongue in her mouth then kissed her lips. "You're an amazing woman. You know that, right?"

She nodded and spoke with confidence, "Yes, I do."

Jacob seized his wife's captivating eyes and peered deep into them with loving adoration. Seeing the glory he felt that he did not deserve, he silently thanked God for his blessing. Following, Jacob murmured, "I'm so in love you, Alex. Please don't ever leave me."

Grinning at his bizarre request, Alexandre impishly replied, "With a full package like you, why would I have a need to leave?"

Jacob snickered at her quip then returned the mischievous smirk. Afterwards, his mouth dropped to her chin, neck, and bare shoulders as he freed himself from the confines of his belt, pants, and boxer briefs. Lowering his head to the fullness of her breasts, Jacob shifted her panties, entered her body, and held her hips. He growled his delight and moved in her warmth until they both cried out in ecstasy.

*** *** ***

Early Saturday afternoon, Alexandre was the first to descend Jacob's vehicle after he placed it in park. She quickly pushed down the tail of her dress and announced, "I am going to walk ahead so that I can hopefully secure a space in front of the fountain. Look for me in the area of our favorite spot."

"Okay," Jacob and Jaamyas both responded in unison, walking to the rear of the sport utility vehicle.

After she placed the large, canvas tote on her shoulders, Alexandre briskly walked toward the park.

"Thank, God, you're on time," she breathlessly panted to Lance when she arrived at the fountain—their agreed meeting landmark that stood tall in the center of the park and cascaded water from its peak.

"Of course I am…Why wouldn't I be? Once a Marine, always a Mar-"

"Because I've been trying to reach you for the last two hours," she retorted in aggravation.

"I forgot my phone and didn't want to be late by going back for it."

She exhaled loudly, pushed back the loose hairs that fell from her ponytail, and explained, "Look, we are going to have to reschedule." She peered over her shoulder and found that neither Jacob nor Jaamyas was in sight.

"What? Why?"

She returned her gaze to him. "Because Jacob is here…That's why I was trying to reach you."

Lance shrugged. "Okay. So, it will be the four us now. That's not a problem."

"It is a problem, Lance," she urged, growing more aggravated by his nonchalance. "I can't risk-"

"I'm not leaving, Alex, if that is where this conversation is leading to," he affirmed. "You promised me this day to spend with our son and I am going to make you honor it…It's the least you can do considering."

Alexandre respired deeply and audibly. She searched his eyes for a glimmer of empathy while asking, "So, there is no swaying your decision?"

Lance huffed at the affect she still had on him. He turned from her hypnotic eyes and responded, "No, not this time, Alex." He faced her and admonished, "You're just going to have t-"

"COACH!" Jaamyas exclaimed, rushing through a group of trees to the left of Alexandre—an obviously shortcut that he had discovered during one of his earlier explorations.

"Hey, you!" Coach Carter greeted and returned the embrace that Jaamyas gave him when he reached him.

"Good to see you again," Jacob greeted as he shifted items to his left hand and extended his right.

Coach Carter received Jacob's hand and firmly shook it. "Likewise...Do you need help with that?"

"No, I'm okay—thanks." Jacob released his hand and equally distributed the weight in his hands again. "What brings you out this way?"

Coach Carter ran his hand down his abdomen to flatten the fold in his yellow, button-down shirt and eased his hands in his khaki shorts. "It's a beautiful day to spend in the park," he merely responded.

"Indeed it is. I couldn't agree more," Jacob concurred.

"I've, ugh, I've invited him to hang out with us," Alexandre stated.

"Awesome!" Jaamyas gleefully responded. "Coach, do you want to explore with me? I want to show you something."

Coach Carter laughed. "Sure, I guess." He looked at Alexandre who gave a nod of approval.

"Here you go, Jacob," Jaamyas offered, unloading the contents he held onto Jacob. He then took the forearm of his coach and led him toward the trees.

Alexandre shook her head and chuckled. She extended her hand to offer aid, but Jacob refused.

"It's okay, babe. I've got it. You just lead the way."

She leaned in to touch his lips with hers and then led the way up the green terrain.

Several steps into their hike, Jacob asked, "Soooo, am I to continue to think that serendipity prompted the meeting with Coach Carter at the fountain or are you going to finally confess that you orchestrated this?"

"I'm sorry?" She asked, feigning her confusion.

"Don't be coy, Alexandre. This supposed chance meeting has the Honorable Judge Denton-Hall all over it."

"Oookaaaay. Fiiiinnne." She huffed and finally relented, "I did have a hand in planning today's meeting."

Jacob exhaled his frustrated confusion. "I don't understand why you would keep this information from me."

Once in the shade of the tree, Alexandre stopped to meet his gaze. "Because I did not want to upset you."

"Upset me?" He loosened his grip on the red and white gingham blanket when Alexandre reached for it. "Why would you think that this meeting would upset me?"

She shrugged and spread the wide blanket on the soft grass. "I don't know. I guess because Jay has been wanting to spend more time with his coach and I am not yet comfortable with them being alone, and I didn't want you to be put-off by the idea."

"Put-off?" Jacob lowered the picnic basket and board games to the checkered covering. When he stood erect, he elucidated, "I'm not intimidated by our son's desire to spend time with a positive role model, Alex. I would actually encourage it—it takes a village."

After smoothing her hair back into her thick ponytail and forcing loose strands behind her ear, Alexandre spoke, "I'm sorry that I misjudged the situation."

Jacob inhaled deeply and exhaled loudly. Her show of contrition now made him feel like the villain. "You're not alone in this anymore, Alex. I am his father now. I can shoulder a lot more if you would just let me—even if it means me overseeing play dates."

Alexandre nodded then chuckled lightheartedly in hopes that they were now past the unplanned uncomfortableness. Following, she knelt to the ground, mindful to carefully fan her dress over her bare legs. Jacob lowered himself next to her and watched as she retrieved card games from her large tote.

"What's the status of the adoption proceedings?" Jacob boldly introduced into the conversation with no warning.

She lowered her eyes over her lids and sunk her shoulders when she remembered that the document remained unread and unsigned in the compartment of her briefcase. The many demands of work had, first, thrust the tasks to the back of her mind; and, now, the resurgence of Lance have completely obliterated them.

"Well…" she started as she opened her eyes, but avoided his.

"You didn't file them, did you?" He finished for her.

"…I'm sorry."

"Damnit, Alex," he uttered in heated vexation. "You gave me your word."

"I know, I know. With everything that is going on at court, I just forgot…I'm so sorry."

Alexandre extended her hand to caress his cheek, but Jacob pushed her hand away and turned from her. Looking forward at the fountain, he deliberated on their impasse. He wanted to demand the return of the adoption papers so that he himself could ensure that they would be filed. Unfortunately, however, Jacob knew that he could not move forward without her consent. Therefore, once again, as with the majority of factors in her life, Alexandre possessed the power of the pen.

Uncomfortable with the silence, Alexandre attempted to assuage his irritation and anger by stating, "Maybe my absentmindedness is a blessing in disguise. Thinking it over now, we never had a real discussion as a family about this."

Jacob considered the truthfulness of her statement and concluded that no amount of family discussions would equate to being a "real discussion" in Alexandre's opinion.

When Jacob spoke nothing in response, Alexandre continued her monologue. "It's not as easy as it seems, Jacob…Yes, Jaamyas is old enough to give consent, and, in the state of North Carolina, it is needed in adoption proceedings. But, again, no one has had a serious conversation about this. It all kind of just unfolded so unexpectedly and quick and…and Jaamyas just signed a bunch of papers without a full understanding of what he was doing."

Jacob finally pivoted his head, squinted his eyes, and responded to her. "Why does any of that matter? You know how I feel about him, Alexandre. You had to have known on some level that I would want to make my fatherhood legal."

Alexandre shrugged. "Maybe, but we never talked about it."

"I don't take any of this lightly. And you of all people know that I totally commit to everything I do.

"I know, Jacob, but-"

"I love him, Alex, and he loves me. What more is there to talk about?"

Alexandre forced warm air from her nostrils and thought of a response that would clearly convey her point. "Yes, he does, Jacob. Jaamyas loves you immensely. But he also loves his science teacher, Coach Daniels, and, now, Coach Carter. Jay is notorious for forming emotional attachments to any man who shows him genuine interest."

"You know what I mean, Alex, and you know that my relationship with him is different. I am his father."

Alexandre closed her eyes and breathed. When she opened them, she peered at her husband's exasperated visage. "I know, Jacob. I…I just want to have an in-depth conversation with him about it. I want him to be aware of his options so *he* won't make this decision lightly."

"Why do I get the feeling that this is becoming less about him and more about you?"

Alexandre twisted her face at the accusation. "What? Of course, it isn't."

Jacob looked her over in disbelief. He knew that her reticence was attributed to something more than what she was conveying, and he needed to know what it was. "…Okay, then let's have the discussion today."

"Today?"

"Yes, today. When he returns from his exploration."

"No, absolutely not," she immediately objected. "Not in front of our guest."

"Then tonight and I don't want to hear that-"

"We're back!" Jaamyas announced, rushing towards them with glee.

Alexandre smiled as she clandestinely thanked God and her son for the much-needed interference. "I see. How was it?"

Jaamyas breathlessly dropped to the corner next to Jacob, leaving the last available corner next to Alexandre for Coach Carter.

"It was great, Mom. You should've come."

"Perhaps next time."

"You have quite the explorer on your hands," Coach Carter lauded. "He very well may be next Matthew Henson."

Suppressing his discontent with Alexandre, Jacob grazed the waves on the top of Jaamyas's head with the palm of the hand and responded with pride, "I don't doubt that. He is very strong in science."

A brief, awkward silence fell among them and Alexandre was the first to break it with, "So, who is hungry? There is plenty to eat. I packed sandwiches, chips, sliced vegetables, cookies, hummus and crack-"

"Can we play a game while we eat?" Jaamyas asked.

"Sure. You pick," she responded as she unpacked the basket.

"Spades."

"Again?" Both Alexandre and Jacob questioned in unison.

"You said that I can pick," Jaamyas contested.

Coach Carter contorted his face. "He plays Spades?"

"Like you wouldn't imagine," Jacob responded. "Obviously something he inherited from his mother."

Coach Carter accepted the sandwich, chips, and bottle of water that Alexandre extended to him. He caught her eyes and smiled. "This, I've got to witness."

"Mom's my partner," Jaamyas proclaimed.

"Well, Coach, I guess you and I are left with the unfair disadvantage," Jacob forewarned.

"With that defeatist attitude you are prone to lose," Alexandre mocked.

Jacob shrugged, quashing the last of his anger so that the remainder of the afternoon could be enjoyed by everyone. "You know board games are more my forte." After winking at her, Jacob took her hand then Jaamyas's, gesturing his readiness to bless the food.

Alexandre extended her hand to Coach Carter and watched him retrieve the other hand that belonged to their son. With bowed heads and closed eyes, Jacob led them in prayer. Though it was a common grace that Jacob often recited, Alexandre found it difficult to discern all that he spoke because of the distraction of Coach Carter's thumb's gentle stroke of her folded fingers.

"Amen," they all spoke in unison.

Coach Carter took his time releasing her hand and Alexandre lifted her head to meet the softness of his eyes. In them, she saw loving memories of their youth and passionate moments of their marriage. When a cool chill crept up her spine and enveloped her body, Alexandre quickly brought her hand back to her side and made every effort to avoid his gawk as they enjoyed their meal and card game.

Several hands of Spades later, Coach Carter inquired of Jaamyas, "How did you get so good at this game?"

Jaamyas collected his mother's and his winning book and played his next card. "My mom…and technology," he knowingly responded.

Coach Carter squinted at him. "Technology?"

Jaamyas again collected his mother's and his winning book and played his next card. "Yes, I play against the algorithms of my electronic devices. I find that doing so helps me better predict my opponents' hand based on their playing patterns."

Coach Carter laughed at his well-spoken and intellectual acuity. "Really?"

Jaamyas nodded. "Well, that and the fact that my friends don't play card and board games much. And, I don't have any siblings to play with…At least not yet anyway."

Instantaneously, Alexandre felt all three pairs of eyes melt into her. "Wow! The pressure I'm feeling over here."

They all erupted in laughter.

"You have your god-brother and god-sisters to play with, Jay," Alexandre reminded him to ease the pressure she felt.

Jaamyas shrugged, gave the winning book to Jacob, and responded to his mother, "They'd rather play my game consoles."

"…What about your biological father, did you ever play with him?" Coach Carter asked.

Struck by the question, Alexandre fought hard not to burn a glare into Coach Carter. She knew that he was baiting their son for a reason she did not know and it caused a host of emotions to knot in her abdomen.

Jaamyas somberly shook his head. "He died when I was a baby…so, I never had a father to play with."

Jacob playfully jabbed Jaamyas's bicep and assured, "You have me, kiddo."

Jaamyas feebly grinned and then spoke "I know, but…"

Alarmed by his reservations, Jacob encouraged Jaamyas to speak his mind. "But what, son?"

Alexandre cleared her throat and advised, "Maybe we should table this talk for another time."

Jacob shook his head in dissent, never taking his eyes off the child he claimed as his own. "No, let him speak. It's okay."

Jaamyas met his mother's eyes and searched for answers to the questions he had not yet formed. In spite of life's many changes, his relationship with her was the constant that he had come to heavily rely on. Now that Jacob had been introduced into his life, he was expected to rely on someone that, based on the past tumultuous weeks, was not certain to be a constant.

When courage finally prevailed, Jaamyas lowered his head and confessed, "Sometimes I feel as if you are only around because of Mom and not because of me." He looked at Jacob and explained, "I mean I understand that it's because of your love and marriage that we are a family, but…"

Though Jacob disagreed in part, he held his silence to allow Jaamyas to collect his thoughts.

"…But I also feel that if things were to change between you and Mom, you would feel no obligation to continue to be here for me."

Her son's heartfelt confession snatched Alexandre's breath. Up until the wedding, she had calculated every phase of her relationship with Jacob knowing that each decision would emotionally and psychologically impact Jaamyas. However, Alexandre had given little thought to her son's well-being during their union and certainly gave no consideration to it in the event of their demise.

Flabbergasted, Jacob contemplated Jaamyas's confession and began to reflect on what he must have said or done to cause his misgivings. When nothing immediately came to mind, Jacob spoke, "Wow. I had no idea you felt that way, son, especially since you know how I feel about you."

Jaamyas raised his shoulders. "It's just how I feel— considering the circumstance as of late."

Unsure of what he meant exactly, Jacob ended the charade by simply urging, "Well, how about we change the circumstance?"

Jaamyas squinted at him and inquired, "How?"

"With the adoption; your mother has just confirmed that the court is ready to move forward with it."

"Jacob, we should really talk about this a little mo-" Alexandre attempted to interject as she struggled to repress her anger with how he grossly stretched the truth.

"THAT way," Jacob continued, speaking over her, "no matter what happens between your mother and me—not that anything will—but, in the event it does, you will always be my son and I will always be your father."

Jaamyas glanced at Alexandre and then Jacob. "Really?"

"Yes, really," Jacob assured.

Jaamyas dropped his cards and threw himself in the folds of Jacob's arms. He squeezed his neck tightly and thanked him.

Alexandre looked at Coach Carter and saw the despair on his face. When she caught his eyes, she mouthed the words, "I'm so sorry."

Coach Carter turned from her gaze and watched his son release the man he wanted to acknowledge as father and return to his seat. He now regretted the grace he extended to Alexandre; his loss was inevitably greater than her gain.

Jaamyas inquired, "May I change my name, too, like Mom did?"

Jacob smiled and nodded. "If that is what you want."

Jaamyas nodded and confirmed, "I want to be Denton-Hall as well."

"Nothing will make me happier."

"Oookaaay," Alexandre spoke forcefully to end the exchange. "Let's have a more serious conversation about this at home."

"We don't need to, Mom. Jacob knows what he wants; I know what I want; you are the only one who doesn't know what-"

"JAY!...Hey, Jay!" A peer called out to Jaamyas across the lawn.

Jaamyas turned in the direction of the voice and immediately recognized his friend. He waved at him and then faced Alexandre, "Mom, may I go play with Aaron?"

She shrugged. "Ask your coach. It's his play date."

Jaamyas darted his eyes to his coach, "May I?"

Coach Carter smiled and nodded toward his friend. "Of course. Go have fun."

Jaamyas embraced his coach and thanked him before rushing toward his new playmate.

Refusing to allow the awkward silence settle too comfortably among them, Alexandre cleared her throat and spoke, "That was quite the picnic conversation…I apologize, Coach Carter, if it made you uncomfortable and you felt out of place."

Coach Carter sipped from his water bottle then responded, "No need for an apology. Adolescents seldom genuinely speak their minds. So, when there is an opportunity for them to open up, it should be seized."

Jacob smiled as he helped himself to chocolate chip cookie. "I appreciate that, coach. I couldn't agree more."

Alexandre rolled her eyes as she recovered the playing cards and placed them in the box. She then retrieved the bottle of merlot and red wine glasses from the basket. After offering a drink to both men, who politely declined, Alexandre poured herself a full glass of courage—the element she needed most to endure the remainder of the afternoon with both her husbands.

"So, Coach Carter, when you're not with the kids, what do you do in your spare time? Have a special lady in your life?" Jacob asked.

Coach Carter grinned while he took a moment to ponder the latter question. He then replied to the former, saying, "I play golf. You play?"

Jacob shook his head. "I'm not much of a fan, but I have been known, on occasion, to putt a few rounds with the partners."

"No surprise there. Golf is an excellent game for social networking."

"As is basketball—which is more of my sport."

Coach Carter nodded. "As for the special lady, there is one I have my eye on."

"Really?" Jacob questioned genuinely inquisitive.

Coach Carter chuckled. "Nothing much to report yet, but there could be in weeks to come."

Alexandre sipped her wine as she absentmindedly listened to their dialogue and watched her son throw a football with his comrade.

"What do you think about that, babe?" Jacob asked, bringing her attention back to the conversation.

She looked at him. "I'm sorry. What?"

"Dinner with Coach Carter and his lady friend."

Alexandre met Coach Carter's eyes and searched them for the truth. Despite the legitimacy of his relationship and dinner request, Alexandre discovered that she possessed an intense yearning to meet the mysterious lady friend. Keeping Coach Carter's gaze, she sipped from her glass, then responded, "...Of course. Just let me know the date and I will confirm it with our calendar."

"Thanks, but it will be some time from now. She and I are still getting acquainted."

She nodded and finished the last of her wine.

"So, how did the two of you meet?" Coach Carter inquired.

Alexandre and Jacob looked at each other and chuckled.

In spite of his growing envy, Coach Carter grinned. "Must be some story."

"It is actually," Jacob concurred, reflecting on the Friday evening he had just retired from work.

"It is not," Alexandre bashfully disagreed. "We met at a gas station. I pulled up in a rental to the pump next to him and-"

"And she couldn't find the gas tank release."

Alexandre rolled her eyes at the embarrassing reveal. "Didn't I mention I was in a rental? And exhausted from a long day in court? And in a rush to a fundraising event that I was obscenely late for?"

"And a beautiful, distressed damsel dressed in a royal blue evening gown," Jacob added in a way that he knew would vex her.

She shook her head as she turned her eyes upward. She then smiled when he winked at her.

"Anyway," Jacob continued, "she asked for my help to locate the gas release...It was tucked away beneath the wheel. Honestly, it took me some time to find it."

"So, just like that? You become her hero and husband?" Coach Carter surmised.

Jacob drank from his water bottle and then shook his head. "Well, it did take a hell-of-a-lot of work on my part, but, in short, husband yes, hero no…Alexandre is not the type of woman that needs saving."

"Well, you did save my fortune that night," Alexandre acknowledged in jest. She looked at Coach Carter and explained, "In haste, I left my credit card at the pump and Jacob followed me to the event to return it to me."

"She invited me to stay as her plus one and we ended up spending the entire evening in the lobby of the hotel talking."

Alexandre met his adoring gawk as they journeyed down memory lane—their eyes communicated the mutual love, trust, and respect they possessed for each other. Undoubtedly, Jacob was more enamored with her than she was of him—just as a man should be—but, in that moment, Alexandre felt herself fall in love with Jacob a second time.

Interrupting their intense gaze, Coach Carter cleared his throat and spoke, "Well, I do believe that is my cue." He met her eyes first and said, "Alex, thank you for a wonderful day in the park." He then shifted his stare to Jacob and expressed, "I appreciate the conversation."

"Of course," Jacob responded for both Alexandre and himself. "I look forward to the next outing."

Coach Carter rose to his feet, smoothed at out the folds in his garments, and began his stroll in the direction of the parking lot. Though he felt Alexandre's eyes on his back, he fought the urge to turn to meet them.

*** *FOUR* ***

"WHAT?" Alexandre hollered in aggravated frustration. She had just ended her contentious call and discovered both her assistant and law clerk standing at her chambers' threshold in silence.

Cynthia recoiled at her tone, but did not speak.

"Y-your counsel on retainer is…is on his way up to-to see you," Leah lowly fumbled.

Alexandre shrugged. "And? So what? Does he have an appointment? What does he want?"

"No-no, he doesn't, but he has said that it's urgent and…and to clear your calendar for the next hour."

After tossing the handset down on her desk, Alexandre retrieved an elastic band from her drawer and proceeded to pull her hair up into a high bun.

"Everything around this damn place is fucking urgent," Alexandre mumbled to herself.

"But it is regarding-" Cynthia began in her attempt to elucidate.

"Please tell Mr. Amato that I am busy and have him put time on my calendar," Alexandre interrupted her.

"I would advise against that, Your Honor," Cynthia nervously, but forcefully spoke.

"Excuse me?" Alexandre inquired of her audacity.

After swallowing the swell in her throat, Cynthia repeated, "I would advise against that."

Alexandre inhaled deeply through her nostrils and then slowly exhaled warm air through them. Following, she calmly asked, "Why? What's the problem?"

Leah and Cynthia exchanged quick glances and then returned their eyes to Alexandre. They both stood in silence.

"WHAT?" Alexandre hollered once more in aggravated frustration. "Will someone please loose the bind on their tongue and tell me what's going on?"

Cynthia parted her lips to speak-

"The Hernandez family have filed their suit against the city," a deep male voice spoke behind the law clerk and assistant.

The two women pivoted to meet the eyes of the suited Italian who now blocked the exit for their escape.

Alexandre nonchalantly shrugged at the expected legal action. "And? We already anticipated that."

"Excuse us, ladies," he politely spoke as he motioned for them to vacate the chambers. After they opportunely retreated, he stepped across the threshold, closed the door behind him, and walked further into the room.

"And the complaint includes the juvenile facility in which you recommended Julio Hernandez be housed."

"So, what? Why are you here? Am I at risk of being named later in this suit?" She offhandedly questioned.

"And others if we don't get ahead of this right now," he honestly retorted. Several years as her legal counsel, he had grown accustomed to employing the firm hand she needed on occasion.

Flabbergasted at the astonishing response, Alexandre slowly lowered herself to her seat. She meditated on all that she had said and done in the Hernandez matter and contemplated how she could have conducted the proceedings differently. In her many years of desiring to assist and rehabilitate troubled youth, Alexandre never predicted that she would be prosecuted for her well-intended actions.

She peered up at the handsome chiseled man whose physique alluded to a schedule that immediately transitioned from library-gym-library to office-gym-office post-law school.

"Be straight with me, Gabriele," Alexandre implored.

"Aren't I always?" He rhetorically asked as he retrieved from his leather briefcase a copy of the complaint and extended it to her. Gabriele then observed her thumb through the pages and quickly scan them.

Alexandre snickered and answered, "No, you're not. Sometimes you have this dreadful habit of concealing things in an effort to protect me." She looked up from the document and met his amber eyes. "So, really be straight with me, Gabriele…How bad can this get for me?"

Gabriele loosened the button of his tailored, navy suit jacket and lowered himself in the chair in front of her desk, placing his briefcase in the other. He then reclined in the seat as he placed the ankle of his right leg on the knee of his left and folded his hands in the seat of his pants.

When he did not immediately reply, Alexandre inquired, "What is the likelihood that this can be contained?"

"If this ends up at your door, I will quash it," Gabriele confidently assured, purposely circumventing her questions. He did not want her to concern herself with matters she compensated him handsomely to resolve. "You are protected by judicial immunity."

Alexandre puffed hot air at the antiquated protection that she believed not only sheltered the good, but the bad and the ugly of the judicial system as well.

"…Against what potential claims?" She reticently inquired.

Her counsel shrugged. "Any number of frivolous claims: judicial misconduct, negligence-"

"Negligence?"

"Your detention center recommendation-"

"My recommendation?!" She interrupted in irritated anger. "Yes, it was my recommendation, Gabriele, but it's not as if I have a variety of five-star detention centers to choose from. I opted for what would keep him close to his family until a final decision about his transfer was made."

Alexandre took a moment to breathe and reflect. When the

moment lapsed, she spoke, "...I just saw the bigger picture and my part within it. I truly thought I was committing a good deed."

Gabriele huffed in empathy and stated as a reminder, "We both know those never go unpunished."

Alexandre shook her head in disbelief. "It took decades to prosecute fellow members on the bench for the kickbacks they received for sentencing children to for-profit-jails—DECADES. And I am busting my ass to genuinely help these children and I am being persecuted for it."

He watched her rest her head on the back of her chair, lower her lids over eyes, inhale deeply through her nostrils, and exhale slowly through her pursed lips.

As she took the time to regain her bearings and contain her fury, Gabriele spoke, "You can tell a lot about a person's morals and values by the decisions they make. I would not be in your corner, Alex, if I thought you were one of questionable character."

Smiling feebly with her eyes still closed, Alexandre responded in deflation, "Thanks, Gabe, but that really doesn't help me much now."

Annoyed by the development of her defeatist disposition prior to them devising a battle plan, he uttered language in his native tongue and then stated, "Were those acts despicable miscarriages of justice? Yes! Will the egregious amount of time it took to prosecute those judges forever be a stain on our justice system? Yes! But you and I both know that you're preaching to the choir, Alex."

When she reopened her eyes, Gabriele maneuvered his body to catch her gaze. He then reminded, "My hue does not afford me those privileges either. Now that we have acknowledged that, let's move on because we do not have time to squander on a discussion of the various racial injustices in this country."

Alexandre looked away from his stern, yet empathic glare and offered no words in response.

"Look, Alex, I'm just trying my best to prepare you for the worst...I really am shooting in the dark here."

Recognizing that her sights were aligned on a friend and not a foe, Alexandre withdrew the weapon of her words. She then respired in distress, recalled his earlier speculation, and anxiously requested, "Please continue. Negligent how?"

"Your decision to house a child in a detention center that was ill-equipped to meet the needs of his mental disabilities will be called into question."

"You've got to be fucking kidding me. Mental disabilities? I thoroughly reviewed his psyche eval.," she contested as she sat up from her reclined position. "He was a well-adjusted adolescent—deviant, but well-adjusted, nonetheless."

Gabriele contrarily shook his head. "You read the report of *one* mental health practitioner. That's it—*one*."

"What...the...fu..." Alexandre uttered in frustration until her voice trailed off. She turned from his gaze and rolled her eyes. Loathing her precarious plight, she began to regret denying the judicial waiver when it was first petitioned.

True to form and without thought, she reached for her pendant and began to race it along the chain around her neck.

"Alexandre, do not stress over this. That is what you are paying me to do. As I mentioned, the claim, if it is filed, will be quashed."

After returning to his stare, she softly spoke in a paraphrase, "Theodore Roosevelt once said that no man is above the law and no man is below it. We, therefore, ask no man's permission when we ask him to obey it. Obedience to the law is demanded as a right, not asked as a favor."

"Alex-" he began in an effort to rebut her regurgitation of the former President's infamous quote.

"No, Gabriele. I cannot—I *will not* hide behind judicial immunity. The mere optics of it will destroy me and I may never recover from it."

Alexandre ignored his look of disapproval and confirmed, "I stand behind my decision."

Begrudgingly conceding, Gabriele adjusted himself in the cushioned chair before he confirmed, "...Then I will find a way to win."

Alexandre observed the disconcerting shift in his temperament and presumed that there was a trade-off that she would be averse to. She learned some time ago that Gabriele was a superb batter and it behooved her to have him on her team. However, he was one who always swung hard to win, not to play fair.

"…But," she pressed, assuming that there was a caveat awaiting to be disclosed.

Gabriele impishly chuckled, spoke an incomprehensible axiom in his native tongue, and then stated in English, "You know me so well."

"Well, I have kept you on retainer for quite some time now. So, I would hope so."

Alexandre's chambers fell silent as she watched him use the back of his hand to smooth over the low-cut hairs of his dark beard. She gleaned that he was unhurriedly deciphering the best way to deliver his objectionable advice.

"You always play fair, Alex. But, to really get ahead of this, we must play underhandedly."

"Absolutely not," Alexandre immediately opposed. "You know that it is not my modus operandi."

"As your counsel, Alex, my job is to ensure that your tactics are not prohibited by law." He retrieved his briefcase, rose from his seat, rebuttoned his jacket, and then added, "As for your actions that may or may not be amoral, I will leave that to your pastor to scrutinize."

Before departing Alexandre's chambers, Gabriele winked at her and assured, "I will be in touch."

Late that evening, Alexandre sat in the cushioned chair of Jaamyas's room and, with the aid of the dim hall lamp light, she watched him sleep—so peacefully, so angelically.

"What are you doing?" Jacob whispered, interrupting her gaze.

She smiled up at him and responded with the same tone, "Just watching him sleep."

He nodded as he crossed his arms at his chest and rested his weight on the door frame. "He tries his best to wait up for you, but most nights he is so exhausted he typically crashes by 9."

Alexandre turned back to her son and gently stroke the top of his head that he tied down with a satin durag. "My sweet prince, my brave warrior; always feels the need to protect me—even from myself."

"He loves you something terrible, Alex; and when you love someone, you protect them." Looking with adoration upon the son who he called his own, Jacob spoke, "Jay's a great kid."

"…Yes, he is," Alexandre confirmed, returning her hand back to her lap. She then spoke with regret, "I missed out on so much just trying to balance everything; and I am still missing out on so much. He is growing so fast…Time truly is a mother's enemy…"

Alexandre's voice trailed off as she recalled her fervent desire to save the world's children. Undeniably, it was a yearning that was seemingly more attainable during her years as a young law student. Now, several years and a teenaged son later, she struggled to secure the safety of her own child let alone the children of the world.

"What's wrong, Alex?" Jacob asked, breaking the silence that fell in the room. By her solemn speech and melancholic disposition, Jacob discerned that something was amiss and it was more than just time lost with Jaamyas.

Alexandre ignored the question and the gentle call of her name that followed. Instead, she observed her sleeping child—flesh of her flesh, bone of her bone—and pondered what her life would be like without him or his without her. Throughout the highs and lows, all they ever continually had was each other. If he was taken from her in death or she from him in prison, Alexandre imagined that-

"Alex," Jacob spoke, touching her hand.

Alexandre turned to him, realizing that he had walked further into the room and knelt before her.

"Talk to me, Alex. Please, talk to me."

"…I've made so many mistakes, Jacob…so many mistakes. I feel that the only thing I have gotten right was bringing him into the world."

Jacob caressed her cheek and held it with the palm of his hand. "That's not true, Alex."

After smiling feebly, she kissed the inside of his hand, and then held it in her lap with the other. "Thank you for saying so."

"What is this really about, Alexandre?"

She inhaled deeply and exhaled loudly through her nostrils. "I am facing the possibility of prosecution...In the Hernandez matter, the family has brought legal action against the city and the juvenile facility. It is probable that I could be named later in the suit."

Though distressed by the appalling news, Jacob suppressed his anxiety to be the strength and comfort that she needed. "Have you sought Gabriele's advice?"

She merely nodded and muttered, "Yes, we spoke in my chambers earlier today...He said that he would take care of it."

"Well, that's solves it. You know Gabriele never loses."

She shook her in opposition. "Not this time, Jacob. This time it is much more than a simple resolve, even for Gabe."

Refusing to permit her to shake his confidence, Jacob spoke, "Well, let us pray to God and have faith that he will."

Alexandre nodded once more and then requested, "Just promise me that no matter what happens to me that you will always be here for Jay. That you will always take care of him."

"Of course. Why wouldn't I?"

Thinking of the many reasons unbeknownst to him as to why he would object to such a promise, Alexandre lowered her lids over her eyes and implored, "Please, Jacob, just promise me. I am entrusting you with the one thing I got right in my life...So, please, just promise me...I need you to say it...I need to hear it."

"Open your eyes, Alex." Once she followed his directive, Jacob met her gaze and spoke to her soul, "I promise that, no matter what, I will always be here for Jay."

Feebly grinning, Alexandre whispered, "Thank you, Jacob."

*** *** ***

Alexandre entered the foyer and immediately began to scrutinize the fully furnished, corporate suite. "This is quite the accommodations you have here," she uttered in admiration.

Lance secured the door then walked further in the unit behind her. "It's not home, but it's doable for now. I just needed something monthly that you would be comfortable with Jaamyas visiting."

"...Always the forward thinker," she commented under her breath, turning on her heels to face him.

"Something to drink?" Lance offered.

Alexandre shook her head. "No, thank you. I can't stay long. I just wanted to finally come by like I kept promising I would. Thursdays and Fridays are typically my lighter days, but for some reason today has been a day from hell."

"Well, thanks for the pressing your way." He peered deep into her eyes and professed, "Alexandre, I really want to start spending more time with my son. Time at the center no longer suffices for me, particularly since school has resumed and Jay's visits to the center are less frequent."

She respired audibly at his well-known intentions and responded, "I know, Lance. I know—and, thank you for being so patient through all of this. I know that none of this is easy—not for either of us, especially you."

"Especially with the adoption fiasco," he added as a painful reminder.

Alexandre nodded in concurrence and repeated, "Especially with the adoption fiasco..." She cleared her throat and hesitantly informed, "Obviously, I-I...I haven't filed the papers for...for the obvious reason."

Lance tipped his head in knowing acknowledgment.

"Again, I'm so sorry..."

In lieu of a reply, Lance stretched his lips into a forbearing smile. He then considered all that he had to be forgiven for and concluded that granting her a pardon was the minimum he could do to right the various wrongs he had committed against her. Unbeknownst to Alexandre, Lance was willing and prepared to do much more. All that he needed was the opportunity to regain the family he forsook thirteen years ago.

Interrupting the brief silence that fell between them, Alexandre inquired, "May I please see the rest of the unit, particularly where you intend Jay to sleep?"

Lance nodded. "Of course."

After showing her the lower level that included a kitchen with stainless steel appliances; half-bathroom; living space with gas fireplace; mounted flat screen television; several light fixtures; dinning set; sofa; loveseat; coffee and end tables, Lance led Alexandre to the upper level. He observed as she carefully inspected the two furnished junior rooms that shared a joined bathroom; and he watched while she opened and closed the storage space of the chest of drawers as well as the closets.

Content with the accommodations, Alexandre peered at Lance and nodded. "This is more than suitable for him."

Lance breathed a sigh of relief, grinned, and optimistically inquired, "So, how would you like the unveiling to occur?"

Alexandre shrugged. "I'm not sure. I'm still thinking on it. Jacob still doesn't know the truth about you…I figured that, in the interim, Jay could spend a few hours or nights with you."

Elated, he expressed his gratitude by saying, "Thank you, Alexandre. That really does mean a lot to me."

She nodded her head to recognize his appreciation. "Is your room far from here?"

"Just down the hall…But, I can still get to him quickly if he needs me."

Alexandre was comforted, but needed more assurance. "May I see it?"

"Of course." Lance led her down the hall to the master bedroom and bath.

Once in the room, Alexandre took in the immaculately kept space. The bed was made, clothes neatly organized in drawers and hung in the closet, furniture was dusted, bathroom was clean, and all toiletries were appropriately placed about the counter and shelves. She was instantaneously reminded of how easy it was to share a space with him.

"…Definitely true to form," Alexandre murmured. She turned to step out of the threshold of the bathroom door and collided into Lance who stood close behind her.

He held her lower back to keep her from falling. "…Always a Marine," Lance responded to her low utterance despite knowing that he was not meant to hear it.

She looked up at him and spoke, "Semper fidelis."

"Semper fidelis," Lance stated in return. He then held her soft gaze until he slowly lowered his mouth onto hers.

At the familiar touch of his lips, a fire burned in Alexandre's belly and a chill rose in her spine. Instinctively, her mouth opened to taste his and a low moan escaped her. She felt Lance wrap his arms firmly around her waist and slowly guide her further into the bedroom.

Lance dropped his mouth to her ear and whispered, "I've missed you, Alexandre...I've missed you so much."

Alexandre closed her eyes and recalled the many lonely nights she spent in their marital bed. She wrapped her arms around his neck and confessed, "I've missed you, too."

Lance kissed the space just above her collarbone—her second most sensitive spot. He then lowered his fingers under her skirt and into her underwear to stroke her first most sensitive spot.

"Lance," Alexandre pleaded, pushing his hand away. "...Please...Please, I can't do this...I'm married."

Lance dipped his tongue into her mouth and kissed her lips. Then, without hurry, he traced his fingertips along her biceps, forearms, and finally lifted her hands to hold in his with interwoven fingers. When his firm grip diverted his attention to the metal bands on her left ring finger, Lance effortlessly removed them and released them to the wooden floor.

Meeting her eyes, he finally replied, "I know you are, Alex—married to me."

Ignoring the sound of the bouncing platinum and the concern of where they finally landed, Alexandre weakly smiled at the unfathomable truth.

"...You're supposed to be dead," she whispered.

Lance dropped his hand to her small waist and held her close as he worked her legs further apart with his knee. He then lowered his second hand to gently ease a finger inside her body. "Do I feel dead to you?"

Alexandre gripped his shoulders in response to the intense ecstasy that overwhelmed her when he gently stroked her G-Spot.

"Answer me," he huskily demanded in her ear.

She held him close and answered, "No."

Lance left her warmth, lifted her from her feet, and rested her on the king size bed. He methodically removed her black heels and lowered his head between her thighs.

Alexandre placed her legs on his shoulders and held his head as he held her thong to the side and danced his tongue on her swollen femininity. "…Please, Lance…Please don't tease me."

Lance grinned at the memories of their heightened passion in which he would occasionally torment her. "…I won't…I promise." With that, he pulsated his tongue on her in the way he recalled precipitated an orgasm so fervid that her entire body quivered.

After her release, Lance slowly kissed his way back up her body, stopping to peck his diamond heart that rested in the space between her breasts. He then kissed her mouth as he freed himself. When he slowly entered her, he was immediately enveloped with familiar pleasure.

"Alexandre," Lance moaned, taking her hand into his. He kissed the back of it then held it tight.

She wrapped her legs around his strong waist and moved with each of his thrusts. Chills moved up her spine and reverberated throughout her entire body. When deep plunges accompanied the suckles at the dip just above her collarbone, Alexandre tightened the grip of his hand and clenched more the claw of his back as she erupted with pleasure again.

Lance ignored the pain in his hand and at his back. He instead reveled in the delight he had delivered her a second time. Releasing her hand, he stroked the hair from her forehead and gazed into her eyes. In them, he saw both the girl he was enamored with in his youth and the woman he had promised to love his entire adulthood.

"…I love you, Alexandre," he confessed. "…I still love you…I've never stopped loving you."

Tears swelled in her eyes and slowly rolled back into her hair. She wrapped her arms around his neck and held him close until he released inside of her all that he had caged for thirteen years.

After leaving her body, Lance moved on his back and pulled her rest to on him. He finger-combed her tresses with one hand and held her left hand with his other. Following a lingering kiss at the base of her ring finger, he firmly held her hand against his racing heart.

In the room's stillness, they both reflected on their fervent tryst. Though not sinful, it was indeed morally wrong.

"I should get going," Alexandre spoke, finally breaking the silence.

Despite his longing for her to remain in the warmth of his arms and the comfort of his bed, Lance fought the urge to contest her departure. He understood the magnitude of her situation at home and gleaned that what they just shared exacerbated her plight.

Kissing her forehead, Lance responded, "Okay…Give me a minute and I will walk you out."

At home, Alexandre stood in the shower of the master bathroom and cried. She had tried, to no avail, to scrub Lance's scent from her hair, passion from her skin, and love from her pores. Tears flowed incessantly from thoughts of her arduous plight. She considered a resolution and then contemplated an alternate decision to that resolution. No matter the selected choice, someone she held close was destined to be devastated.

"Alex," Jacob called out to her after hearing her distressing cries. He walked further into master bathroom and stood outside the steamed, glass, shower door.

Alexandre immediately silenced her cries and stepped under the water in an attempt to conceal her depressed eyes.

"Alex, are you okay?"

"…No, not really," she confessed. "I, uh, I had a rough day."

Without invitation, Jacob disrobed and stepped into the shower behind her. "So, you took a shower to hide your tears from me?"

Alexandre laughed halfheartedly to conceal her misery. "I see there is no getting one over you."

He pushed back her wet hair that the hot water had transformed back into tight coils and asked, "I'm your husband, Alex. Why would you want to?"

Alexandre erupted into another heartfelt cry and walked into Jacob's extended arms. She rested her head in his muscular chest and declared, "I don't deserve you."

Jacob kissed her forehead under the hot water that rained on them both. "No, you are God's gift to me. So, it is I that don't deserve you."

His statement worsened her guilt and she wept harder.

Jacob firmly held her close, holding back his own tears. He loathed witnessing her so distressed, but hated more that he could not absolve her of the weight that saddled her shoulders.

He kissed her forehead again and pleaded, "Please talk to me, Alex. Tell me what's going on...Tell me how I can help you."

Alexandre lifted her head from his chest, kissed his lips, and then stepped out of his embrace. "I'm okay, babe...I will be okay."

"No, you're not, Alex. I can tell you're not."

She kissed him again and requested, "Please don't push."

Jacob exhaled loudly in frustration and then begrudgingly relented. "Okay...okay."

Alexandre conjured a seductive grin in effort to assuage his irritation and enticed, "I'll wait up for you."

Although vexed by her unspoken troubles, Jacob halfheartedly smiled at the innuendo. He gently swatted the fullness of her right buttock and assured, "I will be out in a minute."

Alexandre nodded as she stepped out of the shower to, first, complete the remainder of her nighttime routine and, then, nestle into bed.

A brief moment later, Jacob climbed into bed next to Alexandre to find her drifting to sleep on her side. He pulled her close to him, kissed her cheek, and nuzzled close to her damp hair that was pulled back into a shaggy ponytail and tied down with a satin scarf.

"Babe," he whispered in her ear.

"Hmm."

"I was thinking."

"About what?" She sleepily inquired.

"You taking some time off."

"Is that so?"

"Yes, with my promotion I can manage our expenses on my own for quite a while."

Alexandre adjusted her weight on her hip and responded in her light sleep, "I couldn't let you do that, Jacob, especially since a great portion of our expenses derive from Jay's care."

"We would do it anyway in a year when we expand the family. Let's just start now. You can take a sabbatical and we can just start now."

Alexandre's eyes abruptly opened and she turned on her back to face him. "Are you kidding me?"

Jacob adjusted himself to her new position. "No, I'm not…I hate to see you so stressed from work, and I know that you will go crazy without a project."

"A baby is not a project, Jacob. It's a life…A life that demands a lifetime commitment."

"You know what I mean, Alex. I just think-"

"No, Jacob, no. We agreed to wait a year. So, let's just wait the year."

Jacob respired with dissatisfied annoyance. Though he yearned to argue his point further, he could not bring himself to rescind the agreement they both entered into prior to the wedding.

"…Fine…fine," he lowly uttered as he reclined on his back and closed his eyes.

A new wave of guilt overwhelmed her and Alexandre found it difficult to drift back to sleep, particularly since Jacob laid next to her feeling defeated in his attempt to console her.

"…But waiting doesn't mean," she began as she lifted her short satin gown above her waist and straddled him, "we can't practice making one until then."

Alexandre kissed his lips and guided him into her warmth. She watched as his aggravation gave way to gratification as she moved on him until he filled her with his seed.

*** *** ***

The next morning, the shrilling sound of the alarm clock startled her awake and Alexandre struggled to gain her bearings at the noise. With her eyes closed, she stretched her hand toward the nightstand and clumsily searched for the loud culprit. When several items fell to the floor and behind the furniture, Alexandre groaned and finally opened her eyes.

She switched the alarm off and then observed the time. "Oh my g—Jaamyas!"

Alexandre descended her bed in a hurry, grabbing her satin robe at the foot of it. "Jaamyas, wake up son! We slept in!" She exclaimed as she placed her robe on in haste.

Alexandre exited her room, rushed down the hall, and entered her son's bedroom. "Jaamyas?"

His bed was made and the room was empty. She walked in further and found his bathroom empty as well. In a panic, she rushed downstairs to the kitchen.

"Jaamyas!"

In the kitchen, Alexandre found only a plate of fresh cut fruit with pancakes and a note that read:

Good morning, beautiful. I trust you slept well...I set the alarm in lieu of waking you as I typically do. I also took care of Jay and made breakfast so that you could sleep in. Have a wonderful day! –All my love, Jacob

Smiling, Alexandre lifted the plastic wrap from her plate and retrieved a strawberry. She nibbled on it as she made her way to unhurriedly shower and dress for the courthouse.

Lance quickened his step to her side at the bar and lightly kissed her cheek. "Sorry I'm late. I did not mean to keep you waiting, especially after your long day in court." He lowered himself into the barstool next to her. "There was just an incident I had to tend to."

Alexandre shrugged and fingered the stem of her wine glass. "It's fine…As you can see, I started without you."

He peered at her nearly empty red wine glass and commented, "I can see; I should catch up." He raised his index finger in the air until he gained the attention of the suited bartender. "Vodka—no ice, please; and top-off the lady."

"Must have been a challenging day for you or you are anticipating this to be a challenging conversation," Alexandre observed by his potent drink selection. She then raised her glass to her lips.

"A combination of both," he confessed. "But more so the latter than the former."

She completed her beverage and returned the glass to the bar table. "Okay. Well, let's not prolong the inevitable. What is it that you want to talk about?"

"I," he began, but stopped when the bartender returned with Lance's requests.

"Thank you, Kenneth," Alexandre spoke to him as he refilled her wine glass.

He nodded and winked at her then returned to his other patrons.

Lance threw back his shot and then cringed as he swallowed it. He raised his index finger a second time and requested a rum and coke on the rocks.

"Alexandre, I did not come with the intent of reclaiming what we had thirteen years ago. I swear to you that I didn't."

Feeling marginally spurned, she simply muttered, "Okay," before drinking from her glass.

"But that has changed," Lance quickly clarified. "To have Jaamyas is not enough…Not anymore." He met her eyes and declared, "I want you, too…I want a chance at a family—my family."

The alcohol retarded Alexandre's comprehension of his confession. But when the message finally traveled from her ears to her brain, her brain unhurriedly sent the response to her mouth. "…But, I'm married, Lance."

"Yes, you are, and you now have to choose which marriage to dissolve."

When she failed to react to his forward comment, he stated in support of their union, "We had a good marriage, Alex."

"No, Lance, we didn't," she finally spoke in dissent. "We had a *great* marriage, but it only remained great just as long as I played the role of doting wife in your love triangle."

Lance breathed aloud as he clandestinely rolled his eyes at the disgruntled feelings Alexandre continued to harbor. It was unmistakably clear that she still believed herself to be the "other woman" in his committed relationship with the military.

"Alex," he began, although not certain of the words he needed to speak to lessen her discontentment. Throughout their union, Alexandre would incessantly express that she could not compete with his true love. Unfortunately, however, her unhappiness was always met with either hostile denial or cavalier avoidance.

Recalling the many ways in which he ignored her several pleas for reassurance in their marriage, Lance sincerely apologized.

When Alexandre uttered nothing in reply, Lance covered her cool hand with his warm one and reminded, "It's been thirteen years, Alex."

"Yes, it has and-"

"And the Marine Corps is no longer a factor," he interjected, hoping to quash her need to unload a decade-plus of hurts and disappointments.

As the pregnant silence grew between them, Lance reached into the inside pocket of his suit jacket for the platinum rings that she absentmindedly abandoned on his bedroom floor. After placing them on the bar, he used his index and middle fingers to inch them in front of her.

Alexandre lowered her lids over her eyes as she felt her body temperature rise and cheeks flushed. The humiliation of their affair had returned to her and brought along with it the embarrassment of her forgetfulness. She was one who had mastered control and, in a single moment, had forsaken all that she had learned. To simultaneously experience the discomforts that were almost foreign to her throttled Alexandre as if they were untamed garden weeds suffocating a beautiful flower.

Breathing gradual deep breaths, Alexandre slowly opened her eyes. She then retrieved the rings with a trembling hand and eased them on her finger. Feeling unnerved, she struggled to suppress the guilt for not having noticed that the symbols of love, honor, respect, and trust were missing from her left hand. More importantly, she struggled to suppress the guilt for having violated all that the symbols typify.

Kenneth returned with Lance's request, placed a white napkin before him, and set the glass on it.

"Thank you," Lance spoke.

"You're welcome," he replied, stepping away.

"...I hear you, Lance," Alexandre began, "but..." Her voice trailed off as she contemplated the appropriate words to convey her heart.

"But?"

"...But..."

"But what, Alex?"

"...I can't...I can't fully process everything absent a sober mind," she finally deflected.

Lance huffed at her comment. He had hoped for a more definitive answer or, at the very least, a path forward. "I understand, Alex, but you, of all people, know that we cannot postpone the legal ramifications of my reemergence much longer. I have to go back to Texas soon so that I can begin to really deal with this in my home state." He placed a hand on the one that she had rested on her crossed thigh. "It is my hope that my wife will have me when I return."

Alexandre inhaled deeply and exhaled slowly as she slid her hand from beneath his. She then watched as his hand tenderly squeeze the fullness of her leg, move down to the hem of her dress, and graze her bare knee. Lance then raised his glass to his mouth for a long drink.

Ignoring his professed desire, Alexandre admitted, "With the exception of pseudocide, I know of no precedent in this matter."

Lance scoffed at her response and sipped again from his glass. True to form in everything, she had deliberated as an attorney.

"Well, we don't have to resolve the matter tonight. It's Friday and the courts are closed until Monday," Lance mocked in concession. He completed his drink and set the glass on the damp napkin in front of him. "So, tell me about the challenging day you had."

"Excuse me?"

Lance pivoted and peered at her visage. "I can tell by your glazed eyes that that is not your second glass of wine tonight."

Alexandre dropped her eyes and shrugged her shoulders. "I don't want to talk about it."

"Fair enough. We can transition the conversation to talk of how I can help you decompress from your challenging day."

Alexandre shook her head. "…You're so bad, Mr. Denton," she commented, chuckling, first, at him, and then at the affect the wine had her disposition.

"And I, in no way, am denying it." Lance surreptitiously stroked her outer calf that was not visible to the other patrons. "I am, however, asking that you be bad with me."

At the resonation of his request, a cool chill rose in Alexandre's spine and enveloped her entire body.

"…Lance, my stint of overnights is over," she merely responded, praying that he did not discern her vacillation with his offer.

"Then I will settle for a few hours."

Alexandre slowly raised her glass to her lips and sipped her beverage to keep from declining or accepting his invitation.

Noticing only a slight apprehension in her, Lance retrieved from the inside pocket of his suit jacket further enticement. He placed one of the two black keycards on the bar table and eased it toward her.

"I took the liberty of reserving your preferred suite…Take your time and think it over." Lance rose from his seat and spoke before his departure, "You know where to find me."

Alexandre closed eyes, inhaled deeply, and exhaled slowly. When she opened them again, she drank from her wine glass and then gazed at the keycard that was beckoning her. The thought of Lance waiting for her upstairs in a sea of velvety sheets and a cloud of soft pillows sent another chill up her spine and through her body.

"Another glass, Your Honor?" The suited bartender inquired, breaking her trance.

Alexandre looked up at him and smiled. "No, thank you, Kenneth. This will be the last for me tonight." She pointed to Lance's empty glasses and then her own. "Please add these to my tab."

He shook his head in dissent. "They have already been taken care of by the gentleman, as well as your open tab."

Alexandre smirked at and contemplated Lance's well-thought intentions—even if she did not make it to his bed, he made sure that he would be the final memory of her night.

"Your Honor?"

"I'm fine, Kenneth. Thanks."

She finished the last of her wine, extended her empty glass to him, and stood with her handbag and the keycard in hand.

"Enjoy your evening," she bid him as she exited.

✱✱✱ *FIVE* ✱✱✱

"Okay, okay," Alexandre attempted to speak over the crowd pressed in her chambers. When no one heeded her polite warning, she hollered, "THAT IS ENOUGH!"

The room fell immediately silent at her intonation, and all gazes shifted to her.

"Will everyone but counsels exit the room please."

Following the departure of several people and her assistant closing the door, Alexandre spoke, "Let me remind you that the purpose of this meeting is not to hear or debate opposing statements." Her eyes darted from the two attorneys on her left to the two attorneys on her right. "I have permitted this meeting so that an amicable agreement could be reached—one that best fits the needs of the child-"

"Your Honor-"

"AND let me remind you," Alexandre spoke over the male prosecutor that attempted to interject her thought, "that our system of juvenile justice is one of rehabilitation and not retribution. So, we all should be considering means with an end of restoring the youth, and not contemplating punishments that have no history of making society feel safe."

"Agreed," the defense counselor offered in support. She then added, "Particularly since we all know that safety is relative in this country, and that most Americans have a disturbingly false sense of security."

"Tell that to the 78-year-old victim whose car was broken into while she attempted to complete her holiday shopping early."

"Her vehicle was not broken into, the doors were left unlocked," she corrected him.

He shrugged at the elucidation. "Okay, unlawful entry—it's still burglary." After turning his gaze to Alexandre, he posed the question, "Your Honor, where is the sense of security if every day Americans cannot enjoy a favorite pastime without the fear of having what they worked hard to acquire is stolen from them?"

"Oh, come on," the female attorney spoke in response. "What this woman really had was a *false* sense of security. I mean, who leaves their car unlocked with expensive electronics in plain sight in a highly trafficked shopping mall? The whole incident reeks of entrapment, in my opinion."

"Well, no one had asked you for your opinion," he hotly retorted. "And if your legal advice is equally inadequate, then you can keep that to yourself as well."

"Okay, counselor," Alexandre interrupted, providing no opportunity for his adversary to respond. During the contentious bickering, it became obvious to her that the lawyers' possessed a myopic focus on the win. As a result, they lost sight of the true purpose of the fight.

After darting her eyes between both legal teams, Alexandre forewarned, "Either we all play nice or we don't play at all, and I will be forced to decide this matter without either of your considerations."

"Forgive me, Your Honor, but I just don't like the blame-the-victim approach that is being presented here."

"Blame-the-victim?"

"Yes, blame-the-"

A knock on the chambers' door preceded its opening with Alexandre's assistant on the other side.

"What is it, Leah?" Alexandre inquired.

"A Detective Gaines would like to speak with you."

Alexandre nodded and spoke, "Of course." She then shifted her gaze to each of the attorneys and offered, "Let's reconvene with cooler heads next week?"

Following the departure of the four attorneys, Alexandre stood to her feet to receive the hand of the detective, dressed in a black suit and white shirt, that entered her chambers.

"Please have a seat." When he lowered himself into the chair that she offered, Alexandre did the same in the chair behind her desk. "How may I help you, detective?"

"Well, I don't know, Judge Denton-Hall. Now that I am here, I think it may be best that my questions be asked and answered down at the station."

"Questions pertaining to what?"

"The Hernandez matter. I am certain that you are aware that the Hernandez family have filed their suit against the city."

"I read the paper," Alexandre simply responded with a nod of her head.

"So, would you mind coming down to the station to answer a few questions?"

"I would actually." Alexandre met his eyes and assured, "I will gladly answer whatever I can here, and whatever I can't, you can contact my attorney."

Detective Gaines smiled at her disposition. People of her caliber where both a pleasure and pain to contend with. They were the occasional challenge that his monotonous tenure among the force needed, but also the vexing impediment to justice.

He cleared his throat and opted to accept her offer to cooperate in her chambers. "I understand that you often volunteer at the detention centers."

"Your understanding would be accurate," she replied then offered as a caveat, "however, I am not the only volunteer, and I am sure that I am not the only court official to volunteer."

He tipped his head in acknowledgement. "Any time volunteered at the detention center to which you sentenced Julio Hernandez?"

"The juvenile justice system does not sentence children, Detective Gaines. We disposition them," Alexandre corrected him.

"But, in any event, I am certain you know the answer to that question, or why else would you be here?"

"I just believe it to be all too peculiar that another incident has occurred that involves an adolescent you *dispositioned* to the exact detention center where you volunteer."

Perplexed, Alexandre contorted her face and inquired, "What are you talking about? What incident?"

"I'm not at liberty to disclose that just yet—for familial reasons."

"What incident?" She inquired more forcefully. "Has another child gone missing? Is another child dead?"

Detective Gaines ignored the questions he believed that he had previously answered by refusing not answer, and clarified, "Your Honor, I am only here to confirm with you the evidence that I found—well, did not find, in the visitor's log."

Alexandre rolled her eyes as she lowly uttered her discontent.

Disregarding her insolence, he stated, "You haven't visited the detention center in a while. Why is that?"

"I've been busy—getting married, raising a son, presiding over a courtroom."

"So, no missed logs?"

"No, no missed logs. I sign in and out every visit." Alexandre huffed in frustration and asked, "Is there a point you are attempting to make here, detective? If there is, I'm grossly missing it."

"There is a po-"

"I had nothing to do with the disappearances or the untimely deaths of these children," she interrupted with her own conclusion, not interested in hearing his point. "The heart I have for them would not permit me to commit such horrid acts."

Unmoved by her emotional interjection, Detective Gaines shrugged. "The same, if not worse, have been done in the name of love. Trust me, in my line of work, there is no end to the horrid acts committed against love ones."

Recalling all that she observed during her many years of service among the juvenile justice system, Alexandre begrudgingly accepted his point. "...Fine, I don't dispute that, but come on.

Really? Soaking wet and bloated, I am 130 pounds. Do you really think I can hoist a child of Julio Hernandez stature to his death?"

"You are a judge, Your Honor; a powerful influencer. And even when you can't influence, the response to your jump command is always how high."

Suppressing her fury, Alexandre responded, "I have never and would never abuse my power in that way. And I resent the tone that you are striking here."

He lifted his hands as if to surrender. "I don't mean to offend, but we are both individuals of law and logic. So, these incidents cannot be just due to chance."

"Excuse me?"

"Meadow's Law."

Alexandre twisted her face in confusion at the reference. Though she possessed some familiarity of the concept, her knowledge of it was limited.

"It's based on the premise that if a particular event is rare, two or more instances of said event occurring to the same individual are so improbable that they are unlikely to be the result of chance," Detective Gaines elucidated after recognizing the bemusement on her visage.

As Alexandre exhaled audibly at the implication of calculated deviant behavior, Detective Gaines watched for any change in Alexandre's disposition. He observed her race the pendant on the chain around her neck and hastily transcribed notes on the legal pad in front of her. When she spoke nothing in reply to supposition, he continued, "Well, of course the notion was originally based on infant deaths in a family, but the same sentiment can be applied in this instance—one death is a tragedy; two are suspicious; and three—well, three are good old-fashioned murders."

She bit down on the tip of her tongue with her front teeth while she stared blankly at his pale skin and dark eyes. The deep cycles beneath the windows of his soul told a tale of a long and stressful career—a career that made him rigid, contentious, and distrusting. Alexandre lowered her eyes and observed that his left hand was devoid of a wedding band—indicative of a life that made him cold, lonely, and bitter. In an attempt to manage her agitation and anger towards him, Alexandre surmised that it was his innate personality in addition to his professional experiences that attributed to his cynical view of not only people, but of the world.

Before the silence settled too long between them, Detective Gaines unveiled, "Julio Hernandez was a right-handed child."

"And?" She questioned, confounded by his statement.

"And the knot that was tied in the rope used to hang him was formed by a left-handed person."

Alexandre tightened the grip of the pen she held in her left hand. When her fingers began to ache from the pressure, she released the pen to the legal pad.

"Are we done here, detective?"

He shook his head. "Just a few more questions-"

"Please forgive me," she forcefully interrupted. "Allow me to restate for clarification purposes—*I am* done here. All future communications can be transmitted through my legal counsel."

"Please, just a few more questions."

Alexandre abruptly stood to reinforce her readiness for him to depart, and quickly gripped the edge of her desk. A fleeting vertigo caused the room to orbit around her.

Detective Gaines stood and stepped towards her. "Are you alright?"

Waving off his assistance, she confirmed, "I'm fine—just the stress of the day, and I stood too quickly."

After she opened her desk drawer to retrieve her attorney's business card, Alexandre extended it to him and instructed, "Please reach out to this contact if you have any additional questions."

Detective Gaines reluctantly received the card and inserted it into the inside of his blazer's pocket. "Thank you. I will," he spoke before departing her chambers.

*** *** ***

"Moooooom, weeeeeee're hooooooome," Jaamyas gleefully sang, rushing into the family room.

Alexandre lowered her wine glass to the end table and her book to her lap. "I heard, and now I can see that," she calmly assured him, hoping to restore tranquility to the room. "How was the football game?"

Jaamyas breathlessly fell into the seat next to her and rested his head on her shoulder. "It was amazing, Mom." He yawned, rubbing his eyes while he fought to conceal his exhaustion. He then encouraged, "You should have been there...It was so much fun."

Alexandre kissed his forehead and watched as he finally closed his eyes. "Maybe next time, son, but I'm glad you had a good time though...Did the Panthers win?"

"Of course not," Jacob answered, entering the room. He greeted her with a kiss and then added, "But, then again, no one was expecting them to in a game against the Cowboys."

Alexandre chuckled and watched Jacob retrieve her glass from the end table to finish the remainder of her red wine. She offered in consolation, "Well, win or lose, you guys had a great time and that is all that matters."

Jaamyas nodded sluggishly in agreement and murmured, "The best time and the best birthday ever."

Alexandre patted the fullness of his thigh to wake him. "Okay, kiddo. Off to shower and bed. It's still a school night."

"...Yes, ma'am." He slowly raised his eyelids and sat erect in his seat. Awaiting the arrival of the energy he needed to retreat upstairs, Jaamyas inquired, "...Mom, did you know that Coach attended A&T, too?"

Taken aback by the question, Alexandre prevaricated, "...Really?...No. No, I didn't."

Jaamyas nodded and rubbed his fatigued eyes another time. "Yeah, he did...But, he was several years ahead of you though." He covered his yawn with his hand and then continued, "So, you probably didn't notice him on campus...Plus, he said that he was an international relations major and studied world systems and the connections between them and...and you were a criminal justice major. Right, mom?" Following another involuntary inhale, Jaamyas restated, "Criminal justice and criminology?"

Alexandre swallowed the knot in her throat and tilted her head in agreement. "That's right, baby...Now, off to shower and bed. We had a deal," she reminded him, deflecting. "So, I want no trouble out of you when it's time to get up in the morning."

"Yes, ma'am," Jaamyas lowly spoke in acknowledgment of their pact. He leaned forward to kiss her cheek, rose to hug Jacob, and wished them both a good night before vacating upstairs.

Jacob claimed the seat next to her and finally kissed her in the way he had desired all day. When their lips parted, he asked, "How was your evening?"

Alexandre grinned and responded, "Exceptionally quiet."

Jacob laughed. "I bet."

"Did you enjoy the game as well?"

Jacob shrugged. "You've been to one game, you've been to them all. I'm just glad that our son enjoyed it…As did Coach Carter, as a matter-of-fact. The two of them have seemed to really hit it off."

Alexandre held her breath for a moment then spoke, "I hope that is okay…You know Jay is quick to form emotional attachments."

After nodding, Jacob responded, "Of course. I'm actually relieved for it. The hours I am working at the firm now, I can't always be around and I know that you have quite a bit on your plate…"

"Buuuut?"

Jacob met her eyes. "What do you mean?"

"I feel there is a but coming. So, what is it? But what?"

He scoffed. "You know me too well."

Alexandre shrugged her shoulders. "I am your wife."

"That you are." He leaned forward to kiss her but she held out her hand to maintain their distance.

"No deflecting," she ordered.

Jacob exhaled. "There is just something mysteriously peculiar about Coach Carter."

Alexandre rolled her eyes and chuckled. "You say that about all of the volunteers at the center until you get to personally know them."

"No, but Coach Carter is different…He is a bit too closeted for my liking. He shares just enough to suppress suspicion, but continues to remain withdrawn."

After closing her book and placing it on the end table next to her wine glass, Alexandre reminded, "Coach Carter is new to the area. He trusts us no more or less than we trust him…Give him time…"

Jacob pondered her suggestion. "…Yeah, I suppose you're right, probably just need more time…He did invite Jay over to his place for pizza and a movie. I don't have any reservations unless you do."

Alexandre took a moment to feign contemplation of the invitation and then replied, "Nope, no reservations from me."

"Okay, I will let him know…I'm going to shower and then go to bed. You're going to be up much longer?"

She shook her head. "I will be up in a minute."

Once Jacob exited the room, Alexandre retrieved her mobile phone from the coffee table in front of her and searched for the number of her son's biological father.

"Hey, it's me," she greeted upon him answering. "Tomorrow, can you meet me?"

*** *** ***

"Thanks again for coming in on a Saturday, Jacob," Phillip, the senior partner, spoke as he rose from the conference room chair at the conclusion of their meeting. "I know the workweek is long enough as it is for you without the additional demands on your time during the weekends."

Jacob shrugged, rising from his own seat. "Think nothing of it." He began to collect the documents that were fanned across the table and added, "My wife and son have a prior engagement today anyway."

Phillip nodded and inquired, "How are things going with the new Mrs.? I read in the papers that she's been within the line of fire for quite some time as of late."

Dismissing his concern, Jacob replied, "Haven't they all among the judiciary?"

"Well, I don't know," Phillip answered. "I suppose so, but it is Judge Denton-Hall that is receiving all of the media attention these days."

Jacob did not care to disclose much of his personal life in the office, particularly as it related to Alexandre's power position among the justice system. However, he did not want to appear ungrateful to the genuine concern. So, he responded, "She is well— all things considered...Thanks for asking."

Phillip nodded and returned, "You're welcome."

Snickers erupted from the two associates with whom Jacob had closely worked throughout his tenure. One finally broke his laughter and jested, "Considering what? The 'Mr. Tall, Dark, and Handsome' that we have spotted her with on occasion?"

Perplexed, Jacob squinted at his colleague. "Come again?"

He chuckled again and mocked, "Come again?"

"Repeat yourself," Jacob forcefully restated.

Jacob's intonation extinguished his colleague's humor and faded his smile. Following the clearing of his throat, he responded, "Nothing, man, nothing...Just forget about it, forget I said anything."

"No, don't stop now. You opened the door, now walk through it," Jacob fiery encouraged.

"Alright, fellas, enough loafing," Phillip intervened in what he believed to be playful banter despite the growing tension between his subordinates. "We have a seven-million-dollar contract that is demanding immediate results...Jacob, I expect something on my desk by Friday."

"Of course," Jacob responded. He watched Phillip exit the conference room through the glass door, but before the associate could walk past him to do the same, Jacob grabbed his arm and asked, "What the hell was that?"

He shoved Jacob's hand from him. "Like I said, it's nothing."

"Well, how about you elaborate on that nothing," Jacob vehemently retorted, closing the space between them.

He huffed. "Wow. She really has you wide open, doesn't she?" He searched Jacob's eyes that were at level with his. "…We warned you about marrying an older woman, especially an older woman like her—new fish always gravitate to her pond…Maybe when you finally find yourself from underneath her, you will see the familiar that she always has around her."

Examining his eyes in return, Jacob hotly questioned, "What the hell does that even mean?"

"It's means nothing, Jacob," the second colleague finally spoke, stepping in between them as he gently nudged them apart. "It all means nothing…We're were just messing with you—like we always do…Right, Darryl?"

"Sure," Darryl spoke without breaking Jacob's intense gaze.

Jacob doubted both their truthfulness, but dismissed them by advising, "I will have your assignments for you on Monday morning…Enjoy the rest of your weekend."

After the two associates vacated the conference room, Jacob lowered himself into a cushioned seat at the conference table. He contemplated the quip and the conceivable truth in it. Prior to his engagement, marriage, and promotion, Jacob and his colleagues had spent a considerable amount of time together playing as hard as they worked. As a result, their relationship transitioned from one that was not only professional, but fraternal as well.

Naturally, however, their relationship changed over time in conjunction with the changes of his marital and professional status. It was indeed an unsettling process, but one that had to occur for Jacob's growth. Nevertheless, he still yet considered the associates close friends and, for this reason, he believed there was merit in their banter.

As Jacob pondered who the "Mr. Tall, Dark, and Handsome" could be, his mind scoured the familiars Alexandre kept in her company. When the image of Coach Carter appeared to mind, he immediately rose from his seat with the files in hand, returned to his office for his keys, and began the journey home.

Alexandre rushed into her bedroom to quickly change her wet clothes. The unexpected rain had robbed her of the minutes she had to spare before arriving to the party.

"Jacob," she spoke, astonished to find him sitting near the window. She hurried to her large walk-in closet to peel off her wet garments and called out, "What are you doing here? I thought you were putting in extra hours at the office today?"

Jacob continued to watch the storm clouds enclose them and he responded, "Something more pressing come up, so I returned home."

Entering the room again with a halter, maxi dress in hand, she inquired, "More pressing? Like what?"

He turned to watch her step into her dress and affix it properly on her body. He ignored her question and instead asked, "Where are you going?"

She ceased smoothing out the folds in her attire and gave Jacob a perplexing look. "Jay has a birthday party today. I told you that."

Jacob rose to his feet and walked towards her. "Will Coach Carter be there?"

Confused by the question, she shrugged and responded, "No...I don't know...Maybe. Why?"

"Because I have just learned that the two of you have been spending an awful lot of time together. In fact, a lot more time than you have led me to believe."

Alexandre nervously exhaled at the revelation. She contemplated a half-truth that would quickly ease his doubts and terminate the conversation. "Jacob, please try to understand-"

"Understand what? That somehow your clandestine visits were about Jay?"

"Yes—no—yes." She huffed and then took a deep breath to compose herself. Her nerves were impeding her ability to think logically.

"Can we talk about this when I get back? I'm already running late." Alexandre entreated.

Angered by the audacity of her request, Jacob retorted, "No, we are talking about this now. I left a 7.3-million-dollar contract on my desk to come home to deal with this now. So, we are going to do just that."

"Jac-"

"I want the truth, Alex!" He interjected, raising his voice over hers.

"No, Jacob, you don't. What you want is for me to invalidate whatever it is that you have heard in the streets."

"And are you telling me that you can't?!"

Alexandre dropped her eyes, but did not reply.

"ANSWER ME!" Jacob exclaimed.

She flinched at his tone and looked up at a face that grossly feared the truth, but could not bear a lie.

"Are you guys okay in here?" Jaamyas inquired, inviting himself into their bedroom.

"Jaamyas, go to your room," Jacob instructed.

"But, I-" he contested.

"NOW!" Both Jacob and Alexandre hollered in unison.

Jaamyas took small steps back towards the exit, but defiantly stood at the threshold.

Jacob returned his gaze to Alexandre and asked, "Who is he, Alexandre? And don't you dare tell me he is just Jay's coach or I swear on everything that I love I will lose it."

Her racing heart beating in her tight throat blocked her ability to promptly speak.

Frustrated by her reticence, Jacob compellingly pried, "Is he a former client?"

Alexandre shook her head and whispered, "No."

"Former co-counsel?"

Alexandre shook her head once more and answered, "No."

"Opposing counsel?"

"No."

"Then who, Alex?...A former classmate? Lover?"

When she did not respond, Jacob knew that he had finally guessed the correct answer. He turned from her and uttered, "...Un-fucking-believable." He pivoted to face her and restated, "...YOU'RE un-fucking-believable."

"Jacob." Alexandre extended her hands to console him, but he pushed them away.

"This entire time that I have been sharing my time and space with this man you knew him to be more than just our son's coach?!" He shook his head in painful dismay and spoke, "I can't believe that you would do this to me…Humiliate me in this way."

"Jacob, please." She reached to touch his face, but he pushed her hand away.

"Don't touch me."

"You guys stop," Jaamyas beseeched, walking further into the room.

Ignoring her son's pleas, Alexandre reached for Jacob's forearm and implored, "Please, Jacob, try to understand…"

Jacob shoved her fingers from his arm and backed from her personal space. "I said do not fucking touch me."

When she made another attempt to embrace him, Jacob slapped her hand from his body, gripped her shoulders, and shunted her into the wall behind her. He held her against the drywall and growled, "Do not fucking touch me!"

Jaamyas rushed to his mother's aid and began to pull and strike at Jacob's arm. "Get off my mom! GET OFF OF HER!"

After Jacob released Alexandre, Jaamyas stepped in the middle of them and pushed at Jacob's torso.

Seeing the innocent eyes of his son and the tear-filled eyes of his wife, Jacob immediately regained his bearings. "I'm so sorry…I…I don't know what came over me…I'm so sorry."

Weary of Jacob's contrition, Jaamyas remained as a blockade for his mother. He was prepared to defend her security with all of the might his anger conjured.

Alexandre's heart wrenched and then sunk as a deafening silence grew among them. Accompanying the quietness was an immense tension that served as a reminder that she was the one to blame for the current unrest in their home.

Inhaling deeply, Alexandre nervously grappled for the courage needed to restore peace in their family, and in their marriage. None of which could be achieved or enjoyed without the truth in its entirety.

"…He…He is Jaamyas's father," Alexandre confessed in a murmur.

Thunder roared above them as each pair of eyes intensely burned into her.

"…Whaaat?" Jacob asked in disbelief.

Trembling, Alexandre wiped her wet face and confirmed, "Coach Carter is Lance Carter Denton…Jaamyas's father."

Jacob slowly backed into their large bed and lowered himself onto it. After taking a moment to allow the news to resonate, he finally asked, "And you've known this the entire time?"

Alexandre shook head. Then with a racing heart and unsettled nerves, she lowly uttered, "No…not the entire time. I only found out the night Jay invited him to dinner."

Jacob recalled the event they hosted several months ago. "Same damn difference, Alex."

"…You're right…I'm so sorry." She placed her hands on Jaamyas's shoulders to comfort him when she noticed a decline in his gallant facade.

Jaamyas instantaneously pivoted and stepped far from her touch. He then pierced a gaze of confusion, betrayal, and disdain while he spoke no words.

"…It all makes sense now," Jacob murmured. "…It all makes damn sense."

Tears fell from Jacob's eyes as the lightening brightened the sky and the sound of thunder filled the bedroom. When there was a break in the rumble, he confessed in a brief monologue, "I always knew that I would forever have to compete with him for your heart. The number of times I would often watch you stare blankly into the void, racing your pendant, and then lie when I would ask you about your thoughts. I knew…I knew and I was okay with it…I was okay with it because I was comforted in knowing that he was no longer among the living—his death mitigated the threat to or marriage…But…but, to know that he is alive changes everything."

Alexandre met his tear-filled eyes and assured, "It doesn't have to, Jacob. Nothing has to change."

"But, it already has, Alexandre."

"No, it-"

"Are you sleeping with him?" Jacob boldly inquired.

Alexandre dropped her eyes and avoided the question. She was too fearful and ashamed to answer, in the presence of her son, what she suspected Jacob already knew to be true.

Jacob's heart sank into his abdomen when her non-verbal response provided the answer to his question. His world, first shattered by the news of her living former husband, was now obliterated by the reveal of their recent intimacies. Deeply aggrieved by the thoughts of Alexandre passionately entangled with her first love, Jacob burst into a solemn cry.

The blood-curdling sounds of Jacob's torment brought tears to the eyes of Alexandre and Jaamyas, but neither of them moved to comfort him. Alexandre was fearful of his reaction to her embrace, and Jaamyas was taken aback by the emotional collapse that he had never witnessed in a man.

After a moment passed, Jacob silenced his weeping and took the time needed to breathe through his heartache and disappointment. He then wiped his eyes and stood to his feet. Looking at his son's wet face, Jacob noticed they shared the same feelings of confusion, rage, and anguish caused by Alexandre's betrayal. Though he would never dismiss Jaamyas's experience, in that moment, Jacob believed that the impact of the treachery was greater for himself. Because more than the trust Alexandre had fragmented with Jaamyas, she had broken a vow with Jacob.

Finally meeting Alexandre's eyes, Jacob spoke with conviction, "…We're done…We're done and…"

His voice trailed off when the gleam of the diamond heart pendant resting in the space between her breasts commanded his attention. While Jacob looked upon it, the token of affection that merely vexed him in the past quickly become the object of his hatred.

"…I'll be back later for my things…but we're through." With that, Jacob walked out of the bedroom and toward the winding stairs.

"Jacob," Jaamyas called out, rushing after him. "Jacob, may I come with you?"

"No," he simply responded. At the front door, Jacob collected his keys from the foyer table then walked out into the light rain.

Finally reaching him before Jacob could open the driver door of his sport utility vehicle, Jaamyas tugged at his arm and pleaded his case.

Inside, Alexandre hurried to her master bathroom and emptied the innards of her stomach into the toilet. She vomited until she coughed and eventually heaved dry air. After flushing the contents, she made her way to the basin and rinsed her mouth, first, with water and, then, with mouthwash. Subsequently, Alexandre eased her way toward the hall, down the stairs, and to the front entrance to locate her son.

"I don't understand why I can't come with you," Jaamyas reasoned.

Jacob looked down at him and conveyed, "Because your mother needs you."

"No, she doesn't. She doesn't need me because she doesn't care."

Noticing the hurt in his son's tone, Jacob encouraged, "That's not true. She does care, Jay."

Jacob opened his vehicle door, but Jaamyas abruptly pushed it close.

"No, she doesn't or else she wouldn't have lied. She lied to me and she lied to you…"

"Jay-" Jacob began, avoiding his stare. He did not want to succumb to the angst in his eyes.

"She's a liar…She's a liar and I hate her. I HATE HER!"

Jacob inhaled deeply and exhaled loudly. "Jay, don't speak ill of your mother that way."

"Why not? You hate her, too."

Although uncertain of how he felt, out of parental obligation Jacob rebutted, "I don't hate her, Jay."

"Yes, you do."

"No, I don't."

"Then why else would you be leaving?"

"For reasons other than hate."

"Then don't go. Stay," Jaamyas pleaded. "Stay and we can work this out as a family."

Jacob shook his head in dissent. "I can't, Jay."

"Why?"

"I just ca-"

"WHY?"

Jacob wiped his eyes but did not respond.

Jaamyas tugged at his arm so that he would be forced to look at him and answer. "WHY?"

Furious by the pressure to work through the pain he was not yet ready to confront, Jacob yanked his forearm from his grip and yelled, "I JUST CAN'T, OKAY?!...Now, for once, without a fight, can you just do what the hell I tell you to and go back in the damn house?!"

Taken aback by Jacob's vocal elevation and language that he had never used with him before, Jaamyas recoiled. Distressed, he slowly backed away from Jacob.

"Jay, I'm sorry...Jay—Jay, I didn't mean it," Jacob contritely admitted as he stepped toward him.

Jaamyas shook his head. "Just leave me alone." He looked at his mother and then Jacob. "The both of you, just leave me alone!" He pivoted on his heels and sprinted in the opposite direction.

"JAAMYAS!" Jacob called after him.

"Don't," Alexandre spoke as the rain began to fall harder on them. "I'll go...This is all my fault anyway. So, I'll go."

Jacob looked at her with contempt and concurred, "Indeed this all is." He stepped into his vehicle, started the engine, and sped away from the hell that he once called home.

Alexandre walked into the foyer and reached into the bowl on the table for her keys. When they were not there, she remembered that she had parked her vehicle in the garage. Just as she stepped into the direction of the mudroom, a sharp pain developed at her temple and an intense vertigo spun her world. Alexandre collapsed to her knees and hit her head on the floor. She whispered her son's name until a deep sleep overcame her.

Alexandre finally came to and lay supine on the floor while she recalled where she was. Slowly easing from her position, pain throbbed at her temple and she quickly remembered the earlier events that triggered her migraine and temporary blackout.

"Jaamyas," she muttered, remembering that she was en route to find her son. Now, in no condition to drive, she walked into the sitting room to phone for assistance.

"Hey, Dad, it's me…No…No…I'm not alright." She wiped her eyes and stifled her cries. "It's Jay…We had a fight and he took off in the storm."

"What do you mean he took off?" Her father inquired hotly in anguish. "Jacob is not with him?"

"No, Jacob and I had a fight and he left as well…Please, Dad, I need your help."

"Of course. What is it that you need?"

"Can you look for him?"

"Yes, I am leaving now. You stay home in the event Jay returns to the house. I will send your mother to sit with you."

"No, please, don't tell Mom. At least don't suggest she come here…Her air of judgment will only add to the feeling of nausea that I am already experiencing…It's just too much."

"I don't want you waiting this out alone, Alex."

"I won't be alone. I will call Seanna."

"Okay. I will call you when I find him. Please do the same if he finds his way home."

"Thanks, Dad, and I will." With that, Alexandre ended the call with her father and dialed the number of her best friend.

The six o'clock hour approached and they remained side-by-side with clenched hands on the sofa of Alexandre's sitting room. As they awaited either of the mobile phones or landline to ring, the silence gradually suffocated the air.

Seanna finally inhaled deeply and exhaled loudly to express her discomfort and increased exasperation. "…Alex, it's been over an hour. I've been here for over an hour."

With little regard for the time, Alexandre did not respond.

Gently squeezing Alexandre's hands, Seanna implored, "Could you at least tell me what's going on? Why did Jay leave? What did you guys fight about?"

Keeping her gaze on her cell phone that was placed on the coffee table in front of her, Alexandre wiped the lone tear that fell down her face and shook her head.

Seanna puffed hot air in frustration. "Alex, please...Please, give me something. You pulled me from my husband and children in a middle of a volatile storm. Tell me something—anything."

Alexandre held her silence.

Seanna released her hands from the grip of hers, retrieved her phone from the table, and stood. "Okay, well, I'm going to help look for my god-son...Sitting here in silence is worsening my anxiety. I will call you if I have anything to report." She turned on her heels and began her walk to exit the room.

"It's Lance," Alexandre finally spoke.

Seanna halted her steps and clandestinely rolled her eyes at Alexandre's historical anchor—the very one that kept her ship moored in a position to see the highlights of the past, but never the possibilities of the future.

After exhaling again her aggravation, but this time with added concern, Seanna turned to face her friend. Following, she compassionately inquired, "What about Lance?"

Alexandre met her eyes and confessed, "He's alive...He's alive, Sea, and he wants his son."

Taken aback by the news, Seanna slowly returned to the seat next to her, asking, "Is this some kind of joke? Because if it is, Alex, I promise you that I'm not humored."

Alexandre scoffed. "...I wish it were...Trust me, I wish it were..."

Seanna watched as her nearly lifelong friend erupt into a cry that quaked her entire body. Though immensely perplexed, she was motivated by empathy and love to reach for Alexandre's hand and hold it firmly. Afterwards, tears fell from her own eyes as Seanna felt the burdensome weight of pain, fear, and sorrow in Alexandre's trembling fingers.

A moment past before Alexandre could calm herself and wipe her cheeks dry with her free hand.

Pulsating the hold of her hand, Seanna murmured, "Alex," to encourage her to speak.

"...I wish this was a joke," Alexandre uttered at last. "...I really do...At least that way my life would be as it was three months ago."

Seanna wiped her own eyes with her free hand and allowed what Alexandre commented to reverberate within her. When it did, she gradually released Alexandre's hand. "...Three months?"

Alexandre did not reply.

"What do you mean three months, Alex?"

Alexandre avoided her gaze and did not respond.

"You mean to tell me that you knew of Lance's resurrection for three months and we are all just learning of it today? Including Jay? Is that why he ran away?"

Again, Alexandre did not respond.

"Answer me!" Seanna demanded.

As she focused on the palmar creases in her hands, Alexandre whispered in deflection, "Not quite three months, but close enough."

"That wasn't the question, Alexandre," Seanna growled through her clenched jaw, more concerned with her answer than the accuracy of the timing.

After inhaling deeply, Alexandre held her breath for four seconds, and then replied with a quivering voice, "...Not everyone. Just Jacob, Jay...," she lifted her tear-filled eyes to Seanna's fiery ones and finished, "...and now you."

Seanna turned away in disgust. "Un-fucking-believable." She returned their gaze and told her, "You're un-fucking-believable."

"Sea, please don't be mad...I can't handle one more person being mad at me."

"Oh no, I'm not mad, Alex. I'm fucking pissed the hell off!...How could you keep this from us—from me? ME?! Of all fucking people; we share EVERYTHING!"

Alexandre burst into another cry. "...I know...I know...I'm so sorry."

Seanna fought her own tears and demanded, "DON'T! Don't you dare..."

Alexandre took Seanna's hand in hers. "Sea, please."

She yanked her hand from Alexandre's grip and shook her head in defiance. "NO...You get no sympathy from me, Alex. You are dead ass wrong for this."

Seanna pondered their three decade-plus friendship and all that they endured together. Throughout life's multiple highs and lows they were each other's close confidante. Only a shared bloodline would make them closer.

"...I can't believe you lied to me, Alex," Seanna lowly uttered in angst as she peered at Alexandre's visage.

Pivoting from her accusatory eyes, Alex corrected, "I did not lie to you, Seanna. I..." She exhaled audibly, then confessed, "I just failed to tell you..."

Seanna huffed at her comment as Alexandre was one whose virtue was tightly hinged to a form of honesty that was predicated on full disclosure; her exemplary decision-making ability required it. Thus, each person in Alexandre's personal and professional spheres were expected to meet her arbitrary standard of truthfulness.

"...A lie of omission is still a lie, Alexandre—you of all people know that."

Seanna shifted her stare to the beautifully polished piano located next to the large window. Despite the distraction of the dark atmosphere outside and the heavy rain, she could still envision Jacob stroking the ivory keys for their listening pleasure. At the thought of the man that was unequivocally enamored with Alexandre, Seanna's heart went out to him. It overwhelmed her to consider how the revelation must have been tormenting Jacob.

"...I...I don't understand, Alex. Why?...Of the many things you could have kept from me: your missing Lance, your longings for Lance, your dreams of Lance; you decided to keep his return from me?...Why?"

When Alexandre failed to respond, Seanna continued, "Your lie is going to devastate more than just the three of us, Alex. Everyone attached to you is going to be hurting for a while because of this one." She pivoted to meet the windows to Alexandre's soul and added, "And what will really pain me the most is that, despite the fact that you and I trust each other with everything, you didn't trust me enough with this; and, I don't even know why. Am I that shitty of a friend?"

"Of course, not," Alexandre objected.

"Then, why, Alex? I could have helped you through this—as with everything else, I could have helped you."

"Sea, I'm so sorry."

Seanna shook her head in dissent. "No, I know you all too well, Alex. You're not sorry; not in the least bit. What you are is regretful that you ran out of time to devise a plan to let this perfectly unfold the way that only Judge Alexandre Kaniece Denton-Hall would have it."

"Sea, plea-"

"I just never thought that, in this lifetime or even the next, I would be a victim of your manipulation."

"Seanna, I've never manipulated you."

"Really? So, garnering my support to postpone the adoption proceedings for at least a year had nothing to do with Lance?"

Unable to recollect the timing of events that surrounded their many conversations, Jacob's petitions, Jaamyas's approval, and Lance's resurgence, Alexandre refrained from answering her question.

Seanna respired in disappointment. Her heart ached and then sunk at the unspoken revelation that she was merely Alexandre's pawn employed to advance her calculated end.

"…I mourned him with you," Seanna spoke as she attempted to understand Alexandre's scheme to protect her family, herself, and her reputation.

Alexandre wiped her eyes and nodded in agreement. "…I know, and I will forever be gratef-"

"No, you don't know, Alexandre," Seanna interjected, reflecting on the memories that entailed her many sacrifices. "Because I am not that kind of friend—the kind of friend that belabors all that I have done for you for vainglorious reasons."

"I know you're not, Sea-"

"BUT," Seanna hotly interrupted. "I am about to be that friend now because I flew all-the-way out to fucking California to be there for you, Alexandre. In fact, I postposed the celebration of my first wedding anniversary so that I could be there for you. So that I could mourn your supposed dead husband for weeks—hell, months—with you!"

After closing her eyes, Alexandre nodded in agreement once more. When she opened her eyes again, she offered, "...You're right...You're absolutely right."

Reminiscing more on all that she forewent to be the help that Alexandre desperately needed, Seanna confessed in a low breath, "...The start of my family—having my own children—was delayed just so that I could be there for you and your child."

Grossly overwhelmed with guilt, Alexandre attempted to explain her actions, "...Lance and I were just trying to-"

Seanna raised her hand to interject. "This has you written all over it, Alexandre. Not Lance—you...I could be wrong, but either way, I don't want the details."

Alexandre heeded her request and halted her explanation. She then allowed the silence to settle between them in hopes that it would calm Seanna's bitterness.

"...At least not now anyway." Torn by the desire to be resentful and the need to forgive, tears fell from Seanna's eyes. Although she was overwhelmed with many emotions, she managed to sorrowfully admit, "...I'm not ready to forgive you."

After nodding in acknowledgement, Alexandre choked, "I understand, but I do hope that one day soon you will. I don't want this mishap to ruin us."

Seanna scoffed at her appeal and the audacity of it. "You love to cleave to this notion that you are different from your colleagues, but you're not, Alexandre. Despite what you may think, you are just like them."

Alexandre parted her lips to contest the unjust attack on her character, but Seanna halted the attempt by speaking, "Just because you don't push for policies that favor the rich and the privilege does not mean that you do not propagate some type of agenda—be it for yourself or those children you like to believe you are protecting."

Taking a deep breath, Seanna seized a moment to garner the courage to express with candor, "I'm sick of it. I'm sick of it all. And, truthfully, Alexandre, I'm sick of you..." When her voice trailed off, they, once again, sat among the deafening silence as they reckoned their thoughts and listened to the sniffles that accompanied their quiet cries.

"...I-I," Seanna began in stammer while struggling with her anguish. It vexed her to display mercy, but her heart would not permit Alexandre to endure her hardship alone. Consequently, Seanna swallowed the burning knot of emotions in her throat and took her best friend's hand into hers. She then squeezed it and met Alexandre's eyes, "But I won't leave you to deal with this terrifying wait alone...I'll stay until my god-son is returned home safely."

Alexandre wiped her eyes, feebly smiled, and whispered, "Thank you. Thank you so much, Seanna. I really do appre-"

Jacob pushed open the front door for Jaamyas to enter ahead of him. "I know, son, and I completely understand, but your mother needs you to be here with her. She needs..." His voice gradually quieted when Alexandre rushed to them, Seanna trailing behind her.

"Thank God you're okay," Alexandre stated as she embraced her damp, stoic son whose anger would not allow him to return the affection.

Jaamyas pulled his mother's arms from his shoulders and stepped away from her warmth. He looked at Jacob with discontent and then took off, without a word, up the stairs and to his room. They all flinched at the sound of the slammed door that ricocheted throughout the halls.

Jacob finally nodded and spoke, "Seanna," to acknowledge her presence.

"Hello, Jacob," she murmured, peering into his red, weary eyes. The beating muscle in her chest ached from the pain and sorrow she witnessed in them. Wiping her own eyes, Seanna pardoned herself, "I...I will head home now." She gently stroked Jacob's triceps in comforting support as she stepped past him, and opened the door.

"Seanna," Alexandre called out to her.

Seanna stopped, but refused to face her longtime companion.

"Thank you," Alexandre finally spoke.

Seanna said nothing in reply. Instead, she closed the door behind her and hurried to her car in the torrential downpour.

"From the looks of it, I take it she didn't know either," Jacob assumed.

"She didn't...I didn't tell her because-"

"Don't," Jacob interrupted. Though he yearned for the truth and the justification for all that she had done, he was not yet ready to listen to all that she had to reveal. "...Just don't."

She nodded in concession.

A pregnant silence grew between them and Jacob's eyes dropped to the diamond pendant that rested in the space between her breasts. Instantly, he began to despise it more than he ever had in the past.

"Jay took several buses into the city," Jacob offered in an attempt to dispel the silence and change the subject. "He came to the condo."

Alexandre nodded. She appreciated the fact that Jaamyas had heeded her lessons on taking public transportation. However, in divergence with the wave of gratitude, she did not appreciate his failure to execute her instruction only in the event of an emergency. The thought of Jaamyas's use of her teachings to flee their home at their moment of discord exasperated her.

After deeply respiring, Alexandre recalled that she was the cause of their familial conflict. So, she suppressed her anger and genuinely spoke, "Thank you for bringing him home."

"I only did it because I knew you would worry and I didn't want you calling me all night...He asked to stay with me." He met her eyes and forewarned, "The next time he comes to me, I won't refuse him." Jacob moved toward the stairs, but stopped when Alexandre grabbed his forearm.

"Jacob, please," Alexandre beseeched. "I-"

Jacob pushed her fingers from him with his free hand. "I'm only here for a few of my things, Alex...I'll call whenever I'm ready to talk."

✯✯✯ *SIX* ✯✯✯

For the second time that day, Alexandre flushed the contents of her stomach and heaved dry air until the nausea passed. She then groaned her misery as she slowly paced to her bathroom sink. After, first, rinsing her mouth with water and, then, mouthwash, Alexandre pressed cool water on face and neck.

"What is wrong with you, Alexandre?" She asked her reflection in the large vanity mirror. Her skin was clammy and pale, and her eyes were weary and red.

"God, please help me," Alexandre prayed when a mild vertigo rotated the room. She lowered her lids over her eyes and calmly breathed until the spinning ceased.

"I'm so sorry," she muttered to her body, realizing that her neglect permitted worry, stress, sorrow, and regret to devastate her immune system—making her susceptible to whatever virus she contracted.

Reminiscing out loud, Alexandre recalled, "I haven't felt this sick since I was pregnant with Jaa…"

Alexandre words gradually silenced as she struggled to recall when she had last taken her oral contraception…

She had not taken it that morning or…

The morning before or…

"No…no, no, no. Please, God, no," she beseeched, exiting her master bathroom in haste. She rushed to her nightstand to retrieve her compact. It was not near the lamp where she typically kept it.

She yanked open the drawer and frantically shuffled through its contents. It was not there.

Her panic aided her triumph in the struggle with the hefty nightstand. She pulled the polished wood forward and found lodged between it and the bed a pen, highlighter, and small legal pad. After placing the items on the down comforter, Alexandre wrenched forward the furniture a few more inches and continued her search behind it. She retrieved a book and placed it on the tabletop. Following, she noticed the black circular case she was searching for.

With a racing heart and trembling fingers, Alexandre collected the compact and slowly opened it…She had missed the last sixteen days of pills.

As Alexandre lowered herself to the edge of the bed, she released a heartfelt cry and continued to weep until her abdomen ached. She was now confident that what she held in her hand was confirmation of a new life flourishing within her and not a virus overpowering her compromised immune system.

Quieting her sobs, Alexandre wiped her eyes and began to contemplate the contentious plight she was bringing an innocent child into—one in which she was uncertain of its father.

*** *** ***

"Hello, George. How are you?"

The suited concierge stood and greeted her, "Judge Denton-Hall, what a pleasure. It's been quite some time since I've seen you last."

Alexandre smiled and agreed, "Indeed it has. How are you and your beautiful family?"

"Well, ma'am; all is well. Thank you so much for asking. How are you?"

"The same, and thank you for asking…Is he in?"

He nodded. "He is. Hasn't left since returning from the office."

"Thanks, George. I will let myself up."

"Of course, ma'am. Enjoy your evening."

"You do the same."

Alexandre walked past the immaculately kept and inviting lobby to the elevator bay. When the first of the six opened, she stepped on, and selected the penthouse level. The doors gradually closed and her heart began to palpitate. As each glowing number lifted her higher to her destination, the throb in chest rose to her throat.

She closed her eyes and exercised her square breathing technique to steady her nerves. While she did so, Alexandre reminded herself of all that she learned with her first pregnancy— primarily, stress was not good for the baby. When the bell chimed and the doors separated, she opened her eyes and descended the elevator.

Though she had made the journey several times before, the walk to the end of the hall seemed exceedingly long. So long that each step she took gave Alexandre a moment to contemplate her return to the elevator bay. Several excuses fueled her timidity, but the reasons for her visit, encouraged her to overcome her cowardice.

Finally at Jacob's door, Alexandre inhaled deeply through her nostrils and exhaled slowly through pursed lips. She then raised her trembling fist to knock. It was not until her third knock went unanswered, did she remember that she possessed a key.

"Jacob?" She inquired after she unsecured and cautiously opened the door.

No response.

Alexandre stepped into the unit then closed and secured the door. "Jacob, are you home?"

Again, no response.

She took in a panoramic view of the tidy and faultlessly decorated condo. Small steps took her further into her second home and she found everything as she last remembered it. Pictures of his family, her family, and their family hung on the walls along with priceless art. Jacob had changed nothing during the separation, and, to Alexandre, that was a revelation that gave her hope of reconciliation.

"Ja-" Alexandre stopped when she noticed him in the living room. He was slouched, with a short glass in his hand, on his oversized sectional positioned in front of the fireplace and large mounted television.

Standing in front of him, she asked, "Did you not hear me knocking?"

When he failed to answer, Alexandre stated, "Jacob, I was calling you."

Jacob swirled the dark liquor around the ice cubes, sipped from the glass, and continued to stare at the black screen of his television.

"What are you doing here, Alexandre?"

She was pained and taken aback by his callous question. "...I'm conducting a wellness check on my husband."

He scoffed, drank from his glass, and confirmed, "You checked, I'm well, now leave."

In defiance, Alexandre lowered herself next to him, placed her keys in her handbag, and then set it on the floor.

"We need to talk, Jacob."

"I told you I will call when I am ready to talk."

"And will that be? It's been several weeks...If you weren't so private, I would have called your brother."

"Do not bring my family into this," Jacob admonished. He then swallowed from his glass and added, "It's hard enough trying to make sense of this shit myself."

"Well, I don't know what more to do, Jacob...I call, but you don't respond. I text, but you don't respond. I email, but you don't respond. You NEVER respond, Jacob."

Before taking another sip of what calmed his rage and numbed his pain, Jacob ignored her recollection of his avoidance behavior and finally replied to her question, "I don't know when I will be ready to talk, Alexandre, but you don't get to decide."

Alexandre respired audibly. If it had not been for the second reason for her visit, she would have left Jacob to continue in the drinking of his emotions. At the thought of the news she had to deliver, her heart began to race again. Biding time, Alexandre pushed a lock of hair behind her ear then massaged the palmar creases in her right hand.

"…How are you doing, Jacob?" She asked.

He drank from his glass and ignored her.

"Jacob."

He finally turned to meet her eyes and saw the agony that mirrored his. "Take a guess, Alexandre."

She shrugged. "I don't know. I…I mean I suppose I could guess, but I rather not. I would prefer that you talk to me. So…So, please…Please, just tell me—tell me anything…I just need you to talk to me, Jacob." She paused to tame her quivering voice then lowly uttered, "…This silent treatment is killing me. It is emotionally and mentally killing me."

Turning from the face that he once could not cease gawking, Jacob looked to the window in the corner. Despite the closed blinds, the early evening sunlight illuminated the room. It was a brightness that he used to adore, but have now come to loath.

"How can I, Alexandre?...I can't even stand to look at you, more or less talk to you."

An unexpected bawl escaped her and Alexandre attempted, to no avail, to collect herself.

The sound of her sobs brought tears to own his eyes and Jacob quickly wiped them way with the back of his hand. He then struggled to drown his grief with another swallow of cognac.

A moment past before Alexandre finally quieted her cries and wiped her face dry with her hands. A thick silence swelled in the room as she awaited the arrival of her courage.

When bravery finally set, she confessed, "I'm pregnant, Jacob."

Jacob lowered his lids over his eyes and allowed the news to resound in his mind. Had the news come several months earlier he would have been elated by the delivery of it.

Perturbed by his silence, Alexandre tried to explain, "…I…I missed a few pills…and...and now I'm pregnant."

Jacob opened his eyes, drank from his glass, and rhetorically inquired, "Is it mine?"

"…I don't know."

Though he anticipated her admission, it still saddened him. Alexandre had once again sabotaged what he earnestly desired.

Cavalierly raising his shoulders, Jacob smugly responded, "Of course, you don't."

His words pierced her to the core and Alexandre struggled to speak, "…I…I don't know what to say, Jacob. I have truly made a mess of things and…and I…I can't seem to apologize enough."

He swallowed the last of his libation and placed the glass on the coaster on the coffee table in front of him.

"Then stop," he advised, leaning his back into the cushion of the sofa.

"Excuse me?"

"Then stop fucking apologizing," he restated. "There's no point…It won't restore what we had—what I worked my ass off the last three years to build."

Jacob attempted, to no avail, to wipe the frustration from his face as he recalled, "The night you accepted my proposal you told me that the only thing that I could give you that you could not buy for yourself was my life." He turned his gaze to her and choked, "I have been giving you that from the moment you said yes, Alexandre…And for what? To have you and your lover obliterate it in a matter of months?"

"…He isn't my lover, Jacob. He is—was—my husband."

Jacob sneered. "You're right. I stand corrected." He leaned forward to retrieve the bottle of cognac on the table and refilled his glass.

After he reclined again into the cushion behind him, Jacob swirled the brown liquid around the ice cubes and sipped from the glass. "…I am the lover," he agonizingly acknowledged.

Reflecting on his numerous aspirations and achievements, Jacob explained in a decelerated but coherent monologue, "…My entire life, all I ever wanted was a family of my own…It did not matter to me how God packaged it; I just wanted something that was mine…The stellar grades in school, the long hours at work, it was always for the family I prayed for."

He swallowed his beverage to its end and then conceded, "…I suppose now it was all for naught."

Alexandre took the glass from his hand and set it on the table away from his reach. "Please, Jacob, try to understand."

"Understand what? That my wife is a habitual liar and compulsive cheat? That it took the murmurs in the street to compel her to tell me the fucking truth?"

The intense pangs caused by his crass observation formed fresh tears that unyieldingly fell from Alexandre's eyes. Her hands maneuvered quickly to dab at the hurt, sorrow, shame, and regret, but the rivulets that traveled down her face were more expeditious.

"I'm…I'm going to head out…Uumm. If you could please respond to the fall festival invitation, I would appreciate it…Jaamyas is fearful of your rejection, so he won't ask you himself."

Jacob spoke nothing in response.

Alexandre gripped the handles of her bag and stood to leave.

"Alexandre," Jacob called out to her as she turned and walked away from him.

She turned on her heels and looked upon his visage despite his avoidance of her eyes.

"Please tell my son that I will be there."

Alexandre sighed in relief. She had been the source of a lot of disruption and uncertainty in Jaamyas's life, and a strained relationship with Jacob was not one that she was willing to allow. Thus, despite her broken union, Alexandre was determined to do everything within her power to maintain the bond that her son had with the father he had yearned to call his own.

"I will," she confirmed. Unsure of his feelings towards her and his thoughts of their future, she merely bid, "Take care, Jacob."

*** *** ***

"Amen," they all spoke in unison after Alexandre's father, sitting at the head of the table, recited grace. Serving dishes were then passed around the table so that each person could select their desired portion of roasted potatoes, green beans, caramelized carrots, fried fish, and sweet rolls.

Typical of most Sunday afternoons, following worship service, Seanna's household met Alexandre's household at her parents' house for dinner. Atypical of most Sunday afternoons, neither Jacob nor Seanna or her husband was present.

"Who is he?" The four-year-old asked above a whisper as her amber eyes were fixated on the man at the end of the extended dinner table. He was seated in front of Alexandre as they both sat next to her Alexandre's father.

"He's Jay's real dad," her firstborn brother, sitting next to her, answered. After assisting her with the green beans, he extended the dish to Jaamyas in front of him.

Contorting her face in confusion, she furthered inquired, "So, Jacob isn't his dad anymore?"

"Be quiet, Rayne," her older sister across from her commanded. "You ask too many questions."

"It's okay," Jaamyas finally muttered, defending his youngest god-sister. "She is just curious."

"Curious is an accurate assessment, Jay," his grandfather commented as he placed the cloth napkin on his lap and received the rolls from Alexandre. "As we are all curious."

"Victor, please," his wife beseeched from the opposite end of the table. "Can we not do this at dinner?"

"Yes, Daddy, please," Alexandre concurred. She knew that the conversation would unleash years of disappointments, frustrations, and hurts. And, although it was a conversation that needed to be had, Alexandre preferred that it did not occur during Sunday dinner and certainly not in the presence of children—particularly Jaamyas.

Victor chewed and swallowed a forkful of potatoes and responded. "I think it's appropriate dinner conversation. The question was posed at the dinner table after all."

"Victor, Lance may not want to discuss-"

"It's fine, Mrs. Leigh," Lance interjected. "I don't mind answering. I am sure everyone here is curious to know. So, now is as good as time as any to appease the curiosity."

"Well, in that case," Victor spoke, "You can start with what are your intentions? Have you come to take my daughter and my grandson because that sure as hell is not going to happen."

"Victor-" Cheryl spoke, hoping to silence her husband.

"With all due respect, sir, Jaamyas may be your grandson, but he is my son. Where he goes and stays is decided by his mother and me."

Alexandre glared at Lance and shook her head in admonition. She had purposely disclosed Lance's reemergence to her parents telephonically and waited several weeks before allowing them to meet in person. The purpose of her delaying the reacquaintance was to avoid the fiery exchange they were currently encountering. Nonetheless, despite her warnings that her father was baiting him, Lance had successfully hooked the line. Whether or not the baited hook was intentional on Lance's part, that, she did not know.

Suppressing his agitation, Victor chuckled and then sipped iced tea from his glass. "I've been Jay's father since the day he was born. In fact, until Jacob's blessed arrival, I was the only father he knew."

Victor turned to Lance and inquired, "Have you met Jacob?"

Lance did not respond.

Victor lowered his glass back to the table and resumed consuming his meal. Between chews, he stated, "I'm sure you have. He is Alex's husband after all—a good man; sticks around, you know; takes care of his family."

"Daddy, please," Alexandre begged, reaching out to touch his forearm. "Can we please have this conversation later?"

"Sure, just as long as it is understood that he is not taking my grandson anywhere. Now, I may not have a say in Alexandre's coming and goings, but that boy there," he pointed in Jaamyas's direction with his cutting knife, "is mine. I am his father and he stays with me."

When Lance cleared his throat to contest, Victor lowered his utensil, glared vehemently at him, and reminded, "While you were out playing G.I. Joe, I was being the father that Jay needed for the last thirteen years."

Lance huffed in disbelief. He placed his napkin in his untouched plate and pushed it away from him. "Playing G. I. Joe?"

"You heard me. I did not stutter."

"Mr. Leigh, I know that you had I have never seen eye-to-eye on anything. And I would venture to say that you never cared for me-"

"And you would be accurate in the assessment," Victor interjected before consuming again his meal.

Ignoring his father-in-law's retort, Lance continued, elevating his tone, "But at the very least, I am owed your respect. From the day I said 'I do' I have taken care of your daughter and our son. I may not have also been physically around, but damnit I was there taking care of them. Even in my supposed death they were well-off. So DO NOT make it seem as if I abandoned my family. I was honorably fighting in a war to protect your rights, your freedoms, your civil liberties!"

Without thought, Victor calmly lowered his knife and fork in his plate. He then retrieved his napkin wiped his mouth and placed it at the side of his plate. Finally, he abruptly gripped Lance's business shirt at the shoulders, lifted him from his seat, and shoved him into the nearest wall. The table cloth that was inadvertently tucked into the seat of Victor's pants, accompanied his stride, sending food plates, drink glasses, and serving dishes to the floor.

"You left your pregnant wife so that you could volunteer for a war whose only purpose was to make the rich richer!" Victor growled hotly. "Where is the honor in that, huh?!"

Victor awaited Lance's response as he continued to hold his shirt at its shoulders despite Lance's firm grip of his wrists. He ignored his wife's calling of his name and daughter's voice ushering the children out of the dining room.

When no answer was provided, Victor shoved Lance into the wall another time and repeated, "Where is the honor is that?!"

Marginally equal in stature, both men stood at eye level. Fuming, their nostrils flared while they glared at each other. In Lance's eyes, Victor saw a man who never felt good enough in spite of his best efforts; he could never measure-up to the man he felt deserving of his daughter. In Victor's eyes, Lance saw the anger and disappointment of having relinquished his most precious possession—his greatest achievement—to a man who immaturely and selfishly abandoned her.

Respectfully, Lance released his grip, lowered his hands, and uttered, "I'm…I'm sorry, sir."

The sincerity in Lance's eyes and the crack in voice, prompted Victor to release his hold and drop his hands. "Get out…Get out of my house now and don't ever return. In fact, if I *never* see you again, it will be too soon."

As the vehicle that Lance had rented during his visit slowed to a stop in Seanna's driveway, Alexandre contemplated confronting the other dragon that needed slaying her in life. Because she still grappled with the strain of their friendship, Alexandre was not yet ready to explain the impromptu dinner reservations made to fill the bellies left empty after the fiasco at her parents' home.

"Jay, please walk Trevor, Malia, and Rayne to the door," Alexandre requested, finally ending the suffocating silence.

"Yes, ma'am," Jaamyas spoke. He then disassembled his seatbelt, opened the car door, and assisted his god-sister on the step that lowered from the beneath the truck. After watching Trevor do the same for his second god-sister on the opposite side, Jaamyas closed the door.

"I'm so sorry," Lance uttered following the closing of the doors.

Alexandre gazed out her passenger window and questioned, "Sorry for what, Lance?"

Lance pondered her inquiry for a brief moment. He had garnered that she was not only exhausted by the menace he had become in her life, but also wearied by the seemingly empty apologies. Nevertheless, Lance felt obligated to contritely respond, "For the part I played in ruining dinner." He placed his hand under her chin and gently turned her face to him. "For the part I played in ruining our forever after."

Water filled her eyes at his repentance. It was the first time since their nuptials he verbally recognized her anger, her frustration, her disappointment, her sacrifice, and her loss.

His fingers smoothed away the rivulets of tears that ran down her cheeks. "I was, and in many ways still am, a selfish asshole. I see it now; I know it now."

Alexandre removed his hand from her face. "No, you weren't. You were just-"

"A selfish asshole. Don't defend me, Alex, because I was. I really was and your father new knew it and your mother felt it, but you," he took her hand and held it, "Alexandre, you never believed it."

Lance reflected on the immediate years that followed his college graduation. "I was a young Marine with a plan and I expected you to complacently fall in line with that plan." He reminisced of and exhaled loudly at the egotistic ingrate he was once was. "...In addition to that, I was a Marine with a chip on my shoulder. I had something to prove to your father, your mother, my commander, and myself...Trust me, I know what I was; you...you just refused to believe it."

Despite her tears, Alexandre feebly grinned and explained, "I was a naïve girl in love. I only saw the best in you."

"I know, and because of that I should have been proving myself to you. Or, at the very least, I should have exhibited some grand gesture to acknowledge all that you had forfeited for me." Lance raised his shoulders and then admitted, "But, of course, my pride wouldn't allow it..."

His voice trailed off as he carefully considered his words in spite of his disorderly thoughts. Upon gaining his composure, Lance confessed, "I loved you, Alex. God knows that I loved you—hell, from the moment I met you, I deeply longed for you. But...but, truthfully, I...I always believed you to be a deviation from the well-crafted blue-print I formulated for my life."

Although taken aback by the unexpected confession, the truth was no surprise to Alexandre. Lance was meticulous to a fault in all that he planned—a quality that she, too, possessed. It was one of her many attractions to him. It was why they worked. It was why they were the ideal team.

After remaining stoic in her silence for a moment, Alexandre finally uttered "I-"

The vehicle door swung open and Jaamyas climbed in speaking, "Mom, God-mom Sea said thank you for dropping them off. She is still not ready to speak with-"

Jaamyas words halted after he closed the door, leaned into his mother's seat, and watched her quickly wipe her face. "Mom, are you okay?"

"Yeah, I'm fine, Jay."

"Then why are you crying?" He pressed in disbelief. He pivoted his head to burn his glare into Lance who he thought to be the culprit of his mother's distress.

"I'm just upset with you grandfather—that's all, but I'm fine," she assured. "Now, sit back and put your safety belt on so that we can go home."

With the exception of the soft gospel tunes humming the through the speakers, the car ride was silent. In that silence, the three of them relived their unique experiences of the last few hours, days, weeks, and months.

"I feel out of place," Lance confessed after parking the car. "I don't know if I should walk you in or sit in the truck until you safely enter the house."

"It's okay. We will be fine." Alexandre turned her head to the back seat and requested of their son, "Go ahead inside and start getting ready for school and then bed."

Jaamyas held her eyes with worry. Though he still despised her for the disruption she caused to their family, he hated more the suffering he could unmistakably see in her visage.

Giving him a bogus smile, she stated, "I'm fine, Jay, and will be in a minute. Go ahead in."

Jaamyas nodded. "Yes, ma'am." As he opened the car door, he heard his father wish him a good night. Without facing him, Jaamyas wished him the same, exited the vehicle, closed the door, and started toward the front door.

"Jay doesn't know the truth about your deployment. I never wanted him to feel abandoned by his father. So, I always told him that you were a hero who died honorably after receiving special orders to go to war."

Lance lowered his lids over his eyes. Even in her sorrow and disenchantment, she still presented him as a man to be honored, respected, and loved.

"Thank you," he stated slightly above a whisper. "...Though I suppose after tonight, the truth will have to be explained to him?"

Alexandre shrugged and then assured, "It's your truth to tell, Lance, not mine. But he will have questions. Jay is a very precocious child and, when things are not logically sound, he will ask a host of questions. And when he does, that will be your opportunity to tell the true version of your life story."

Understanding the unspoken request, Lance nodded and turned to look out the windshield.

A quietness fell between them, but before it settled too long, Alexandre boldly confessed, "I'm pregnant, Lance."

He turned to face her, and to make sure he heard her correctly, he inquired, "What?"

"I'm pregnant," she repeated, "and the child may be yours."

The thought of a second chance to experience all that he missed with his first child brought a smile to his face. "That's wonderful news."

"Is it?"

"Why wouldn't it be? It's another blessing, another life, another-"

"Reminder of my infidelity?"

"Alex-"

"I'm not making any demands of you, Lance. I just thought you had a right to know. Jacob knows, Jaamyas knows, so, now, you know. I just needed you to know before anyone else."

Lance nodded though unsure of her statement of her lack of demands. He yearned for her to be demanding, and to make requests that he be present and accountable every step of the way. From the fact that she did not articulate these demands, Lance gleaned that she was not yet in a mental and emotional space to make those requests known.

After swallowing the knot in his throat, he murmured, "I appreciate that...You...You are keeping it, right?"

By his tone, Alexandre concluded that the question was more of an appeal than an ask. "...I am. I couldn't live with myself if I terminated the pregnancy, especially if I could not conceive again afterwards."

Lance exhaled gradually in relief. "Whatever you need, just let me know. I mean it, Alex, I am here every step of the way this time. I promise."

Alexandre slowly closed her eyes as Lance leaned in to lower his lips on hers. As the chills rose in her spine and traveled throughout her body, she recalled his many spoken words that returned void in the past. Shattered vow after shattered vow, he eventually obliterated her confidence in him. For that reason then, and her cause now, Alexandre could not wholly rely on Lance or readily permit herself to grant him the benefit of the doubt.

Pulling her mouth from his, Alexandre opened her eyes and searched Lance's for his truth, sincerity, and commitment. Without a doubt, her self-sufficiency ensured that she and the children will be okay if he decided to vanish; but her vulnerable heart yearned for him to make the decision to stay.

When the exploration into the windows of his soul became impossible due to the clouded layers of their history, Alexandre finally spoke, "Have a good night, Lance," before she exited the truck and walked toward the front door of her home.

*** *SEVEN* ***

"I dragged you out of the office because I get the sense that something is off with you," Phillip spoke with great concern as they took seats at the bar of the restaurant in their firm's building.

The unexpected observation caused Jacob shift his weight in the barstool, but he offered no response.

Ignoring Jacob's silence, Phillip acknowledged, "You're turning around projects at a rate that you never have before."

"And that's a bad thing?" Jacob inquired perplexed.

"For business—no, but for your marriage—yes. You are newly wedded, Jacob, and you're spending all this time at the office."

Jacob shrugged to dismiss his keen assessment. "...Just more on my plate with the promotion. I am just trying to stay on top of it all."

"Are you sure that's it?"

Jacob did not respond to the question he knew to be a probe compelled by skepticism.

"...Because what I see," Phillip began in spite of Jacob's reticence, "is a young man on a path that I am all too familiar with—

one that leads to two messy divorces; a shitload of alimony payments; and string of rapacious, accessible women beseeching to have your last name."

Before Jacob could contest, a female bartender arrived, placing white napkins in front of them. "Hey, Phil. What's your poison?"

"Hello, Jessica. Give me a rum and coke and a food menu; and add to my tab whatever it is that my friend here wants."

She looked at Jacob and awaited his response.

"Cognac, please, with little ice."

Jessica nodded then stepped away to quickly fulfill their requests.

"So, are we going to continue to dance around the fire or be men and walk through it—together?" Phillip asked.

Jacob inhaled deeply and exhaled loudly. He then looked up at Phillip, a man he considered a second father, and began to share all that he had not yet shared with his biological father.

"Do you still love her?" Phillip asked at the conclusion of Jacob's monologue.

"Of course, I still love her," Jacob answered without reservation. He sipped from his glass then confirmed, "She is the love of my life."

"Then find a way to forgive her and move on. Otherwise, you risk losing her and everything you worked so hard to forge with her."

"…I don't know, Phil. It all sounds easier said than done."

Phillip sneered. "Trust me, it's not easy—it's not easy at all. In fact, it's fucking hard." He sipped from his beverage and cynically added, "When it comes to marriage, there are better odds in Vegas and I have a record of losses to prove it."

Jacob huffed at the metaphor.

Halting his brief rant before it transitioned into a protracted monologue of his own, Phillip took a moment to scrutinize Jacob's despondent visage. The infidelity that transpired in his marriage had not only broken his heart, but also his spirit. Both were pains that Phillip was all too familiar with when his first wife sought comfort in another man.

Recognizing that what Jacob needed was not a companion in misery, but a counselor of hope and restoration, Phillip encouraged, "...But, every-once-in-while, there is a union worth making the bet on."

Jacob took a moment to ponder Phillip's advice intently, considering whether Alexandre was still worth the gamble. Though she remained the love of his life, he was not certain if he was willing another time to bet with his heart. In fact, he was not certain if he was willing to remain a wagerer in her unfavorable game of chance.

When Jacob spoke no words in reply to his offerings, Phillip candidly stated, "Look, nothing worth fighting for is easy, and anyone who tells you differently is a damn liar."

Jacob vigorously rubbed his forehead in distress. "Phil-"

"No, don't Phil me, Jacob," he interjected in effort to halt a litany of Jacob's excuses. "Either you choose to fight or you choose the alternative. And what's the alternative for you? Another man playing the role of head-of-household to your family?"

Jacob respired audibly at the question and then mumbled under his breath, "I'm not so sure it was ever my family to have."

"Bullshit. The way you lauded that beautiful wife and intelligent stepson of yours, that is your family. And the new baby only adds to the joy of your family."

Jacob feebly grinned. "...Yeah, I suppose...But I still question paternity."

Phillip shrugged. "And you have every reason to—it's your right. But, Jacob, don't let it rob you of this experience. It only happens once per child and you will regret missing out, especially if the child is yours."

"And if it's not?"

Phillip shrugged once more as he thought for a moment. He empathetically contemplated the advice he would have liked to receive if he were in Jacob's position. "...You love your wife, so that means loving all that comes with her and all that comes from her."

The wise counsel that ached Jacob's heart compelled him to consume a long swallow from his glass. "...I need time. I'm not ready to consider all that was said and done a wash."

Phillip placed a hand on Jacob's forearm and firmly squeezed it in support. "That is understandable, but be mindful not to take too much time."

"How does one determine that? What length of time is too much time?"

Raising his hand from Jacob's arm, Phillip rubbed his brow and responded, "Well, from what you shared, the former husband is looking to stake his claim. So, I suppose any amount of time that will permit him to do so successfully is too much time."

Jacob nodded and meditated on the guidance.

Before the silence lingered too long between them, Phillip sipped from his glass then inquired, "How is the Mrs.? What are her thoughts on all of this?"

Jacob raised his shoulders with nonchalance, realizing that he has yet to give Alexandre the opportunity to convey to him all that she was thinking and feeling. "She says that I need to understand."

"Well, do you? Do you understand?"

Before answering, Jacob downed the remainder of his beverage and returned the glass to the wet napkin on the bar. "...I do...I understand that I was not enough for her."

Phillip chuckled at his simple response. "To the contrary, Jacob, you are enough. You are actually everything she needs— that's why she chose you...Now, everything she wants, is something entirely different. But, then again, in this life, we are not promised everything we want. So, it is an unjust burden to place on our spouses when we expect or even demand that they fulfill our every want."

Jacob deliberated the wealth of wisdom afforded him by the man almost thirty years his senior. Not quite sure what to do with the knowledge bestowed upon him, he rose from his seat while speaking, "...I'm, uh, I'm going to walk back to the office to get some work done.

Phillip glanced at the hands that pointed to 9:42 on his wristwatch and then responded, "It's really late."

"Yeah, I know...But, working late keeps me together while I'm falling apart."

Comprehending all too well the paradox, Phillip encouraged, "Well, don't stay too much longer."

"I don't plan to." Jacob placed his hand on Phillip's shoulder and squeezed it firmly to convey his appreciation of his many offerings. "Thanks for the drink."

*** *** ***

Jacob immediately noticed her upon his entrance of the gymnasium's vestibule. She stood four inches taller in the heels she wore that were partially hidden by her fitted denim jeans. The black blazer gave her a professional look despite the white t-shirt that hugged her breasts and bore the name of Jaamyas's school.

The conversation in which she engaged with the other parents made her laugh and the sound of it warmed Jacob's heart. He had missed her laughter and, more importantly, he had missed her.

"Hello, Alex," Jacob greeted as he made the final steps towards her after the other parents left her company.

Astonished by his arrival, Alexandre stuttered, "Ja-Jacob, you…you came…"

"I told you I would."

"Yeah…I know, but…"

"Here are the tickets," Lance announced, rushing back to the table. "I'm told these are the last two rolls."

Alexandre received them and said, "Thank you."

When Lance lifted his gaze to see what captured hers, he finally noticed Jacob. Speaking first, Lance greeted, "Hello, Jacob."

"Coach Carter," Jacob returned, meeting the eyes that were a few inches above his own.

"Listen, Jacob," Lance began in an attempt to break the silence and ease the awkwardness, "I just want to apologize…It was never my intent to-"

"Please, let's not make this about us," Jacob interrupted him. "I'm only here for my—our—son. I gave him my word that I would be here. He is the only reason why I am here."

"Of course. I will go find him for you," Lance replied, stepping away again.

Not able to contain his curiosity, Jacob asked, "Are the two of you-"

"No," Alexandre immediately objected not needing him to complete his thought before she concluded his supposition. "No…we are…we are just trying to navigate our way through this co-parenting situation we now find ourselves in." She peered deep into his eyes and confirmed, "That's it, Jacob. That's it, and that's all."

Jacob nodded then pointed at the rolls in her hand to divert the conversation. "Are those admission tickets?"

"Yes—I mean no. Jay paid for your ticket and your shirt with his own money…He, uh, he never lost hope that you were coming."

Nervously dropping her eyes down to her hands, Alexandre struggled until she finally removed the shrink-wrap while stating, "These—these are actually, uh, one dollar raffle tickets for a few prizes for the kids." She met his gaze and completed, "The remaining funds go toward scholarships."

"Seems to me to be a worthy cause. Have the drawings begun? Is it too late to purchase tickets?"

"Yes, but no."

Confounded, Jacob squinted his eyes as he tried to decode her response.

"The drawings have begun, but they are throughout the evening. So, you can still buy tickets," Alexandre clarified.

"Got it." Jacob went into the inside pocket of his sport coat for his wallet. "I will buy a hundred of them."

Alexandre chuckled. "A hundred tickets?"

Jacob shrugged, "I figured a hundred will increase my son's odds of winning something."

Alexandre rolled her eyes at his benevolence. "You're spoiling him."

"I know, but it's easy to do with a kid like hi-"

"JACOB!" Jaamyas exclaimed at the sight of him. He rushed to throw his arms around his torso. "I knew you would come. I just knew it!"

Jacob returned the hug and kissed the top of his head. "Of course, I would. I gave my word, didn't I?"

Releasing him, Jaamyas spoke, "I have your shirt and admission ticket."

After he retrieved his bookbag from behind the table curtain, Jaamyas removed the shirt and ticket, giving the former to Jacob and the latter to Alexandre.

"Thank you, son," Jacob spoke, removing his sport coat and placing it on the table. He then quickly pulled the white t-shirt over the one he currently wore and placed his sport coat back on. After he adjusted the shirt over his denim jeans, he asked, "How do I look?"

Jaamyas laughed. "Like all the other parents."

Jacob snickered at his quip and playfully jabbed him in the jaw.

"Come watch me bob for apples," Jaamyas demanded, grabbing Jacob's hand leading him away from his mother and Lance.

When Alexandre noticed the melancholic look on Lance's face, she gently touched his forearm. "Give him time, Lance. Jacob is the only father he knows."

Lance nodded. "I know and I understand, but..." His voice trailed off.

"But, it still hurts?"

He nodded again. "I'm just getting him back and I already have to let him go."

"Trust me. Jay is not a child you can let go. He is like a barnacle."

Lance feebly smiled at her attempt to cheer him. He then suppressed his ill-feelings and returned to assisting her with the management of ticket sales.

"Mooooooom," Jaamyas sang later in the evening as he approached her. "We're running low on ice. If it's okay with you, Mrs. Towson would like Elijah and me to walk over to the convenience store to purchase more."

Vexed by her son's rude interruption, Alexandre pardoned herself from the parent with whom she was speaking, and simply responded, "Sure, Jay." Afterwards, she walked to where Lance stood to retrieve a twenty-dollar bill from the cash register box.

Extending the currency to Jaamyas, she commanded, "Get four bags and bring back the change and the receipt."

Jaamyas collected the money and tucked it in his pocket as he nodded in acknowledgment of his mother's directives.

"Please be careful crossing the street, Jay."

He huffed at her plea. "Okay, Mom."

"And cross at the crosswalk."

Jaamyas turned on his heels and clandestinely rolled his eyes. "Okaaay, Mom."

"And stay off your phone!" She called out to him while he and his companion exited the double doors of the vestibule.

"OKAY, MOM," he called back to her as the doors closed behind them.

"Sorry," she spoke to Lance. I feel like I have to always remind him of these things. He is so easily distracted at times."

Lance impishly grinned then responded, "As am I."

Alexandre blushed. "I see that old habits do die hard."

"They do indeed."

An hour later, Lance inquired of Jacob as he approached them in the foyer, "Heading out already?"

Jacob forced his second arm into his sport coat and then pulled it on his shoulders. "Yeah, I figured I…" his voice trailed off when he met Alexandre's saddened eyes.

"Abscond while you are ahead?" Lance finished for him.

Jacob broke their gaze and answered him, "Yes, or least before Jay spends all of my money and Mrs. Towson exhausts all of my energy."

The three of them laughed lightheartedly at his wit, a gesture they were all appreciative of.

When the laughter gave way to silence, Jacob met Alexandre's stare another time and requested, "A moment please, Alex?"

"Of course. I will walk you out." She extended the last of the raffle tickets to Lance and asked, "Could you man the station until I return?"

Lance received the bundle from her as he tilted his head forward and merely replied, "Yes."

In the cool night air, Alexandre folded her arms across her breasts and walked close to Jacob's warmth en route to his car. Though it was he that requested the meeting, she was the first to speak, "Thank you, again, for keeping your word, Jacob...I know...I know that being here tonight was probably not the easiest thing for you to do, but it means the world to Jay. It really does and...and I don't know if you noticed or not, but he was ecstatic to see you."

Jacob shrugged at her rambling of appreciation and offered in response, "I am nothing if not a man of my word."

"I know, but-"

"Alexandre," Jacob interjected, knowing that her palavering was an attempt to engage him. "I know we still need to talk—to have a serious conversation about the situation we find ourselves in, but I am not ready. So, we don't have to fill the void with small talk."

"...Oh...okay."

"...I just need more time to muster the courage to endure all that you have to say to me. In addition to that, there are a host of questions that I have for you, but I am not yet ready for your responses to them. So, for now, I will refrain from asking...I only invited you out here to share that with you...I figured you are owed that much."

"...Thank you, Jacob," she uttered with nothing more to say to his unexpected candor.

"You're welcome," he returned as their walk slowed to a stop at the driver's door of his luxury sedan. Jacob then pivoted to face her stating, "Alex, I really do hope that you understand; and not just understand, but support and respect my decision."

She thought for a moment and then reasoned, "…I do. Well, in part, but I do need-"

True to her role as an officer of the court, Alexandre partitioned her concurrence. She was always mindful to never agree wholeheartedly on certain matters in the event she needed to recant.

"Damn it, Alex, this is not about you, and what you need, and what you want," Jacob forcefully interrupted, recalling that Alexandre possessed the wherewithal to mold people to her will. Therefore, it was necessary for him to halt her attempt to exercise her practice with him. "This is about me dealing in my own time, and in my own way, with the truckload of shit you selfishly dropped at my front door."

Alexandre respired deeply to remain calm and contrite despite his premature attack. "…What I was just trying to say is that, though I partially understand, I do need you to know that I support and respect your decision. Because if the roles were reversed and you were the guilty party, I, too, would need the time to process my thoughts and emotions as well."

Astounded by the concession that was atypical of her character, Jacob spoke nothing in response. In the many years that they have been acquainted, he had grown accustomed to Alexandre's inability to relinquish her authoritarian persona. Consequently, every facet of her life; his life; their life, had become an extension of her courtroom. Not even for the sake of him coping with their marital issues in his own manner could Alexandre release control, and it immensely agitated Jacob.

He watched her lower her arms to her side as if to surrender her defenses, and listened to her confess, "Without a doubt, my legal power position spews into our marriage—and it's not an excuse for my actions, and I'm not even saying that it's right, but it is an explanation as to why I push—I push often and I push hard…But, I just push because I feel that it's needed even when it's not wanted…and, now, I am pushing because you're missed, Jacob."

Jacob allowed a moment for the words she spoke to resonate with him. When enough time passed, he inquired, "Missed by whom, Alexandre?"

Taken aback by the question, she asked in return, "By whom do you think?"

Jacob shrugged then responded, "I don't know. That's why I asked, because, by man's insatiable nature, we always want more than what we have until what we have becomes no more."

Alexandre huffed at the allusion that her deep yearning of his presence was only motivated by the agony of his absence—that she desired more outside of him when he was with her and now that he was gone all that she desired was him. "…I miss you, Jacob," she finally retorted. "For myriad reasons I miss you. But above them all, I miss you because I love you."

With aid from the lights of the lampposts, Jacob could see the sincerity in her face. It was a face that, despite his occasional ill-feelings, was as beautiful as the evening he first met her. However, on this evening, her beautiful face glowed. Jacob longed to touch her, but the pain that ached his chest prevented him from expressing, in any manner, anything that he felt. He especially could not articulate the love his broken heart still possessed for her.

After clearing his throat, Jacob asked, "Do you want a ride back to the entrance?"

Though grossly disappointed, Alexandre stifled her distress at the lack of his response to her affirmation. In her terse monologue, she had given her caution to the wind and vulnerably confessed her wrongdoings and stated her yearnings, and, still yet, Jacob had rejected her.

She pridefully shook her head at his offer despite the chill in the air that subtly quivered her body to generate warmth. Alexandre preferred to shiver in the night's cold offerings as she walked to the entrance than to do the same among Jacob's cold offerings as he transported her to the entrance.

"No. No, thank you," she politely declined. "But, please drive safely back to the city."

Refusing to press her acceptance of his invitation, Jacob merely remarked, "Enjoy your evening, Alexandre." He then entered his vehicle, started the ignition, and exited the school's parking lot.

*** *** ***

"Jacob," Alexandre spoke in astonishment after she opened the front door to the ringing bell. He stood before her in a tailored black suit, white shirt, and paisley tie and handkerchief.

"Hello, Alex."

Bemused, she inquired, "Why...Why didn't you just use your key?"

Jacob glanced over his shoulder at the vehicle in the driveway. "I didn't want to intrude on you and your guest."

She scoffed at the superfluous gesture. "It's not an intrusion, Jacob. This is still your home." Alexandre side-stepped and motioned for him to enter. After she closed the door behind him, she explained, "Lance is here helping Jay prepare for his Halloween party for his class."

Jacob simply nodded, hoping that his eyes did not disclose his jealousy and disappointment. "I didn't come to stay. I just wanted to grab my navy suit for tomorrow. It's not at the condo. So, I assume it's here."

Concealing her own discontent caused by the true purpose of his visit, Alexandre replied, "No, it's fine. No problem at all...I'm...I'm sure it is upstairs." She nervously pushed a lock of hair behind her ear and then lowered her hand to stroke her lower abdomen.

Jacob's eyes followed her hand to her womb. Though there was not much to see, the thought of life growing in her excited him and he yearned to touch it—to touch her. Regrettably, he was halted by the many uncertainties of their union and the unresolved tension between them.

"...I'm just going to grab the suit and be on my way."

"Are you sure you can't stay? Jaamyas will be elated to have you here."

"No—I mean—yes, I am sure. I've got another contract meeting early in the morning and—"

"JACOB!" Jaamyas exclaimed, rushing into the foyer. "I thought that was your voice."

Jaamyas hugged his torso.

Immediately returning the embrace, Jacob spoke, "Hey, kiddo. How are you?"

Jaamyas released him and peered into his eyes. "My class is having a Halloween—well, fall festival—party tomorrow and we're decorating homemade sugar cookies for me to share."

Disappointed again by the realization that this would be the first Halloween that they did not don costumes, cover the house with decorations, and gift candy to trick-or-treaters, Jacob simply responded, "So, I hear. Sounds like fun."

"One more would make it merrier," Jaamyas coaxed.

Jacob chuckled at Jaamyas's regurgitation of the axiom he often recited to him. He would speak it in an effort to encourage Jaamyas to invite his friends to their male-bonding outings.

"Not tonight, Jay. It's already after seven and I've got an early meeting in the morning," Jacob politely declined as he gently smoothed the waves in Jaamyas's hair.

"Coooome ooooon," Jaamyas dragged relentlessly. "Pleeeeease…Please, just one cookie. You can decorate a pumpkin for me and I will do a ghost for you."

Jacob met Alexandre's eyes hoping for a merciful interference, but she offered none. "Okay," Jacob finally conceded in a loud exhale, "but one cookie and then I have to go."

"Yes!" Jaamyas spoke with excitement. "I will set up your workspace while you wash your hands." With that, he returned to the kitchen.

"Thank you," Alexandre whispered.

Jacob simply nodded and walked to the half-bathroom to wash his hands. He civilly greeted Lance en route.

In his slow return to the kitchen, Jacob watched as Lance offered Alexandre a bite of his meticulously decorated cookie. After first declining, she eventually gave into his persistence and leaned to sample his treat. Before her lips could touch it, Lance pushed the cookie into her face, smearing green and orange icing on her mouth and nose.

The kitchen erupted with laughter.

Alexandre wiped the confection from her face with her hand. "I knew you were going to do that. You always did that to me." She playfully fought with the strength of Lance's arms as she struggled to paint his face with the colorful icing on her fingers.

"I'm sorry. I'm sorry," Lance spoke through his laughter.

Jacob cleared his throat. "So, where do you want me, Jay?"

Jaamyas pointed to a set-up next to him, but in front of Alexandre. "Right here next to me."

"You got it." Jacob removed his suit jacket and placed it on the back of bar chair. He then unbuttoned and rolled up the sleeves of his shirt as he scanned the decorating options before him.

"Mom, you still have icing on your face," Jaamyas advised, breaking the brief silence among them.

Alexandre dabbed her face. "Where?"

Jaamyas giggled. "All over."

"Let me see," Lance instructed, turning her head to face him. He smiled, retrieved the dish towel next to him, and began to tenderly dab away the imperfections.

Uncomfortable by his display of affection, Alexandre collected the towel from him saying, "I've got it, Lance...Thanks."

Jacob caught her eyes for a brief moment before she quickly terminated their stare.

"You know what, Jay?" Jacob began. "...On second thought, I think I am just going to head on out."

"Whaaaat? Whyyyy?" Jaamyas whined.

"I'm so sorry, Jay. I really am. It's just late and I really do have an early start in the morning...Maybe another time. Okay?"

Jaamyas nodded and glumly mimicked, "Okay."

"Everyone, have a good evening." Jacob grabbed his jacket from the chair and walked toward the front entrance. Alexandre quickly followed.

"What about your suit?" She inquired.

Jacob swung open the front door and stepped outside. "I don't need it."

Alexandre closed the door behind her. "But you came all this way for it."

While keeping his stride toward his car, Jacob responded, "I know, but I will wear something else."

"Jacob, please," she grabbed his hand and turned him to face her. "Please."

Though he tried, he could not help but gaze into her beautiful eyes. He took his thumb and gently wiped the last of the frosting that was on her cheek.

"Thank you."

He smiled feebly and wished, "Enjoy your night, Alex."

Alexandre huffed in frustration when he turned to continue the walk to his vehicle. "Do you think that this situation is easy for me?"

Taken aback by the question, he turned to face her and responded, "What the hell kind of question is that?"

"I...I don't know. I just think that sometimes-"

"No, I don't think that this is easy for you, Alexandre. I would be a fool not to understand that this is a challenge—probably the greatest challenge you have ever encountered in your life...But, I need you to understand that this is not easy for me, too. That watching you with him is killing me."

"Jacob, we are only trying to navigate our way through this co-parenting plight we find ourselves in," she reminded him. "That in and of itself is difficult."

Jacob huffed incredulously at her rehearsed explanation. "Perhaps if you believed that that was all that this was, then maybe I would believe it, too...But, it's more—so much more, Alex. I know it, you know it." He nodded toward the house where Lance remained and completed, "and he knows it."

"...And with the baby-" Jacob continued, transitioning the conversation to the second of his concerns.

"That may not even be his. It could be yours—I'm yours, Jacob," she reminded in desperation.

Though doubtful, he smiled weakly at the thought. "I wish I could believe that..."

"What more can I do? Tell me, Jacob, and I will do it...I will have an amniocentesis conducted if knowledge of paternity will calm your doubts and expedite our reconciliation."

Jacob shook his head. "I could not ask you to do that. I wouldn't even allow you to do that...Your pregnancy is already high risk."

"Then what, Jacob? What do you want?"

"I want us—four months ago," he answered without hesitation.

Alexandre slowly closed her eyes in an attempt to prevent the tears from falling. Her efforts failed.

"…But that want is impossible for you to fulfill, so grant me another."

She opened her eyes, wiped her face, and spoke, "Anything you want."

"Grant my petition for an annulment."

His request snatched her breath and suffocated an immediate response. Alexandre was blind-sided by his request as she had hoped that their marriage could be restored—that their love would mend all that was shattered.

Jacob turned from the broken spirit that he saw in her eyes and elucidated, "I have given it a lot of thought and it is what I want."

"Jacob, please," she beseeched.

Ignoring her plea, he reasoned, "You once told me that a part of you died when Lance was officially declared dead. Now that he is alive, perhaps that part of you has revived. So, I believe that you owe it to yourself to explore that revival—you both do."

After he respired through his heartache, Jacob continued with the unselfish proclamation, "I am freeing you to explore whatever it is that the two of you feel like the war and time has robbed you of."

"…Jacob…Jacob, please…Please don't do this," Alexandre implored between cries.

"Don't, Alex…Please don't make this harder than what it already is." He returned to their gaze. "I will always be here for you, for Jaamyas, and even for the baby, but…But, I just can't do it as your husband. Not anymore."

Devastated by his meager offering, Alexandre inquired between cries, "Why are you doing this, Jacob?" When he failed to immediately respond, she reminded him of his earlier vow to her, "You said that you would never abandon me."

Though he was taken aback by her use of his words to manipulate him, Jacob suppressed his surprise, regained his bearings, and clarified, "This isn't abandonment, Alex. This is me being forced out—being forced out of our home, being forced out of our marriage."

Alexandre peered upon Jacob's indignant façade. By the angst in his eyes she ascertained that his concession did not derive from feelings of nobility as she had initially thought, but of resentment.

After wiping her face dry, she admonished, "Don't do this."

"Don't do what, Alex?"

"Make this decision with an angry heart."

"My heart is not angry, Alexandre. It is broken."

"Well, don't do it with a broken heart either, Jacob."

Jacob pondered the warnings that she had just expressed. It was a few of many that she had become accustomed to sharing as an arbitrator. Opting to selfishly ignore her admonitions, Jacob simply replied, "The sooner I relinquish my ties to this catastrophe the sooner I can begin to heal."

Alexandre shook her head in contrast and cautioned, "A broken heart cannot heal if it is guarded."

Jacob exhaled loudly in exasperation. As in the past, their conversation transitioned from one of despair and contrition to control and manipulation. "…I am only protecting it from you, Alex."

Stunned again by his admission, Alexandre was unable to forge the words to possibly change his mind. When defeat finally resonated within her, she erupted in a distressing cry.

Jacob gathered her in his arms and held her quivering body until her cries were silenced. He then lowered his mouth to hers in a lingering kiss. When their lips parted, he whispered, "Goodbye, Alexandre."

✯✯✯ 𝓔𝓘𝓖𝓗𝓣 ✯✯✯

"Jacob," Taylor spoke as she walked through his opened office door. "I have made the requested modifications to the contract. However, I need your signature before processing it."

Jacob looked up from the designs on his desk, rubbed his weary eyes, and simply replied, "Okay." He extended his hand to retrieve the manila folder from the paralegal and asked, "Where do I sign?"

After he placed the folder on the surface in front of him, Taylor smoothed out the folds of her high-waist midi skirt and leaned over him. She was mindful not to make the motion sexually suggestive.

Taylor opened the folder and turned to the first signature page. "Here," she indicated with her perfectly manicured index finger.

Jacob selected a blue pen from his mesh pencil cup and scribbled his name where she instructed.

Taylor flipped through several pages and stopped on another signature page to advise, "Here…Here—but not here, Phillip signs here."

Alexandre arrived at the threshold of Jacob's office and immediately halted her entrance. Noticing his company, she patiently watched and waited as Taylor instructed Jacob.

"There's more?" Jacob huffed, growing exhausted by her demands.

Taylor chuckled. "Just a few more." She turned to the final page and spoke, "Initial here and then sign and date here."

Jacob did as she commanded, closed the folder, and gifted it back to her. "Thanks, Taylor. I really do appreciate all of your hard work on this project, especially since you are using your holiday breaks to help us out until we hire someone new...I know that it can't be easy spending your Thanksgiving break here right after midterms."

Taylor merely shrugged her shoulders and commented, "I don't mind. Besides, you are paying me handsomely to be here." She then met his gaze, stretched her lips into a wide grin, and added, "Let's just hope that my replacement works as hard as I do for you."

Jacob dropped his eyes and laughed to himself. Despite his many rebukes, Taylor refused to refrain her sly innuendoes. "...Yeah, one could only hope," he merely remarked.

"Enjoy the rest of your day, Jacob."

"You, too, Taylor."

When she pivoted on her heels, Taylor noticed in surprise Alexandre standing at the door. Her smile faded immediately as she fought to subdue her shock.

Walking toward the exit, Taylor meekly greeted, "Judge Denton-Hall."

"Ms. Greene," Alexandre spoke in return. She kept her glare on the paralegal although she deliberately avoided her eyes.

After side-stepping to allow Taylor to exit, Alexandre entered the office and closed the door behind her. She watched as Jacob respectfully stood to his feet.

"So," she began, "does the entire firm know about our demise or just your paralegal?"

Jacob puffed air and slowly shook his head in disappointment. He was dismayed by her lack of a proper greeting and her callous inquiry.

In lieu of a response that had an equally harsh tone, he answered, "Neither because, one, it is none of their business and, two, I would never do that to you—tarnish your name and your reputation."

His reply overwhelmed Alexandre with guilt. Despite the feelings of shame that was prompted by her assumption and accusation, she did not apologize. Instead, Alexandre spoke with light humor, "Well, I suppose I do enough of that on my own…at least that is what is stated in the newsprint."

Jacob shoved his fists in the pockets of his pants to conceal his irritation—he was not moved by her banter. Following a deep inhale and an audible exhale, he asked, "What do what, Alex? Why are you here?"

She walked further into the office and stopped in front of his desk. "I called your assistant and blocked off two hours on your calendar…I want to take you to lunch."

His cheeks flushed from his fury and he attempted, to no avail, to wipe the frustration from his face. "I can't believe you did that, Alex, and…and that Nicole aided you in your effort."

"Don't be mad with her, Jacob," Alexandre quickly petitioned on the behalf of his assistant. "I told her it was a surprise."

"I am not mad at her, just frustrated," he clarified. "…It is not clear to me where either of your loyalties lie."

Confounded by his reaction to what she believed to be a kind gesture, Alexandre apologized, "I'm sorry, Jacob. I did not know that my well-intentions would upset you like this."

Jacob's eyes burned into hers. In them, he saw a woman that he had not met before—she was egotistical as well as calculating, but presented herself as a faultless victim. "I'm upset by your incessant need to advance things in your time, on your terms—even after you said you would support and respect my decision to move at my own pace. I'm upset by your use of your judicial clout to strongarm people to your will…Damn it, Alex. Why can't you just understand that I need a moment to deal with everything in my own time, in my own way?...You—you just keep pressing me to rush to a resolve. It's not right. It's not right and it's not fair."

"Jacob-"

He turned his head from her and he vehemently declined, "I'm not having lunch with you, Alexandre."

Once she swallowed the disappointment that swelled in her throat, Alexandre muttered, "…Okay."

Jacob met her eyes once more and witnessed the pain and suffering in them. His own heart aching, he lowered his gaze and lowly confessed, "I'm not ready…I'm not ready to be around you, to look at you, talk to you…I'm just not ready."

"Okay," Alexandre again muttered, conceding on the matter of lunch. However, she was still yet unwilling to concede her fight for their marriage. So, she consequently inquired, "But what about counseling?"

When Jacob offered no reply to the unexpected request, Alexandre relentlessly, but gingerly pressed, "Will you consider counseling?"

Aggravated by the pressure, Jacob initially responded, "No," but then equivocally spoke, "maybe…I don't know," after he contemplated the appeal.

"You don't have to answer now," Alexandre assured, finding hope in his vacillation. "It is a lot for me to request of you…Just…Just promise me you will consider it, before you file the annulment papers."

Jacob vigorously rubbed his forehead as he considered her petition. What she was asking of him tested the strength of his faith, the bounds of his trust, and the depth of his love. He looked upon her solemn visage and responded, "…I'm sorry, Alex, but I can't do that…I can't make that promise."

Disheartened by his choice that devastated her more than protected him, Alexandre's aching heart sunk. Nodding, she uttered, "I…I understand, Jacob…I really do, but…" She swallowed the second knot that formed in her throat and blinked back the tears to conceal the twinge in her chest. "…But please still consider it anyway—for me, for us."

When he shook his head in protest, she reminded, "We were once so happy, Jacob, and I know that we can get back to it—if you would just forgive me…"

Taken aback by her forceful suggestion, he questioned, "If we were so happy, Alex, then why did you feel the need to betray me?"

Despondent and abashed, Alexandre could not bring herself to answer his question. Instead, she held his stare until the overwhelming guilt prompted her to lower hers.

"...I went to God for you, Alex," Jacob confessed, disrupting the uncomfortable silence that fell in the room. It was a truth that he refrained from disclosing, even in his wedding vows.

Alexandre returned her eyes to his and inquired with confusion, "What?"

"From the moment we met I—I wanted you." He cleared his throat and elaborated, "You were absolutely everything I desired in a wife. So, I went to God and prayed for you. I promised Him that I would do all that I needed to prove myself worthy of you if...if...only He would grant me the opportunity to have you."

Surprised by the revelation, Alexandre responded, "I had no idea. You never told me this. Why have you never told me this?"

"Would it have made a difference, Alexandre?"

She considered his question, as well as their vows, and her actions that desecrated them. "...No, I suppose not," she whispered.

"The moment you accepted my marriage proposal was by far the happiest in my life...Then..." He voiced cracked when he spoke, "Then in another moment you obliterated that happiness...The woman I love, cherish, adore, and trust destroyed me."

Jacob tried, to no avail, to wipe the frustration from his face. Contrary to his desire to express his thoughts and emotions in his own time, he found himself, once again, bending to her will to communicate according to her timeline. He exhaled in annoyance at the unshakable hold she maintained on his heart.

"I'm so sorry that I did this to you, Jacob. I wish I could go back. If only I could go back, I would and undo what I did."

After chuckling halfheartedly at the offer, he elucidated, "Just because you wish it doesn't make it so, Alexandre. I know that a part of you longs for a portion of what you had with your first husband. I would be remiss to think that you could forsake your history."

"Jacob, Lance and I are history."

He weakly grinned at her perception of the truth that he ascertained to be a falsehood. No love as deep, innocent, and passionate as hers and Lance's could have ever been quashed by war or death. Jacob begrudgingly recognized that he was merely the casualty in the battle their two souls fought in an effort to reunite.

After struggling with the bulge that formed in his throat, Jacob successfully swallowed it and professed, "It is not so much the infidelity as it is the lie, Alex…I…I suppose, on some celestial compassionate level, I can be sympathetic and forgive you of your tryst, but it is the lie—the lying that I cannot forgive." He peered into windows of her soul and vehemently spoke, "It makes me despise you."

"Jacob, please-"

"I now regret the day that we met, Alex," he boldly stated. "I wish," he breathed deeply and completed, "I wish that I had immediately walked away that night after I returned your credit card to you."

Flabbergasted by Jacob's admission, Alexandre lowly whispered, "…Wow," in response to the shocking purge of his emotions. Gently pressing the tears that fell from her eyes into her cheeks with the back of her hand, she added, "No amount of counseling would have prepared me for that disclosure."

Jacob ignored the ache in his chest and shrugged off his growing remorse. "Had we remained strangers we both would have avoided this agony."

Alexandre pondered his observation then questioned, "But would we though?"

"Would we what?"

"Avoided the agony?"

"Yes, I would like to believe so."

She shook her head in dissent. "Well, I don't."

Jacob rolled his eyes; she was forever contrary. "Of course, you don't," he uttered.

"I don't because I believe it would have just been a different type of pain. The pain of regret. Not knowing. Loneliness…No love."

Jacob scoffed at the insinuation. "Don't 'Alfred Tennyson' me, Alex."

"I'm not, Jacob—you haven't lost love," Alexandre spoke to refute his cynicism.

"But I've lost you, Alexandre," he retorted, vexed by her unwavering faith that their marriage, their family, their love could return to the level of security they once enjoyed.

Alexandre lowered her eyes and, in lieu of an attempt to disabuse him of his belief, she diverted the conversation. "Uumm, Jay, is…He, uumm, is really struggling with all of this—our separation, the news of the annulment…He—he is now less attentive in school, just quit the team, and has totally isolated himself at church and at home."

Refusing to engage in the blaming pendulum, Jacob took ownership in his part in their familial plight and considered the impact on Jaamyas. "Tell me what it is that you want me to do, Alex."

"Can you spend time with him this weekend?"

"Won't he be with his father?"

Alexandre shook his head. "He has left—I mean—he has returned to Texas for a spell. He has a lot to contend with."

"As do we all."

"Yes, but what does any of it have to do with you and your relationship with Jay?"

Jacob offered no reply to her question.

"Jacob, you promised to always be there for him," Alexandre reminded him.

He puffed hot air incredulously at her audacity. "Wow. Did you really just go there?"

"Jacob, I-"

"You know I made that promise without having knowledge of all the facts, Alexandre," he angrily spoke over her. "Facts you knowingly withheld from me."

"So, what Jaamyas pays for what I've done?"

"We all do, Alex! That is the point you are not getting—everyone connected to you pays!"

After allowing the silence to calm his rage, Jacob reminded her, "You made a choice, Alexandre. No matter how good or bad it was, you made it. And, now, we all must live with it—no matter our guilt or innocence."

Jacob reflected on his earlier petition made shortly after their nuptials and stated matter of factly, "…At least I now know the true reason why you never filed the adoption papers."

Alexandre exhaled aloud. She was more irritated with his inaccurate suspicion than annoyed with his steadfast persistence.

"Lance isn't the reason, Jacob," Alexandre spoke in an effort to correct him of his erroneous assumption. "…I mean, he is now, but wasn't before…Now…" Her voice trailed off as she contemplated the harsh reality and the pain that many will suffer from it, particularly Jacob.

Following a deep breath, Alexandre braved the delivery of the news that altered the course of his desired aspiration. "Now, Lance would have to terminate his parental rights, and I don't foresee him doing that." She met his eyes and restated, "He won't do that."

Suppressing his anguish and concealing his disappointment, Jacob mumbled, "Just like I said, everyone connected to you pays."

A pregnant silence swelled in the office as his words resonated with her and a tranquil calmness overcame him. After exhaling the last of his grief, Jacob glanced at his wristwatch and concluded that the fifteen minutes that he had afforded Alexandre was more than enough of his time. "I will pick Jaamyas up on Saturday morning and spend the day with him."

She nodded. "Okay. What time?"

"I'm not sure yet, but I will call Friday night to confirm." Jacob walked to his door and opened it to indicate his readiness for her to vacate.

Alexandre walked to the exit and peered into his eyes. "Thank you, Jacob."

"No need to thank me. Jay is my son, and no matter what becomes of us he will always be my son."

She nodded another time and then spoke, "Enjoy the rest of your day."

"You do the same, Alexandre." He quickly closed the door behind her before the tears he held at bay, flooded his eyes and rolled down his face.

*** *** ***

As they walked along the bank of the lake, each holding their own fishing rod and tackle box, Jacob spoke, "…You're not much for conversation today."

Jaamyas said nothing in response.

"You've been fairly quiet the entire ride here—just reading your books…That's not like you, Jay."

Jaamyas settled into their familiar spot then finally broke his silence, "There isn't much to talk about."

"Well, your mother has told me different."

Jaamyas huffed and clandestinely rolled his eyes. As he adjusted his fall coat and the fisherman hat that Jacob gifted him during their first fishing expedition, he murmured, "What does she know?"

Though it pained Jacob to defend Alexandre, he could not permit Jaamyas's insolence to go unchecked. "She's your mother, Jay. She happens to know a lot."

Hooking his live bait just as Jacob instructed him years ago, Jaamyas inquired, "Why are you even protecting her? You don't love her anymore."

"Jay, that is not true."

"It is true. And I know it to be true because you don't want to be her husband anymore; just like you don't want to be my father anymore—you are divorcing us. That is why she has me spending all this time with Coach Carter now."

Taken aback by Jaamyas's inaccurate assessment of their familial demise, Jacob considered the appropriate words to assuage his cognitive dissonance. Unequivocally, he loved his wife and loved his son—they were his family. Regrettably, however, by no fault of his own, they were no longer his family to have. He had to let them go.

Realizing that it was futile to argue a point with an adolescent overwhelmed with rage, bitterness, and dejection, Jacob merely retorted, "None of that is true, Jay. None of it. I do…"

Jacob voice trailed off when Jaamyas turned to meet his eyes. In them, he saw a desperate plea for a reconciliation that would return his homelife back to the one he once enjoyed—a reconciliation that was not likely to occur.

"…You know what? Let's not make this about me because this is not about me. This is about you, Jay, and you should want to spend time with your biological father."

"Why?" Jaamyas asked in a tone that was more of a protest than an inquisition.

"Because in knowing him you get to know more about yourself."

Disheartened by what he believed to be Jacob's concession, Jaamyas turned from his gaze, shrugged his shoulders, and cynically responded, "I'm not interested. He left before; he will leave again. Only this time he would have ruined my life in the process."

Jacob exhaled loudly at the stubbornness that Jaamyas undoubtedly inherited from Alexandre. Refusing to concede in his effort to engage him in conversation, Jacob diverted the topic by inquiring, "So, your mother tells me that you quit the team. Is this true?"

Jaamyas casted his fishing rod into the lake and reeled in the line. He shrugged once more before answering, "Mom is making a bigger deal of it than it has it be."

"Perhaps, but, then again, perhaps not. You love the game—always have."

"I just don't want to play anymore. Okay? And I don't want to spend our time together talking about it."

"I understand and that is fair. I just want to make sure that this is a decision you are making because of your loss of interest in the sport, not because of Coach Car—I mean, your father."

Jaamyas did not respond to Jacob's assumption. Instead, he observed the calm waters and spoke off-topic, "She cries a lot and is sad all the time…She blames it on the baby and hormones, but I know it's because she misses you."

The revelation pained Jacob's heart and he responded, "I'm sad, too, buddy…I'm sorry for all of this…that…that you even have to endure any of this."

"Then just forgive her. If you are truly sorry, then just forgive her and come home."

"It's not that easy, Jay."

"Yes, it is," Jaamyas contested is desperation as the tears formed in his eyes.

"No, Jay, it isn't."

"Yes, Jacob, it is. Seventy times seven."

Jacob respired deeply and considered the Biblical teaching he had often reminded Jaamyas of following each spat he had encountered with his playmates. "…This is different, Jay. So, no, it isn't."

"Why?"

Jacob took in the fledgling who knew very little concerning matters of the heart and merely responded, "Because…"

"Because why?!" Jaamyas pressed.

"Just because, Jay."

Discontent with his reply, Jaamyas recited his mother's infamous axiom, "Because is not an answer! Because why?!"

"Because she hurt me!" Jacob hollered.

When Jaamyas flinched at his intonation, Jacob lowered his tone and restated more quietly, "Your mother broke my heart…She really hurt me."

Jaamyas's tears fell to his cheeks and rolled to his quivering chin. With hesitation, he inquired, "…So, that's it?…You will divorce and we won't be a family anymore?"

Jacob inhaled deeply and exhaled slowly. In lieu of a simple response to Jaamyas's direct questions, he offered, "There is a mythological belief that people once had two heads and four legs."

Jaamyas contemplated Jacob's random statement and grinned through his tears. "…Whaaaaat?"

Jacob returned the grin. "I know; silly, right? But it's what many believed…Anyway, people once had two heads and four legs until a lightning bolt separated them."

"A lightning bolt?"

Jacob nodded and confirmed, "A lightning bolt."

"Hmmm," Jaamyas responded, considering why anyone would believe such an implausible tale.

"But, even though these people were separated, they continually longed for each other."

"Why?"

"Because they shared the same soul." He turned to Jaamyas and elucidated, "You see, they became two bodies, but they still remained one soul."

"So, they each had half a soul," Jaamyas surmised.

"Exactly, and people can spend their entire lives searching for the other half of their soul to become whole again and never find it…but not your mother." After wiping his eyes and swallowing the knot in his throat, Jacob choked, "A long time ago, Jay, your mother found hers…and…and I'm not him, your father is…He is her soul mate."

*** *** ***

Alexandre unsecured and opened her front door shortly after the ringing of the bell announced a visitor.

"Jacob," she greeted, concealing her excitement of his surprised visit.

"Hello, Alexandre."

"Please, come in," she invited as she widened the door for his entrance.

Jacob declined, shaking his head. "I'm not staying."

"Oh," Alexandre breathed dismayed.

"Is Jay home? He left these library books in my car on Saturday and I just came to return them."

"No, he is out with his fath—Lance," she responded and quickly restated, "he is out with Lance. They should be back in hour or so, if you can wait. I'm sure Jay would be happy to see you."

Jacob shook his head once more. "I can't stay, Alex." He extended the books to her. "Just let him know he owes me big for this one."

Alexandre retrieved the three books and scanned the titles. "His science class is exploring ecosystems. So, he has been reading all these books on the great wonders of the rainforest and the ocean," she explained with light humor.

After nodding, Jacob bid, "Enjoy your evening, Alexandre," before pivoting to return to his vehicle.

"So, you really came all this way just to return Jay's library books?"

He turned back to her gaze and simply answered, "I did."

Though devastated by his response, she suppressed it as she did not believe that what he spoke was true. "I could have met you in the city, Jacob. You did not have to come all this way."

Jacob merely shrugged and explained, "I waited out the traffic, so the commute was not that bad. Besides my intent was to see Jay—not you."

Alexandre lowered her eyes at the harsh revelation and uttered, "Duly noted."

"I did not mean that to be a slight to you, Alex. It's just that..." He respired deeply and confessed, "It's just that Jay and I have had better days than we did on Saturday and I just wanted to check in on him. Otherwise, I would have just taken the books to the school."

"He has told me the same thing—not in those exact words—but something similar...Do you want to talk-"

"No, I don't want to talk about it, especially not with you, Alex."

"But you will talk about it with my son?" She hotly inquired infuriated by his decision to discuss their adult problems with her adolescent son. "Do you know how disconcerting it is to hear what truly you feel about me from a thirteen-year-old child?"

"Probably not as disconcerting as finding out from two colleagues that your wife is having an affair."

Alexandre held her tongue at his quick-witted rebuttal. Though his pain was conceivably greater than hers, she did not want to engage in an argument to measure it, especially not at her door.

Jacob inhaled deeply and exhaled audibly to allow his breath to calm him. "...Look, Alexandre, I did not come here to pick a fight—truly, I didn't. I just wanted to drop off the books and conduct a wellness check on Jay. You said that he is out with his father, so I assume he is fine now that Lance is back in town."

"Please don't do that, Jacob."

Jacob puffed in frustration. He had already stayed past the time he had allotted for this visit. True to form, he had allowed her conversation to draw him in. "Do what, Alex?"

"Allow your ill-feelings towards me destroy the relationship, the bond you forged with Jaamyas. He loves you, Jacob. You know that he loves you."

Jacob considered the request. "I don't know how much longer I can do this, Alex. I'm trying, but, honestly, I just don't know."

Without the need for him to elaborate, Alexandre understood his plight. "Please, just come inside so that we can talk."

Shaking his head, he replied, "I really can't. I have plans."

"Then dinner, maybe? I'm free this weekend."

"…Maybe…I don't know. I will let you know after I think on it and check my calendar."

Alexandre feebly smiled. "Okay."

"Enjoy your night, Alex."

"Thanks—you, too."

*** *** ***

Alexandre chuckled at his wit as they enjoyed the last of their main course and awaited the arrival of their dessert. After sipping from her water glass, she snickered again. He always had a way of making her feel as if she was the most important person in the room. Sometimes the affection made her blush, other times it made her smile, but all the time it made her feel adored.

"…I don't know about that one. I will have to think on it a little more, Lance."

Her calling him his name cut through Jacob like a sharp blade. Despite the many efforts he exerted to ensure they both enjoyed the evening, her mind was still with her first husband.

Alexandre gasped at her error and immediately reached across the table to touch his hand. "I'm so sorry, Jacob."

Jacob abruptly moved his hand from underneath hers. First disappointed, then offended, and finally enraged, he sought to conclude their date. He retrieved his wallet from the inside of his suit jacket pocket and urged, "Let's, uh…Let's call it a night."

Alexandre watched as Jacob gathered several hundred-dollar bills and placed them on the table. Grappling with her own disappointment, she nodded in acquiescence and lowly uttered, "Okay." She then stood without the assistance Jacob typically offered, collected her clutch, and followed him to the entrance of the restaurant.

Jacob extended his ticket to the valet and nodded in response when the suited gentleman spoke, "It will be a moment, sir. I'm waiting for drivers to return."

As they stepped away from the small crowd, Alexandre shivered from the cool night air and regretted not donning a trench coat. Once alone, she rewrapped her pashmina scarf around the bodice of her cocktail dress and bare arms. She then watched as the stoic Jacob avoided looking at her.

"I'm sorry, Jacob," she apologized again. Following, she attempted to explain the Freudian slip.

Jacob shoved his fists in his pockets of his pants to conceal his frustration. "Please, stop, Alexandre," he calmly requested. "I don't want to hear it." He glanced at her. "I don't want to hear you."

Alexandre gently tugged at his muscular bicep to turn him to face her. "Jacob, please try to understand-"

He shrugged her hand off him. "Understand what, Alex?"

She parted her lips to speak, but no words were uttered.

"You keep telling me that I need understand, and I keep hearing that I need to understand, but I don't quite understand just what it is exactly that I am to understand."

When Alexandre continued to hold her silence, Jacob seized the opportunity to reflect on their history. "…I understand now…I didn't then, but I do now," he confessed following his period of intense thinking.

Contorting her face in confusion, Alexandre asked, "What are you talking about?"

"I'm talking about the fact that from the moment I decided to pursue you, you have controlled every facet of our relationship. The terms of our courtship, my introduction to and time spent with Jaamyas, the merging of our lives, the wedding, when we have children—everything. You literally controlled everything."

Jacob turned from her and meditated on their past years together. After exhaling loudly, he spoke with regret, "…Against my better judgment, and, now, to my own detriment, I allowed you to control everything."

With only himself to blame for feeding the beast that another man created, he scoffed and recalled, "I made far too many concessions with you, Alexandre, and it has ruined us."

Alexandre turned her head away in disgrace when Jacob shifted his body towards her. She could not bear to meet his eyes. He had adequately assessed her need for control, and in varying ways she had treated him like an older son rather than respected him like the young, but mature husband that he was.

Jacob shifted his gaze from the top of her head to the approaching headlights. He then pivoted and observed as the vehicle slowed to a stop near its owners. As he watched the gentleman open the door for his lady, Jacob reminisced on the several changes, personal and professional, he made to accommodate a life with her. Standing now alone holding the shortest end of the stick, Jacob concluded that all that he sacrificed was for naught.

"…I immediately took my place in line and marched to your cadence," Jacob admitted.

"Jacob-" she began in contest.

"It's undeniable, Alex. I know it; you know it; everyone connected to us knows it." He shifted his body back towards her and rationalized his doings, "At least then I had a reason."

Alexandre concurred that Jacob had made many adjustments to have Jaamyas and her in his life. However, they were no more than what any other man would have done in pursuit of her.

Tilting her head to him, she inquired more about his reasons by asking, "Which was?"

Jacob furiously glared at her. The audacity of her question not only insulted him, but minimized the feelings he possessed and the work that he conducted for her. Alexandre was no low hanging fruit. To the contrary, she was the luscious red apple at the pinnacle of the tree—the delectable fruit he desired. However, unlike most men, Jacob did not hack down the tree to obtain what he yearned for. Instead, he diligently climbed it all while encouraging it to grow.

"…Because I loved you and loved seeing you happy," Jacob finally answered after he suffocated his rage. "I knew that being in control gave you peace; it gave you comfort. And that made you happy."

"…I made a mistake, Jacob," Alexandre contritely uttered in contest. Believing that his efforts were not in vain, she added "I have made plenty of mistakes and will make plenty more. Please…Please don't crucify me for being human."

"Crucify you?!" Jacob exclaimed, ignoring the eyes that his raised intonation attracted. As he deeply breathed to lower his voice, he reminisced on the acts she committed that were not mere human mistakes, but emotional crimes.

"Yes, crucify me."

Jacob yanked his hands from the pockets that kept them warm and pointed at himself while growling, "I am the one with the broken heart, a wrecked marriage, and a child with questionable paternity on the way! Crucify you?! No, I want to BURN you, Alexandre."

He turned from her weary eyes as he felt the tears swell in his own, yearning with everything in him to despise her. A large bulge formed in his throat, but Jacob still managed to choke, "…But…but, my heart won't let me…I still love you. Despite everything, I still love you, Alexandre."

Tears fell from her eyes as Alexandre allowed his confession to resonate within her. To be a recipient of such unconditional, romantic love was unprecedented and overwhelming, and she was uncertain of how to receive it or comfort the giver of it.

Absent the right words to express her sincerest contrition, Alexandre secretly prayed, to no avail, for the expedient arrival of their vehicle. The busy autumn night had them waiting longer than she cared to—forcing her to be in the presence of her scorned second husband, immense guilt, terrible sadness, and haunting thoughts. In spite of her many years of education, training, and experience with children, she found herself inept to console adults, particularly an adult male that she had wronged.

Jacob broke their silence when he chuckled halfheartedly. "The situation is almost laughable when you really think about it...When you really think about it and consider all of the counsel advising me against marrying an older woman of your caliber, it is almost laughable."

Alexandre was taken aback by the revelation that he had kept from her. She herself had received unsolicited guidance about her marriage to a younger man—all of which she had shared with him. Jacob had in return assured her that the age difference would never negatively impact their union. Now, at the cusp of their marital demise, Alexandre began to think that that was a lie and she was a fool to believe that lie.

Alexandre pushed behind her ear the curl that fell from her hair pin and confessed in a murmur, "Things always came easy for me with Lance...I suppose maybe a part of me misses that...yearns for it, maybe."

Infuriated by the unwarranted comparison, Jacob hotly questioned, "And life is an insurmountable challenge with me?"

"That's not what I meant, Jacob...That's not what I meant at all."

"Then what the hell else is that supposed to mean, Alex?"

"I meant...never mind...I don't expect you to understand. Jacob, you're young."

"Don't. Don't you dare. Don't you fucking dare go there with that I'm too young bullshit, Alexandre. Because I am not...I'm not too young to be a partner and manage a team of associates. I'm not too young to manage two households-" He began to count off his fingers, "managing your new car payment, insurance on all three of our vehicles, two mortgages, and Jaamyas's tuition."

"Jac-" Alexandre attempted to interject to clarify her statement.

"I'm certainly not too young to father a child that is not mine, but I publicly acknowledge as my own. And I sure as hell am not too young in the bedroom when I am fuc-"

Jacob stopped short of his abusive tirade, remembering that the woman before him was his wife, his rib, his queen and any harm he brought to her he brought upon himself.

"You know what. Let's...Let's just stop talking," Jacob suggested. "We will get the car, I'll get you home, and that will be the end of our night..."

*** NINE ***

"Come in and make it quick," Alexandre ordered Monday afternoon.

"Your Honor," Leah greeted, entering her chambers with a vase filled with roses. "These just arrived for you, but they have no card."

Alexandre looked up from her document and removed her glasses. Her breath immediately slowed at the sight of the black floral arrangement. "...They don't need one...The color says it all."

Confounded, her assistant inquired, "Come again?"

Alexandre stood to receive the vase and placed it on her desk. "Floriography, it is a way of communicating through flowers."

"Interesting," Leah intriguingly spoke. "So, what are these conveying?"

"Death, hatred, the advent of tragedy—take your pick, although none of them are favorable."

Leah lowly gasped. "...Oh no. I'm so sorry...Do...do you want me to discard them?"

Alexandre shook her head. "There is no point. The message was delivered all the same." She fingered the smooth petals of the bunch and lauded, "They are beautiful roses though—despite color. So, I will just, uh," she cleared her throat and swallowed. "I will just set them aside as I did the hate-card I received last week."

Perplexed by Alexandre's actions, Leah watched her admire the arrangement and inquired, "Your Honor, why do you hold on to such disparaging messages and tokens of animosity?"

Alexandre shrugged while she simultaneously pondered the question. After considering the cause of her actions, she responded, "I suppose it keeps me humble. These gifts remind me that, no matter how beloved I think I am, I, too, should know that I am equally despised."

"But, Your Honor, these are not gifts. These are threats."

Alexandre shrugged another time and commented, "I suppose it's relative to the recipient."

"Well, relativity aside, I think we should inform security about this."

Following her chuckle to the suggestion, Alexandre met her eyes and asked, "And request they do what? Hold all my mail and halt all my deliveries?...That would be absurd, Leah, particularly since everything is already scanned prior to its delivery to me."

Alexandre reminisced on her failed attempt to restore employment of the officer she requested to be terminated. "Besides I am not on their list of favorites right now anyway. So, I am certain they are in no position to conduct special favors for me."

"You don't think…" Leah's voice gradually quieted at the notion of a law enforcement agent retaliating against an officer of the court.

Assuming Leah's incomplete thought, Alexandre lowered her eyes and cavalierly spoke, "Absolutely not…It's…it's probably a disgruntled tax payer peeved by a decision I made." She then seized a moment to reflect on the earlier guidance offered by her mentor and colleagues and further explained, "Apparently, these actions are so commonplace that they have become a part of the job."

After meeting her assistant's eyes once more, Alexandre offered with an air of confidence, "So, trust me when I say that if I can't handle the occasional mudslinging or unwelcomed favor, then I need to resign my position on the bench."

LaKeisha LaKay

Leah nodded in deference, but was not wholly convinced. In passing, she had learned of the threats that other court officials have encountered, but none were as disconcerting as the ones Alexandre had been subjected to.

Transitioning the unpleasant conversation, Alexandre walked to her coat rack and stated, "I'm going to go for a walk and will pick up lunch while I'm out." She retrieved her trench coat and slipped it over her fitted sweaterdress.

"But it's raining."

As she buttoned and tied her coat, Alexandre assured, "I will be fine. The bistro is just a few blocks away and I have an umbrella."

"Well, I will call ahead for your usual. At least that way you won't have to wait."

"Thank you, Leah. I won't be more than an hour." She placed her leather tote on her shoulder, gripped the handle of her large umbrella, and exited the door.

The fifteen-minute walk calmed her nerves, but did nothing to ease her mind. Thoughts of the perpetual subtle threats tortured her psyche and vexed her spirit.

"Thank you," she graciously spoke to the gentleman that held the door for her. Alexandre quickly lowered her umbrella and crossed the threshold of the French bistro. She then greeted the hostess and confirmed, "Pick-up for Denton-Hall, please."

"Of course, Your Honor. I will check on that for you."

"Alex?"

Alexandre pivoted to the familiar call of her name. "Jacob, hey."

"Hey."

"What are you doing on this side of the city? We didn't have plans, did we?"

"No. No, we didn't."

Alexandre exhaled loudly in relief. "Oh, thank God." She laughed at herself then asked again, "So, what brings you out this way?"

"Lunch with a colleague," he simply responded.

"I'm all set," Jacob's colleague announced, returning from the restroom and back at his side. "Thanks so much for waiting.

There was no way I was going to survive the drive back to the office."

"No problem...Alex, this is Bianca Rivera—the newest associate at the firm."

Alexandre feebly smiled as she nodded and took in the beautiful Hispanic woman.

"Bianca, this is my—Judge Alexandre Denton-Hall," Jacob fumbled, unsure of how to present his future former wife.

Bianca's hazel eyes grew in admiration. "Wow, Your Honor, such a pleasure to meet you." She extended her well-manicured hand.

Alexandre suppressed her jealously, received Bianca's right hand, and briefly shook it. "A pleasure indeed."

"Your order, Judge Denton-Hall," the hostess spoke as she offered Alexandre the handle of the paper tote bag.

"You know what? I'm not hungry after all, but please still bill the card on file."

Jacob retrieved the bag from the perplexed hostess, thanked her, and then closed the gap between Alexandre. "What are you doing, Alex?" He murmured. "You have to eat—if not for you, then for the baby."

"Then you eat it," Alexandre commanded. She turned on her heels and exited the restaurant.

Jacob faced Bianca, extended the bag to her, and requested, "Please give me a moment."

"Alexandre!" He called out after her in the light rain. "Alexandre, stop!"

She halted her steps and turned to him. "What, Jacob?"

"Let me take you back to the courthouse."

"I'm fine. Pregnancy does not preclude my legs from working."

"But you're in heels and it's raining."

"They're boots and I have my umbrella." She pivoted to depart.

"Alex."

She faced him and hotly inquired, "Of all the restaurants in the city, why this one?!"

Jacob wiped the raindrops from his face and shrugged. "I don't know. It's her first day. She said she liked French cuisine and this was the only place I could think of."

"And you couldn't search for someplace else?"

"No...I don't know...Maybe, but I didn't."

Alexandre huffed in incredulity. "Unbelievable."

"Despite what you may think, Alexandre, the city of Charlotte is not your courtroom. You don't get to arbitrate all that transpires within it."

"Duly noted." She pivoted once more and began her walk back to the courthouse, ignoring the calling of her name.

*** *** ***

"Jacob Hall," he announced after retrieving the ringing phone on his desk.

"Jacob, it's Stan. How are you?"

"Well, thanks. How are you?"

"Good, thanks. Listen, it's been several days. So, I'm calling to put your feet to the fire on the draft I sent you."

Jacob exhaled audibly.

Discerning Jacob's reticence, Stanley reminded him, "When you retained me as your attorney, you were adamant about 'the sooner, the better.'"

"...Look, I know...I just-"

"Did you look the annulment documents over?" Stanley asked, immediately curtailing Jacob's typical barrage of excuses.

"I scanned them, yes."

"Okay, good. If there are no modifications, then I will prep the final version for signature, and then move forward with filing the documents and serving your wife."

Again, Jacob exhaled loudly. This time in aggravated confusion. "No, wait...Don't file anything yet. Have a courier deliver the draft to her for her review."

Stanley awaited the passing of his indignation before he inquired, "You're kidding me, right?"

"No, Stan, I'm not," Jacob spoke firmly. "I want to be certain that she will be okay…That she and the children will be okay."

"This is an annulment, Jacob, not a divorce. It just requires that the court recognizes your marriage as invalid despite her husband being declared deceased."

"I know, I know. I still want to do what is right—what she believes to be fair…I need that piece of mind."

Stanley rolled his eyes and shook his head with skepticism. He had always known his comrade to be a bleeding heart, but thought that the facts surrounding the dissolution of his marriage would alter his philanthropic character. Having grossly misjudged the plight, Stanley regretted agreeing to serve as counsel for proceedings he expected to be quick. "…Fine. It's your dime," he finally retorted.

Jacob sneered at the callous remark and concurred, "Yes, it is and I am paying you to spend it how I see fit."

Stanley respired deeply and obliged, "Okay, I will have-"

"Quick—turn on the television!" Nicole breathlessly exclaimed, rushing into Jacob's office.

Jacob alarmingly took in his disheveled assistant who was habitually poised and polished. "What?"

"The local news—turn to it."

"Stan, I have to go. Text me when the draft is delivered."

After lowering the handset back into the base, Jacob retrieved the remote to the television gifted to him by his colleagues. He swiveled in the direction of the mounted flat screen, powered it on, and toggled to the local news.

"—No, at this time we cannot confirm that the incidents are related."

"But, Chief Saunders," a reporter spoke above the aggressive mob that thronged the courthouse entry. "We were initially led to believe that the Hernandez matter was a targeted, one-off incident—first, presumed a suicide; now, confirmed a murder."

"Chief, to add to that," another correspondent began, "a new source has asserted that each of these youths were of cases in which the Honorable Judge Denton-Hall presided. So, how can you now not confirm that these incidents are related?"

Blindsided by the inquiry, the police chief wiped his brow with a handkerchief and loosened the black tie around his neck. He then took a moment to regain his bearings as he prudently contemplated the concealed information that had been leaked.

"...I...I will not comment on that," Chief Saunders responded. "But, I will confirm that all leads are being followed."

"Chief, should we be concerned with a third incident?"

"No, I do not believe that-" Chief Saunders began to answer before he was interrupted.

"Now that we know that these facilities are not conducive for children, will these facilities be closed?"

"I am not the authority who makes those decisions," Chief Saunders merely replied. Following, he was barraged with a host of hostile questions.

"Is Judge Denton-Hall available for a statement?"

"Is it true that Judge Denton-Hall knew that Hernandez was not fit for judicial waiver, but she continued with the proceedings nonetheless?"

"I cannot speak for the Honorable Judge Denton-Hall. Please direct all questions to her or her representative," the police chief instructed.

Despite the chief's guidance, the media relentlessly persisted, "Should we be concerned with verdicts rendered from this bench or any others?"

"How will Your Honor respond if named in the suit against the city?"

"Will the city-"

Jacob muted the television and turned to Nicole. "Has anyone from the courthouse made a statement?"

Nicole shrugged her shoulders. "No—I mean, I don't know...Not that I am aware. But, then again, I was only in the cafeteria briefly."

Jacob nodded and cleared his throat. He lowered his gaze and requested, "Please cancel any meetings that I have today."

"Are you heading out?"

He shook his head. "No…Yes…Maybe." Jacob massaged the tension at his temple with his fingertips and exhaled. "…I don't know…I just need a moment to process what I've just heard."

"…Okay. Do you need anything?"

Jacob shook his head once more. "No. Thanks…Just please close the door behind you."

"Of course." Nicole exited, doing as he requested.

*** *** ***

"Mother, what are you doing?" Alexandre greeted in aggravation after taking in the suited woman standing at her threshold. Even with the additional pounds, Dr. Cheryl Leigh remained an aged-perfect, reflection of her daughter.

"About five seconds from using my key if you didn't answer this door."

"That key is for emergencies only—you know that."

"Well, according to my grandson, this is an emergency."

Alexandre rolled her eyes, widened the door, and side-stepped to allow her to enter. She huffed at the thought of her plans for a quiet Saturday afternoon being obliterated.

"I saw that," her mother admonished.

"You always do," Alexandre muttered. She closed and secured the door then plodded her way back to the family room.

"From the looks of it, it doesn't appear that you have been doing much yourself." She scrutinized the leggings Alexandre wore along with her blue and gold alma mater sweatshirt.

Alexandre settled back into the comfortable corner of her oversized sofa and covered herself with her favorite crocheted afghan. "Don't start, Mother. I am now in my second trimester."

"And?"

"And," Alexandre began as she resumed playing the movie she was streaming and reached for her pint of ice cream on her coffee table, "this baby has fast-tracked its growth."

"And?"

Alexandre surreptitiously turned her eyes upward. "And I am tired, and hungry, and horn-" she stopped short of completing her sentence, remembering who she was conversing with. She indulged in a spoonful of the sweet treat and finished, "...all the time."

Her mother snatched the carton from her hand and slammed it down on the table. She then took the remote and powered off the television. "That is no reason for you to be slothful...and certainly not gluttonous."

"Mother, please," Alexandre whined as she fell back into the pillows and covered her head.

Cheryl lowered herself into the cushion next to her daughter and yanked the covering from her head. "This ends now, Alexandre. If not for your career or your marriage, then for your two innocent children who need you."

"Mom, please. Can't I just have a moment—this moment to be vulnerable, this moment to break."

"No. No, you cannot," Cheryl vehemently responded to Alexandre's absurd request.

"Why?"

"Because I am your mother and you are my daughter...Because you are Alexandre."

Alexandre rolled her eyes. "You mean the reminder of the son you always wanted, but never had?"

"Why do you incessantly cleave to that lie?"

"Because it's not a lie, Mother."

"It *is* a lie and if you feel differently, then it is your own conscience because I have said or done nothing to warrant that egregious tale."

Alexandre laughed with cynicism. "Oh, please, you were always withdrawn and consumed with other priorities as a microbiologist...It was clear a long time ago that I was not what you ultimately wanted."

Her mother puffed hot air. "...Alex, from the moment you were born, you and your father were each other's favorites. After your weaning, it was clear that I had served my purpose."

Alexandre rolled her eyes another time. "Don't be so melodramatic. I was a child—you couldn't possibly have taken anything I said or did seriously."

"And why not? You're no child now and still nothing has changed. You never call or confide in me—only your father. It's always been your father."

Alexandre was slightly taken aback by the assessment. Undoubtedly, she favored her father over her mother, but in no way did she loved her mother any less. "Well, it's because…because you're so manipulative and controlling; so…so callous and critical. You were then and you are now."

"And you weren't? Despite what you may think or even see in your courtroom, Alex, teenaged girls are the cruelest creations on this earth. You were no exception…I just kept hoping that you would grow out of it—that we would one day have the mother-daughter relationship that I had always dreamed of."

When Alexandre did not react, her mother continued, "Your father coddled and spoiled you to the core. If you were to be prepared for the world at all it had to be me to have done it. That is why I was stern with you. I played the mean parent so that your father could continue to play the nice one."

"I'm not listening to this," Alexandre spoke as she rose from her seat. She refused to partake in a conversation that disparaged her hero. "I'm stressed enough as it is."

"I'm not done talking."

"Well, I am."

"Alexandre Kaniece, sit your ass back in that seat or you will get a thrashing that my granddaughter will feel until she's 41."

Alexandre halted her steps, turned to the woman that gave her life, and chuckled at the threat. She then lowered herself back to her seat in obeisance. "Really, Mom? Thrashing?"

Cheryl removed her black blazer and rested it on the arm of the sofa. "I know who I am speaking to, I must choose my words wisely."

Alexandre respired audibly. "Why do we always do this, Mom?"

"Because we are one and the same."

Alexandre sneered and remarked, "I'm nothing like you."

"Oh, yes, you are, baby. Keep living and having babies, and you will eventually see just how much."

They simultaneously reached for the carton of butter pecan ice cream on the table.

"Go ahead," Alexandre offered in deference.

Cheryl took a spoonful for herself, offered her daughter a dallop, and then placed the carton back on the table.

"Do you know why I named you Alexandre?"

Alexandre rolled her eyes and repeated what she believed to be true her entire existence, "Because you desperately wanted a son."

Cheryl huffed at the cognitive dissonance that would not allow her daughter to relinquish the falsehood. She placed a decorative pillow on her lap and motioned Alexandre to rest her head on it. As she gently stroked Alexandre's tight curls that were pulled back into a loose ponytail, she fell in love again with her daughter's natural hair.

"No, that is not the reason and I fault myself for you believing it…Hindsight now 20/20, I guess I really should have pushed harder against it." After taking a deep breath, Cheryl finally divulged, "I named you Alexandre because after 6 failed pregnancies, you were my lucky number 7—the charge that completed my life, motherhood…I knew you were destined for greatness the moment you transitioned into the third trimester."

Alexandre took a moment to allow the revelation to resonate within her. The truth now unveiled made her regret the undue hostile contentions between them. "…And after I was born?"

Cheryl chuckled then responded, "Oh, you were hell on two legs."

Alexandre laughed at her mother's quip.

"My goodness, you were such a fighter. And, in many ways, you still are—you just don't fight me as much anymore."

Reflecting on her transitional years from childhood, adolescence, and adulthood, Alexandre silently agreed.

Cheryl grinned and then encouraged, "Like your great predecessor, you cannot be defeated, Alexandre. Yes, there will be opponents with unfamiliar fighting techniques, but you will adapt—you always do."

Alexandre rose from her mother's lap and peered into her eyes. "Why am I just now hearing this? Why didn't you tell me this years ago?"

Cheryl cupped her daughter's chin with her soft, warm hand and answered, "Because, like your mother, you are stubborn."

Alexandre turned from her mother's touch. She knew that what she had spoken was true—it did not matter if her mother had confronted her with the verity ten, twenty, or even thirty years ago, Alexandre was too stubborn to receive it. "…Ugh, the thought of having a girl—another one of us—is terrifying."

Cheryl gently caressed her back. "That is the least of your worries, Alex. Your priority now is the environment you are bringing her into."

As tears formed in her eyes, Alexandre returned to her mother's gaze and confessed, "I'm afraid, Mom…I'm afraid, and confused, and I really just don't know what to do—or who to choose."

Wiping the water that ran down Alexandre's face, Cheryl advised, "Choose you, baby, and everything else will fall into place."

"Hello, Jacob," Alexandre saluted after she opened the door later that evening.

"Hello, Alex. May I come in?"

"Of course," she replied, waving him in from the unseasonably frigid temperature. She closed and secured the door behind him.

"I didn't plan to drop in on you like this. I…I, uh, I just needed a drive to clear my head and ended up here."

Alexandre smiled. "There is no need for you to explain. Jacob, I have told you before that this is still your home."

"Until it's not, right?"

Poorly attempting to conceal the sting of his comment, Alexandre merely agreed, "…Right…I suppose you're right."

"Look, Alex, I didn't come here to discuss the annulment or even the next steps concerning visitation with Jay and the baby. I…I just wanted to see you. Honestly, I just wanted to check in on you and Jay and make sure everything is okay. Based on the media, I know that things are…are difficult at work."

"Thank you, Jacob. I really appreciate that." She breathed through the heartache and announced, "Jay is locked away in the study completing homework or maybe in his room reading." She shrugged. "That's pretty much his routine these days…I'm in the family room if you care to join me."

"Sure," he spoke then followed her into the warmth of the room.

Alexandre lowered herself into her seat and watched as Jacob added wood to the dying fire without her needing to ask. She then folded her book closed and placed it on the end table so that Jacob could sit next to her.

"No tree this year? I know you traditionally like to have the decorations up the weekend before Thanksgiving," Jacob observed after he sat in the space she cleared for him.

"Unfortunately, not this year. Jay, doesn't want them up and doesn't want to celebrate." She respired audibly and acknowledged, "My parents and I will be so fortunate if he graces us with his presence on Thanksgiving Day…I mean I can force him to appear, but what's the point? An absent content son is probably more enjoyable than a present onerous one."

"I can speak to him if you want."

Alexandre shook her head. "Not unless there is a promise to be here somewhere in that conversation." She looked into his eyes and, with a quiver in her voice, conveyed, "He told me there are no holidays without you."

"I'm so sorry, Alex," he contritely spoke as his heart ached for her.

"Don't be," Alexandre responded, reaching for her crystal flute on the end table. "I created this mess."

"Should you be drinking? Your pregnancy is already high risk," Jacob reminded her.

Alexandre replaced her glass on the table after a few swallows. "It's just sparkling cider. It doesn't harm the baby, but, surprisingly, it somehow manages to soothe me when I am feeling anxious." She shrugged at the nonsensical logic of her explanation. "It sounds crazy, I know, but it works."

Jacob shook his head in dissent. "There is nothing crazy about anything you said." He took her hand and held it. "What's crazy is that you feel that you have to shoulder everything alone." He gently squeezed her hand and spoke, "You're not alone, Alex. I've told you this multiple times before."

"You are dissolving our marriage, Jacob," she reminded him. "How can I trust that you will still be here, especially if this baby is not yours?"

Pained by the question, a knot grew in his throat and he released her hand, bringing his back to his body. After taking a moment to suppress his agony, Jacob swallowed the bulge in his throat and answered, "Because before there was a marital vow to always be here, I was always here. I was devoted to you and our son for three years—and you know that, Alex."

"Jacob, I cannot watch you love another woman," Alexandre boldly declared after briefly considering all that he stated. "To witness you love and create a family with someone else, I just can't."

Blindsided by her egocentric revelation, Jacob puffed hot air and retorted, "Trust me, I understand the emotional anguish."

"Then walk away," Alexandre recommended, disregarding his slight.

"What?"

"If this baby is not yours, then walk away."

"I can't believe that you are suggesting that to me. Of all the suggestions to make, you state that one?"

"Trust me, neither can I, but it really is for the best for all of us—especially the children."

"Alex, walking away is not what I want."

"And an annulment is not what I want."

"So, you are punishing me?"

"No, Jacob, I am not punishing you. I'm offering you an out."

"I won't want a fucking out, Alexandre! What I want is my damn fam-"

Alexandre watched him stop short of his profession. She allowed a moment for him to complete his thought, but when silence befell him, Alexandre stated, "Then have your family, Jacob. Either with me or some other woman, but you can't have both."

"This is not fair."

"I know it isn't, Jacob, and I am so sorry for all of it. I truly am, but this is where we are and a decision has to be made. I pray to God that you decide to choose me, us, our family, but I truly understand if you don't." She breathed deeply and admitted, "Yes, Lance was the great love of my past, but you are my future, Jacob. I want you—you and I are good together."

Jacob pondered all that she had said and realized more in that instance that, even with his best efforts, he could never equally measure against the great love of her past. "The thing about great loves, Alex, is that they are a tough act to follow—not even the good ones stand a chance."

"Jac-"

"I'm going to say hello to Jay and then head out. Let me know if there is anything you want me to take care of before I leave."

He rose from his seat and exited the room.

✳✳✳ *TEN* ✳✳✳

"Your Honor, my apologies. I didn't think you would still be here this late—it's almost eleven o'clock."

Alexandre looked up from her report to see the custodian standing at the threshold with her cart of supplies.

"It's quite alright, Ms. Rodriguez...I was on my way out, but was held back by something."

"Please, Your Honor, it's Soledad. You may call me Soledad."

Alexandre smiled at the request of the middle-aged Latina. The dark colored smock that overlayed her casual clothes poorly hid her inherited curves. "Only if you call me Alex."

"Your Honor, I couldn't, I-"

"I insist." She removed her reading glasses and invited, "Please come in. I don't have anything in the wastebasket, but I would certainly enjoy your company while I shutdown for the night."

Soledad walked further into the dimly lit chambers and stood in front the executive desk. When Alexandre motioned for her to sit, she lowered herself into the closest seat.

"How are you enjoying this new position?" Alexandre inquired as she returned documents to their corresponding folders.

Soledad shrugged and pushed behind her ear the black strands of hair that fell from her loose bun. "It's a moonlighting opportunity. The evening hours are flexible and the extra income helps with my children's expenses."

Alexandre chuckled then echoed her sentiment, "Yeah, they do tend to become more expensive as they grow. Don't they?"

Nodding, Soledad responded, "They do and each new addition compounds the expenses." She reflected on the children she had borne and sighed. "But they are indeed a blessing, each adding their own dynamic to the family...You will soon see with your second child."

"How did you-"

Soledad tilted her head toward the frames on her desk. "The photos, ma'am."

Alexandre smiled. "I often forget those are there."

"He is a handsome young man...Are you hoping for a girl this time around?"

Alexandre dropped her hand to the swell of her womb and her eyes followed. Absent-mindedly, she confessed, "I was hoping not to be pregnant at all." She closed her eyes and immediately regretted the words soon after they left her lips. "Wow...That was crass...I...I didn't mean it...It's just that..."

"It's okay, Your Honor. Your honesty doesn't make you a bad mother. It makes you human...Besides, not all of my children were planned..."

A brief awkward silence fell in the chambers and Alexandre attempted to usher it out by stating, "So moonlighting, huh? What is it that you do during the day?"

"I am a sec-"

The mobile phone ringing on her desk interrupted her response. Alexandre retrieved it to see that it was Jacob calling and she immediately silenced it. She assumed that Jaamyas contacted him and he was now calling to give her grief concerning her long work day.

"I'm so sorry," Alexandre contritely expressed.

"Think nothing of it."

Marginally disheveled by the interruption, Alexandre met her eyes and encouraged, "Please continue. How many children do you have?"

Soledad smiled at the redirection of the conversation and went with it. "Four—I mean three…I lost one…"

Gasping at the tragedy, Alexandre uttered with compassion, "I'm so sorry."

Nodding, Soledad replied, "Thank you."

"How long ago? What happened—I mean, that is if you don't mind my asking."

"It's fine," she confirmed as she shrugged her shoulders. "It's been a couple of years now, and he-"

The office phone ringing on Alexandre's desk interrupted her response. Alexandre reluctantly peered at the name and number that glowed in the display. It was Jacob calling.

Alexandre exhaled aloud. "I'm so sorry, Soledad. I really am, but I must take this call."

"It's quite alright, Your Honor. I need to finish my rounds anyway…Thank you for the conversation. Enjoy your evening."

"You as well, Soledad. Have a good night," Alexandre bid her as she watched her depart the chambers. After accepting Jacob's call, Alexandre absentmindedly greeted out of habit, "I'm on my way out the door right now, Jacob."

"I find that hard to believe considering I am walking through your door right now."

Alexandre watched the door widened until Jacob appeared. She immediately flushed when the sight of his muscular physique in his tailored suit sent a chill up her spine. When her extremities began to tingle and her skin warm, Alexandre grew uncomfortable by her body's steadfast response to him.

She bashfully lowered her eyes. It remained unclear to her whether or not it was proper to cleave to such feelings for a man who was dissolving their marriage.

Jacob impishly grinned at the ignominy she attempted to conceal. Though it pleased him to know that she possessed fond emotions for him, he had no intentions of acting on them.

After closing the door behind him, he teased, "Happy to see me?"

Alexandre stood to her feet. "More like surprised...Jay called you?"

Jacob contorted his face at the rhetorical question. "Of course, Jay called me."

She shook her head at her overzealous son. Of the many choice contacts who he could have called, he contacted Jacob—the one that would have the greatest influence on her.

"I am going to have to talk to security about your visitation and parking privileges," Alexandre jokingly warned.

Jacob snickered. "If you did that, then I wouldn't be able to surprise you with this." He briefly held up, so that she could see, the brown paper tote that bore the name of her frequented French bistro, then lowered it.

"You didn't?"

"I did."

"Poulet au cidre?"

"Oui, avec frites," he responded in the French language they both spoke fluently.

"You're too good to me," she lauded as her mouth salivated at the thought of the tasty cuisine of creamy apple cider chicken and fried potatoes. "How did you convince Chef Antoine to prepare this so late in the evening?"

Jacob shrugged. "Nothing special in particular. I think it was more his Breton nature than anything I said. You know the French believe food to be sacred and shared-"

"With those you love," they finished in unison. The silence that followed allowed them both to reflect on their former plans to finally travel to the city of love—together. Now, with the uncertainty of their marital status, the improbability of a second honeymoon in Paris greatly increased.

Despite his grief, Jacob held her eyes and weakly smiled. He then nodded as he extended her the bag.

Alexandre lowly spoke, "Thank you," while she received the brown paper tote.

"You're welcome," Jacob uttered. Then, in an effort to encourage her departure, he stated, "I'm sure it will taste much better at home though."

Alexandre placed the meal on her desk as she considered his innuendo. "Yes, I'm sure it will…I'm so sorry that Jay called you. He should not have done that. I will talk to him."

"It's fine, Alex," Jacob sincerely assured. Before silence had an opportunity to make their meeting awkward, Jacob inquired, "May I walk you out?"

She shook her head and declined what would potentially be an uncomfortable ride in the elevator and distressing walk in the garage. "I'm still working. I have a few fires to put out."

Jacob meagerly smiled. "So much for 'on your way out the door right now.'"

Alexandre smiled halfheartedly in return. "You know me…True to form."

He nodded concurringly. "Have a good night, Alex."

*** *** ***

Sitting at the window of a popular brick-oven pizzeria, Alexandre awaited the arrival of her best friend. When the bells chimed, her eyes darted towards the entrance. It was a group of teenagers heavily layered for the unexpected December flurries.

Anxiously vexed, she glanced at her watch and saw that it was a quarter after six—their meeting was scheduled for five-thirty. If the rendezvous had been with any other companion, Alexandre would have left the establishment forty minutes ago. However, this meeting was with her lifelong confidante and, though her invitation remained unanswered, Alexandre held out hope that Seanna would not forsake her attempt to make amends.

When the bells chimed again, Alexandre peered around the group waiting to be seated and saw Seanna dressed in layers. Alexandre rose from her seat and waved her to the table.

"Thank you for coming," Alexandre greeted.

"Well, as you can tell by the time, I almost didn't."

"It's okay. I figured you were stuck in traffic or something," Alexandre spoke dismissing the possibility of her longtime friend standing her up. "I would have waited all night if I had to."

"Please let's not make this about us," Seanna requested, ignoring the offer to embrace as they typically did when greeting each other. She lowered herself to the cushion seat at the table. "This is about my god-son—you called, I came."

Alexandre nodded. "I understand." She returned to her seat and lowly repeated, "Thanks, again, either way."

Seanna nodded toward the swell of her belly. "It appears that congratulations are in order."

Alexandre puffed at the insinuation of another big secret kept between the best-of-friends. "Sea, you wouldn't take my calls or return any of my messages…And…and I didn't want you to find out any other way but from me—in-person."

Seanna exhaled loudly. "Well, congratulations. I'm sure Jacob is elated that your guilt compelled you to concede on your one year wait for pregnancy."

Alexandre dropped her gaze and lowly shared, "…It may not be his baby."

Seanna contorted her face and questioned, "…What?"

She met her eyes once more and repeated another way, "Lance could be the father."

Despite Seanna's brain commanding her legs to rise and leave, she obliged the heart that pleaded with her to stay. Not wanting to discuss Alexandre's infidelity that had compounded her lies and betrayal, Seanna spoke, "The kids have never spent a Christmas apart. So, I presume you requested this meeting to come to some temporary truce for the sake of the children?"

"You and I have never gone longer than a few days without talking let alone three months. It's been hell, Sea. I miss you; Jay misses you—and his siblings. This conflict between us has become a strain on them…"

"Okay, and?" Seanna hotly inquired, impatiently waiting for her to arrive at the crux of her argument.

"…And…and I was just kind of hoping that-"

"Fine," Seanna yielded in an effort to silence the start of Alexandre's monologue. "We will get through Christmas for the sake of the children."

Though she was expecting more, Alexandre begrudgingly nodded and accepted the favor. "Thank you," she meekly uttered. Alexandre then reached for Seanna's hand but returned to her upright position when Seanna quickly removed her hands from the table and placed them in her lap.

"…I'm sorry," Alexandre contritely offered, supposing that she offended Seanna by the gesture.

"Good evening, ladies. My name is Roman and I will be your attendant. Could I start you with drinks and appetizers or are you ready to order?"

Seanna shook her head. "No, thank you. I won't be staying— dining."

Alexandre looked at her with disappointed eyes. "Sea?"

"You know what? Could you just give us another minute?"

"Sure."

Seanna waited for the staff member to leave their table before she spoke to Alexandre, "I'm not here to break bread, Alex. I'm here at the petition of my husband so that you will finally stop calling. So let us discuss whatever it is that you want to discuss and I can go on with my night."

Alexandre turned from her glare and sat in silence. She nervously traced the palmar creases of her right hand with her the thumb of her left and contemplated her response. For the first time during their rift, she realized that their thirty-five-year friendship was potentially coming to an end.

"I believe this year Christmas is at your house, correct?" Seanna spoke, breaking the uncomfortable stillness between them.

Alexandre nodded with her gaze still turned from her. "Yeah, but let's do it at yours if you don't mind. Jay doesn't want to decorate. So, the house won't be very festive."

After deeply respiring, Seanna questioned with conviction, "What have you done, Alex?"

Alexandre finally met her gaze. Offended by the question and her sanctimonious air, she retorted, "I haven't done anything, but try to make the best of the quasi-Machiavellian experience I am encountering in my life."

Seanna shook her head in disbelief at her lack of ownership and shifted blame. "No, Alex, you have done a hell-of-a-lot—to Jay, to Jacob, and to Lance. And, for the record, Lance did not fake his death. He was a prisoner of war."

"I kno-"

"Besides, you of all people, the astute historian, know that Machiavelli's bogus death is a rumor."

"Are you finished?"

"No, I'm not. I've been reading the paper and watching the news. Things are not good for you, Alex. Now more than ever, your entire life is on stage for the world to view…And, you pretending that nothing is wrong—that you have done nothing wrong, is the greatest performance of it all."

Seanna rose from her seat indicating that she had no intentions of allowing Alexandre to rebut all that she had mentioned. "Please text or email my god-son's wish list and I will see you Christmas morning."

*** *** ***

"I'll get it," Jaamyas announced as he galloped down the stairs.

"No, you won't," Alexandre stated, disabusing him of his efforts. She walked to the front door ahead of him and spoke, "I will get it. You go back upstairs and get dressed."

Jaamyas looked down at his jeans and sweatshirt. "I am dressed."

Alexandre snickered at his defiant perception of business casual and then dissented, "Not for family Christmas photos, you're not."

"Moooom," he whined.

"Not today, Jay, please," Alexandre beseeched as she unsecured and then opened the door. "Merry Christmas," she greeted.

"Merry Christmas. Special delivery for Alexandre Denton-Hall."

Alexandre squinted her eyes in suspicion and inquired, "Home deliveries on Christmas morning?"

"Mail never stops, ma'am." The uniformed courier extended the electronic tablet for her to sign.

"I see." She received the tablet, signed with the stylus pen where indicated, and returned the tablet to him. "Thank you," she muttered, accepting the sizeable gift-wrapped package.

"You're welcome, ma'am. Enjoy your holiday."

"Thank you, and you as well." She nudged the door with her elbow and entreated, "Lock the door, please, Jay."

Jaamyas stepped to do as his mother requested as he watched her depart to the kitchen. "What is it, Mom?"

"I don't know, Jay."

"Who is it from? Is it from Jacob? Are we going to see him today after all?"

Alexandre deeply respired to suppress her annoyance with his series of questions. She placed the package on the marble island and carefully removed the card.

Jaamyas scurried to her side and pulled the box in front of him. Though he desperately wanted to yank off the red bow and tear through the gold paper, he repressed the urge after recalling his mother's instruction to always read the card first—doing so was not only polite, but also provided insight to the gift.

"Careful, Jay, the label reads 'perishable'."

After breaking the seal of the envelope, she removed the card and recited, "My holiday wish for you: may you have the courage to leave behind all that you are not, and the strength to reveal who you truly are."

Alexandre flipped the card in search of a signature as she briefly considered the cryptic message. When no signature was found, she finally permitted, "Go ahead, open it."

Without hesitation, Jaamyas tugged at the bow and ripped the gold paper. When the Styrofoam cube was unveiled, Jaamyas twisted his face in confusion. "A cooler? What type of gift is this? Why would anyone get you a cooler? We already have several of these."

Alexandre rolled her eyes and pulled the white container back in front of her. "It's what's inside the cooler that is the gift, Jay."

"Oh…I knew that."

She beamed a smile at him. "Of course, you did—just like you know what's inside this cooler."

"Not worth the trouble if it's not an ice cream cake."

Alexandre chuckled at the child replica of herself and responded, "You wish."

Jaamyas shook his head in opposition. "Not just any wish—a *Christmas* wish."

Tickled by his distinction, she chuckled once more as her manicured nails picked at the clear packing tape. "Okay, boy genius."

After she successfully peeled back the seal, Alexandre methodically maneuvered, with both hands, the snug top off and placed it on the counter. She then began to push away ice cubes until her gift was revealed.

"Gross!" Jaamyas exclaimed.

Alexandre snatched back her frozen hands and gasped in horror. "…Jay…Jay, upstairs."

"Who sent you that? Why would someone send that in the mail?"

"Jay, upstairs, NOW!"

"But-"

"Jaamyas Antwan Denton, do not make me tell you again!"

Alexandre inhaled deeply and exhaled slowly to calm herself, realizing that she was speaking from emotions that were not conjured by him. "…We are leaving in thirty minutes. So, please, Jay, just go upstairs and change."

"Yes, ma'am," he muttered prior to walking away.

Once she confirmed his exit, Alexandre released her fear, frustration, and anger in a nervous pant. A barrage of thoughts plagued her mind and raced her heart as worry and stress overcame her. More than herself, she was concerned with the safety and security of her son.

After the moment she allowed herself to be human had passed, Alexandre took a deep breath and transformed back to the shero her son needed her to be. She forced the top back on the cooler and then went to prepare to dispose deep in her backyard the most repulsive gift she had ever received—an eviscerated catfish.

"So, this is where you have retreated," Seanna spoke, exiting the holiday festivities in the family room and entering the kitchen. After pressing down the folds of her red cashmere sweater dress, she pulled out and then lowered herself onto the cushioned seat next to Alexandre at the breakfast nook.

Alexandre looked up from fingering the stem of her sparkling cider glass. "I'm at the mercy of your court." She returned her gaze back to her glass and murmured, "I don't want to do or say anything to rescind your grace."

Seanna chuckled at her jargon. True to form, in every occasion, Alexandre spoke as an attorney. "...I'm on my third martini, Alex...I think it's safe to assume that you have been granted clemency." She retrieved the toothpick from her glass and extended the olive to Alexandre—a customary practice they employed to quash disputes.

Alexandre respired in relief and accepted the olive. Once she ate it, she embraced her best friend and whispered, "Thank you."

"You're welcome." Upon releasing her, Seanna confessed, "Don't be mad, but Jaamyas told me about this morning."

Alexandre rubbed her forehead in distress and exhaled audibly. "I told him not to say anything."

"Why would you expect him to keep such a secret, Alex? He is just a child; a child who is worried about you."

Alexandre rolled her eyes and muttered, "...Yeah, my Wednesday child."

Seanna ignored the subtle reference to the poem that suggested that children born on Wednesday were full of woe. Although Jaamyas did possess the ability to strongly empathize for others and often bore their sadness, she did not believe that these personalities were attributed to him being born on a Wednesday.

"Alex-"

"It was just a gutted fish, Seanna," Alexandre abruptly stated desperate to end the conversation.

"What is this I hear about a gutted fish?" A deep, familiar voice inquired.

Seanna turned her eyes upward in annoyance at the untimely and unwelcomed interruption. "You miss nothing, my dear husband." She gawked as his tall, athletic stature strode to stand next to her.

"After fourteen years of marriage, is that not the expectation?" He retrieved his wife's martini glass from her hand and sipped from it. "Anyway, back to this gutted fish...I'm no oneirocritic, but don't fish dreams allude to pregnancy?" He pondered for a moment and, when no one offered an answer to his question, he concluded, "Perhaps a gutted fish is symbolic of a miscarriage or pregnancy termination."

The kitchen fell invidiously silent as Alexandre and Seanna stared blankly him. Instantly, his short, bronze hair and amber eyes appeared more pronounced as his fading summer tan grew paler with embarrassment.

Seanna yanked her glass from her husband's grip and ignored the droplets that fell to the marble. "It wasn't a dream, Brent. It was a real-life occurrence."

"Really?" Brent asked while adjusting the collar to his white, long-sleeved shirt. He now felt more uncomfortable in his business casual attire.

Alexandre nodded. "Yes...Someone gifted it to me this morning."

Brent twisted his face in ambiguity and probed, "What?...Why? Why would someone do something so sinister?"

Alexandre shrugged. After a long swallow from her glass, she responded, "I don't know...I just need it to stop—my chambers is one thing, but my home is completely another...Jay was at the house—he saw it."

"Oh, my g…" Brent's voice trailed off as he contemplated all that she said. "Wait, what do you mean at your chambers? Today's event isn't your first threat?"

Alexandre shook her head. "…If we can even call them threats."

Brent inquired, "Well, what else would you call them, Alexandre?"

She broke their uncomfortable stare and replied with nonchalance, "I don't know. Maybe-"

"Do you think it is the same person who mysteriously sent you the tulips?" Seanna interjected.

Alexandre shook her head another time. "No…Turns out that Lance sent me those."

At the mention of the resurrected, the room fell awkwardly quiet. It was a matter that remained undiscussed among them, resulting in burdensome thoughts and repressed emotions.

Brent was the first to clear his throat and offer, "We should probably contact law enforcement."

"No, please don't," Alexandre immediately objected. "Jay is experiencing a tough holiday season as it is…I-I don't want this event to compound things for him—or even me."

Brent loathed that her concern did not extend beyond herself or her son. "Compound more than what?"

"Brent-" Seanna attempted to interject, recognizing that Alexandre's selfishness had now exacerbated her husband's anger and frustration.

Brent rose his palm to silence her. "No, Sea, we are all family here and this needs to be said."

Seanna abruptly lowered his hand, vexed by his insolence, and retorted, "Yes, but does it have to be now? It's Christmas for crying out loud."

Brent darted his eyes between those of his wife's and those of her best friend's. Despite the many nights he could recall extinguishing her anger, calming her fears, consoling her heartbreak, wiping her tears, and encouraging her faith, Brent knew that Seanna would defend Alexandre "'til death."

"No," he finally responded as he shrugged his shoulders with apathy. "I suppose it can wait until after Christmas, or at least until another Gerald Curry shooting occurs right outside the courthouse," he added with sarcasm.

His cruel innuendo stressed Seanna and she attempted, to no avail, to rub the feeling from her forehead. "Brent, it's Christmas…Let's just table this for another time."

"Yes, please," Alexandre concurred prior to swallowing from her glass. She returned it to the marble, met Brent's eyes, and beseeched, "Please."

"Sure," Brent smugly conceded. He pondered the request another moment and then slyly stated, "…I suppose we can...for now…or at least until a disgruntled ex-convict breaks into your home, duck tapes you to a chair, and threatens revenge by shooting you to death."

Brent's impertinence exasperated Alexandre, causing her to rise from her seat and exclaim, "How can you be so callous?!"

"Callous?"

"Yes, callous!"

Offended by the accusation, Brent expressed what they all knew to be true, "We live in a nation in which a growing number of the population has *no* respect for authority. And I'm callous? Bullshit, Alexandre."

"Brent, please let's-" Seanna gingerly began in an attempt to usher peace into their conversation.

His fury burning in his chest, Brent knowingly interjected Seanna's calming efforts with, "These people believe that they can do and say whatever they want because they *feel* like it, and they hide behind their misconstrued perceptions of the First Amendment. I know it and you know it, too, Alexandre. You're just too damn gullible to acknowledge it."

Alexandre dismissed his well stated argument and ignored the crude slight made concerning her naivety. Instead, she focused on his cavalier recollection of the attacks of the members of the justice system and how it minimized the hardship endured by the victims.

"…Maybe I am," Alexandre replied, shrugging her shoulders. "But at least I am not heartless. Those were real-life events that should never be considered lightly. And for you to speak of them with an air of nonchalance is disrespectful in and of itself."

Brent shook his head at Alexandre's penchant to circumvent issues that she had no desire to discuss. Her classic avoidant behaviors were the reason why he had always thought her to be a better politician than an officer of the court. In his many years of knowing her, Alexandre managed to abscond every fight she could not win.

After snickering through his irritation, Brent clarified, "The only person that is taking these and other impending events lightly, Alexandre, is you!"

"Me?!"

"You guys-" Seanna stated in an effort to assuage their fury despite the increased intoxicating affect her beverage had on her.

"Yes, you!" Brent hollered at Alexandre.

Alexandre scoffed and rejoined, "You're out of line, Brent McCoy. You have totally lost it!"

"You guys, please stop fi-"

"I've lost it?!" He shouted over the voice that tried to defuse the heated quarrel.

"Yes, you!" Alexandre spat.

"You are the one who tends to forget just how vulnerable judges are, and I have lost it?! New flash, Judge Denton-Hall, it is your silence and complacency that are exacerbating the legal chaos that we are currently experiencing in this country! But I guess it will take another disgruntled client shooting up a law firm before you act—or, better yet, a courthouse."

Seanna abruptly rose from her seat, shouting, "DAMN IT, YOU GUYS. THAT IS ENOUGH!" When she heard the children abruptly stop their play in the family room, Seanna lowered her voice and repeated, "That is enough—the both of you."

A brief silence cooled the hot tempers fuming in the room. While Seanna fixated her eyes on Brent, he maintained his glare with Alexandre.

At last, Brent spoke to his wife, "…You're right, it is enough. Enough of the bullshit she keeps taking you through." With that, he walked out the kitchen, allowing the stomp of his heels to convey his dissatisfaction with the discussion's end.

Seanna returned to her seat and contritely murmured, "Alex, I'm so sorry…He's just-"

"No, don't, Sea." Alexandre struggled, but finally swallowed the hard knot in her throat. She lowered herself back to the bar seat and lowly uttered, "...He's right. I have been so short-sighted and selfish. I have literally taken you and everyone else close to me through hell."

Seanna reached for her hand and firmly held it. Although she agreed with all that Alexandre commented, she felt no need to verbally concur. Instead, Seanna sought to seize the opportunity to discourage Alexandre's unyielding tenacity. "Everything broken can't be fixed, Alex. You've got to know when to cast certain things away."

Alexandre downed the remainder of her beverage then rose to her feet. "Maybe...or at least find someone better to fix it."

Seanna shook her head as she released Alexandre's hand. "What does that even mean, Alex?...What are you going to do?"

"You know me. I am nothing if not a woman with a plan."

"Please, Alex," Seanna beseeched in desperation. "You. Are. Pregnant," she reminded her, emphasizing each word. "Think about your child."

"I am thinking of my chi-"

"No...No, you're thinking of yourself just as you always do."

"That's not true, Sea, and you know it. In fact, I am thinking of both my children."

Seanna rolled her eyes and huffed at her remark. She parted her lips to respond but a fleeting vertigo halted her. "...Look," she began again once the spiraling of the kitchen ceased, "I'm too inebriated to have this conversation now. How about we both just go and enjoy what's left of the holiday, we can finish this in the morning?"

"No, I'm finished actually—with both the holiday and this conversation."

Seanna closed her eyes in frustration, worry, and regret. There was no getting through to Alexandre when she was like this. As per usual, Seanna felt that she had no option but to concede. "You are my best friend, Alex, and I don't—I can't lose you...Just promise me that you will be safe."

*** *ELEVEN* ***

Alexandre watched as the private investigator folded the yellow paper of his legal pad behind its cardboard and fervently continued to transcribe notes on a blank sheet. His office was cold, bare, and uninviting, but appeared to possess the accoutrements necessary to maintain the stellar reputation that proceeded him.

Unable to cope with the deafening silence any longer, Alexandre shifted her weight in the uncomfortable wooden chair that was positioned in front of his dated oak desk, cleared her throat, and spoke, "I can provide more details if you need them."

The retired police officer looked over his reading glasses, shook his head, and responded, "No, I believe I have everything I need…except…," he flipped and scanned through the pages of his notes, then continued, "I'm just not clear on who you are requesting that I follow."

Alexandre stared blankly at the attractive brown-skinned sexagenarian who, with the exception of his bald head shaven by senescence and not choice, appeared to be in excellent health. She respired audibly and nervously spoke, "Me."

He looked up from his legal pad and repeated, "You."

She nodded. "Yes, me…I…I know it sounds absurd, but that…that is what I need."

"…You need me to follow you?" He first sneered at the unusual request; then contemplated it; and, before finally dismissing it, he entertained the idea, asking, "For how long?"

Alexandre rose her shoulders with uncertainty and answered, "Until this is resolved."

He released a noticeably long breath. The seriousness in her tone and stoniness of her disposition gave him an incalculable cause for concern. She was requesting the impossible.

After folding the papers back to the front of the legal pad, the private investigator lowered it on the desk. He then recapped his fountain pen and tossed it on the wavy yellow pages. "This has the potential of becoming very costly."

Alexandre reached for her wallet in the leather tote placed in the chair next to her. "I understand and I am prepared to pay."

Shaking his head in dissent, he removed his reading glasses from his face, folded the temples, and placed them on his desk. "You don't understand, Mrs. Denton-Hall-"

"Alex," she forcefully reminded him.

"Alex," he restated. "I am a one-man operation. I cannot forsake my other clients just to trail you. I'm no babysitter." He reclined in his own wooden chair, then inquired in a manner that was more suggestive than inquisitory, "Wouldn't you prefer this be a police matter?

"No," Alexandre spoke without hesitation. She shook her head, adding, "No, this *matter* has received enough media attention as it is. So, I need this investigation to be discreet—no police and no one can know that I hired you, or that I am being followed…You must clandestinely find yourself in and out of the same space that I am in."

Once more, he chuckled at her incredible appeal. "Unless disguised as your bodyguard or a bailiff, in and out of the juvenile courtroom is not happening—those proceedings are generally informal and private—they are not open to the public. You know that, Alex."

"Then feign being my bodyguard," she merely resolved.

He shook his head and repeated, "I'm no babysitter."

Alexandre huffed with nervous disappointment and frustration. "…Then what am I supposed to do?" She solemnly choked. "I feel as if this is far more than my career. My life—my family—is in jeopardy."

His years of service among law enforcement muted his investigatory alerts. Far too often, complainants presented themselves as victims absent the necessary evidence to corroborate their case.

To simply alleviate her unsubstantiated worry, the investigator advised, "Then get an alarm."

Aggrieved by the dismissive suggestion, Alexandre retorted, "I have an alarm."

"Then get a dog." He glanced at the hands of his wristwatch and noticed they were nearing the end of their one-hour consultation. "They are actually better than alarms."

After initially rolling her eyes at the suggestion, Alexandre snickered at his argument. It resembled the one that Jaamyas made years ago when he petitioned her for a pet.

"Really?" She questioned with more sarcasm than cynicism.

"Yes," he answered, ignoring her mockery. "An alarm alerts you when danger is already at your door; a dog will alert you prior to danger's arrival."

Though she followed the logic of his explanation, Alexandre discharged it and retorted, "I will soon have a new baby to contend with. I do not need a new puppy along with it…Besides, I'm allergic."

He dismissed her excuses by responding, "Then get one that is hypoallergic."

Alexandre rolled her eyes another time at the investigator's ignorant response as no dog breed was wholly sans allergens. The number of proteins found in pet saliva alone was enough for an emergency room visit.

Shaking her head, Alexandre steadfastly affirmed, "I'm not getting a dog."

Wearied by their impasse, the private investigator made no additional attempts to sway her decision. Instead, he allowed the office to fall silent as he carefully assessed the potential client seated in front of him. From their brief encounter, he gleaned that

Alexandre was a woman who was more accustomed to persuading than being persuaded, and any effort to alter her unmalleable decision would be exhaustingly futile.

Alexandre sat rigid in her chair while her pensive gaze focused on the wall behind the investigator. The clutter pinned on the cork bulletin board mirrored her life—a flood of demands, priorities-to-do, and things-to-remember held at bay by weakening levees.

"I have never been a person who has been afraid of much." She met the gawk that he kept on her and confessed, "But this…this really frightens me."

He watched her lower her lids over her eyes and inhale deeply, hold her breath for spell, and then exhale slowly. She repeated the breathing pattern before opening her eyes and adding, "I think more than anything I am afraid for my children."

"…I understand, Alex, truly I do…and on some level I can even empathize, but-"

"You don't want to help me," Alexandre's voice cracked, concluding the statement for him. She fought hard to hold back the tears that swelled in her eyes.

Hearing the despondency in her voice, he spoke gingerly, "It's not that I don't want to help you; it's more that I can't help you…I really do think that you should take this to the police department…Not much stupefies me, but this—this I think is so much greater than what I can do."

Alexandre shook her head in opposition as she opened her wallet to her checks and began to inscribe the requirements. After she completed the amount portions with a figure several hundred dollars above his standard rate, Alexandre tore the paper slip at its perforation, and extended it to him. She was confident that all that he needed was financial encouragement. However, to her dismay, he did not receive the check, but Alexandre remained obstinate. She placed it on his desk and slid it towards him.

With no interest in what she offered the private investigator slid the check back towards her. "Mrs. Denton-Hall-"

"ALEX," she interrupted with exasperation; angered, first, by his refusal of her retainer and, second, by his failure to address her by her preferred name.

"...Please...call me Alex," Alexandre reminded more calmly.

He forgave her unspoken apology when she lowered her eyes in contrition. Understanding her immense level of stress and aggravation, the investigator showed her compassion rather than the exit.

"Alex," he gently spoke. When she did not respond to the call of her name, he beseeched, "Alex, please look at me as I say this to you."

Alexandre met his glare and listened as he stated, "There is no amount that you can pay that will convince me to take this on. I appreciate whomever recommended me to you. I really do, but...but what you need..." His voice trailed off as he prudently thought of his next words, "is a task force."

Her heart dropped in her chest at the same moment tears fell from her eyes. Distressed, she cried to herself as she reflected on all that vexed her—a tumultuous career, a failing marriage, rekindled nuptials, filial battles, a strained friendsh-

The life in her womb kicked firmly, abruptly ending her period of sulking. Alexandre moved her hand to the swell of her abdomen and feebly smiled in spite of her tears. She inhaled deeply and exhaled slowly then pressed her face dry with the back of her hand.

Observing the rivulets of water that traveled down her cheeks and the brokenness that had replaced the strength of her spirit, compassion overwhelmed his heart. He finally conceded commanding, "...Get me a list."

"Pardon?" Alexandre inquired in the midst of returning her wallet to her tote and retrieving several pocket tissues. She dabbed her wet face dry and gently wiped her nose.

The investigator exhaled, confident that he would soon regret repeating his request. "Much information has been leaked and you believe it to be an internal breech. So, get me a list of persons with whom you regularly interact."

Alexandre contemplated his petition for a moment then finally replied, "Such a list is not feasible. I regularly interact with several people—known and unknown to me."

"Well, start with a list of those that you do know."

She breathed in incredulity. "To what end? Is the intent to interrogate each person?"

He shrugged. "It might be."

Shaking her head, Alexandre disclosed, "I am not a favorite in Mecklenburg. I know with certainty that building security despises me since I had a hand in an officer's termination, my law clerk loathes my judicial decisions and perceives me to be soft-on-crime, and my colleagues on the bench have distance themselves from me because of all the unfavorable attention." She took a deep breath before adding, "And that's just the first legal pad of names...Trust me, I have more foes than friends."

He laughed halfheartedly at her final statement and commented, "It is imprudent of you to think you have friends at all." Peering deep into her eyes he advised, "...Alex, an effectual leader has no friends—just followers and foes."

Ignoring the slight that alluded to her naïveté, Alexandre held his gaze and confirmed, "Well, either way, I have more foes."

The investigator turned from their stare. After he looked down at his hand-written notes, he respired loudly, and vigorously rubbed his forehead with the pad of his fingertips. "...Again, Alex, I am not sure how I can help you."

Incensed by the false hope that he had just given her, she spoke vehemently, "How you can help me?!...Someone is trying to destroy me, maybe even kill me. I need you to find who this person is before they succeed in their efforts. THAT is how you can help me!"

In an effort to allow the quietness of the room to calm her, the private investigator did not immediately respond. Instead, he retrieved the check, scrutinized the amount she offered for his services, and placed it on top of his notes. "I will dress in different disguises and do some probing to see what I can find out for you."

Alexandre released the air she held trapped in her lungs in a sigh of relief. "...Thank you."

"Don't thank me, yet. You haven't received my final invoice.

She nodded and reassured, "I will pay whatever you deem is fair." When he did not respond, Alexandre inquired, "Anything else?"

Returning the head gesture, he merely answered, "Yes." He then looked far into the windows of her soul and continued his response, "Once we determine a viable lead, we turn it over to the authorities."

"But-"

"No, Alex," he immediately interjected. "This is not a request. It is a condition. Either you agree with it or I resign. I am running a reputable business here, and executing street justice is not one of my offerings."

At the suggestion of impropriety, a bulge quickly swelled in her throat, the temperature rose in the room, and the four walls began to enclose her. Alexandre had not given much thought to the end that she sought until the investigator had made an allusion to one. As a result, she began to ponder, for a brief moment, her true intentions.

At the least, Alexandre wanted for herself: peace of mind; and, at the most, she wanted for her children: security and protection. How such feats were accomplished were of no immediate concern to her. For, in that moment, Alexandre recognized that she had given and sacrificed much for children that were not her own. Consequently, she would be remiss not to do the same for children that were her own.

With her priorities no longer in disarray, Alexandre's intentions flushed her skin. Unequivocally, she was not one who subscribed to the tenets of Hammurabi's Code. It was her earnest belief that the execution of an "eye for an eye" was a never-ending pendulum of revenge. She did, however, favor justice in any manner that deterred the strong from exploiting and harming the weak. And, in this instance, her children were the weak.

After succeeding in downing the knot in her esophagus, Alexandre replied, "...I understand and I would never ask..." Her voice trailed off when she noticed that his visage only displayed concern for her response to his condition and nothing more. Relenting, she cleared her throat and recited what he wanted to hear, "Okay, we will find a lead and will turn it over to the authorities.

At the receipt of their verbal contract, the private investigator rose from his seat, smoothed out the folds of his white business shirt and black pants, and responded, "Good—I will start working on this tomorrow, and you start working on that list."

"Okay," she said slowly standing to her feet.

"I will walk you out."

*** *** ***

Alexandre chuckled as she rose from her seat. "Yeah, you do that and get the door while you're at it, too. I'm sure it's for you— all this food here and you're ordering takeout on New Year's Eve."

Lance laughed at himself along with her and explained, "Hey, I want what I want."

She rolled her eyes and shook her head. "…I'm going to the restroom."

Lance watched her disappear down the hall as he retrieved his wallet from the inside of his jacket and returned it to the arm of the chair. He then walked to the front door, unsecured it and swung it open.

"Happy New Ye-" Lance stopped short of his well wishes when he was greeted with a bouquet of roses. "Jacob."

He lowered the flowers, astonished to see his nemesis standing at the threshold. "Lance." Jacob adjusted the jacket of his suit and cleared his throat. "Alexandre available?"

"Yeah. Sure. Come on in." Lance widened the door, permitted Jacob to enter, and closed and secured it. He then stepped back in front of him and began to ramble, "Everyone left about an hour or so after dinner, and Jaamyas left with Seanna and the family. Alexandre is in the restroom, but will be out shortly. May…May I get you something?"

Jacob shook his head at the audacity of the question— inquiring if he needed anything in a home that was once his. "…No, but if the two of you are busy, I can come back another time."

"No, no not at all."

"Are you sure?" Jacob pressed. "Because I declined her dinner invitation for another event, but, halfway through it, I changed my mind. So, Alex is not expecting me."

Lance ran his hand over his muscular torso to press down the crease in his tailored black sweater. "No, we were just uh…watching a movie after cleaning up after dinner."

Jacob huffed and spoke with jealously under his breath, "Always Mr. Helpful."

"Excuse me?"

"…Nothing."

"No, it's something." Lance dissented and then encouraged, "In fact, you and I are long overdue for a conversation. Now is as good of a time as any."

Jacob rolled his eyes at his pompous nerve. "With respect, *Coach Carter*, I have shit to say to you."

Lance sneered, offended, first, by Jacob's allusion to his earlier ruse and, second, by Jacob's rejection of his genuine attempt to make amends. In response, Lance callously retorted, "Wow. Such language from the man who has been playing the role of replacement to *my* family."

Fuming with rage, Jacob met his gaze and growled, "Don't be angered by the fact that I recovered your fumble."

After shrugging his shoulders in nonchalance, Lance asked, "And all to what end?" He stepped to close the minuscule gap between them and confirmed, "I am told that you are forfeiting the game. So, either way, I win."

Jacob's anger clinched his jaw tighter than his fist, but he relaxed them both when he heard a door open.

"Sorry, sorry. I'm so sorry," Alexandre contritely spoke as she rushed out of her room and started toward and down the stairs. "I just had to get out of those pants and into something more comfortable. This little girl is expanding me at double the rate Jaamyas did. Maternity waistband my aaas—Jacob. Jacob what are you doing here? You said you weren't coming."

He tossed the flowers on the foyer table and walked to her—intentionally knocking shoulders with Lance en route. "We need to talk."

"Oh, okay."

Jacob took her by the hand and led her back upstairs. Once in the room that they both once shared, he closed the door behind her and kissed her—fervently, desperately, and aggressively.

Alexandre pressed her back into the cool door and attempted to break from his overbearing lips. "Jacob…Jacob…Jacob, please." She finally grabbed his face and looked deep into his eyes. "Jacob!"

"What? Are you not still my wife?"

Taken aback by the question, she exhaled in disbelief and responded, "I don't know. Am I?"

In lieu of a reply, Jacob searched her eyes for any inkling of restoration. Despite all that he believed and all that he threatened, he still desired a life and a family with her.

"What has gotten into you, Jacob?" Alexandre asked once she grew exhausted of the silence. "This isn't you—storming in here like some madman, barraging me with overbearing kisses…What's going on with you?"

Jacob turned from her gaze and stepped from her personal space. He then walked to a seat at the window, lowered himself in it, and place his head in hands. "I don't know…I just don't know anymore."

Alexandre walked to the seat in front of him and, too, lowered herself in it. Following, she removed his hands from his face and held them.

"I went to the courthouse yesterday," he shared.

"…Okay," Alexandre lowly uttered.

He eased his hands out of hers. "I went to finally file the annulment papers. It…It was something I personally wanted to do once my attorney received them back from you; so, I went."

She struggled with the knot that grew in her throat. When she at last swallowed it, Alexandre nodded her head in acceptance of the dreaded and inevitable dissolution of their union.

"…But…but I couldn't do it…I drove all the way there, parked the car, made it to the clerk of court and…and I couldn't do it."

"Ja-"

"Is this really it? Are we really over?

Unsure of how to answer as the choice was ultimately his to make, Alexandre attempted to respond, "Jacob, I think-"

"Was I just the temporary replacement?"

Alexandre twisted her face at his nonsensical inquiry. "Replacement? What? Why would think that?"

"Just answer the question, Alex," he pressed.

She searched his weary eyes and saw the agony behind them. Recalling his brief encounter in the foyer with her first husband, Alexandre questioned, "What did Lance say to you?"

"I don't care about what he said to me, Alex. I care about what you tell me."

"No, Jacob, you are not a temporary replacement. You were—are—an amazing husband and a terrific father."

Jacob puffed hot air in disbelief. "Then what happened to us?"

"I happened, Jacob. I...I made a horrible mistake and destroyed what we were building together." She stroked his cheek and added, "I don't deserve absolution, but please forgive me. For all that I have done and said to hurt and disappoint you, please forgive me...You deserved none of it, and I am truly sorry."

He took her hand and held it. "Alex, I forgave you a long time ago."

Tears filled her eyes as she kissed the back of his hand. In his compassion, she realized more, at that moment, that their marriage was indeed one of the great things that had occurred in her life. To that end, in consideration of his amorous heart and congenial character, Alexandre admitted to herself that she had to release him before she destroyed him.

"...Jacob..." Alexandre unnervingly began before her voice trailed off. It pained her immensely to yield to the fact that she had to let Jacob go.

An uncomfortable warmth enveloped her body as she felt the tears form in her eyes. Peering into his, Alexandre garnered that Jacob needed a love that was going to restore and uplift him and not break and hurt him. Consequently, freeing him to find a love just as formerly described was the final selfless act she could do for him. Of the many great things that Jacob deserved, he deserved that much.

"...File the papers, Jacob."

Confused, Jacob's forlorn eyes searched her red ones as he questioned, "What?"

Alexandre nodded to assure that he heard her correctly. As she feebly smiled, she repeated, "It's okay…File the papers."

Jacob felt as if the oxygen in his lungs was bludgeoned from his body. In his failure to file the annulment papers with the clerk of court, he had hoped to the point of expectation that they could reconcile—that he would forgive her, she would love him, and they would start anew. The thought of her desiring something different suffocated him.

Breaking the unbearable silence that grew in the room, Alexandre offered, "I just-"

"Is that what you really want?" Jacob interjected, finally capturing his breath.

Once confident of her decision—the decision to be with him, Alexandre was no longer certain of what she wanted. She was conflicted by the way she remained in love with her second husband, but was still enamored by her first. It was quite the entanglement in which she, the Type A, play-by-the-rules, executor of justice, would have never fathomed her unscrupulous involvement. It was uncommon, uncertain, and unsafe. For these reasons, Alexandre knew that she had to set Jacob free.

"…Yes," Alexandre finally responded in a murmur despite not knowing whether it was the response she should lead with.

Jacob burst into a heartfelt cry. He lowered his head into his hands and then her lap. As he released his diverging emotions, he felt the gently touch of Alexandre's hands on the back of his head. He sobbed at the loss of everything he held sacred: friendship, family, and love.

After a moment passed, Jacob rose his head, wiped his eyes, and questioned, "What about the baby?" in an attempt to reason with Alexandre. "What about Jay?" He pressed despite knowing that his son and daughter were no resolution for their marital problems. Nevertheless, in desperation, Jacob employed the children as a temporary fix. "Our children-"

Alexandre shook her head. "They—we'll—be fine…Just…" She inhaled deeply and exhaled loudly. "Just walk away, Jacob, and start anew."

"Just like that? Like nothing ever happened?"

Nodding her head, Alexandre replied, "That is the whole idea behind an annulment…The very premise in which it is built on—like nothing ever happened…"

Jacob lowered his lids over his eyes to prevent, to no avail, the rivulets of water streaming down his cheeks. Alexandre's words regarding the conditions of the annulment first, loudly echoed in his ears, then, resonated with his mind, and finally, penetrated his heart. Although all that she spoke resounded loudly, it did not subdue the chime of his watch that indicated the twelve o'clock hour.

After opening his eyes, he gently cupped Alexandre's face, and touched her lips with his. "Happy New Year," he muttered before rising from his seat to vacate the room, leave the house, and depart her life.

*** TWELVE ***

In her chambers on a frosty Monday morning, Alexandre watched the private investigator adjust his black frames on his nose and the press badge around his neck.

"You couldn't have found a more inconspicuous disguise?" She inquired in a tone that conveyed her dissatisfaction.

He shrugged off her disapproval and then defended his decision, "Press surrounds this building and swarms the halls. I thought I'd fit right in."

She rolled her eyes and then stated, "There is a flaw in your plan."

"And what would that flaw be?"

"I don't speak to the press," she answered, disabusing him of his logic.

He squinted his eyes at her remark. "I do recall you in a few televised press conferences."

"Alone," Alexandre clarified. "I do not speak to the press alone."

The investigator dismissed her concern and leaned forward to place the list she had given him several weeks prior on her desk. "That list was fruitless."

"Nothing?"

"Nothing," he confirmed.

"What about Officer Ross?" Alexandre asked him of the former law enforcement officer whose termination she successfully sought.

"Nothing. I followed him, observed him, and even questioned him—there is nothing there," the investigator confirmed.

Astonished to the point of disbelief, she pressed, "Are you certain?"

"Unequivocally…He did, however, admit that he is still enraged by his dismissal, but nothing to the degree that would cause him to seek retribution. He also reiterated, just as you already mentioned, that you are not a favorite among these corridors. Any number of people in and outside this courthouse could be seeking vengeance."

Alexandre lowered her head in disappointment and rubbed her forehead in frustration. "…I can't believe this…I cannot fucking believe this…Someone is sabotaging me and there is not a damn thing I can do about it."

"May I be frank with you?"

She met his eyes, chuckled halfheartedly, and inquired, "You mean you haven't been so thus far?"

"Not in the way I am going to now. You're not going to like what you going to hear."

After she respired deeply, Alexandre confessed, "I don't trust people who tell me what I like to hear."

"Touché…" The investigator contemplated the delivery of his curt message, then finally spoke, "You have a lot on your plate, Alexandre: an impending divorce, a high-risk pregnancy, a crumbling career, and a hostile stalker. You need to lay low—take a sabbatical and just lay low. Leave the country. Go to Europe; you can have your baby there."

Alexandre erupted in laughter at the suggestion she initially thought to be a jest. "You can't be serious."

His stoic facial expression did not alter.

"Seriously, are you serious?"

"I am very serious."

She shook her head in dissent. "Absolutely not...Europe? No way."

"The continent does not matter. It could be Europe, Asia, Africa, wherever. The point is to get you and children someplace safe until this blows-over."

"You mean run and hide?"

"What I mean is protect and survive."

Alexandre briefly considered his response, quickly dismissed it, and then spoke, "I can't...I can't do that—uproot my life, uproot my son."

Disappointed, but not surprised by her response, he reached inside his black blazer for his slim wallet and retrieved the check she had given him. He placed it on the desk and slid it to her. "Then, there is nothing more that I can do for you."

"Nothing more you can do? Then what I am supposed to do?"

He shrugged. "Arm yourself, hire guards, put some fire under the asses of law enforcement."

Alexandre sat in silence and considered all that he had advised. Though none of his recommendations were feasible, she appreciated his efforts. So, she eased the check back towards him and insisted, "Please, keep it—for your troubles."

The investigator feebly grinned at the benevolent gesture. Though he rightfully earned the sum afforded to him, he did not feel at ease receiving payment for services that rendered no results. Consequently, feelings of discomfort began to overwhelm him.

"Please," Alexandre beseeched, noticing his reticence.

He collected the check and return it to his wallet and the wallet to his jacket. Following he inquired, "What do you know of Cynthia Sackie?"

"My law clerk?"

He nodded.

She raised her shoulders. "I don't know...My previous law clerk vetted and hired her."

He huffed at the hiring and onboarding processes that he was all too familiar with. It was one that required little to no interaction with the employer with whom the employee will be working.

"Well, keep an eye on her," the investigator forewarned.

Alexandre held his intense gaze and questioned, "Why do you suggest that?"

"Because she comes from a long line of right-winged politicians and litigators."

"And?"

"And? I don't need an and, but since you're asking, I am talking about the epitome of conservativism." He used the index finger of his right hand to count off the fingers on the left hand, "Pro-life, pro-second amendment, pro-capital punishment, anti-social programs, anti-universal healthcare, anti-gun control, anti-"

"Is there a point to all of this?"

"You don't think it odd that a woman of that caliber, of such pedigree, would accept a clerkship with the most compassionate judge in all of North Carolina?"

She thought on his question for a brief moment and finally answered, "No, I don't."

Vexed by her naïveté, the private investigator rose from his seat. After he pulled down the creases in his denim, pressed the folds in his business shirt, and adjusted his blazer, he recommended, "Then you should."

"And why is that?"

"Because powerful women tend to have powerful enemies," he spoke with authority. "…There may not be anything there criminally, but I am inclined to believe that she has an agenda."

Alexandre shook her head in dissent, refusing to believe that a trusted ally was guilty of nefarious activities. "I think you're wrong."

With an unwavering air of confidence he spoke, "I rarely am," prior to exiting her chambers.

*** *** ***

LaKeisha LaKay

"Judge Denton—I'm sorry—Judge Denton-Hall," the uniformed officer greeted when Alexandre approached the window. "Yours is a face that I haven't seen in a while."

Alexandre received the pen and clipboard he extended to her through the glass opening. She completed the required information on the visitor's log and then quickly scanned the names above hers and a few pages prior. "Well, you know, I have been busy getting married, getting divorced," she gestured to the swell of her womb, "and getting pregnant."

After widening his eyes at the unexpected honesty, the officer of the detention center retrieved the clipboard and pen, and merely spoke, "Yeah, I suppose that is enough to keep anyone busy."

Alexandre chuckled to ease the uncomfortable tension between them. "That is why I could use some normalcy in the new year…Is my typical classroom available?"

"I'm not sure, but even if it is, your students may not be. It's been a while so they will have to be scouted."

Alexandre shrugged, brushing of his subtle attempt to discourage her volunteering efforts. "I have time and I don't mind the wait."

"Of course, you do, and, of course, you don't," he spoke with sarcasm. "If we all had the kind of time as our volunteers-"

"Then your routine checks would be more frequent?" Alexandre smugly remarked before he could complete his thought. "Or at least every 15 to 20 minutes as required by law?"

He swallowed the bulge that swelled in his esophagus as he stared blankly at Alexandre. He then responded defensively, "The work we do and the services we provide are limited by the number of zookeepers we have on staff."

Alexandre huffed incredulously. "Cute…real cute."

The officer shrugged in mockery, still offended by her insinuation that he and his staff were indolent. "Even on our worst day, we still fare better than the best days of the detention centers that are ranked the most deplorable in this country."

Alexandre shook her head while she glared at him in disgust. He, like so many others, believed that the youth housed in the facility were miscreants not worthy of redemption or forgiveness.

They were merely a squander of taxpayers' dollars and undeserving of another chance.

Recalling that the previous generation attributed to the plight of the current generation, she vehemently spat, "If that is your barometer of success, then you need to be hung at the gallows."

He resisted the urge to respond with a snide comment that would allude to the newsprint that unmercifully questioned her character and intentions. Despite his ill feelings of her and hers of him, he knew that she genuinely cared about all the children she encountered. She poured into vessels that were empty; encouraged spirits that were broken; and loved hearts that were forsaken. His animosity, no matter how fervent, could not deny these truths.

"I will check on your room and round up your brutes," he finally responded.

Alexandre flashed a bogus smile and halfheartedly spoke, "Thank you…And, if you don't mind, I will take a look at the visitor's logs for the past few months."

"Why would I mind? We don't work around here."

Recognizing that her request was more a favor than an obligation, as it was outside the bounds of her legal authority, she ignored the invitation to squabble further.

"Thank you," Alexandre sang. She expressed her gratitude a second time when he exited his office and delivered into her hands a stack of files.

Alexandre opened the first file of the deck and began to skim the visitor entries. As she reviewed the records for familiar names, she massaged the pain in her lower back. Different from her first pregnancy, her second pregnancy did not allow her much time on her feet. She needed to find a seat before the pain enveloped her entire body.

Taking the files into her hands, she pivoted on her heels and collided into the body behind her.

"I'm so sorry," she contritely spoke, watching him retrieve the files that she dropped.

Standing erect, he offered, "It's no prob…"

"Officer Ross," Alexandre greeted in astonishment.

"It's just Eric now, Judge Denton-Hall," he corrected, reminding her of her recommendation that abruptly ended his law enforcement career.

"...R-right. Of course," she stammered, recalling with regret her decision made in haste.

He peered down at her, contemplating all that he wanted to convey. Though he had rehearsed this moment several times before, he was now conflicted by what he wanted to speak first.

"Listen, Eric, I'm so sorry about your termination. The whole incident unfolded so quickly and I...I was just acting in anger...I did try to make things right by-"

"Don't," he interrupted as he extended her the files. "Just don't."

Alexandre received the files and nodded in deference, but still offered, "Please if there is anything, anything at all that I can do just-"

"You don't think you've done enough?"

"Excuse me?"

"The greatest show of power is not found in the swing of the sword or, in your case, the stroke of the pen...It is the waver of the tongue." When she offered no retort, he continued, "Sometimes there is no means to undo the damage done when we speak in anger."

Alexandre felt her face flush while she considered his comment and the full ramifications of her actions. She accepted the fact that her persuasive diatribe was expressed in rage and it had influenced the outcome she ultimately desired—his termination. However, as an impartial adjudicator, she believed that all that she said, despite its delivery, to be warranted by the unlawful acts he committed.

"Look," she began to elucidate, "I respect that you don't agree with my actions but I did act in the way that I believed best at that time."

"Indeed, you did. You always do."

Before an awkward silence could settle between them, Alexandre exhaled audibly and inquired, "What are you doing here, Officer Ross—Eric?"

He searched her eyes for sincerity and finally responded, "I have a meeting with an acquaintance."

Confused by his gaze that burned into her, she clarifyingly probed, "Who? Me?"

He chuckled at her audacity. "You and I are not acquaintances."

Alexandre cleared her throat and stammered in embarrassment, "N-No, of course…I mean, of course we are not—well, at least not anymore…Sorry, sorry. I didn't mean to imply that…" Her voice trailed off as she took a moment and breathed through her crippling nervousness. The hard pounding of her heart could be heard in her ears as her concern of the unknown exacerbated.

Looking down on her with a blank stare, he smugly commented, "What baffles me most about you is that you think too highly of yourself as you judge others."

Taken aback by his random assessment, Alexandre rejoined, "That is not true. I have a reputation for-"

"You use your words as your weapon of choice," he interrupted her to complete his own thought. "But for what benefit, if you cannot exercise restraint?"

"Excuse me?"

"You can't control your mouth, your temper, your emotions—and, quite frankly-"

"Are you threatened by me?" She inquired in offense as she knew such statements of control would have never been made of her male counterparts.

He snickered at the suggestion. "Not in the least. But what I am is disgusted. Those characteristics are unbecoming of a woman of your caliber."

"Of my caliber?"

"Of position…of distinction…of power."

She looked upon his unemotional face and then peered into his impassive eyes. They were both dark, cold, and rigid. His appearance in addition to his misogynistic tone unveiled that he was neither concerned by the wrong she had committed against him nor unmoved by her attempts to make things right. Instead, he was fretful of the power position she possessed both in and out of the courtroom, and such agitation made him dangerous—possibly sociopathic. Because of her many years in the legal profession, Alexandre could easily discern that people of his kind were liable to cause harm either to themselves, or worse, cause harm to others. A man of his caliber did not seek justice; he sought revenge.

After clearing her throat, Alexandre announced, "…I have a class to teach…Take care…"

*** *** ***

After Cynthia pulled her blond hair over her right shoulder in annoyance, she placed her hands on her waist. She contemplated for a moment then asked aloud to herself, "You've got to be kidding me. It was just here…Where is it?"

She quickly scanned the desk again to see several expanding files, manila folders, and voluminous documents. She had thumbed through them all and had not succeeded in locating what she was in search for.

"It has got to be here somewhere—a case file does not grow legs and walk," Cynthia self-encouraged as she began to pull open the desk's drawers and rummage through them. Nothing.

She pivoted to the credenza's drawers and fumbled through its contents until she reached the bottom drawer. It would not immediately open. Stubbornly, Cynthia employed her might in hopes of shaking the drawer open. "Come on, come on."

"What the hell are you doing, Cynthia?" Alexandre asked after she widened the door to her chambers.

Cynthia jumped and held her right hand above her left breast. Her heart raced after being startled by the unexpected voice. "Your Honor, I thought you had left for the evening."

"I did," she replied, walking further into the dimly lit room. "But then I got all the way to the garage and realized that I had forgotten my keys."

Cynthia quickly scanned the desk and discovered the keys on the corner of it. She retrieved and extended them to Alexandre. "Here they are," nervously spoke.

Alexandre walked further into the room, gathered the keys from Cynthia's trembling palm, and placed them in her leather tote.

Peering deep into her green eyes, Alexandre spoke, "You still have not answered my question. What the hell are you doing?"

"I, uh, I…" Cynthia stammered, cleared her throat, and attempted to respond, "I was looking…"

"Looking for what?" Alexandre hotly inquired, growing more suspicious of her intentions as she struggled to reply. Alexandre began to reflect on what the private investigator had unveiled to her:

"She comes from a long line of right-winged politicians and litigators…I am talking about the epitome of conservativism—pro-life, pro-second amendment, pro-capital punishment…It's odd that a woman of that caliber, of such pedigree, would accept a clerkship with the most compassionate judge in all of North Carolina."

"Your Honor, it's not what you think."

"You don't know what I am thinking."

"You're right, I…I don't. I-I was just looking-"

"For more information to sell to the press?"

"What? No. I…I would never breach confidentiality or-or compromise your trust."

"Not even for your family?"

Though perplexed by the question, Cynthia replied, "No, of course, not."

"You're lying."

Taken aback by the accusation, Cynthia refuted, "No, Your Honor, I am not."

"Yes, you are." Alexandre huffed in despair at how grossly mistaken she was concerning many things. "I speculated that the threats, the leaks, the attacks all came from within these walls. I just never imagined that the perpetrator would be someone this close to me. How could you, Cynthia?...I trusted you. I went as far as developing a personal interest in cultivating you."

"Your Honor, you are gravely mistaken. We may not have always agreed, but I have always been on your side. I went against what I believed to defend you on multiple occasions."

Alexandre shook her head in disbelief and then confessed, "I've seen your sign-ins at the detention center. You've become quite the regular there."

"...You've...you've been following me?"

"No, I haven't been following you, Cynthia. But what I have been doing is following my suspensions and obtaining answers when it is prudent for me to do so."

Cynthia struggled with the swell in her throat as she considered the accusations against her. Though she believed them to be unjust and unfounded, she swallowed hard her pride and the desire to offer a spirited contest. Instead, Cynthia calmly elucidated, "...Like you, I volunteer at the detention center as well." She peered deep into Alexandre's eyes and confessed, "In fact, it was your leadership that encouraged me to do so."

Keeping her gaze, Alexandre deliberated all that she shared. All things considered, there was a possibility of truthfulness in Cynthia's narrative, and it echoed loudly in her ear. Unfortunately, however, the case that the private investigator presented and the facts that he disclosed seemingly resounded louder.

Alexandre raised her shoulders in a cavalier manner and responded, "I do not believe you."

Cynthia panted in a way as if the oxygen was bludgeoned from her body. "...B-but...but why?"

"Because a private investigator warned me about you. I did not heed his admonition and I see now that it was to my own detriment...Two children are now dead because of you and I am the whipping boy for it all."

The law clerk twisted her face at Alexandre's egregious summation. Despite the many falsehoods embedded in it, Cynthia opted to disregard the inaccurate assumption of her involvement in the youths' deaths so that she could focus on Alexandre's admission of her investigation.

"Y-you had a private investigator look into me?"

"Get out," Alexandre demanded in lieu of responding to her question.

"Your Hon-"

"Get out now and do not return. You're fired, Cynthia. You're fired and I am reporting you as a viable lead to the authorities, and I will see to it that you are disbarred."

Cynthia gasped at the command as well as the threats, and frantically contemplated a well-composed explanation that would alter Alexandre's decision. As she slowly removed that lanyard from around her neck, she finally offered in a confession, "...I was only looking for the Johnson file. I recalled his mother was out of work and his father left some time ago."

After she removed her credentials from the clip and began to maneuver the office keys from the metal ring, Cynthia added, "My uncle is now on the hiring board of the sports complex. I was going to funnel her contact information to him."

Alexandre was astounded by the unscrupulous, yet compassionate gesture. Throughout her few years on the bench, many have had entered her chambers demanding something; very few have had entered offering much of anything. Indeed, it was refreshing to have a young member of the court system with the desire to give back. Nevertheless, Alexandre's suspicions would not permit her to rescind the threat of termination. In her new position between a rock and a hard place, Alexandre could not afford to equivocate.

"Please leave," Alexandre uttered.

Cynthia placed the items on the desk and began to step from behind it. When she was at Alexandre's side, she stood shoulder-to-shoulder and spoke, "I appreciate the opportunity to have worked with you. I learned more from you these past several months than I did in the three years of law school."

Alexandre held her breath to refrain from speaking.

Cynthia lowered her head in disappointment when Alexandre spoke nothing in return.

"Take care of yourself, Your Honor," she genuinely spoke, knowing that she was not the culprit that Alexandre assumed her to be.

Cynthia then existed the chambers, closing the door behind her.

*** *** ***

Alexandre held Seanna in an embrace as close as her pregnancy bulge would allow. In that moment, her warmth was more than a greeting from a best friend, but comfort from a trusted confidante.

Once she released her, Alexandre spoke, "Thank you so much for meeting me for lunch."

Seanna nodded. "Of course. You gave the impression that it was dire." She peered deep into friend's eyes for confirmation. When none was found, she added, "But, then again, everything with you is dire."

Alexandre rolled her eyes at the quip.

To stave off offense, Seanna chuckled then added, "I'm just kidding…We needed to meet. It's long overdue considering the fair amount of craziness the new year has ushered in."

"Tell me about it," Alexandre concurred. Afterwards, she gestured with her hand toward the glass entrance and inquired, "Shall we go in? Hopefully, we still have our reservation considering the length of time I had you waiting."

Seanna shrugged off her subtle apology, opened the door, and allowed her to enter first. "We are all accustomed to your tardiness. It's the burden we bear for being acquainted with someone in such a high-powered position."

Alexandre snickered at her sarcasm as she greeted and then followed the hostess who escorted them to their table.

"So," Seanna began after they removed their winter layers and settled in their seats at the linen covered table. "What is so unurgent that required this urgent lunch?"

"Well…" Alexandre started then paused to reflect on all that had transpired since they last saw each other Christmas Day.

Following that holiday, their conversations have had been sparce—undoubtedly, the result, in part, of them still trying to recover from their irreconcilable differences.

Detecting her longtime comrade's apprehension, Seanna searched Alexandre's visage. Her forlorn eyes yearned to convey a message that her quivering lips were too reticent to do so. "…What? What is it, Alex? Is it Jay?"

Alexandre shook her head, cleared her throat, and responded, "No…"

Lowering her gaze, Alexandre allowed a moment to past so that she could consider the cross she needed the most help bearing. When her courage set, she met Seanna's glare once more and confessed, "…It's Jacob. He—well, he and I are moving forward with the annulment."

Seanna exhaled audibly her heartache and disappointment; her shoulders sunk in the deflation. In spite of her understanding of Jacob's desire to terminate the marriage, Seanna had held out hope that he would reconsider reconciliation. Similar to Alexandre and Jaamyas, Jacob was family to her, too. To lose any family was painful, but to lose the family you get to choose was heart wrenching.

"How are you feeling? Are you okay?"

Before Alexandre could answer the questions, Seanna asked, "Is this something that you really want?"

Alexandre parted her lips to respond, but a suited attendant arrived to fill their water glasses. In the time that it took him to retrieve their drink and food orders, she deliberated her true thoughts and genuine emotions.

"…I'm okay…Honestly, I am at peace with it now. In the beginning, I was very selfish in wanting him to stay, but, now…now, I realize he doesn't deserve this. He is a good man and deserves so much better."

"Better than you?" Seanna abruptly questioned in unbelief. She took in the beautiful woman across from her and saw a warm, benevolent, and compassionate soul; a woman of drive, passion, and many accolades.

"There is no better than you, Alexandre, because you are the best. It just so happens that this decision was determined to be the better for everyone—not just Jacob."

"…Thank you," Alexandre uttered in response as she feebly smiled. While she appreciated the support of the friend who would defend her to the death, she was not in a position to believe all that Seanna spoke.

"So," Seanna spoke, interrupting the brief silence. "You and Lance are going to revive what you had 13 years ago?"

Alexandre did not reply.

"Is that even possible? Is he even the same person?"

Alexandre shrugged. "I don't know…It's so unsettling for me because I don't know the answer to those or any other questions." She respired and candidly shared, "…And, to be frank, Sea, I am scared shitless."

Seanna burst into a heartfelt laughter. "…Yeah, I bet. Operating within so many unknowns is out of character for you."

"Shut up," Alexandre retorted, turning her eyes upward and chuckling herself.

Once their laughter calmed, Seanna asked, "Why Lance?"

"I'm sorry?"

"Why are you choosing Lance?" Seanna restated. "Is it for Jay?"

Alexandre lowered her gaze as she pondered the question and her reply to it. Undoubtedly, Seanna knew her too well as she was not a woman to permit a decision to made without her casting a vote. To the contrary, in all decisions, Alexandre was a woman who always possessed the controlling vote.

"No, surprisingly, no. I can honestly say that I am doing this for me." She met Seanna eyes and confessed, "I love him, Sea. I always have—I never stopped."

Seanna tried to comprehend from where her friend's thoughts and emotions derive, but she struggled with the logic of both. "I'm sorry, Alex. I just don't get it—I don't. I mean, like your father, I will never forgive him for what he did 13 years ago."

Stretching her lips into a bogus grin, Alexandre acknowledged, "I know. You are and will forever will be Team Alex and I love you for it, but…"

"But you need my acceptance of this?"

"I don't need it, but I would like to have it."

Seanna disregarded her correction and asked, "How is my god-son coping with all of this?"

"We haven't talked much about it. But you know Jay, he is a go-with-the-flow type of kid. For the time being, he spends time with both Jacob and Lance."

"And do you?"

"And do I what?"

Seanna rolled her eyes at Alexandre's propensity to circumvent questions that she had no desire to answer. "Do you spend time with both Jacob and Lance…I'm curious to know more of the former than the latter."

Alexandre breathed deeply as she contemplated the best way to respond to her inquiry. "…Yes, in the beginning and…and, truthfully, I would still like to, but…"

"But what?"

"But, ultimately, it's not my decision to make. It's Jacob's and I can't make the decision for him—especially if this baby is not his, and if he decides to start a life with someone else."

Reflecting on all that Alexandre was compromising for the sake of something that had no guarantee of materializing, Seanna blatantly asked, "What is it about Lance, Alex?"

When she parted her lips to response, but no words where uttered, Seanna pressed, "Please don't say love because it has to be something so much more than that; especially since you are willing to throw away all that you accomplished the last four years with Jacob…So, what is it? Help me understand—make it make sense to me."

Alexandre inhaled deeply and exhaled loudly while she thought of a response that would accurately express all that she felt. "…With Jacob, I am the most important person in the room. With Lance, I was with the smartest person in the room."

Seanna started blankly at her with confusion.

"Lance has the ability to navigate any situation," Alexandre elucidated. "He was always very skillful in that regard and it makes him tactical yet spontaneous—so full of adventure…With him, I am at ease. With him, I know everything and everyone is taken care of."

Seanna looked upon her with perplexed and sorrowful eyes. She could not comprehend why Alexandre would opt for a brilliant leader with diffused loyalty than a devoted partner committed solely to her.

"You are a mother with a career, Alex," Seanna reminded her. "You need stability; you need the assurance that your husband is going to always be there…" She reached for Alexandre's hand that rested on the table. "You need to be the most important person in the room today, tomorrow, and forever."

Before Alexandre could contest her friend's subtle recommendation to remain in her marriage with Jacob, their hot plates arrived. Seanna released her hand so that her dish could be placed in front of her. After Alexandre received hers, they rejoined hands, recited grace, and then enjoyed their meal as they engaged in a lighthearted conversation concerning their children's spring break.

"I'm so glad that there is nothing on the docket for the remainder of the day," Alexandre commented, chewing then swallowing the last morceau of food. "I'm so exhausted."

"Then just go home," Seanna recommended while completing the tip and signing the receipt for both their meals.

"I can't. I have a few status calls."

Seanna removed her napkin from her lap, dabbed at the corners of her mouth, then placed it next to her empty plate. "I swear you work too hard, Alex."

Alexandre chuckled. "And I swear you would not say that to me if I were a man."

"Damn right," she retorted with authority, "because that is their charge for sin, not ours." Seanna stood and then lowered her gaze to the swell of Alexandre's womb. "You will receive your just due in a few months."

Alexandre rolled her eyes at the reminder of her impending labor pains. "Well, not all of us can be a successful real estate agent with a prominent investment banking husband," she jested, accepting her friend's hand for assistance to rise from her seat.

Donning her layers again for the frigid temps outdoors, Seanna responded, "Hard work is not a stranger to any of us, and you of all people know that all that glitters is not gold."

"But it is oh so pretty to look at," they spoke in unison, laughing as they walked towards the exit.

"So, when are you taking maternity leave?"

Alexandre shrugged. "I don't know. I would prefer to work up to my due date in late May, early June, but I am certain that is not going to happen."

"Alex, please," Seanna uttered with concern. "Do not do that. It's not safe for you or the baby."

Ignoring the recommendation, Alexandre stepped out into the cold air and inquired, "Where did you park?"

Seanna pointed to her silver sedan a few steps from the restaurant's entrance. "You?"

Alexandre shoved her gloved hands into the pockets of her long, wool coat and nodded toward her vehicle farther away. "Across the street."

"Okay, I will walk you to your car."

"No, don't. It's fine."

"I know it's fine—that's why I am doing it."

Allowing no contest, Seanna slipped her hand into the fold of Alexandre's elbow to walk linked-arms to the crosswalk.

"So, I was thinking that after the baby is born-" Alexandre began.

They smiled and nodded in appreciation at the driver who stopped his vehicle in adherence to the pedestrian crossing law.

"After the baby is born that, this summer, we-"

"WATCH OUT!" Seanna exclaimed, unlinking their arms.

As they cleared the first car, a second vehicle drove towards them with excessive speed. Seanna instantaneously recoiled onto the hood of the first car, yanking Alexandre along with her.

Warm air was forced from her lungs when Alexandre's back slammed against the driver's door. She hunched in agony, panting in horrid disbelief.

"Are you okay?!" The driver frantically questioned. He cautiously opened his door and went to Seanna's aid first. "Are you okay?"

Seanna nodded. She accepted his hand and slowly rose from her supine position on his hood. "…I'm fine…"

They journeyed slowly to the location that Alexandre stood. Seeing the look of distress and fear on her friend's visage, Seanna threw her weight onto Alexandre for a firm embrace.

"Thank God you're okay," Seanna breathed.

Alexandre nodded and confirmed, "I'm okay…Are you okay?"

Overwhelmed with emotions, Seanna could not respond. Though she considered herself to be a great friend, Alexandre was an extraordinary one. The thought of losing her primary confidante—the one who kept her secrets, supported her aspirations, and loved her despite her many shortcomings, wrenched her heart. Seanna burst into a solemn cry and squeezed Alexandre's layered body tighter.

"…I'm okay," Alexandre muttered, attempting to calm her. "…I'm okay."

A crowd began to encircle them and inquiries about their safety followed. Silencing their cries, but not loosening their hold, Alexandre and Seanna assured the throng of their wellbeing.

"I can't believe they didn't stop," a witness spoke in astonishment. "…I mean, what the hell? It's a pedestrian crosswalk in a strip mall for Pete's sake.

"Who speeds through a fucking pedestrian crosswalk like that?" A second spectator angrily questioned. "This is some bullshit."

"I agree. People need to slow-the-fuck down. Someone could have gotten killed…Did anyone capture the plates?"

"I did—I took a photo, but the reflective plate covers distort the picture. It's still a good photo of the car that I can give the police," a voice from the crowd responded. "I've called them and they're on their way."

Alexandre quieted her suspicions as she suppressed the urge to comment on what she believed to be a meticulously timed event crafted by one who was enraged. Because she had been the recipient of multiple expressions of hate, Alexandre could not dismiss the near-death occurrence as happenstance. However, unlike the past several months in which Alexandre speculated that her nemesis merely wanted to destroy her, she was now convinced that her adversary wanted her dead.

Following the reflection of past omens, thoughts of future demises emerged and they agonized Alexandre for several reasons. Among her greatest concerns was the belief that her son would soon be a motherless-child and her daughter would experience death before her first breath. Compounding Alexandre's misery were considerations of Seanna, who was frightfully caught in the crossfire of an instance that could have left her children motherless as well.

At that moment, Jacob's truth expressed during their earlier spat began to clearly resound in Alexandre's ears, *"Everyone connected to you pays."*

*** *THIRTEEN* ***

"Judge Denton-Hall, what a pleasure to see you," the psychiatrist greeted, rising from her desk after Alexandre walked into her office.

"Likewise, Dr. Ahmed."

"Almost six months this time…"

Alexandre offered no reply to her observation despite knowing that her physician was seeking one.

"…I am seeing you less and less; even your check-in calls are becoming more infrequent."

After she settled into the cushion of the loveseat, Alexandre shrugged her shoulders with little care. She had far more to contend with than irregular therapy sessions. "I've been busy…I'm sorry."

"No need to be apologetic," Dr. Ahmed encouraged, walking towards her. "I understand the demands on your time. I'm just elated that you finally made time for your mental and emotional wellness, *and* that you kept the appointment."

Uncertain of whether her final comment was a slight or a jest, Alexandre made an attempt to explain the after-hours visit,

"Things are really hectic right now. I could not commit to anything before seven."

Dr. Ahmed uncovered her head, folded her hijab, and placed it on the arm of her sofa. She then lowered herself into the cushioned sofa seat in front of Alexandre.

"It's fine, Alex," she softly spoke, reaching to touch her knee in solidarity. "Really, it's fine."

Alexandre stretched her lips into a phony grin and offered, "Thank you."

"No need to thank me," Dr. Ahmed said as she reclined in her seat. "It's what your excellent insurance is paying me for."

Alexandre rolled her eyes, shook her head, and chuckled at her wit.

"No, but, seriously," Dr. Ahmed began to elucidate, "I had paperwork to complete and waiting for you here ensured that I would get it done. Things are impossible at home with four children and a husband demanding my time and attention."

"So, you were here waiting alone?"

Dismissing Alexandre's concern, she raised her shoulders. "Only for the last hour. My assistant left around six…The building has amazing security. So, I feel safe."

Realizing that she was projecting her own anxieties and fears onto her physician, Alexandre merely nodded. She lowered her lids over her eyes and began to exercise her square breathing technique to a calm her anxiousness.

Dr. Ahmed unhurriedly watched as her patient inhaled for four seconds, held the air in her lungs for four seconds, and then exhaled for four seconds. When she finally lifted her lids, Dr. Ahmed scrutinized Alexandre's appearance. Though her skin radiated, her eyes were distressed. As her longtime therapist, she surmised that Alexandre was maintaining a healthy diet, but not a balanced circadian rhythm.

"You're not sleeping much. Are you?"

"I sleep when I can, and when I can, I sleep well."

Dr. Ahmed nodded in acknowledgment. Following, she inquired, "So, what's the reason for your visit tonight? What is it that you would like to work through."

Alexandre contemplated the question. As she reminisced on all that transpired since her last visit and everything she could gripe about, she was careful to avoid Dr. Ahmed's stare. Though the physician's persona was compassionate and understanding, it offered no forgiveness for self-pity.

Calmly waiting in silence for a reaction, Dr. Ahmed's gaze broadened to Alexandre's disposition. She not only appeared fatigued, but stressed and disheveled as well—all characteristics that were uncommon for her.

After clearing her throat to break the silence, Dr. Ahmed confessed, "I read in the paper that a lawsuit has recently been filed against you."

She awaited an acknowledgement from Alexandre. When none was given, Dr. Ahmed continued, "Some have loosely compared you to the juvenile court judges in Pennsylvania who were involved in the kids-for-cash scandal."

Alexandre rolled her eyes and shook her head as she huffed in repugnance. She was, first, disgusted by the comparison and, second, the tragedy. In the state that was home to the "city of brotherly love", Alexandre's distant colleagues received kickbacks for sentencing juveniles to for-profit jails. Thoughts of the corruption that disgraced the honorable bench enraged Alexandre again and her face began to tighten and flush.

"What are you thinking? How are you feeling in this moment?" Dr. Ahmed probed.

Alexandre shrugged as she considered the millions of dollars ordered to be paid in restitution and how it paled in comparison to the millions of lives devastated by the mercenary deeds. In that moment, what she thought was that the court officials were grossly under-sanctioned; what she felt was that they deserved more—they deserved prison.

"…I suppose as anyone else knowledgeable of this miscarriage of justice would…" Alexandre initially responded in the most politically correct form that she could offer.

Dr. Ahmed contorted her face at her answer. She knew Alexandre too well to accept it as her genuine reaction.

"Honestly, Alex. I want you to reply honestly."

Alexandre pondered more the question. After examining her honest thoughts and true feelings, she admitted, "...I'm furious—pissed as hell, actually..." Her voice trailed off as she considered the inquiry in greater depth. "...But, honestly and somewhat selfishly, I think I am a little more incensed by the newsprint comparison."

"And why is that?"

"Because I am nothing like them," Alexandre retorted, agitated by the rhetorical question.

Dr. Ahmed nodded in concurrence. "Alex, I know you; and I know that this is not who you are." She leaned forward and placed her cool hand on the warm one that Alexandre rested on her knee. "Unequivocally, I believe that you have no part of any malfeasance, professional or personal."

When nothing was said in response to her message, the psychiatrist gave her patient's hand a gentle squeeze. She had hoped that the gesture would serve as a reminder that she was not her enemy.

"I am more than confident that you will be vindicated, Alex. You're a good person and justice always prevails for the good."

Alexandre parted her lips to rejoin, but immediately reconsidered the myriad thoughts she wanted to convey. Though they were similarly situated in many respects, she believed that their differing ancestorial ties separated them—for several hundreds of years Alexandre's lineage dwelled in a nation in which justice was not only blind, but was blinded by falsehoods.

Keeping her therapist's gaze, Alexandre, in lieu of speaking, attempted to ascertain whether the words Dr. Ahmed spoke were done so in an effort to persuade her or convince herself. Though truer words had never been spoken, Alexandre could tell no difference from friend and foe in that current plight. And throughout her legal tenure she has been taught that, though trust could be earned, loyalty was inevitably fragile.

When Dr. Ahmed's intent could not be determined, Alexandre slowly slid her hand from beneath hers, cleared her throat, and continued to hold her silence.

Dr. Ahmed reclined back to her original seated position and watched Alexandre sit quietly. After allowing a brief moment to past, she offered, "…We can talk more about this if you want."

"Talk about what? I mean, what is there left to talk about?" Alexandre questioned in increasing aggravation. "It's all there in black and white—even what the public is feeling is right there," she gestured with her hand toward the folded publication on the end table, "literally in black and white."

Dr. Ahmed pivoted her head in the direction of Alexandre's gesture. She retrieved the newspaper and inquired, "But is the newspaper *reporting* a feeling in the public or *creating* a feeling in the public?"

While she waited for Alexandre's response, Dr. Ahmed tossed the subscription in the nearby waste basket that was still filled with the facial tissues of her prior patient. When her current patient gave no response, she answered the question herself, "Because I am of the mind and opinion that the vast majority of the public feels that you are doing the very best you can with the resources that you have. You have an immensely tough job, Alex—one that requires you to make tough decisions every day."

Alexandre raised her shoulders in nonchalance. She refused to accept the generous rationalization that Dr. Ahmed offered because, throughout Alexandre's tutelage, she had learned that the head was heaviest of the one that wore the crown. In additional to this realization, Alexandre learned that success was always a team effort to be celebrated, but failure was solely a leader's cross to bear alone. Without a doubt, Alexandre's head was heavy and she was alone.

"…It is a tremendous amount of power that can either develop a life or destroy one," Alexandre finally stated, acknowledging that no matter the confines she had to work within, she would be faulted for every poor outcome of her judgments.

"Exactly," the psychiatrist agreed. "And I don't envy you, Alexandre, I really don't."

When Alexandre said nothing more, Dr. Ahmed suggested, "So, let's transition to that. Let's talk about how the pressures of work make you feel."

Alexandre shook her head and abruptly dissented, "I don't want to talk about work."

Taken aback by the unexpected opposition, Dr. Ahmed inhaled deeply then calmly conceded, "...Okay...Well, what do you want to talk about?"

Alexandre brought her hand to her neck and began to race the diamond pendant on its chain as she offered no answer.

"Alex, obviously you want to talk. Something has brought you to my office tonight and I cannot help you unless you tell me what-"

"I'm pregnant."

Dr. Ahmed lowered her gaze to swell of her womb that she did not notice before. Until that moment, it was concealed well by the layers Alexandre wore.

Confused by the revelation, the physician thought for a moment and then attempted to clarify by asking, "But I thought you were waiting a year? That you wanted you, Jacob, and Jaamyas to acclimate as a family first."

"That was the plan."

"Then what changed your mind."

Alexandre exhaled loudly and smugly retorted, "Several missed pills and a positive pregnancy test."

Dr. Ahmed discerned from Alexandre's tone that she was in need of a reprieve from the badgering. So, she halted her probing questions and afforded Alexandre the time she needed to recover.

As they sat in silence, the psychiatrist watched as her patient lowered her hand at her neck. She then began to use the thumb of her left hand to vigorously rub the palmar creases of her right.

"...I'm sorry," Alexandre finally stated with genuine contrition. "...I have not been myself lately."

"It's fine, Alex."

"No, it's not fine, Priya," Alexandre forcefully acknowledged, refusing to accept an excuse for her discourteous behavior. "My responses have been curt and gratuitous...Perhaps tonight wasn't the best time for a session."

Dr. Ahmed smiled sweetly. "Tonight is the perfect time for a session. It is what works for you and, look, you are here—you didn't cancel."

Alexandre smiled feebly, but spoke nothing in reply to her observation.

"...So, you're pregnant—not in the time that you wanted, but it is ultimately what you wanted. So, congratulations to both you and Jacob. I wish you both-"

"It's not his child."

When Alexandre watched her therapist squint her eyes in confusion, she clarified, "I mean, it could be I am just not certain."

Perplexed, Dr. Ahmed did not mince words by asking, "Who is the other possibility?"

Alexandre turned from her gaze without providing an answer to her question.

"...Were you sexually assaulted?" The psychiatrist gingerly probed.

Alexandre shook her head.

After eliminating the possibility of forcible rape, Dr. Ahmed deduced, "...An affair?"

She watched Alexandre lower her head as she hesitated to respond. By the distress in her patient's countenance and uncomfortable shift in her weight, Dr. Ahmed was able to determine the answer to her inquiry. Exhaling in disbelief, she lowly uttered, "Oh, Alex...What happened? You just married." She leaned her body forward to capture Alexandre's eyes. "Were you—are you unhappy in the marriage?"

Alexandre quickly wiped the tears from her eyes, ignoring the box of tissues on the end table next to her. "...No...No, Jacob is great, the marriage is great. I...I just made a huge mistake, that's all."

When the tears incessantly fell from her eyes, Alexandre relented and pulled a few tissues from the box. As she dabbed at her face, she spoke, "I did not come here tonight to be reminded of it or to be judged for it."

"You're right, Alex, but I'm not judging. I'm sorry if I gave you the impression that I am...It's just..." Still baffled by the confession, Dr. Ahmed explained, "It's just that that type of behavior is so out of character for you, Alexandre. You're not one to lose control, bend the rules...break a vow..."

Alexandre spoke no words in response.

"…Please talk to me. I cannot help you or guide you through this if you do not talk to me…What's really going on with you, Alex?"

When Alexandre failed to rejoin, Dr. Ahmed took in a deep breath in hopes that it would provide the wherewithal needed to assist her conveniently mute patient. After swallowing her growing exasperation, she asked, "Have you at least told Jacob about the affair and the uncertainty of the child's paternity?"

"Yes, I have."

"And what about the other potential father? Have you told him?"

"Yes."

"And Jaamyas?"

"He knows as well—everything."

Alexandre watched her psychiatrist move her long tresses to one shoulder as she reached for the notebook and pen that were placed on the table next to her. After penning a few notes, Dr. Ahmed asked her, "So, which of these elements do you want to confront tonight—the husband, the son, or the lover?"

Taking a moment to ponder the question, Alexandre inhaled deeply through her nostrils and exhaled audibly through her mouth. She then replied, "…Let's start with the lover…Afterall, it all started with him almost twenty years ago."

Dr. Ahmed ceased writing and lifted her eyes to meet Alexandre's. "What are you talking about?"

"I'm talking about Lance."

Dr. Ahmed respired loudly. "Alex-"

"He is not dead, Priya."

"Alex, I know that it is hard to lose someone you love and, in your case, it's even harder to first be abandoned by the one you lost. But if you are fixated on regressing by returning to old demons, then I am not certain that I can help you any longer, especially not with the use of talk therapy. I-"

"I'm not regressing, I am professing," Alexandre spoke, raising her voice over hers. "Lance is alive and he is potentially the father of my child."

Immediately, the office fell uncomfortably silent. Thick in the air were tension and incredulity.

When the agitation between them calmed, Alexandre expounded, "He was a prisoner of war…The entire time I was led and convinced to believe that he was dead, but he wasn't…He was alive. He was alive the entire time, Priya."

Flabbergasted, Dr. Ahmed absent-mindedly released her pen onto the notebook. When it rolled and fell to the hardwood floor, she did not bother to retrieve it. She cleared her throat to offset the awkward silence. "…Something tells me that this is not an illusion."

"It's not. I wish it were, but it's not…At least if it were, then I would not be caught between two marriages and an unwanted pregnancy. One with questionable paternity at that."

After clearing her throat another time, Dr. Ahmed stated, "Okay, well, let's start-"

Alexandre shook her head as she rose to her feet. "No, I'm done talking. I don't want to talk about this anymore."

"Alexandre," the psychiatrist spoke rising to her feet as well. "You cannot employ avoidance as a coping mechanism. You will-"

"I don't want to talk about this anymore," Alexandre restated with an elevated tone. She peered deep into the physician's eyes and emphasized, "Anymore."

"Fair enough," Dr. Ahmed conceded, concerned that too much pressure would cause another long-term absence. "…I suspect you will return whenever you are ready to talk again."

Alexandre shook her head. It was time to severe ties with the woman that knew far too much, and knew her far too well. "Not likely," she spoke in a tone that conveyed her desire to finally end the doctor-patient relationship. "…Thank you for everything, Dr. Ahmed."

After tossing her soiled tissues in the waste basket, she pivoted on her heels to exit the office.

"Alex," Dr. Ahmed called after her, dropping her notebook in the seat she once occupied. "Alex, wait."

She followed Alexandre to the dimly lit and desolate lobby. "Alex, please."

Alexandre ignored the calling of her name as she increased her steps to the double glass doors that exited to the elevator bay. Once in the hallway, she frantically pushed the plastic button to call for an elevator. When the doors opened, she immediately stepped in just as the custodian with a large cart was attempting to hastily step out.

Startled by the unexpected occupant, Alexandre recoiled and her stiletto slipped from beneath her. She fell backwards to the cold, linoleum floor—her lower back making contact with the hard surface first, followed by her shoulders, then head.

The custodian yanked off her headphones and rushed to Alexandre's side. "I'm so sorry…I'm so sorry. I didn't see you. I'm so sorry." She looked up at Dr. Ahmed, who hurried to offer assistance, and explained to her, "I didn't see her."

Kneeling next to Alexandre, Dr. Ahmed asked, "Are you okay?"

Alexandre grimaced at the pain in her lower back as she tried to conceal her discomfort. "It's okay. I'm fine." She took the hand that was extended to her and began the slow rise to her feet. When the agony quickly traveled to her womb, she winced—releasing a low cry.

Dr. Ahmed firmly held Alexandre's hand as she squeezed it. She used additional might to keep Alexandre from falling to the floor another time when she hunched in anguish.

"Alexandre, are you okay? Is it the baby? Should I call for help?"

After shaking her head, Alexandre breathed through the pain until it faded. "I'm okay," she finally responded. "Just startled, but I'm okay."

"Are you sure?"

Alexandre nodded.

"I'm so sorry. I'm so very sorry," the custodian softly spoke.

"It's fine, I'm fine," Alexandre assured. She then released her physician's hand, stepped to the wall, and called for another elevator so that she could depart the building.

*** *** ***

Alexandre accepted the tissues the nurse proffered and wiped the gel from her swollen abdomen. She then slowly rose to a seated position on the examination table.

"Are you sure don't want a sonogram?"

After nodding, Alexandre replied, "I'm sure."

"Okay." The nurse penned a few notes in Alexandre's medical file then closed it. "I will let the doctor know that you are ready for her."

"Thank you." Alexandre watched her stand from the rolling stool, adjust her printed scrubs, and walk out of the examination room with the manila folder in her hand.

Once the door was closed, Alexandre sat in the chilled room in silence, fighting to push the recent sight of the baby out of her mind and the heartbeat from her ears. Torn by the need to be detached from and the desire to bond with the life growing in her, tears swelled in her eyes. She quickly wiped them away when the door swung open after a rapid knock.

"Alex, so glad that you could finally fit your visit into your schedule."

Alexandre exhaled loudly, unmoved by her judgmental tone. "Hello, Dr. Ming."

The slender Asian physician ignored the greeting as she lowered herself onto the stool the nurse once occupied. She removed the pen from the pocket of her white coat and scribbled notes in the medical file.

"The baby's heartbeat is strong and her development looks good."

Exhaling in relief while giving a silent prayer of thanks, Alexandre surprised herself with the reaction to the positive report. On a level not yet known to her, she did appreciate the unexpected blessing. "...So, the spotting..."

"Is not uncommon and not yet perilous, and may just be cervical irritation or the result of rigorous activity, heavy lifting, or a fall. In any event, it is something that I want you to take seriously."

"So, the baby is fine?" Alexandre inquired, summing the physician's response.

"Yes, Alex, the baby is fine—no abnormalities or placental abruption; everything is fine."

Alexandre sighed in relief once more.

"But you're not, Alex."

"I'm not what?"

"You're not fine."

"What do you mean? What does that even mean?"

"It means that your numbers are not where I would like them to be," Dr. Ming responded, concerned that Alexandre was not heeding her earlier advice and subtle warnings.

Alexandre sneered. "Then that will make them parallel with everything else in my life."

"I'm being serious, Alex."

"As am I."

Using the rubber heels of her leather flats, Dr. Ming rolled herself in front of Alexandre so that their eyes could meet. She then admonished, "You could lose this baby, Alex, and any chance of having another."

The warmth in the room grew in conjunction with the silence as the physician's comments resonated with Alexandre. While she considered how her home, career, and life were in turmoil, Alexandre also agonized at the thought of another dependent vying for her attention. Undoubtedly, Lance's baby…no—Jacob's baby…wait—her baby…the fetus growing in her womb was inevitably compounding her challenges and complicating her life.

Nevertheless, despite her earnest desire for matters returning to the way they were prior to Lance's arrival, Alexandre appreciated the hope that accompanied new beginnings. Thoughts of possibly carrying, delivering, and nurturing Jacob's child provided her with an unexpected surge of hope in their restoration beyond their congenial acts exercised in the best interest of Jaamyas.

"What can I do?" Alexandre finally asked after she exhaled aloud. Regardless of the uncertainties concerning her tumultuous marriage and various misgivings with the unplanned pregnancy, she knew unequivocally that she did not want her infant to be aborted.

"Reduce your stress, get some rest, take a long vacation—get off your feet."

Alexandre laughed at the seemingly simple suggestions. "I suppose I can do all of that."

"Good-"

"In my next life."

After closing the manila folder, Dr. Ming huffed in concession and finally advised, "Then let's just schedule a cesarean because I don't foresee you carrying this baby to term. It's too risky for you to attempt it—for the both of you, it's just far too risky."

Alexandre shook her head in dissent. "Dr. Ming, I appreciate your medical opinion. I really do, but I can't—I won't be coaxed into something I don't feel comfortable with. And you know I loathe the idea of being cut open."

"Yes, Alexandre, I know you have concerns with the anesthesia and post-op medications, and the harmful impacts they could possibly have on your baby, but-"

"Hold that thought," Alexandre requested when the phone in her leather handbag rang. She rose from the examination table and strode to the chair in the corner of the room. After her hand fumbled frantically in her bag, she retrieved the culprit of the noise and answered it.

"Hey, Jacob, thanks so much for calling me back. Can you give me a minute?" Alexandre muted the line before Jacob could reply, and then spoke to her physician, "I'm so sorry, but I've got to take this."

"Alex-" Dr. Ming protested, knowing that Alexandre's health and the health of her fetus could not be placed on hold.

Alexandre placed her handbag on her shoulder and stepped toward the door. "I know that your consultation is important, but so is this call. So, I really have to go." She opened the door and finally spoke, "I will schedule another appointment soon."

Unmuting the phone as she walked through the clinic to its exit, Alexandre apologized, "I'm so sorry about that, Jacob. I was in a middle of thing that I had to wrap."

"Do you need me to call back? Is everything okay?"

"No—yes—yes, everything is okay."

Hearing the distress in her voice, Jacob pressed, "Alex-"

"I promise, Jacob, everything is fine," Alexandre interrupted. She panted breathlessly as she walked briskly to her car in the frigid temperatures. She regretted her stubbornness in not putting on again her scarf and coat.

"Listen, as luck would have it, when I called you earlier about Jay you were the only one on the pick-up list available to get him. But not too long ago, I had received a request for a continuance. So, I am ending my workday early. I don't need you to pick him up after all. I can do it," she explained.

"Are you sure? I don't mind. I had planned to make it a night with him."

Noticing the white folded sheet pinned to her windshield, Alexandre uttered to herself, "Damnit…The last thing I need right now is parking ticket."

"Alex?"

"Yeah—no—yeah, I'm sure. I'm actually already en route," she prevaricated as she yanked the paper from underneath the wiper and quickly entered her vehicle. After unfolding the sheet, she realized it was not a ticket, but a handwritten note.

"Jacob, something just came up…I…I have to go." Alexandre ended the call before he had an opportunity to protest. Ignoring Jacob's call-backs, she read again and pondered the restatement of President Lincoln's infamous quote, *"Those that deny justice for others, do not deserve it for themselves."*

*** *FOURTEEN* ***

"Moooooom," Jaamyas sang another time as he walked down the hall and through the double doors of her bedroom.

"In here, Jay," she called out to him.

Jaamyas followed the sound of her voice into her master bathroom.

"Geeeez, Mom," he spoke in aggravation as he immediately covered his eyes and turned his back to her. She was soaking in a tub of bubbles. "You're naked."

Alexandre chuckled at his adolescent disgust. "You can't even see anything," she assured. "I'm completely covered in foam."

"It doesn't matter. It's the principle."

"You've seen me naked before, Jay."

"Not since I was a toddler," he reminded her. "Besides, I prefer the sight of God's glory of women *not* related to me."

Alexandre rolled her eyes at the quip she was confident he had learned from his school peers. "So much for the protection and insolation of the Christian private school," she mumbled.

After retrieving the bath towel placed on the side of the tub, Alexandre stretched it over her body, and then announced, "There—I'm covered."

Jaamyas gradually lowered his hand from his face and pivoted to confirm her proclamation. He then walked further into the room with a document and pen in his hands. "May I go with my class next month to Discovery Place?"

"Again, Jay? Didn't you go last year?"

"Last year was Discovery Place Nature. This year is Discovery Place Science," he elucidated.

She contemplated the school trip. Despite the number of chaperones that they will have on the visit to the museum, Alexandre felt unease with him being in the city with all the havoc that was transpiring. Moreover, as a lover of all things science, Jaamyas possessed a penchant for wandering off and exploring for extended periods of time with or without permission. Finally, to compound her worries, her son was socially dynamic—he was so from the moment he was born. Thus, despite her many teachings and admonishments, Jaamyas knew no strangers.

"Please, Mom," he beseeched, knowing that her silence was an indication that she was contemplating the most genial way to deny his request.

"I don't know, Jay...I have to think about it some more."

Alexandre's statement interpreted in the mind of the young teenager meant that her response was closer to a no than a yes. And any wayward behavior between now and the day of the event would be used as the cause to disallow his attendance. To circumvent the possibility, Jaamyas understood that he needed his mother to commit to an answer in his favor at that very moment.

"Pleeeeeeeez, Mooooooom," he begged in a song.

Alexandre ignored his pitchy plea.

"Pleeeeeeeez, Mooooooom," he sang again and then added, "I won't do any independent exploration—at least not without permission—I promise...Pleeeeeeeez."

Alexandre rolled her eyes. If she did not grant him permission now, it would be the longest thirty days of her life until she conceded.

"Fine, Jay. Just leave permission slip on the counter and I will sign it later."

He fought hard to suppress his excitement and simply smiled as he spoke, "Thanks, Mom."

Alexandre chuckled at his poor attempt to conceal his glee. Jaamyas's exuberant displays following the permission of "freedom" often made her feel as if she was not only an overprotective parent, but overbearing mother. Contemplating the fact that, for thirteen years, he was her only child and she was his only guardian, Alexandre felt vindicated of her parental stronghold.

"You're welcome, son," she finally uttered in return.

After Jaamyas did as he was instructed, he faced his mother to see her cupping water in her hands and pouring it over her covered swollen belly.

"Does it hurt?" He asked.

Alexandre looked up at him and asked in return, "Does what hurt?"

Jaamyas nodded toward her bulge and answered, "Being stretched out like that?"

She shook her head and replied, "It's uncomfortable sometimes, but it doesn't hurt…The real pain will come when she is ready to come out."

He nodded. "…What are we going to call her?"

She shrugged. "I don't know yet. What you do think we should call her?"

He shrugged. "I don't know."

"How about this, I come up with a name and you come up with a name and that will be her first and middle name?"

Jaamyas grinned at the idea. "Okay." He hesitated for a moment, but with courage asked, "What will be her last name?" When his mother did not immediately answer, he clarified by inquiring, "Will she be a Denton or a Hall?"

Alexandre turned from his gaze and released a long ignominious breath as she considered the question and how best to respond to it. Although much shame accompanied her chastening fall from grace, she was determined not to withhold the truth from her son. "…I don't know, Jay…We won't know until she gets here."

Jaamyas nodded, comprehending the unstated implications. Since the return of his biological father, no one has discussed with him in-depth the unadulterated truth concerning their family demise. As a result, he was forced to piece together what we gleaned from spirited arguments and emotional conversations among the many adults in his life.

"It doesn't matter," he assured her. "…It's always been just you and me anyway. Now, it will be just us three."

After turning to look up at him, she grinned. "How did I get to be so lucky to be blessed with a son like you?"

Meditating on all that his mother had sacrificed and altered for him, Jaamyas corrected, "No, I'm the blessed one, Mom." He then pivoted toward the room door and stated before he exited, "I will be in the study if you need me."

*** *** ***

"So, what was originally believed to be true several hundreds of years ago," the male orator of the Discovery Place Science Museum began, "has since been proven to be…"

Jaamyas covered with his hand the yawn that was triggered by boredom, and then groaned to himself in disappointment. His school's visit to the museum was nothing as he had expected. Unbeknownst to him, the entire morning of the field trip was planned to the hour by the museum guides and school instructors. As a result, he was left with no time to explore on his own.

Sluggishly strolling several feet behind his class to the next exhibit, Jaamyas's boredom exacerbated with each "fun fact" the tour guide breathed. Consequently, another groan escaped Jaamyas while he pondered all that he could learn on his own self-guided tour. All that was needed was permission from his chaperone and an opportunity to separate from the group.

"Ms. Thomas, I am going to view the fish habitat," Jaamyas announced to his class instructor after he lowly pardoned himself and maneuvered through a sea of his peers.

Transfixed by the guide and the words he spoke, she merely responded, "Are you asking me or telling me?"

"I'm sorry, Ms. Thomas. May I please go view the fish habitat?"

She pivoted her gaze to him as she breathed deeply and considered the request. Her attention as well as patience were already stretched by the other students. Adding to the challenge was the casual dress that made her students less identifiable from those of other academies. Without a doubt, she did not have the energy to entertain the worry that typically accompanies Jaamyas's exploratory appetite.

"I don't know, Jay. Our lunch hour is approaching and I don't want to expend time searching for you, especially with you out of school uniform."

He quickly glanced at the navy sweater that layered his light blue, buttoned shirt, denim jeans, and leather shoes and returned his gaze to her. "You won't have to you. I won't wander off—I promise."

She respired with skepticism. Though well-intentioned, Jaamyas's promises often became futile when his curiosity overwhelmed him.

"Please," he beseeched.

Peering into the eyes of her best pupil, she relented. "Fine, Jay. The fish habitat only—no wandering off."

His lips stretch into a wide smile. "Thank you."

"You're welcome," she responded as she watched him turn on his heels and walk out of her view.

On his own, Jaamyas took in the scenic display of aquatic life. He explored with his hands all that was permissible to touch and absorbed with his eyes all the information posted on the signage. Each sector presented different offerings of sea life, and the further Jaamyas walked into the habitat the more he was free to learn at his own pace. As spectators gradually exited the area for their meal break, Jaamyas's learning opportunities grew because he no longer had to share the space.

Noticing Jaamyas's captivation with the large aquarium, a tall, muscular man walked over and stood next to him.

"Aren't they beautiful?" The stranger inquired.

Jaamyas kept his eyes on the majestic fish, nodded, and then replied to the deep male voice, "They are."

"They're guppies."

Jaamyas looked up at the brown-skinned stranger and contorted his face. "They're what?"

He chuckled and then restated, "Rainbow fish."

"Oh," Jaamyas merely responded, returning his gaze to the glass.

"Members of the Poeciliidae family, they are live-bearing freshwater fish—meaning that-"

"They give birth to live, free-swimming young," Jaamyas completed for him.

"Exactly." He peered down at Jaamyas, who kept his stare fixed on the exhibit, and smiled. "You're a bright young man."

Jaamyas shrugged, dismissing the compliment. "Just read it in a book somewhere."

He chuckled at his modesty. "Then you must really like to read."

"It's one of many pastimes."

"Anything in particular?"

"No, not really, but I do enjoy almost anything related to science."

The man nodded and then allowed a brief silence to fall between them as they both observed the colorful fish in the water. For human amusement, the guppies swam aimlessly within the confines of their purgatory.

Ending the silence, the stranger stated, "The irony of their lifespan is that they live longer in captivity."

Jaamyas contemplated the statement as he was uncertain if it was a fact. Following, he inquired, "How is that ironic?"

"Because a caged animal never reaches its full potential." He looked down at Jaamyas once more and asked, "Where is the blessing in long life if it is lived in a box?"

Though Jaamyas understood his logic, he was unclear as to whether or not they were still discussing fish.

"I'm sorry. I don't follow," Jaamyas finally confessed.

He grinned. "That's understandable. I feel the same way at times about crime, law, and justice, particularly anything related to juvenile justice."

At the subtle reference to his mother's field of study and practice, Jaamyas peered up at him. He took in his profile and attire and then conducted a panoramic view of the room. The crowd had dwindled immensely and they were now the only spectators in that section of the habitat.

Though his heart raced, Jaamyas remained calm. "I have to go now."

"So soon? I was just beginning to enjoy your company."

"Y-yes, my-my class is waiting for me," Jaamyas stammered, attempting to walk around the human barricade.

He blocked Jaamyas's sidestep. "I understand…I mean, if your class is waiting, then you must go." When Jaamyas spoke nothing in response to his probing statement, he followed with the request, "Please give your mother my regards."

Jaamyas swallowed the knot in his throat. No longer feeling secure in his environment, he immediately reflected on his mother's instructions on how to navigate "stranger danger." Being more than an arm's reach of the unfamiliar man, Jaamyas was prepared to drop to the ground and scream to deter an abduction attempt.

"D-do I…do I know you?" Jaamyas stuttered through the rapid pulse that could be heard in his ears.

He smirked at Jaamyas's look of confusion. It was one that was ready to accept in deference any knowledge of their prior meeting, but still questioned the validity of their acquaintance.

"I've seen you a few times in your mother's chambers," he answered Jaamyas.

"Who are you?"

In lieu of an answer, he stepped to close the space between them and commanded, "Just tell her an old friend says, 'hello.'"

"Jay, we are heading out now for lunch," Ms. Thomas, standing at the entrance, spoke into the desolate room.

"Okay," he uttered in response to his instructor then spoke to the stranger, "an old friend?"

"A former badge," he elucidated.

"Badge?"

"Law enforcement officer," he expounded more for the young genius who still had much to learn of the world outside the realm of science.

"Jaamyas, now," Ms. Thomas insisted.

"Go catch up with your class…Enjoy your lunch." He pivoted his step and walked in the direction of the next exhibit.

*** *** ***

"You always blow things out of proportion," Jaamyas commented, walking through door of the mudroom.

"I don't always blow things out of proportion, Jay," Alexandre called after him.

He hurriedly removed his shoes in the mudroom, adjusted his bookbag on shoulders, and continued into the kitchen—eager to abscond his mother's insufferable presence. "Yes, you do. That's exactly why I didn't want to tell you."

"Excuse me?" She placed her keys in her purse and then positioned her purse on the cushioned bench. After removing her heels, Alexandre trailed her onerous child. "Get back here, young man. I am still talking to you."

Jaamyas begrudgingly turned to face his mother. Holding the straps of his bag at his shoulders, he avoided her eyes.

"What did you say to me?"

He did not reply.

"Heeeelloooo, I am not talking to myself."

"…Nothing," he finally muttered in response.

"Oh, so now it's nothing?" When he did not reply, Alexandre hotly retorted, "You're on punishment, Jay."

His eyes met her glare. "What? Why? What did I do?"

"We had an agreement and you reneged."

Reflecting on their multiple conversations concerning the field trip, Jaamyas did not recall the agreement in the way that his mother remembered it. "I did not renege. I asked Ms. Thomas for permission to go see-"

"I don't care what permission you asked for. You were to stay with your class!"

Frustrated with her willingness to listen to him, Jaamyas lowered his eyes to refrain from spewing a disrespectful rejoin.

"No more field trips for the remainder of the school year, Jay."

He shrugged his shoulder in nonchalance. Feeling dejected from defeat, he smugly replied, "The school year is almost over anyway. So, I don't care."

"I can make it make next year, too, smart ass."

"Okay." With that, Jaamyas pivoted on his heels and began his journey to his bedroom.

"I'm still talking to you," she spoke to his back, trailing him to the foyer. When he did not halt his step to heed her warning, she yanked him by his bookbag and pulled him to face her again.

"What?!" Jaamyas questioned in the most respectful way he could conjure as he battled emotions of rage, frustration, and hatred.

Taken aback by his tone, Alexandre released his bag, gripped his white business shirt and blue tie, and tugged him into her.

"Don't you 'what' me, Jaamyas. I am your mother!" She growled.

Jaamyas looked upon the woman who gave him life. As he met her gaze, he considered the fact that she had not been acting like the mother that he had known all his life—not since the wedding, not since the resurgence of his biological father, and not since her pregnancy. Although he could not comprehend why all these events had changed her, Jaamyas knew unequivocally that they had changed the dynamics of their relationship.

Matching the fury in her eyes, he questioned in defiance, "And?"

Alexandre saw the anger in his eyes and it shattered her heart. In acknowledging that she was responsible for the person he was becoming, she recognized what she had become herself when she saw his school uniform crumpled in her fist. She released him and fought the urge to apologize. In spite of her many wrongdoings, his acts of disobedience and disrespect were unacceptable.

She watched him take a few steps back from her. And after a calming deep breath, Alexandre spoke, "And you don't walk away when I am talking to you and you most certainly do not keep secrets from me."

"I wasn't walking away. I thought you were finished," Jaamyas contested in exacerbation and then inquired in annoyance, "And what secrets? I told you what happened at the museum."

"No, Jay," she began to correct him, "what you told me several days after the fact was-"

"Was the truth. Why does it matter how long it took me to tell you? It's not a big deal—nothing happened, I am safe. Why won't you just listen? Why can't you just believe me?"

"How can I believe you when-"

"You keep me treating me like a child and-"

"Well, you keep acting like a-"

"I am not a child, I am a-"

"You're a what, Jay? A ma-"

"Hey, hey, hey," Jacob spoke over their resounding voices.

Alexandre and Jaamyas lifted their heads to peer at the top of the stairs.

"Jacob, what are you doing here?" Alexandre inquired.

Descending the steps, Jacob reminded her, "I told you that I would move more items today."

Alexandre's fingertips vigorously rubbed her forehead as she recalled his intent to transition his belongings from their home back to his penthouse.

"I'm sorry, Jacob. I forgot."

"It's fine...If now is not the best time, I can come back another day."

"Yes, please, if you don't mind, come back another day...That would be best."

Jacob nodded in deference and allowed the silence to relax his son and soon-to-be ex-wife. Before the quietness settled too long among them, Jacob gazed upon Jaamyas then Alexandre. He then calming questioned, "What's going on, you guys?"

"Mom-"

"Jay-"

They both spoke each other's name in unison and continued to speak over each other, increasing intonation in effort to be heard.

"Guys," Jacob moderately spoke in a failed attempt to interject. "Guys…GUYS…GUYS, ENOUGH!"

Jacob's deep voice ricocheted off the walls of the foyer and it immediately halted the heated discord. He then stated more calmly, "I can't understand either of you if you both speak at the same time."

Despite discerning that Jaamyas was once again the victim of Alexandre's unwarranted deeds, Jacob opted to hear her position first. He turned to Jaamyas and requested, "Jay, could you please give your mother and me a moment?"

Without responding, Jaamyas walked past the both of them and stamped up the stairs in anger. Once in his room, he slammed the door closed.

Alexandre lowered her lids over her eyes and breathed deeply through her frustration.

"What's going on, Alex?"

Alexandre opened her eyes, huffed in frustration and exhaustion, and then responded, "What isn't going on?"

Absent the time needed to delve deeper into her myriad issues, Jacob clarified, "Between you and Jay."

"What's going is that I have a 13-year-old who despises me."

Though he believed the assessment to be an exaggeration, Jacob remained sensitive to how she felt and offered, "He doesn't despise you, Alex."

"Well, he certainly feels something, Jacob. He is moody, and distant, and short towards me all the time. It gets worse after each visit with his father…I don't even know who he is anymore."

Jacob chuckled lightheartedly. He extended his hands and gently rubbed each of her triceps. "He is a teenager, Alex. If you don't like his attitude, give him a few hours. It is bound to change."

Alexandre weakly smiled. She appreciated the jest, but what she needed more was assistance with parenting. "Could you please talk to him?"

Jacob released her arms and respired audibly. In tandem with Lance's increased efforts to enter into their lives, Jacob was working to exit out of their lives. "Alex, why do you do this?"

"Why do I do what, Jacob?"

"Put me in position to tell you no. I dread it."

"Then don't do it. Don't tell me no."

Jacob inhaled and exhaled deeply through his nostrils. "This is not like you, Alex. You are not being fair." He met her eyes and spoke with conviction, "You made your choice. You chose his father; so, have him talk with him. Or, better yet, take the time and talk to Jay yourself."

"About what? What more is there to talk about because I do talk to him. I talk to him all the time."

"About what? How about what is really going on, Alex, and not your romanticized version of it."

Offended, she retorted, "I resent that."

"Look, Alex-"

"Jacob, I have spoken to him and what I shared was *not* a romanticized version."

In disbelief, he peered deep into her eyes and questioned with conviction, "So, you've spoken to him about the latest perils of your job? Perhaps if you did, Alex, he would understand better your austere parenting style." When she broke their gaze, but did not respond, he pressed, "What about your marriage to Lance? Or better yet, your marriage to me?...And the baby? Have you told him about the questioned paternity of the ba-"

She returned to his gaze and finally answered, "Yes, I have talked to him. I've talked to him about it all...In the best manner that I can, I made sure he knows everything."

Shaking his head in opposition, Jacob dissented, "I know you, Alex. You're talking to him as the little child that you want him to be and not the young man he is becoming."

When she turned from the windows to his soul, Jacob stretched his neck and tilted his head to capture her eyes once more. He then advised, "Tell him everything and tell him the truth, Alexandre. Tell him in the same manner that you would want to receive it, and then listen."

Alexandre lowered her lids over her eyes as she contemplated all that Jacob advised. Without a doubt, she knew that that his sound recommendation included the disclosure of all that was transpiring at the courthouse and the impending dangers that accompanied her judicial role. Nonetheless, Alexandre was not confidant that she could heed his advice. She was a woman of many words, but could not conjure the ones most appropriate to explain to her child the threats against their lives—even if they substantiated her strict mannerisms.

Opening her eyes, Alexandre resolved that even the worst parents possessed the desire to safeguard their children from the many evils of the world. And, though she was not parental perfection, Alexandre knew that she was not among the worst—despite falling short of the best. Therefore, she, too, yearned for her children to be safe. However, unlike parents with less notable lives, Alexandre's high profile afforded her the right to protect in the way she deemed necessary and the liberty to omit the truth or admit the truth whenever she needed. Only circumstances, not people, would dictate her choices.

Regrettably for Alexandre, Jaamyas was a child replica of her. And, as he aged, he greatly desired that she allowed for more than just situations to dictate her decisions. Jaamyas longed for Alexandre to learn to consider his thoughts and emotions. Above all, he wanted her to heed him in the same manner he witnessed less accomplished mothers with their sons.

"...I don't know, Jacob," Alexandre finally murmured with reticence. She was certain that, as it related to her child, refraining to disclose or choosing to disclose the unadulterated truth would make no difference. Jaamyas possessed and firmly cleaved to many preconceived notions about her parental style and choices, and nothing she said would alter them.

"...He is just...just so angry, and bitter, and sad on and off all the time. There is no getting through to him when he is like this."

Suppressing the urge to acknowledge that Jaamyas's mannerisms resembled hers, Jacob merely advised, "And it will only worsen if you continue to lie to him, Alex."

"I do not lie to my son," she countered fervently.

Jacob exhaled audibly, vexed in the way she misconstrued his statement. "You of all people know that a lie of omission is still a lie, Alexandre."

Deflated, Alexandre loudly respired and finally confessed, "I don't know if I'm ready, Jacob…I have obliterated the stability and security he has enjoyed his entire life. I don't possess the adequate responses to the tough questions he asks me."

"No one is requiring that you have the all the answers, Alex. The request is just that you first listen."

"Listen?"

"Yes, listen."

"I am the parent, Jacob—his mother. He needs to listen to me."

"Listen to what exactly, Alexandre?"

She pondered the question for a quick moment and then responded, "That his adolescent struggle surpasses that of a typical black boy in this country. That there are people that will harm him to get to me."

"And you don't think he already knows this, Alex? That he doesn't have an understanding of all that concerns you? Do you really believe that he is that naïve?"

Uncertain of what her son knew or believed about the depths of her worry, Alexandre failed to answer Jacob's questions. Instead, she suppressed her feelings of maternal disconnect and reiterated, "I just need him to understand that this world is full of evil and that evil will hurt him just to get to me…He doesn't need to know anything more than that—he is a child."

Assuming that he no longer possessed the parental right to suggest otherwise, Jacob begrudgingly accepted her decision. He then seized the opportunity to segue to the topic of safety.

"Have you purchased a firearm?"

Alexandre rolled her eyes and turned to walk into the family room. She did not want to revisit their earlier conversations concerning weapons in their household; but if she was forced to do so, she did not want to debate the matter in the foyer where their voices carried throughout the halls.

"No, Jacob, I have not," she merely responded as she sat on and reclined into the cushions of the sofa. Closing her eyes, she reveled in the comfort the cool softness gave her aching lower back.

Jacob lowered himself on the ottoman positioned in front of her and slowly took her feet into his hands. Massaging gently one and then the other, he spoke, "Alex, despite your position on gun control, or the lack thereof in this country, you cannot negate the fact that you need means to protect yourself."

Alexandre slowly opened her eyes and looked at him. She saw the deep concern on his countenance and reflected on their earlier dates. Jacob was astonished by the realization that she had never fired a gun or even held one, so he insisted on teaching her both concepts during several visits at a shooting range.

"It's not just protection for you, but for the children as well...You have said yourself that this world is evil."

"I do not want guns in my home, Jacob. You know that...It's not an environment conducive for children."

"Neither is a home that is invaded by an intruder with one," he rejoined.

Alexandre turned from his glare. Jacob had made a well-stated argument, but she declined the invitation to acknowledge it. In prior conversations of a similar topic, she was able to respond that he—the perfect first-line of defense along with an array of other strategically placed weapons, and a security system were all their home needed in their gated community. Regrettably, however, the status of their homelife and level of security had changed. So, that response could no longer be made.

"...No," she unequivocally reiterated. "I don't want my children-"

"I have firearms in the penthouse. You know that, Alex. Out of respect for you, I have not brought them here. But Jay has been around them, he has seen them, and he has handled them. He understands the responsibilities that accompany gun ownership."

Avoiding the abyss of circular arguments surrounding the Second Amendment, Alexandre replied once more, "No. Not in my home and not around my children."

Disappointed, but not surprised by her response, Jacob offered, "Then your chambers."

Alexandre met the seriousness of his eyes. To ensure that she heard him correctly, she asked, "What?"

He lowered her feet to the floor and moved the ottoman and himself closer to her. He wanted no space between them as he conveyed, "We can get you registered and I can purchase something for you to keep in your chambers. You can store it in the same locked drawer that you have your folding knife and pepper spray. No one will know but the two of us."

"Jacob, I can't do-"

Jacob took each of her hands and held them in each one of his. "Please, Alex, please…For me…We may no longer be the family that I desired us to be, but that doesn't mean that I stopped caring…I need to know that you are safe—with or without me."

Alexandre contemplated his request and finally conceded.

*** FIFTEEN ***

"Alexandre."

Her eyes raised to the familiar call of her name. "Lance."

"Hey."

"Hey," she echoed.

"Hello, Jaamyas."

"Hey, Coach," he merely responded then returned his attention to the content on his phone.

Lance suppressed the ache caused by his son's coldness and met again Alexandre's gaze.

"Jay, don't be rude."

Jaamyas looked up from his phone another time, shrugged his shoulders, and inquired, "Rude how? I said 'hey'."

Alexandre responded to the denial of his insolence with the rolling of her eyes. Afterwards, she watched as her son lowered his gaze to his device and then returned her stare to Lance.

"How are you do-" they spoke in unison and then snickered.

"You go first," Lance deferred to her.

"I'm as well as can be expected." Alexandre gestured toward her sizeable protrusion. "All things considered."

"You look incredible, Alex," he adoringly lauded, restraining his affections.

She blushed at what she believed to be an underserved compliment and responded, "Thank you."

"You're welcome."

"...And you, how are you?"

"I'm okay."

Alexandre nodded as she reflected on her calendar of events. "...We...we didn't have plans today, did we?...This pregnancy brain of mine has me even more forgetful these days."

Lance grinned and shook his head. "No...No, we didn't." He nodded toward Jaamyas who stood at Alexandre's side still distracted by technology. "I actually was in search of fishing gear. Now that spring is officially here, it is my hope that Jay and I could have some father-son time out on the lake."

His eyes now fixed on his son, Lance offered, "...I know that you and Jacob typically go together, but perhaps you and I try it as well?"

"I think that to be a wonderful idea. Don't you, Jay?" Alexandre asked.

Jaamyas looked up from his phone, stretched his lips into a bogus smile, and merely responded, "Of course." He then broke the gaze he held with Lance and met his mother's eyes. "May I go over to Mr. Petrelli's?"

Alexandre rolled her eyes another time. She could not discern if she was more vexed by his brazenness or his air of imposition. "The antique store again, Jay?"

After suppressing the urge to turn his own eyes upward, Jaamyas explained, "It's for my diorama."

She exhaled audible. "Fine, Jay, but make it quick. I did not plan to spend all day at this strip mall. I still have to get home and prepare dinner."

"Yes, ma'am," he quickly spoke to expedite his departure from his parents.

Lance chuckled as he watched Jaamyas take a few steps past them. "Teenagers."

Alexandre shook her head as she turned her eyes upward and uttered, "Tell me about it. I want my three-year-old back—the period right after the terrible twos but just before all the back talk and eye rolls."

Stifling his laughter, Lance merely nodded as he secretly coveted those moments upon which she was griping. They were all moments he had missed.

As he awaited a vehicle to speed past him, Jaamyas shoved his phone into his pocket. He then descended the sidewalk and started across the street—disregarding the pedestrian crosswalk.

"So, anyway, I'm sorry," Alexandre apologized to Lance.

"The crosswalk, Jay," Lance called out to him then returned to Alexandre and inquired, "Sorry for what?"

"The phone-tag. I haven't put much effort into keeping in touch after your recent return from Texas," Alexandre admitted.

"The crosswalk, Jay," Lance called out to him again then returned to Alexandre and responded, "It's fine, Alex. It really is. I know you are busy and have a lot going on."

Though she appreciated the olive branch, Alexandre felt as if she owed him an explanation. "It's just that I've had so much to contend with as of late and-"

"Jay, the crosswalk—cross at the crosswalk."

Jaamyas rolled his eyes and ignored the directive of his father. He kept his stride in the middle of the street until the chime in his pocket diverted his attention to his phone. Jaamyas slowed his steps to retrieve it and view the message.

"I'm not making excuses," Alexandre offered, "but it really has been a trying time the last few weeks...But enough of that, when are you thinking of taking Jay to the lake? His spring break is in two weeks. Maybe then?"

"That's fine, Alex. Whatever time you think is best."

"Okay, I will let y-"

"Car. CAR. CAAAAR." Lance rushed after Jaamyas as the distracted driver of a blue sedan quickly approached him.

Jaamyas looked up from the message on his phone and immediately froze in fear. A powerful thrust from behind lunged him forward and he fell to the asphalt.

Lance's body planed several feet in the air before it landed on the windshield, rolled off the hood and onto the ground.

"Oh my g—someone, please, please call for help!" Alexandre wailed as she quickly plodded towards her husband.

"Lance, Lance, Lance," she called to him once she made it to his side.

Lance attempted to rise, but the pain kept him to the ground.

"No, no, no. Don't move, don't move. Don't try to move."

"I'm so sorry…I didn't see them…They were in the middle of the road and I didn't see them…" The driver cried over all the commotion of the witnesses.

"…Ja-Jay…," Lance uttered.

Alexandre looked over her shoulder to confirm that their son was well. Fellow shoppers had helped him to his feet, examined him, and was now consoling him.

"He is fine."

Lance nodded then began to drift to sleep.

"Help is on the way. Just try to stay awake."

Lance opened his eyes, nodded, and slowly lowered his lids over his eyes again.

"Lance, please…Please, Lance…" She rapidly tapped his face to revive his consciousness. "…Don't you dare leave me again."

Lance opened his eyes and weakly grinned. He slowly placed his hand at his heart and confirmed, "I…I never left you the…the first time, Alex."

Alexandre returned the feeble smile and uttered, "…I know…I know…but please, just…just hang in there."

Lance pondered her request as he winced at the sharp pain in his chest and coughed blood. Of the many near-death experiences he had encountered in his lifetime, he knew that this instance would be his final occurrence. In the past, he had pressed through each dire circumstance and every major injury so that he could make amends with his wife and established a relationship with his son. Now that he had achieved these goals, Lance believed that he could finally succumb to the ultimate strain on his body.

When the pressure in his chest gave the indication that his lungs were filling with fluid, Lance coughed, to no avail, to clear his air passage. He coughed another time and blood spilled from his lips, confirming that he was slowly drowning in his own blood.

Lance groaned his discomfort and dissented, "No...No, this...this is it...It's time..."

Alexandre erupted into a heartfelt cry. "No, please, please..."

Lance shook his head.

As she watched her husband lie supine within an inch of his life, Alexandre knew with certainty that this was their end. To contest it would be futile. So, she nervously inhaled the fate she reluctantly had to accept and lowly uttered, "...Okay."

"...Thank...Thank you for...for the...opportunity to know...know m-my son," Lance murmured as his breath shortened and heartbeat slowed.

Although she possessed no faith that a miracle would occur, Alexandre silently prayed for one. She then wiped his mouth with her hand and then used the back of it to wipe her eyes.

When Lance groaned his misery, Alexandre retrieved his left hand, kissed the base of his ring finger, and firmly held his hand against her heart. She attempted to smile through her angst while she ignored Jaamyas's call of her name and the faint sound of emergency responders' sirens.

"...P-please...n-never...let him for-." He coughed blood, feeling the life gradually depart from him. "For...get me."

"You're his father. You not only gave him life, you saved it. How could he ever forget you?...I will never forget you."

Lance feebly smiled and with his last breath he uttered to his wife—his one true love and family, "...Semper fi..."

Jaamyas finally broke free of the many hands that held him from returning to the scene of the accident, and rushed to his mother's side. Upon his arrival, he placed a hand on Lance's torso and immediately discerned that the spirit had already left his body. Overwhelmed with devastation by the loss of his beloved coach and father, Jaamyas released a wail that, first, traveled through Alexandre's ears; then, nicked her heart; and, finally, pierced her soul.

He threw his arms around the fullness of his mother's belly and remorsefully bellowed, "This is all my fault...This is all my fault..."

Absent the appropriate words to console Jaamyas's grief when she was struggling with her own, Alexandre merely held her son close and rocked him.

"…I didn't even get to say good-bye, Mom," he mourned as his emotion transition from remorse to regret. "…I didn't even to say good-bye…"

Jaamyas lifted his eyes to meet his mother's gaze and confessed, "…I loved him and I didn't even get to tell him."

Fighting the urge to erupt into her own solemn cry, Alexandre freed herself from his tight embrace then used the tail of her shirt to wipe his face—the very face that morphed more into his father's each day.

"I know, son, I know," she consoled. "…I loved him, too."

"…Do…do you think he knew?"

Alexandre weakly smiled and nodded. "Of course, he did, son…He knew and he loved you back even more."

Jaamyas lowered his face into her breasts and cried, reciting again his remorse and regrets until law enforcement arrived and escorted them from the scene.

*** *** ***

"We therefore commit this body to the ground, earth to earth, ashes to ashes, dust to dust; in sure and certain hope of the resurrection to eternal life," the priest recited as he slowly released soil onto the lowered casket.

Alexandre restrained her emotions as Lance's mother burst into a heartfelt cry that moved all in attendance at the burial.

"Death, no matter the swiftness or the immense time we have to prepare for it, is never a matter easily grappled. For this reason, we should always take comfort in knowing that our Father who loves us has graciously shared with us, for a time, His creation. For it is from God we came and to God we will return."

At the officiant's nodding cue, Jaamyas stepped forward to lower his red rose into the hole in the ground. Once he stood erect, he adjusted the jacket of his black suit and spoke, "The great philosopher, Marcus Aurelius, proposed that every man lives only this present time and that all the rest of his life is either past or uncertain…That short interval is the time which every man lives; and short, too, is the longest post humous fame—and even this is only continued by a succession of poor human beings, who will also very soon die…"

Jaamyas, overwhelmed with emotions, wiped the tears that fell from his eyes and shifted his gaze to Alexandre. Peering into the windows of his mother's soul, Jaamyas recalled her earlier tutelage that whenever someone special leaves, the special things they leave behind should be cherished.

"…I don't know the time that I will die," Jaamyas started in conclusion while pivoting his head to his father's final resting place, "but, because of you, Coach, that time was not eight days ago. I promise you that your memory, your legacy will not fade in the distance—it's impossible, because you will always live on in me…"

Breaking the uncomfortable stillness, the priest held his hand above the congregation and prayed, "Please, go in peace, go in love, and, most importantly, go with God."

As the groundskeepers lowered the cherry wood casket further into the ground and covered it with the earth, several guests shared their condolences with Alexandre. She endured all the well wishes and heartfelt apologies despite her desire to rudely retreat back to her preferred isolation.

Her stoic disposition was disrupted when a familiar courtroom foe stepped into her personal space.

"Your Honor, a word please."

Noticing her ill-ease, Jacob moved to intervene.

Alexandre held out her palm to halt Jacob's gallant attempt and spoke with assurance, "I'm fine. I will meet you at the car."

Jacob nodded in deference then stepped in line with the procession of mourners who slowly walked to the parked vehicles.

"You've got five minutes," Alexandre offered the attorney.

"Thank you. I'll take it."

Feeling the rays of the sun scorch her flesh, Alexandre turned on her toes to seek refuge under a large oak tree. Her nemesis closely followed.

"How are you doing?" He cordially asked in a manner that was more obligatory than sincere.

"I just put to rest my first husband for the second time, counselor. How do you suppose I am doing?"

"…You're right…That was an imprudent and insensitive question."

Alexandre exhaled loudly with impatience; first, with the unusual oppressive heat of spring and, second, with his stalled intentions. In less melancholic circumstances, she enjoyed small talk; it was a fool-proof way to build rapport, establish connections, and strengthen relationships. However, on the day in which the world was unrelenting and cruel, she was not one for pleasantries.

"Please cut to the chase, Mr. Cannon. I have a repass to attend."

He cleared his throat and shifted his weight. His face then flushed with embarrassment at her unwavering ability to read him so well both in and outside the courtroom. "…Your caseload, are you staying all your cases or allowing your colleagues to preside over them?"

Allowing herself a moment to ponder the question, she recalled what of interest to him awaited her judgment. "All my cases or just the Bonner matter?"

His copper skin flushed at the inquisition. Despite his attempt to be gingerly diplomatic, Alexandre quashed his evasiveness. Clearing his throat, he justified his concern by reminding, "Well, it is a high-profile case."

Alexandre rolled her red, weary eyes. "No matter the infamy, it's a juvenile matter under my jurisdiction."

"But you've taken a sabbatical."

"I've taken bereavement," she corrected. "Or are we no longer a nation in which we are permitted ample time to mourn the dead?"

"Look," he began, avoiding the emendation and her question, "all I mean is that this is an election year. The decision on this case can make or break a lot of positions."

"As pariens patraie for all the children who come into my courtroom, political security is the least of my worries, regardless of public scrutiny and regardless if I appear soft on crime."

After puffing hot air at her classic textbook response, he vehemently rejoined, "And will that same sentiment extend to Hannah Rubio?"

Alexandre suppressed the sting of his comment—it was indeed a low blow he inflicted to validate his argument. Swallowing the knot in her throat, she responded, "She was a reckless teenager who was distracted by a text message while speeding through a strip mall. You tell me what type of punitive sentence she deserves for killing my husband?"

"Certainly not vehicular homicide," he answered and then captured her eyes and held it as he spoke with conviction, "You and I both know that that is what the state will go for if she is transferred from the juvenile justice system."

Alexandre shrugged in nonchalance despite her inner conflict. Never had she encountered such an emotionally jarring case that made her question her morals, values, and beliefs. For the first time during her tenure on the bench, Alexandre desired retribution over rehabilitation. Her sudden transformation sickened her and she tried to shrug it off with another raise of her shoulders.

"…It's not my case. So, it is out of my hands," she finally spoke.

He shook his head in disbelief and dissented, "No, but you can petition your colleague to show the same level of compassion and leniency you afford the juveniles that matriculate your courtroom."

Alexandre stared blankly at him while she pondered his subtle request for a favorable victim impact statement. She had given little thought to drafting one, especially not one advantageous to his client. "…Like I said, it's out of my hands." She stepped to walk around him, but he shifted his weight to block her path.

"Come on, Alex, you can't be serious…" he pressed with the use of her short-name in hopes that their personal connection would sway her decision. "…She's sixteen. A Class D felony could put her in prison until she is 29."

She turned her head from his gaze and took in the countless headstones that protruded from the lawn. She pondered how many souls were put to rest by the careless actions of others. "Who exactly are you here for, Trevor?" She met is eyes once more and inquired, "Your client or your friend?"

Uncertain of the gist of her inquiry, he prudently responded by asking, "Why not both?"

"Because you are failing both!"

He exhaled audibly at the disparaging observation and contemplated a clever retort. "…Look, I'm sorry if-"

"Your friendship may have dwindled much after college, but Lance always loved you," Alexandre ardently interjected. "He loved you like a brother, Trevor."

Trevor adjusted his tailored black suit as the guilt and shame made it feel smaller in size. He recalled his four years at North Carolina A&T, and remembered that he and Lance had entered as strangers, stayed as roommates, and departed as brothers in the same fraternity and in life. "…I'm sorry, Alex."

"Indeed, you are…I mean, why else would you be here on the day that I put my husband six feet into the ground to ask that I show compassion for the miscreant who put him there?"

Trevor exhaled audibly another time and considered the accuracy of Alexandre's summation. Undoubtedly, she was right—he was failing his friend by impeding his widow's period to mourn and heal, and failing his client, as Alexandre was in no position to make a compassionate appeal in the juvenile matter. If anything, the reverse could be true—Alexandre's appeal would be one of callousness.

When he offered no response to her question, Alexandre spoke, "thank you for coming to pay your respects, counselor," stepped from under the tree, and walked toward the black limousine in which her family awaited her.

After the crowd of the repass dwindled, Jacob swallowed the last of his liquid courage and approached the lone Seanna in the formal dining room.

"Sea," he called out to her.

"Yes," she responded, keeping to her task with wrapping the prepared dishes with aluminum foil.

Jacob cleared his throat and boldly announced, "When you leave, I need you to take Jaamyas."

"Sure, take him where?"

"…Home…with you."

Seanna looked up from her hands and asked, "What?"

"I need you-"

"No, I heard you," Seanna interjected. "I just needed a moment to wrap my mind around your audacity."

"Seanna, please."

In lieu of an answer, she held his eyes in hope of deciphering his motives.

"Please," he merely beseeched, offering no cause for his request.

Though reticent, Seanna respired and questioned, "For how long, Jacob?"

"I don't know. A couple of weeks—few—several."

She huffed with worry and probed, "Does Alex know about this?"

Jacob shook his head. "No, she doesn't."

Seanna lowered her eyes and resumed in her efforts to tidy her best friend's home as she rambled, "I don't know about this, Jacob… Alex and I have not too long recovered from being on-the-outs. I am not trying to experience that again…Especially, when it comes to her child. With all that is going on, she is like a hawk on its prey."

"Let me worry about Alex, Sea. I just need you to take Jay."

Seanna met eyes and exhaled loudly as she contemplated his demand. "…And what about Jaamyas? We're talking about a kid who does not spend more than two nights away from his mother. Hell, he refuses to go to sport camps unless he can come home every day."

"He did it for the wedding," he reminded her.

"Yes, and that was one hell-of-a-bribe you had to pay him, too. Along with whatever else you promised him."

Jacob closed his eyes and slowly breathed through his nostrils. Though faintly inebriated, he could still recall, as if it were yesterday, the various pre-marital agreements he made with his son.

Upon opening his eyes, Jacob inquired, "If I can get him to agree, will you take him?"

"That's one hell-of-an-if, Jacob, and you know it."

Ignoring her cynicism, Jacob repeated, "Will you take him?"

Seanna respired loudly then spoke with doubt and apprehension, "…Of course, I will take him, Jacob. He is my god-son."

"Thank you."

"You're welcome."

"Jay, may I have moment, please?" Jacob requested later, walking into the kitchen.

"Sure," Jaamyas responded. He placed his glass on the kitchen counter, excused his absence among his god-siblings, and followed him into the sitting room.

"Please, sit," Jacob gestured toward the loveseat.

Jaamyas took in the seriousness of stepfather's countenance and the rigid square of his stance. "I'll stand, if you're standing," he declined.

Jacob meagerly smiled at his silent request to be treated as a man and not a child. "Fair enough," he spoke as he lowered himself into the cushion. Jaamyas followed suit and sat close to him.

"I need a favor from you, Jay."

Jaamyas could recall on one hand the number of favors Jacob requested of him in the three years they had known each other. As a result, he ascertained that Jacob's current request was one that was serious.

"What is it?"

Jacob contemplated the best way to articulate the demand, knowing that Jaamyas rarely obliged without contest.

"…When Seanna leaves, I need you to go and stay with her."

Jaamyas felt the color and warmth leave his face. "Whaaat? Why? What for?"

Jacob broke their gaze as he clenched his folded hand and ignored Jaamyas's questions. Instead, he uttered, "Jay, I know I am asking a lot, but-"

Jaamyas rose from his seat. "No, absolutely not. No."

"Pleas-"

"No, I'm not leaving my mother alone."

Jacob gently gripped his forearm and lowered him back to the loveseat. "Please, Jay, she won't be alone."

"She will be alone, if I leave her."

"No, she won't, Jay."

"How do you know?"

"Because I'll stay with her."

A pregnant silence grew in the room as Jaamyas seized a moment to carefully contemplate Jacob's statement. Although he was uncertain of Jacob's true intentions with his mother, Jaamyas was willing to concede if his objectives included the reconciliation of their marriage.

Peering deep into his stepfather's eyes, Jaamyas asked, "...For how long?"

"I don't know. For however long she needs me."

Jaamyas shook his head in disbelief. "No."

"Jay-"

"That's not an answer I can rely on," Jaamyas honestly retorted.

Though Jacob knew his stepson's skepticism was the result of a series of heartaches and disappointments, he was still devastated and offended by Jaamyas's lack of faith in him. "When have you not been able to rely on me, Jay?"

When Jaamyas offered no response, Jacob pressed, "How many times, Jaamyas?"

Unable to respond with an answer greater than zero, Jaamyas lowered his eyes, ignored the question, and, instead, shared with hesitation, "...Nana says death is contagious—that...that the death of someone we love makes us want to die, too."

Fighting back the tears that formed in his eyes, Jaamyas met Jacob's gaze and confessed, "I—I don't know if that is true or not, but...but what I do know is that I don't want to lose my mother,

Jacob…Despite everything, she is all I ever had. I need her and she needs me."

Jacob vigorously rubbed his brow in frustration as he carefully considered an adequate rebuttal. He not only needed to counter the wives' tale that his mother-in-law stated, but also had to provide assurance to his son whose comfortable and secure lifeboat had, first, capsized and was now sinking.

Following an audible respiration, Jacob offered to all that Jaamyas believed, "Your mother will be fine, Jay. But what she needs is the guarantee that you are safe and looked after…Please, do not compound her stress by sacrificing your security and wellness just to take care of her…Let me do that. Let me take care of her."

The room fell silent once more while Jaamyas pondered all that Jacob had spoken and the logic of it. "…You can't leave her, Jacob."

"You have my word, I won't."

"Ever," Jaamyas emphasized.

The unexpected demand caused a knot to swell in Jacob's throat and he struggled to swallow it.

"Ever, Jacob," Jaamyas repeated staring into his stepfather's weary eyes. "Promise me."

"Jay-" Jacob began, weary of making promises he could not honor.

"No," Jaamyas forcefully interjected. "You want something; now, I want something…Man-to-man, I want you to promise me."

The look in his young eyes conveyed to Jacob that Jaamyas's request spoke to the period beyond his mother's time of mourning. It was a petition to, once again, cleave to the marriage vow that had been exchanged in Aruba—to be parted only by death.

Inhaling deeply through his nostrils, Jacob turned from Jaamyas's gaze and wholly contemplated the request. As he held the air captive in his lungs, Jacob reminisced of the past year and all that transpired, particularly the various transgressions committed against him. To forgive so that they could be cordial to each other was one matter, but to forget so that they could move forward together was another.

"…Jacob," Jaamyas lowly uttered, breaking the long, uncomfortable silence in the room.

Exhaling through pursed lips, Jacob finally released all that remained harbored in his heart. He then met again Jaamyas's eyes, nodded, and affirmed, "I promise."

Jaamyas smiled feebly at the vow. Though he had suspected Jacob's reticence, Jaamyas found comfort in the fact that he had no viable reason to doubt his stepfather or deny his petition to trust him. They possessed a solid history of their word bonding them—Jacob had never broken a promise to him.

"...Okay," Jaamyas conceded at last after relinquishing the last of his reservations that he attributed to his ambivalence to having to trust his mother's well-being in hands that were not his own, or that of his grandfather's.

After nervously respiring audibly, Jaamyas spoke to execute their pact, "I will go pack my bag."

"Thank you."

"You're welcome."

Jacob exhaled his own anxious relief after Jaamyas rose from his seat and exited the room. He then whispered thanks to God that the fight he had prepared for was not as arduous as he had anticipated.

Alexandre held her lids over her eyes with hopes that her disregard for the knock on her bedroom door would prompt the intruder to retreat.

"Alex, it's me and I'm not leaving," Jacob confirmed after deducing that she was intentionally ignoring his respectful petition to open the door.

Alexandre opened her eyes, adjusted her body in her cushioned chair at the window, and then granted him permission to enter.

"I thought you would have left with the others," she greeted him once he opened the door and stepped into the room.

He closed the door behind him and shook his head. "I don't want you to be alone."

She lowered her hands to the swell of her womb and rubbed the life within it. "I'm not alone...I have Jay."

Jacob shook his head another time and reluctantly disabuse her of her belief. "I asked Seanna to take him."

Alexandre lowered her elevated feet to the floor. "What?"

"Alex, before you-"

"Why? Why would you do that, Jacob?"

"I wanted-"

"I want my son back in this house."

"Alex, please."

"Do not 'Alex, please' me. I want my son back in this house and I want him back now."

Empathetic to her concerns with Jaamyas's well-being, Jacob assured, "He will be fine."

"I don't care about him being fine, Jacob. I want him to be safe and I want him here with me."

He respired audibly, exasperated at, first, her obstinacy and, second, her selfishness. Vigorously rubbing his forehead as he suppressed his frustration, Jacob reasoned, "He needs to be a kid around other kids, Alexandre. Please, allow him to be a kid."

When she held her silence, Jacob acknowledged, "There is no one way that people grieve. Being apart from you will permit Jay to grieve in his own way as a kid should, to grieve without the additional worry of caring for you."

Though his argument was sound, Alexandre disagreed. "No, I want my son back in this house." After a brief struggle with her weight, she rose from her seat and conveyed, "I'm going to go get him."

"And then what?!" Jacob hotly inquired. "Have him miss classes and practices because he will be shouldered with the burden of consoling and caring for you?"

"I have never placed and will never place such a burden on my son!"

"Then don't start now!" He warned, recognizing that what she spoke was true at the moment. However, it was likely to change if they were not temporarily separated. Jaamyas was unwaveringly committed to her.

Alexandre held her head as a fleeting vertigo spun the room. She slowly returned to her seat and inhaled deep breaths until the rotation stopped.

Jacob took the seat in front of her. "Are you okay?"

Suppressing her nausea, she nodded and answered, "I guess this is all a little too much excitement for the baby."

He leaned forward and touched her warm, hard, protrusion and spoke, "I would have to agree." Meeting her eyes, he implored, "I ask for so little, Alex. Please…Please, let me have this."

She placed her hand on his and then finally nodded in concession. "…But, you don't have to stay. I can have my mother return…or even Lance's family—their flight doesn't leave until tomorrow night."

"No, I want to."

Confused by his acts of benevolence, she searched his eyes and questioned, "But, why?"

Jacob offered no answer.

"…After all that I have done to you…why?"

He took her hand and kissed the back of it. "When I make the conscience choice to cleave to how much I love you rather than all that you have done to me, it's actually not that difficult."

She stroked his cheek that was now stubbled with a five o'clock shadow then held it. "I don't deserve you."

Jacob huffed as he took her hand from his face and gripped it gently, but firmly. Unable to recite his typical good fortune he found in her, he lowered his eyes, and simply stated, "And I am not sure what I deserve anymore."

✱✱✱ *SIXTEEN* ✱✱✱

"Here you are," Jacob announced after finally locating Alexandre in her home office. She sat in a cushioned chair in the seating area positioned near the window in front of shelves of books.

Alexandre quickly wiped her eyes dry, meagerly smiled up at him, and confirmed, "Here I am." She adjusted the decorative pillow higher on her belly and placed the cordless phone on top of it. "How was work?"

Jacob lowered himself into the end of the loveseat that was closest to her. "I don't want to talk about work." He watched her lower her gaze and finger the phone's rubber buttons. "How are you?" When she did not immediately respond, he attempted to lighten the air by jesting, "The house isn't on fire, so I assume you managed your first day alone pretty well."

Alexandre grinned, but held her eyes on the black handset. In lieu of replying to his question, she began to wonder how long before the red light would appear indicating that the phone needed to be returned to its base.

"I wasn't aware that you had planned to work today," Jacob remarked.

She lifted her head to meet his stare and assured, "I didn't work today…I just came in here to look for something and then Jay called…" Alexandre wiped her eyes dry once more and shared, "He misses me and wants to come home."

Jacob took a deep breath and held it for a moment to refrain from abandoning his support of hers and Jaamyas's separation. He, along with many others, believed it best for their healing. "Don't swim against the current, Alexandre. You will only exhaust yourself."

Ignoring his subtle encouragement to embrace the process, she diverted the conversation by announcing, "Jay went back to school today; he said he needed the distraction."

He nodded to acknowledge the announcement and then asked, "And what about you? Do you need a distraction?"

Alexandre shook her head. "…What I need is a host of answers."

Perplexed by her reply, Jacob contorted his face and inquired, "To what type of questions?"

She shrugged. "To the typical whys people ask in times like this: Why me? Why him? Why us? Why now? Why the pain and suffering?…Why bring him back just to take him away again?"

Unsure of how to lend comfort, Jacob sat in silence and listened. It was the first time since the tragic loss of Lance that she had verbally expressed any emotion. So, he opted to just listen.

Alexandre sneered in embarrassment. "…I made a complete and utter mess of what you and I built in hopes of rekindling what Lance and I once had, and now…now he is gone." She wiped the tears that fell from her eyes. "I know God did not do this, but He did allow this to happen for a reason…I just need to know the reason and, because of who I am, I need that reason *now* and need that reason to make sense to me."

Jacob inhaled deeply and exhaled audibly through his nostrils. Finally, deciding to speak before her weakened faith became lost, he offered, "Alex, you are not a 'milk-drinking' Christian."

In lieu of responding to him, Alexandre opted to momentarily meditate on the Biblical message concerning faith maturity. Undoubtedly, life and all its turbulent circumstances developed her into a 'meat-eater.' Namely, life's trials had made her strong; and when new tribulations weakened her, her faith guided her to the ultimate source of all strength.

"…You know we all belong to Him. And only for a moment does He shares us and then He calls us back again." Jacob reached for her hand and gripped it firmly. "What happened to Lance was a terrible thing, but I believe that a greater good will come from it." He lifted her face with their held hands and comforted, "But until that good manifests, take heart in knowing that, as a believer, Lance has not perished—he will have everlasting life."

Despite her red weary eyes, Alexandre smiled at and reflected on John's recollection of the gospel. "…John 3:16, that's my favorite scripture."

Jacob lowered their hands and rested them on the pillow. "And that's saying a lot considering you don't have a favorite anything." He smoothed back her hair that she had pulled into a ponytail—the most she had done with it since the burial. "…That is what makes you such a great judge—you're impartial to a fault."

Alexandre chuckled. "I'm sure that many would disagree."

"I'm sure they would," he concurred with the truthfulness of her jest.

Diverting the subject, Jacob asked, "…What do you say about us going out to dinner tonight? It will be a chance for you to get out of the house for a bit." He awaited her response, but when she did not readily offer one, he further enticed, "We can take the back road drive into the city—pay Chef Antoine a visit."

At the suggestion she shook her head while she removed his hand from her hair. "I'm not ready to go out. To be among the public, I'm just not ready."

Jacob huffed with frustrated disappointment. "Alex, your period of mourning doesn't have to end. I just want you to get out of this house; to get some fresh air."

"And I just want you to understand that I need to move in my own time, Jacob."

Taken aback by the irony of her request, he released her hand and attempted to wipe the distress from his face. "Alex-"

"I don't expect you to understand, Jacob," she crudely interjected.

Jacob breathed in aggravation at her dismissal. "Here you go again with that."

"With what?"

"That dismissive statement about how you think that I don't understa-"

"Because you don't."

"Because it's never clear what you think I don't understand, Alexandre..."

Jacob truncated his rebuttal in an attempt to allow her an opportunity to respond. When she offered none, he asked, "What is it that you think I don't understand, Alex? Is it pain? Is it disappointment?"

Alexandre held her silence.

"Or is it just everything that accompanies a loss? Because I can tell you right now, Alexandre, that just because you still have a pulse doesn't mean I haven't lost you. It just means you're not dead."

Giving no thought to his attestation, Alexandre elucidated, "...I don't expect you to understand because you hated him."

The harsh accusation astonished Jacob and he, first, disabused her of her assumption by stating, "I did not hate him, Alex. He was the biological father of our son. How could I hate him?" Jacob then corrected her belief by emphasizing, "What I hated was what the two of you did to me—to us—to our family."

Alexandre huffed at the delivery of his message. It inaccurately implied that Lance's and her actions were malicious and calculated. "What we did was nothing we planned, Jacob. It just happened. It happened and I waited to tell you. But, honestly, Jacob, had I told you sooner would it have really made a difference?"

Jacob felt his body temperature rise at the same rate of his anger. He detested her haughty question for three reasons. First, it obscured the fact that the truth was unveiled by individuals who had not been her or Lance. Second, the question did not consider the fact that had the two of been forthcoming about their intent to revisit their past, Jacob could have removed himself as a blockade in their journey. And finally, it failed to consider that, undoubtedly, the agony, disappointment, and shame experienced by all parties could have been mitigated.

"…Yes, Alexandre, it would have…Perhaps you will understand that once you have concluded your period of mourning."

"This is so much more than just mourning my dead husband—I mean, Lance—" she corrected after noticing the sting of her comment on Jacob's countenance.

Jacob folded his arms across his chest. He then encouraged her to continue, "Then what is it?"

"…This is about all the other headaches that I have to contend with…About how I am being tried by a jury of the public for disappearances and deaths I know nothing about. I am taunted almost daily by threats; and I am in constant question of myself, my decisions, my actions—always asking if I am doing the correct thing by serving these children or am I contributing to the harm being done."

She paused briefly to breathe and reflect on the last three years of her career on the bench. "…There is no delicate balance. All family separation is bad for children and there are no cautionary tales to prevent the ramifications of separations—the system is badly broken and the children suffer from this brokenness."

After lowering her head into the palms of her hands, Alexandre lastly uttered, "And…and the media is constantly baiting me, expecting a response to Hannah Rubio's adjudication…"

No longer sympathetic to her suffering after hearing her litany of excuses, Jacob questioned, "Well?"

She lifted her head and met his eyes. "Well, what?"

"Well, what is your response?"

Alexandre looked away, rolling her eyes. "…Not you, too."

"Not me what?…I'm on your side, Alexandre. I've always been on your side. But the universe did not stop just because your world halted. People's lives and liberties are at stake and that has not changed because life happened to you."

Despite the desire to belabor his point, Jacob relented after seeing the brokenness in her visage. He took a deep breath and forced the air through his nostrils as he allowed the silence to usher tranquility into the room.

When a moment passed, Jacob extended his hand, turned her face to him, and spoke gingerly, "Look, I understand that grief is a lifelong journey and it's a process that is more circular than linear.

So, I'm not suggesting you return to work before you're ready, but I am suggesting that if you have a response that can potentially seal the fate of that young girl, then you make it known, Alex."

After wiping with his thumb the tears that fell from her eyes, Jacob dropped his hand to hers, held it, and met her gaze once more. "Do not allow these equivocators who know so little about you, your morals, your values, or your beliefs, to speak for you." He leaned in to press his forehead against hers and whispered on her lips, "Alex, that is not the woman I married…That is not the woman that I am still in love with." He then kissed her long enough for a chill to swell in his spine, but short enough before his emotions overcame him.

Alexandre watched Jacob rise from his seat and exit her office. As she peered out the window that overlooked the backyard, she contemplated every word Jacob spoke. She reflected on the life she lived and the legacy she wanted to leave behind. She considered all that she continued to cleave to, both spiritually and professionally, irrespective of the strong differing opinions of others.

When it was finally unveiled that her issue with Hannah Rubio was not one of absolution, but of forgiveness, Alexandre stood to her feet and plodded to her desk. She lowered herself in front of her laptop and began to draft a request to deny judicial waiver.

*** *** ***

Jacob entered the front door of the house just as Gabriele was approaching to exit it. After he placed his leather briefcase in the foyer closet, Jacob greeted the attorney with a firm handshake and inquired, "How is it going?"

Gabriele responded first in Italian then vented, "Her defense would be so much easier if she weren't so stubborn…Still, it is not anything that I can't handle."

He placed a hand on Jacob's triceps and firmly squeezed it. "Please try to reason with her," Gabriele lowly spoke partly in jest as he peered deep into Jacob's eyes.

Jacob sneered and replied, "If you as her legal counsel can't, then I as her husband have a snowball's chance..."

Gabriele chuckled then stated, "Touché...I will be in touch, my friend."

Jacob expressed his gratitude while he politely opened the door. After Gabriele's exit, he secured the entrance and stared blankly at the mahogany, reflecting on the attorney's comments.

"Thanks for showing him out," Alexandre stated as she strolled into the foyer. I would have done it, but had to take a call."

Jacob pivoted in the direction of her voice and nodded in response to her appreciation. He then asked, "How did your meeting go?"

She merely shrugged and answered, "I have been officially named in a lawsuit, but Gabriele has said that he is handling it."

Jacob huffed at her nonchalance. "Gabriele has also said that this handling of it would be a lot smoother if you weren't so obstinate."

Vexed by the subliminal suggestion that she was being unreasonable, Alexandre retorted, "Well, if the two of you already spoke, then why ask me about the meeting?"

"Because we didn't speak, Alex. I'm trying to speak now— to you."

She deeply respired, turned on her heels, and started toward the stairs. "I'm not feeling well. I'm going to lie down...I need a nap."

"Alex," Jacob called after her. When she did not halt her steps, he called out another time and began to trail her.

"Alex."

Alexandre ignored the repeated call of her name as she walked towards the master bedroom. Before she could enter it, Jacob gripped her wrist and pulled her to face him.

"Do not do this, Alexandre," he angrily demanded.

She yanked her arm free of his grasp and responded, "Do not do what, Jacob?"

"Shut me out!"

When she flinched at his tone, he immediately lowered it. "I'm sorry, Alex." He stepped to close the space between them and cupped her face with his hands. After pressing his forehead on hers, he whispered. "Please don't shut me out. You're not alone in this... I'm here for you, Alexandre...We are in this together."

Alexandre lowered her lids over her eyes as his words resonated with her. "...I know, Jacob...I know and I thank you..."

Overwhelmed with emotions, she touched his lips with hers as she covered his hands with hers. She deepened the kiss when he did not pull away and slowly moved his hands down to her tender, swollen breasts. It had been so long since he had touched her.

"Stop, Alex," Jacob beseeched, attempting to take back control of his hands.

"Please, Jacob," she protested, tightening her grip with hope that he would succumb to her foreplay.

"No, Alex...Alex, stop." When he finally broke free, he stepped from her personal space. "I can't do this."

Devasted by the rejection, but more emotional from the pregnancy hormones, Alexandre vehemently asked, "Who is she, Jacob?!"

Astounded by the inquisition, Jacob simply breathed, "Wow. Really?"

"Yes, really...You haven't touched me in months..."

Jacob was enraged by her wanton accusation, but more exhausted with their interminable fight. As of late, it was a fight to leave, a fight to stay, and a fight to survive their union. Each day in their marriage that had once given him life was now a depletion of his energy.

"And the reason I haven't touched you could not possibly be any other than another woman?" He offhandedly questioned.

"What are you doing here, Jacob?" Alexandre callously questioned in response to his question.

"...Excuse me?"

Ignoring the hurt, disappointment, and anger she witnessed in his eyes, she repeated irately, "What are you doing here, Jacob?"

Jacob contorted his face and squinted his eyes in confusion. Determined to remain the calmer of the two of them, he relaxed his muscles and breathed deeply. "I'm not sure that I know what you mean."

"The cooking, the cleaning, the tending to me? Why?"

"Why? What do you mean why? You're my wife, that's why."

"Oh, please, Jacob. At this point, I'm your wife only in name, certainly not in practice." When he failed to respond to her observation, Alexandre finally confessed to what he already knew to be true, "I've lied to you; cheated on you; embarrassed you; I've done all but physically stab you in the heart and you are still here. Why?"

"I've told you why."

Alexandre shook her head in disbelief—no one in her life, but Jesus Christ, was that forgiving. "I don't believe you, Jacob…I know that this is some sort of sick and sadistic ploy to right the wrongs that I have committed against you. I just know it."

Jacob scoffed at the assertion then rolled his eyes. "You're real a piece of work, Alex. You know that, right? Because you really are, and you're not making sense right now."

"I'm not making sense?"

"Yes, you're not making sense and I cannot talk to you when you're like this." Jacob turned on his heels to retreat to the guestroom. He believed that they needed time and space to pacify their fury.

Alexandre grasped the sleeve of his business shirt and yanked him towards her. "I'm making perfect sense, Jacob," she hotly contested.

Releasing his garment, she peered deep into the windows of his soul and surmised, "I am making sense and I know just what you are doing…I know you want me to get accustomed to you being here so that you can then desert me…You will leave me just like I left you and that will be your ultimate revenge—your way of making things right all while remaining the victim wronged by my infidelity."

Taken aback by the preposterous and vindictive plot she had concocted in her perverse mind, Jacob muttered in a faint whisper, "You're unbelievable, Alex."

"I'm unbelievable?"

"Yes, you're unbelievable," he repeated, elevating his voice with each syllable.

Desperate to end their childlike squabble, Jacob pivoted to depart from her presence; but when her comments gnawed at his core, he halted his steps and rotated his body to face her.

As his eyes pierced hers, Jacob stated, "If that's what you really think of me, Alex, then you have just proven that you don't know me at all."

She shrugged her shoulders at the summation and simply replied, "You're right, I don't know you..."

Jacob stifled the pain caused by her cruel remark. He expended almost four years of his life learning and growing in their love and, now, he could not recognize the woman he was in love with. The woman who introduced herself to him several years ago was warm, amicable, joyous, and tranquil. The unknown stranger who now stood before was cold, bitter, angry, and hostile.

After Jacob fought to swallow the knot that formed in his throat, he spoke, "Well, know this, Alexandre, revenge never makes things right—it only balances the scales for a brief moment...I have nothing to gain by hurting you in the way that you hurt me."

Jacob awaited her response, but she offered none. So, he cleared his throat and respectfully suggested, "Go take your nap, Alex."

Alexandre watched as he turned on his heels and began his journey to the room that he claimed as his own—it was a space that was distant from in hers with a bed apart from her.

"Get out," she commanded to his back.

Jacob arrested his step, turned to meet her hard glare, and questioned, "Excuse me?"

"You heard me, Jacob—get out. I want you out of my house now."

Jacob huffed hot air at the audacity of her demand. He then began to recall the numerous resources expensed to transition her home into a haven for their newly established family. From the moment she accepted his proposal for marriage, all that Jacob owned was hers to have. Consequently, it aggrieved him to now witness her selfish nature increasingly unveil itself at the time of their discord.

Closing the distance between them, Jacob responded with conviction, "If you force me out of *our* home, Alex, I will prove to you that you are not the only that can break a vow. Promise or no promise, I will walk out that door and never return."

Shaken by the threat, Alexandre lowered her eyes and swallowed the bulge in her throat. She had vehemently spoke in anger and frustration, and did not allow herself time to contemplate his reaction to her action.

"...Hopefully, in time, Jay will forgive me," he contritely uttered when a premonition of his stepson's forlorn visage clouded his mind. Jacob immediately began to regret in advance the angst he would cause him.

Alexandre raised her head at the subtle revelation and replied in dismay, "...Well, there we finally have it—the true reason why you are here." She chuckled lightheartedly then continued, "I should have known. You are not here for me, Jacob. You are here because of a promise you made to a 13-year-old child."

Jacob, exhausted by their fight, shrugged at her myopic view of his consideration. "I suppose you're right, Alexandre. If we follow your logic that I couldn't have more than one reason for being here for you, then you are right." He inhaled deeply and exhaled audibly. "I will give you the night. If you still want me gone in the morning, I will leave by the afternoon."

Uninterested in her rebuttal, he turned in the direction of his sanctuary to shower and change.

"I thought you would still be napping," he admitted, widening the door and entering the bedroom. Alexandre had changed into soft pink, maternity nightie and sat in the cushioned chair near the window.

She turned her gaze from the dark abyss to see Jacob, dressed in loungewear, walk towards her. "I never slept...I couldn't."

Jacob did not want to revisit their earlier quarrel. So, focused on the purpose of his entry, he asked, "Are you hungry? I could order-in so you don't have to eat my cooking?"

She grinned, ascertaining that his gesture stemmed from her earlier comment. "I love your cooking, Jacob—you know that," she professed. "It's just that...," she lowered her eyes as her words trailed off. She made a lot of statements that she now regretted and wished she could take back. "...I'm sorry."

He lowered himself to his knees in front of her, took her hands into his, and kissed the back each of them. After lifting her bowed head, he spoke, "I'm sorry, too, Alex. I never considered how my being here impacted you; how it was a constant reminder of your downfall...I-I get it now...I guess...I guess in some ways I was hurting more than helping you."

Alexandre nodded, appreciating his understanding and accepting his apology. "I'm okay, Jacob. Really, I am. So, don't feel obligated to stay." With a heavy heart, she added, "I don't know how Lance's death changes things legally, but, if your annulment request morphs into divorce proceedings by the time our court date arrives, I won't contest it."

"Alex-"

"The court may make you wait until after the baby is born to confirm paternity though."

"She is mine, Alex. I don't need a test to confirm it. The same way that you are mine and Jaamyas is mine, she is mine as well."

Alexandre feebly smiled at his loving and committed heart. In that moment, she recognized that, although the test of paternity was not what Jacob wanted, it was what she needed. Alexandre selfishly needed the truth so that she could always be prepared for his imminent departure.

"...Take the test, Jacob," she offered in the way of advice that was more legal than marital. "Take the test to know for sure, and if she is not yours, then you will be free...free to be with her."

"Alex, there is no her," he blatantly disabused while ignoring her advice concerning a paternity test. "There is only you. For the last several years, it's only been you."

Jacob kissed her forehead and then pressed his against hers. "I never wanted the annulment and certainly don't want a divorce...I love you, Alex. I'm in love with you..."

He held his breath before his emotions had the opportunity to overwhelm him and bring tears to his eyes. Following the regaining of his composure, Jacob confessed, "…I'm too weak to leave—a life without you is unfathomable…"

Alexandre cupped his faced and kissed him until he returned her fervor. The familiar warmth of his lips and taste of his mouth sent a cool chill up her spine and a low moan escaped her.

Jacob lifted her from her seat as he rose from his knees and carried her to the bed. He gently rested her in the center of the mattress and then pressed down the waistband of his lounge pants just enough to free himself. After methodically moving her wet panties to the side, he slowly entered her firm body. He gripped her left hand and pushed it into the mattress, ignoring the discomfort caused by their metal wedding bands pressed together. A few short strokes later his body quivered in a climatic release.

"…I'm…I'm so sorry," he panted in disappointing embarrassment. "I…"

Alexandre met his eyes and smiled. As she gently caressed his face, she whispered, "It's okay." She then pressed him on his back and straddled him. "I've missed you, too," she professed while she eased him back into her warmth and moved until he hardened a second time. She kept moving until climatic releases quaked both their bodies.

*** *** ***

"Mooooooooom," Jaamyas sang, entering the front door early Saturday morning. He tossed his keys into the dish on the foyer table and quickly kicked off his shoes.

"Mooooooooom," he repeated racing to the kitchen. When she was not found, he dashed to her office. "Mom?"

He groaned in impatient excitement as he had not seen his mother in weeks. "Mom, where are you?"

Jaamyas returned to the foyer and jogged up the stairs in pairs. "Mooooooooom." He burst through the master bedroom, giving no mind to a courtesy knock, and fell into the space next to her. "Moooom," he breathed, throwing his arms around the fullness of her belly.

"Hey, kiddo," she sleepily greeted, blinking open her eyes.

Jacob shifted his weight and adjusted his embrace of Alexandre. "Hey, son," he muttered in his sleep.

"Hi, Jacob," Jaamyas responded and then claimed more of his mother's body.

Alexandre snickered quietly at her son's competitive spirit and cautioned, "Watch out for your sister."

"I'm sorry." He kissed the duvet that covered her womb and moved up higher to meet his mother face-to-face. "I've missed you, Mom."

"I've missed you, too, baby." She kissed his forehead and held him near her heart. Taking in the shea scent of his bodywash and lotion, and the peppermint of his toothpaste, she muttered, "I've missed you so much."

"May I come home then?"

Alexandre contemplated the personal and professional recommendations that she and her son should spend time apart; that limited access to each other via phone conversations would allow them to heal from their loss in their separate ways. Though she loathed the suggestion, Alexandre valued the validity of it. Without question, Jaamyas would have spent an immeasurable amount time nursing her grief that he would have failed to nurture his own.

Witnessing now the brightness that had returned to eyes, Alexandre knew that she had made the right decision in conceding. She and her son were now in a place to move forward together. "...Yes, son, you may come home."

"Thank you," he breathed in relief. The earlier responses to his many requests to return home, or even to visit, were always different, but none were ever what he hoped for.

Recalling that she was still in bed, Jaamyas inquired, "Why are you still in bed, Mom? You never sleep-in on the weekends unless you're sick. Are you sick?"

Alexandre stroked the waves in his hair and responded, "No, baby. I'm not sick; just tired—that's all."

"Oh okay. Well, let's be tired together and veg-out in front of the TV."

Alexandre smirked at the idea. Despite wanting to sleep-in in her comfortable king-sized bed, she knew that these infrequent mother-son moments would eventually diminish to none as he aged. So, it behooved her to seize and cherish every opportunity.

"Okay, Jay. Let me shower and change. I will meet you downstairs."

"Awesome. I will let Mama Sea know that she doesn't have to stick around while I pack more clothes, because I am staying."

After smiling at his glowing face, Alexandre encouraged, "Okay, you do that."

*** *** ***

In the immaculately decorated nursery, Jaamyas stood closely to Alexandre at the changing table that was covered with clean laundry.

"These clothes are so tiny," Jaamyas commented, holding a onesie at eye level to inspect it. He then folded it in half and placed it with the others.

Alexandre rolled her eyes and chuckled. Since the start of his offering to assist her, she remained unsure if his attempt to "lend a hand" with folding his sister's garments was more of a help than a hindrance.

Retrieving the half-folded onesie to refold it, Alexandre commented, "Of course they are tiny, Jay. She will be tiny."

Jaamyas contorted his face in disbelief, plucked a t-shirt from the heap, and inquired, "Was I this tiny?"

Alexandre grinned and responded, "Yes, you were…In fact, you were actually very tiny because you were premature…"

Her mind wandered and a quiet stillness fell in the room. She reflected on the several years that preceded his thirteenth birthday until her thoughts hovered around the final months of his gestation. Varying stressors had catapulted her into premature labor. Alexandre recalled that she was anxious by the last weeks of law school, tensed from the preparation of the bar exam, and worried by the absence of her husband. Undoubtedly, it was the grace of God that allowed them both to survive the delivery.

"…You were always so small for your age," Alexandre murmured, finally breaking the short silence.

"Hello," he announced in irritation of his mother's dismal of his current plight. "I am still small."

She shook her head in dissent. "My wallet says otherwise, Jay. You are growing. You may not notice it or choose to believe it, but you are growing."

Though he cleaved to his disbelief, Jaamyas relented, "Maybe, I guess…but I am still the smallest on the team and in my class."

"Yeah, for now, but I am confident that you are going to sprout to the size your father was in no time; especially now that you have transitioned into adolescence."

"Besides," she began to add as an encouraging reminder, "it is the slow and-"

"Strong growth that surpasses the fast and weak one," they spoke in unison.

Jaamyas shrugged at the axiom his mother often recited whenever he expressed his discontent with his stature. Though he remained skeptical, he lacked the concern to refute Alexandre's point. "I just thought I would always be small like you."

His unexpected comment tickled her and she erupted with laughter. When she regained her bearings, Alexandre replied, "Don't insult your mother, Jay. I'm the only one you've got."

Jaamyas clandestinely rolled his eyes and then begrudgingly shared, "You're the envy of all the mothers at my school and the desire of all the horny teenagers who gossip in the locker room. Trust me, Mom, I'm not insulting you."

Alexandre blushed at the revelation as she overlooked the show of insolence that Jaamyas had assumed he had concealed from her. "Well, trust me, I don't want to know what you pre-pubescent boys discuss in the locker room."

Jaamyas laughed. "Please believe me, it's nothing different from the boys of your younger years…Just like you always tell me, time may change, but human desires do not."

Alexandre shook her head as she rolled her eyes at the method in which he applied the wisdom she had bestowed him. Unbeknownst to her, locker room studies were included in the tuition she paid to the private Christian school. In any event, Alexandre was elated to know that Jaamyas was listening and heeding her advice, particularly in the times she was certain that he was not.

Changing the uncomfortable subject and breaking the brief silence, Jaamyas announced, "So, after much thought, I have decided on the name for the baby."

"Oh really? What is it?"

"Amari."

"Amari—that's beautiful. How did you come to decide on it?"

"…Well, I gave much thought to the situation she is being born into." Jaamyas shrugged and then continued, "It's not the best, but she is loved and is still a blessing to our family—'a miracle of God.'"

At the conclusion of his explanation, Alexandre contemplated all that Jaamyas had said. His summation of their household predicament and the familial situation that his little sister would soon be subjected to resonated with her. Though Jaamyas minced words, it was true—this innocent life within her will soon be born into a rocky homelife, an unstable marriage, unknown paternity, and a murdered father.

"…I love it, Jay," she finally spoke and then kissed his forehead. "It's a beautiful name."

Jaamyas's lips stretched into a wide grin at her approval and his heart melted at her affection. He attempted to conceal it but he could not hide that, even in the years of expected teenage rebellion, he still yearned for his mother's approval.

"Have you thought of her first name?" He inquired.

"I have," she simply answered then elaborated, "but I am still deciding. I can't choose between Braelynn and Jaiyana—they both mean strength."

Jaamyas cringed at the thought of potentially sharing his nickname with a sibling. The fact that it would be shared with a girl compounded his worries.

"Another Jay?" He bemoaned in disapproval.

"We could call her Yana, Jay," she offered after realizing his point that she had not considered.

Jaamyas shook his head. "No, my vote is for Braelynn at least then we can call her Lynn. There will be no confusion with Lynn."

Alexandre snickered at his juvenile logic and conceded, "Fine, Jaamyas. Braelynn it is then...I will have a Jay," she confirmed, nudging his triceps in jest, then completed, "and I will have a Lynn."

After exhaling in relief, Jaamyas reflected on his sister's name. "...Our strong miracle of God, Braelynn Amari. It has a nice ring to it...I like it, I like a lot."

"Me, too, son."

"Jay, may I have a moment with your mother please?"

Both Alexandre and Jaamyas abruptly turned to the voice at the door.

"Jacob, I didn't hear you come in," Alexandre professed. "When did you get home?"

Jacob ignored her question as he shifted his gaze at Jaamyas. "Jay, please, give us a moment?"

Jaamyas nodded and lowly spoke, "sure," as he placed the garment down on the changing table and then exited the room.

Once Jacob confirmed Jaamyas's retreat to his bedroom, he walked into the nursery and tossed the document in front of Alexandre.

"What the hell is that, Alex?"

Reading the bold text of the title that answered the complaint filed against her, Alexandre responded, "You were in my office rummaging through my-"

"I was looking for the insurance documents that you supposedly signed, but can't seem to remember to return to me," he finished for her before she had the opportunity to accuse him of invading her privacy.

"Why are you doing this, Alex? Entertaining this lawsuit when you have so many other things to contend with?"

"What do you suppose I do, Jacob? Better yet, what would you like me to do?"

"Quash this…Throw some money at it if you have to. Just make it go away."

"No, absolutely not. That's not who I am, Jacob, and you know that."

"Not who you are?!" He angrily repeated.

Jacob turned from her in frustration to pace the hardwood floor. He was infuriated by the fact that of the many battles she had to choose from she had selected this one—a lawsuit with the potential of becoming a never-ending quagmire. Vigorously rubbing his forehead, he contemplated the best delivery of his curt message.

Halting his steps in front of her, Jacob glared and reminded, "Who you are is a wife and a mother of two children who need you." He lowered his hands to her protruding womb and spoke, "Your fragile condition doesn't allow for any other demands."

Alexandre considered the sound argument he presented and his fervent show of concern. However, her stubbornness would not permit more than a minimal consideration of the facts he regurgitated. Her mind fixed on her decision, she covered his hands with hers, gently squeezed them to acknowledge his trepidation, and then gradually eased them down her bulge until they fell to the air.

"Jacob, even if I were to entertain your request, we are not in a financial position to make this go away. With our existing living expenses, impending medical bills, and approaching family leave, we cannot-"

Jacob dismissed her pessimism with a shrug. "What is the typical settlement paid for a case like this? A quarter million—a half?"

"Jacob, we can't-"

"We can liquidate assets. I will start with selling the penthouse."

His desperate but aggressive show of heroism, caught her breath, and for a moment Alexandre could only gawk at him in adoration.

"I…I-I can't—I mean I-I won't let you do that, Jacob," she murmured, shaking her head. "I know that you really want to bequeath the property to Jay, and I don't want—I won't allow him to suffer any more for my mishaps."

"Alex, there will be other opp-"

"The answer remains no," she reiterated more forcefully.

After respiring in exasperation, Jacob proclaimed, "Then I will sell my car and drive the truck."

She reflected on the gas mileage of the luxury sedan and compared it to that of his sport utility vehicle. Shifted her head from side-to-side in dissent, Alexandre lowered her tone and softly spoke to his generous heart, "No, Jacob…That doesn't even make economic sense."

Deflated by the rejection of his attempts to assist her, Jacob offered in a manner that was more of a plea than a suggestion, "…Then the Steinway."

Alexandre turned from his desperate eyes in an effort to disregard them as she conveyed, "I can't let you do that either…Jacob, you love that piano."

"Not more than I love you, Alex." He used an index finger to gently pivot her face to his. Following, he peered deep into her eyes and whispered, "Not more than I love you."

When she spoke nothing in response, Jacob cleared his throat as he lowered his hand, and confidently assured her of their fiscal stability. "We have quite a few investments that are doing really well. We will be okay."

"…No, Jacob…No…Thanks, but no…I can't—I won't allow you to do any of it."

Infuriated, Jacob inhaled deeply and exhaled loudly. "Alexan-"

"It's not just about the money, Jacob. Paying off these litigious opportunists will set a bad precedent!"

"Damn a bad precedent, Alexandre. I don't care!" He retorted, matching her intonation.

"Well, I do care, Jacob! A settlement will open the floodgates of frivolous lawsuits, especially against officers of the court!"

Jacob captured his tongue between his front teeth to halt his immediate, tyrannical response. As a pregnant silence grew in their daughter's nursery, he fought to suppress his fury. Despite her more pressing obligations, Alexandre was forever thinking and acting as an attorney first.

Wiping the frustration from his visage, Jacob burned his gaze into hers and admonished as his final resort, "…Well, also care about this, Alex, I will not stand by you in this fight. Because I will not watch you destroy yourself, your health, or your wellness for the sake of judicial standards—I won't."

Alexandre struggled with the knot in her throat until she finally swallowed it. The sternness of Jacob's tone and the context of his message startled her. Right or wrong, in concurrence or dissent, he had unwaveringly remained at her side for each trial and every issue. The possibility of losing him as her anchor, and her ship floating adrift in the vast sea of unknowns, brought her fast-moving vessel to an abrupt halt.

She lowered her lids over eyes and began to employ her square breathing technique. As she contemplated all that Jacob had mentioned, Alexandre reflected on her counsel's advice to consider judicial immunity. For the sake of peace, her marriage, and her family, she opened her eyes and lowly spoke, "I will confer with Gabriele about alternative options."

*** *SEVENTEEN* ***

The warmth of the shadow that hovered over her caused her to stir in her sleep. Subconsciously recognizing that the heat derived from another body, she flickered her lids until her tired eyes begrudgingly opened. Slow to adjust to the sunlight beaming into her home office, she caught a glimpse of the silhouette as it departed.

"Jay," Alexandre lowly croaked. After clearing her throat, she spoke, "Jay."

When no one responded, she rose to a seated position on the sofa and gently massaged the ache in her shoulder and neck as she stretched her tendons. The pain from inadvertently napping on uncomfortable furniture would be worse the next morning.

Alexandre noticed the book on the coffee table. It was the very one that had lulled her to sleep. But instead of it being on the floor where she had tiredly left it when it fell from her hands, it was now closed with the bookmark inserted in it. Jaamyas would have never retrieved the book from its fallen location. He often expressed that doing so would contribute to her losing her place in the book. Knowing this revealed her true visitor and Good Samaritan-

"Jacob," she called over her shoulder. She awaited a moment for a response, but no vocal one was given. Instead, she was answered with deafening silence—not even the racket that accompanied movement could be heard.

Alexandre glanced at the hands of her wrist watch and noticed that she had been sleeping longer she had thought.

"Ja-"

Startled, she flinched at the sound of the alarm chime. A hand at her heart, Alexandre paced her breathing as she listened to the announcement that garage door had opened.

"Jacob."

The unusual silence concerned her. Atypical of her family's return home, there was no pattering of feet, boisterous announcement of their arrival, or clamor that occurred with movement. At the hasty thought of an intruder, Alexandre grew anxious and her heart raced in fear. She breathed deeply to calm her paranoia while she carefully considered her subsequent actions. To contact law enforcement without substantial proof of an uninvited guest was would only exacerbate the perception that she had become dangerously irrational. So, against her sound judgement, she opted to first confirm that there was an intruder in the house.

Her back leaned into the plush cushion behind her, Alexandre lowered herself to the floor. Maneuvering her bulging abdomen, she retrieved her Louisville slugger from beneath the furniture, and then used the seat of the sofa to assist her in standing to her bare feet. As she held the bat in her left hand, she unhurriedly crept to exit the office.

"Jacob," she called out, walking down the hall.

When silence was returned, she spoke, "Jaamyas," as she cleared the corner and quietly plodded through the family room towards the kitchen.

Hearing faint clatters in the garage, Alexandre slowed her steps, mindful of any noise that would alert the home invader of her oncoming defense.

Alexandre pressed her back against the wall outside the mudroom to remain out of sight. As she listened intently to the shuffling through the entrance, she directed her focus to the approaching footsteps. Using the sound of the shoes on the hardwood floors, Alexandre echolocated the distance of the intruder. Once their nearness was determined, Alexandre seized the air in her lungs, gripped the maple bat with both hands, and swung with the might that her fear and anger propelled.

In his periphery, he saw the object coming in his direction and ducked. His quick reflexes coupled with her swing aimed inches too high, Alexandre missed his head and hit the entrance frame. He immediately dropped the grocery bags he held in the folds of each of his arms to defend himself.

"What the hell, Alex?!" He questioned in astonishment and rage as he caught the barrel of the bat during her second swing.

"Jacob?"

Jacob overpowered her strength, yanked the Slugger from her grip, and then ripped the baseball cap from his head. "Who else would it be?"

He first peered deep into her eyes and then looked at the damage to the frame that was intended for his cranium. After exhaling audibly, Jacob released her weapon to the floor and ignored the striking sound of wood on wood.

"Who else would it be, Alex?"

Alexandre took in the dark t-shirt and jersey shorts that he typically wore after a shower at the gym as she contemplated a response. Vigorously rubbing her forehead, she relived the last ten minutes that had preceded the incident. Though perplexed, she remained confident that there was an intruder in their home. However, she lacked the indisputable evidence to confirm it.

"I…I don't know…I thought someone was in the house."

Jacob huffed in disbelief, still startled by the unexpected assault. "Someone like who, Alexandre?"

She shrugged. "I'm not sure, but I know someone was here…With me…In the office. I was napping and I saw someone-"

"Napping," he repeated in incredulity. "With the garage door raised and the side door left unlocked?"

She met his gaze. "What?"

"Yes, while you were napping, you left the garage door raised and the side door unlocked."

Alexandre observed Jacob as he gathered the items from the floor and placed them back in the paper bags. While she did that, she began to reflect on the actions that she had taken upon her arrival from the courthouse. She raised the garage door, entered and parked her vehicle on the left side, lowered the garage door, exited and locked her vehicle, unlocked the side door to the house, entered the mudroom, and locked the side door to the house. Although she did not always park her vehicle in the garage, when she did, the routine was the same one she exercised each day. It only differed when she had her son with her.

Alexandre shook head in dissent. "No, I didn't. I'm sure of it."

"Well, it wasn't me," Jacob assured as he walked into the kitchen and lowered the loads onto the island. "And it definitely wasn't Jaamyas."

Alexandre remembered the chime and the announcement of the alarm minutes prior to Jacob's entry. "Where is Jay?"

"You mean where would he still be if I had not picked him up?"

Alexandre lowered her lids over her eyes and quietly cursed at herself. She had just remembered that she had been tasked with retrieving him after practice. "I'm sorry. I…I was reading and I…I fell asleep and slept longer than I anticipated."

"It's fine, Alex. He only had to wait an hour after he couldn't reach you."

"An hour?" She stressed in guilt.

Jacob clandestinely rolled his eyes. He loathed the way she coddled him. "He is fine, Alex. He wasn't waiting alone."

"Where is he now?"

"At Elijah's."

Alexandre nodded. "…I'm sorry, Jacob."

"About what, Alex?"

She watched him store the groceries in haste. She assumed that he was expediting the task to get away from her hysteria. "For my attack on you. I really thought-"

"It's fine, Alex," Jacob spoke in hopes to silence her. He remained too furious to speak about the incident.

"No, it's not fine. I really thought I was in danger. That there was an intruder in our home. So-"

Jacob closed the refrigerator and again stood behind the island that separated them. "So, you were defending yourself, Alex. I get it." Meeting her gaze, he candidly confessed, "Now, what I don't get is why you would leave the house unsecure if you felt so unsafe."

"But, Jacob, I didn't. Someone must have followed me in before the garage door completely lowered and…" Her voice trailed off when she saw the look of disbelief on his face.

"I'm not delirious, Jacob. Someone was in the house. Someone was in my office."

Jacob reminisced on the conversations that he had had with their OB/GYN and recalled the many side effects and complications of pregnancy. Undoubtedly, the hormonal imbalance was attributing to heightened forgetfulness, low energy, exhaustion, paranoia, and psychosis.

Jacob gingerly responded, "I know that you are not crazy, Alex. You have a lot going on professionally and personally, but this excessive paranoia has to end. You're worrying me and you scaring Jay."

"Excessive paranoia?! Jacob, I'm telling you that someone was in the house!"

Opting to remain the calmer of the two of them, Jacob inquired, "Okay, Alex. If that's the case, where is the intruder now?"

Despising his patronizing tone, Alexandre did not respond.

"Have you checked the house? Anything amiss or even missing?"

Again, Alexandre did not respond.

"I suppose if you had agreed to the security cameras I wanted installed prior to my moving in, we could at least review the footage and provide it to the police."

"And I told you that I did not want cameras because this is our home and not a prison," she vehemently spat, vexed that that he, first, recounted their debate at the most inopportune time; and second, failed to acknowledge her concession of the iron fence he had erected in the backyard. Even in that moment, Alexandre remained unclear of its purpose—to keep intruders out or their family caged in.

"And just how home-like is our fortress now, Alexandre?" Jacob mocked. "You consistently live in fear and paranoia, and I now have to contend with getting my head bashed in every time I walk through the door."

Alexandre remembered the incident with the book that had occurred in her home office, and thought to contest his unjust inquisition and inaccurate assessment. "Jacob-"

"This place is starting to closely resemble a prison," he spoke loudly over her, refusing to relinquish his point.

When she offered no words in response, he lowered his intonation and calmly asked, "Have you even called the police?"

She parted her lips to reply but determined it was futile in their argument and for law enforcement. So, Alexandre suppressed her rebuttal and, instead, accepted the possibility that what she was experiencing was, indeed, an apparition.

After inhaling deeply and exhaling audibly, Alexandre finally rejoined, "I will look into having someone come and repair the damage to the doorframe." She then pivoted to return to her office.

"Alex, wait," Jacob pleaded, gently grabbing her wrist to stop her.

He closed the space between them and cupped her face with his hands. "I get it. You are frightened and have every right to be, especially since the changes you have made to increase your security have been minimal at best. But you can't go around batting homeruns every time you are afraid...You could really hurt someone. You could have seriously hurt me."

She contemplated all that he said and recalled the advice of the private investigator she had procured several months prior. "Let's leave the country."

Jacob chuckled. "What?"

"You, Jay, and me. We could leave for France and stay until after the baby is born...We could stay until the end of the summer."

He released his grip of her arm and considered the suggestion along with his current workload. "You aren't serious, are you?"

"I am serious, Jacob. We talked about a visit in the past, so let's just do it now." She searched his eyes and noticed that he was not convinced. "Don't worry about the school year. It's coming to an end, and we can leave right after Jay's final week."

"I'm not concerned about Jay. I'm concerned about you. Are you even fit to travel in your condition?"

Alexandre nodded despite not having a definitive answer as several of her last medical visits concerning her geriatric pregnancy yielded the same results—the fetus was in superior health, but her own health was precarious. Exhausted by the ominous forewarnings, Alexandre postponed multiple times her first third-trimester evaluation.

Jacob observed her disposition while she replied to his inquiry and he grew skeptical. Alexandre had unnervingly shifted her body weight and tucked her hair behind her ear—all tells of a truth that she did not want to disclose. Nevertheless, Jacob conceded the point because he believed it to be futile to belabor an argument that he could easily confirm with their physician. So, instead, he deflected to the other looming ghost they were forced to contend with.

"What about the matter brought against you, Alex? Do you even have the liberty to leave the country?"

Alexandre stretched her lips into a wide grin at his concern. "Stop worrying, Jacob. Look, if you want, I will get Gabriele to confirm it."

Jacob seized a moment to consider her response. Despite his many reservations, he compromised. While nodding, he spoke, "Okay. If Gabriele confirms it, then okay."

"Okay?" She repeated in disbelief.

Taking a moment to consider that a family trip would be good for the three of them—soon-to-be four of them, Jacob confirmed and added, "Okay. This trip can serve as what we need to truly start anew and reconnect."

"I…I couldn't agree more," Alexandre uttered in astonished excitement.

*** *EIGHTEEN* ***

Alexandre breathed a sigh of relief when the vehicle she believed to be gradually trailing her finally passed. Without a doubt, her exhaustion coupled with the dimly lit courtroom garage exacerbated her paranoia—when her steps increased, so did the wheels of the vehicle, when her steps decreased, so did the wheels of the vehicle, and when her steps halted, so did the wheels of the vehicle. Her fear finally subsided when she stepped into the aisle of her parked car and the unsuspecting driver accelerated past her.

Inhaling deeply in practice of her square breathing technique, she attempted to calm her racing her heart. Once she felt she possessed the control needed to proceed home, Alexandre searched her tote for her keys.

"Oh no," she groaned when the keys were not located with the first pass of her hand. Following, she began removing bulk items and placed them on the roof her car.

"Damn it," Alexandre uttered when the bottom of her handbag was visible and no keys were discovered. She then commenced to reflect on her day in an effort to recall every drawer and door that needed to be secured or unsecured with a key.

"Damn it," she uttered once more, suspecting that she had forgotten the keys in her chambers.

Begrudgingly returning items to her tote, Alexandre began to dread the return to the building. The growing discomfort in her lower back and the pain in her feet heightened more her trepidation of the journey. Had it been any other item, she would have abandoned it until the next day.

The brown 9x12 mailing envelope was the last of the items left on her vehicle's hardtop. As she fingered the kraft material, Alexandre recalled its contents. It was a filed copy of the adoption petition that she had finally signed, submitted to the clerk of court, and requested that the matter be expedited. Her earnest desire was that the proceedings would be finalized by Father's Day and Jacob's birthday.

While Alexandre cautiously eased the envelop into her handbag, she pivoted to walk in the direction from which she had come. She ultimately surmised that the quicker she returned with her keys, the sooner she could arrive home to share the news with her husband and son.

Startled by her unexpected return to the chambers, she spoke with a quivering voice, "Your Honor, I thought you had left for the evening. I…I-"

"I did. Well, I was until I got to the garage and realized I forgot my…" Alexandre voice trailed off after realizing that she was offering an explanation to an individual who was not in need of one. Instead, it was the meddler standing behind the desk that owed Alexandre an explanation. The files she held in her hand and what she appeared to be rummaging through was indeed not a part of her job description.

"What are doing in here, Soledad?" She inquired hotly while walking further into her chambers.

Alexandre witnessed the custodian stammer her words, and she grew impatient. Closing the door behind her, she commanded, "Don't bother lying to me because you emptied my wastebasket before I left."

Soledad ceased speaking to consider the question and a sufficient answer to it. As she meditated on the truth, her anger quickly replaced her fear.

"I'm waiting," Alexandre pressed.

Soledad tossed the files on the desk and ignored the sound of the falling picture frames. She respired audibly and then boldly responded, "You know what? You're right. No need to lie. In fact, I am exhausted by all the lying."

Alexandre contorted her face in confusion. "What are you talking about?"

"My name is Soledad Maria Rodriguez."

Alexandre shrugged her shoulders. "…Okay, and?"

"And I'm the mother of Juan-Carlos Sanchez."

Alexandre took a moment to contemplate the name, assuming that it was of great importance to her. When nothing came to her remembrance, she sincerely apologized. "I'm sorry, Soledad, but I don't-"

"Remember," Soledad completed for her. "Yes, I know."

"I'm sorry. Am I supposed to know?"

Soledad chuckled in disbelief at her impoverished memory. It was indicative of Alexandre's minimal consideration for the surviving victim who she wounded more when she pardoned the offender; and, it was evident of her disregard for the families left to mourn the deceased victims.

"Almost two years ago, you made the decision to exonerate the rich, entitled reprobates that killed my son."

Alexandre shook her head in denial as she pondered the accusation. "I…I…"

Silence grew in the room as Alexandre reflected on the several cases that were brought before her during her tenure on the bench. Very few involved the loss of life. Just as she was about to resign her efforts in remembering, Alexandre recalled one matter that came before her her inaugural year on the bench. It was one that, despite the best protections of the juvenile court from the media, had become a high-profile matter.

"…The Mendelson matter?" Alexandre met her eyes and softly spoke, "…You're the mother of the deceased victim in the Mendelson matter?"

Soledad huffed. "At last, some recognition for who I truly am." She yanked off the badge pinned to her dark colored smock and threw it at her. After the badge struck Alexandre's shoulder and fell to the floor, Soledad confessed, "And just to be emphatically clear, I am not a struggling mother moonlighting as a janitor."

Confounded by the many falsehoods, Alexandre inquired, "What?...I don't understand...What? Why?"

"Do you really think I work here parttime to mop floors and empty wastebaskets?"

Now that the rhetorical question had been posed, Alexandre concluded that Soledad's employment was for nefarious reasons rather than the financial ones that she had previously stated. Unfortunately, however, Alexandre had no thoughts as to what those nefarious reasons were.

"Honestly, Soledad, I don't know why you are here or what is going on," Alexandre spoke truthfully.

Soledad rolled her eyes and scoffed at her naiveté.

"Please," Alexandre implored, "why don't you just tell me?"

When she provided no response, Alexandre encouraged, "Please just tell me what's really going on here and, hopefully, we can come to some resolve."

Silence prevailed in the chambers.

"Ms. Rodriguez?"

"Fine!" Soledad exclaimed in aggravation. "Since you cannot seem to remember, I will tell you." She pushed the loose hairs that fell on her face towards her thick ponytail and commenced explaining, "Two years ago, my son was struck and killed by a driver of a candy apple red Lamborghini—three privileged, white teenagers who had been drinking and partying and doing God-knows-what-else-that night in a $400,000 car—a car that is worth more than the house I own."

"...No," Alexandre dissented, now remembering the facts of the case. "The driver was not drinking. He was distracted, but he was not drinking, nor was he under the influence of drugs like the others in the vehicle...He was a good kid...He was the designated driver."

As she had years ago, Soledad ignored all the evidence in the Mendelson matter. "And my son was a good kid. AND MY SON was undistracted that night—rightfully in the pedestrian crosswalk and en route to the bus stop after his closing shift."

The heavy pressure between Alexandre's neck and abdomen made her chest ache. She was uncertain if the discomfort was attributed to the agony her heart felt, or the pain her lungs were experiencing from the air she held trapped in them. Recollecting all the involved parties, Alexandre allowed time for the familial connection to fully resonate with her.

"…That was your son? Juan-Carlos Sanchez was your son?"

Soledad failed to reply to a question that she believed to be already answered. Instead, she confessed, "You infuriate me with your questions that I have clearly provided responses to."

"I'm so sorry. Truly, I am…I-I don't mean to upset you it's just that…" Alexandre's voice trailed off as she contemplated the words that were necessary to console a grieving mother.

"It's just that what?"

"…It's just that…I-I had no idea that that was your son…"

"So, what, knowing my acquaintance then would have altered your decision?"

Shaking her head, Alexandre responded, "No…Honestly, no, it wouldn't…Soledad, that night was such an unfortunate accident."

Soledad huffed at her haughty conclusion and then retorted, "Unfortunate indeed."

"…So, what now?" Alexandre probed, looking down at the files on her desk that Soledad once held in her hands. "You're here to steal their case files?"

"Among other things," she merely replied and then added, "Working here has proven to be more beneficial than I originally thought."

Taken aback by the Soledad's answer, Alexandre stammered, "Beneficial? Beneficial how?…F-for what purpose?"

"For what purpose?" Soledad mocked. She allowed herself a moment to reflect on and chuckled at her well devised plan—a plan she had no intentions of disclosing. Instead, Soledad offered in a disgruntled monologue, "Those entitled shits have all completed their meager community service hours, graduated high school, and gone off to college. They have all aged through the system and there is no getting to them now. They are all living their enriched merry lives as if nothing ever happened—like life did not stop for me the day they killed my son."

"What happened to your son was a real tragedy, and, again, I am sorry for your loss, but life does not stop because a tragedy happens to you." Remembering that Jacob had spoken those very words to her, she added, "Trust me, I know from my own experience."

"You lost a husband," Soledad retorted. "That pales in comparison to the loss of a child."

Alexandre ignored the dismissal of her agony and retorted, "Those boys paid their proverbial debts to society; so, those boys deserve an opportunity to start anew."

"No, what they deserved was a sentence to hell."

Believing that she allowed Soledad the moment she needed to finally recite her victim impact statement, Alexandre was now exhausted by her irrational rant.

"You need to leave, Ms. Rodriguez. You need to leave now and never return."

"Oh, I plan to, Your Honor, but now that you have caught me in the act, you're coming with me."

Alexandre shook her head in opposition. "I'm not going anywhere with you. You are insane."

"Yes, I am and I'm okay with that. I'm okay with that because sometimes being a good mother takes precedent over being a good person."

Weary of her intentions, Alexandre announced, "I'm calling security," as she reached in her handbag for her cell phone. When it was not in the designated compartment or at the bottom of her tote, she presumed that she had left that, too, on her desk.

Soledad revealed the electronic device and inquired, "Looking for this?"

Alexandre's shoulders sank in distress as she refrained from responding.

Soledad tossed the phone in the far corner of the desk and then retrieved Alexandre's keys. "Or what about these?"

Dangling the noisy metal, Soledad taunted, "You really do have a horrible habit of leaving things in places that the wrong hands can get to."

Considering the amount of access the keys granted to her professional and personal life, Alexandre surmised, "…You've been in my home, haven't you?...You somehow managed to copy my keys and you were in my house."

Soledad shrugged. "Maybe, maybe not."

Alexandre deciphered her response and determined for herself that the unsolicited visits to her domicile were attributed to Soledad. Reminiscing on the unfavorable gifts and messages, Alexandre linked those mishaps to the culprit before her, as well.

On one hand, to realize this information provided Alexandre with solace. She was confident that her ill-feelings were not paranoia. However, despite her myriad reservations, it had been easier to write-off her suspicions as hormonal just as the many others who blamed her advanced pregnancy did.

On the other hand, her accurate assumption heightened her concern for her son's safety. Similar to so many children his age, he remained naïve to the evils of the world. However, dissimilar to other children his age, his status as her son subjected him to predatory motives in which he would be used as a ploy for negotiations.

While several thoughts of Jaamyas began to overwhelm her, Alexandre managed to remember the firearm that Jacob had convinced her to conceal in her chambers. It was locked in the drawer of her credenza. So, all that was needed was for her to transition her mental energy in the development of a plan in which she could retrieve it. If given the opportunity, Alexandre knew that she, as had Soledad, would earnestly contemplate being a good mother over a good person.

Opting, first, the attempt to be a good person, Alexandre swallowed the knot in her throat and considered who remained at the courthouse at midnight. Having an unarmed and pregnant disadvantage, she needed assistance diffusing the confrontation that she no longer felt she had control over.

"Look, Ms. Rodriguez, I can't say it enough, I am truly sorry about your son—I really am. I am even more apologetic that you did not like my decision. But you must understand that I had to do what was just in the eyes of the law."

"JUST! My son was abruptly taken from me and those bastards walked free! Where is the justice in that?! Where is my justice?!"

"All parties involved were minors, just reckless teenagers out celebrating prom and the advent of their graduation. Unfortunately, yes, one poor decision made by the distracted driver cost you your son...And...I truly apologize-"

"Would it have been different if the roles were reversed?"

"Excuse me?"

"Would it have made a difference if my son was white and had come from heaps of money and the driver and the drunken teens were Hispanic?"

Alexandre inhaled deeply and exhaled loudly after realizing her angle. "Do you not see that I am a woman of color? Not to mention that my son is also a person of color."

Ignoring the observation, Soledad demanded, "Just answer the damn question!"

"No! No, I will not," Alexandre emphatically rejoined, realizing that Soledad's actions were like so many others among the public who have strong-armed their perception of justice. "I will not encourage this behavior by dignifying that inquiry with a response. The public cannot go rogue every time an officer of the court makes a decision in which they do not agree."

Alexandre boldly closed the space between them as far as the desk would allow, and grabbed the handpiece of her office phone. She hurriedly pushed the red emergency button that dialed security.

Soledad yanked the power cord from the phone. "It's almost insulting that you believe that this night is going to end well for you."

After tossing the handset on the desk, Alexandre courageously spoke, "...I'm not sure what that means, but whatever it is you are going to do, do it quickly, Ms. Rodriguez. I have done nothing to deserve this elongated torment."

Soledad sneered and countered, "Well, you have given me little choice now. My plan has now been completely shot to hell since you unveiled the truth."

"What plan?" Alexandre questioned in confusion. When Soledad did not immediately respond, she inquired further, "You mean the plan to rummage through my files and sell more privileged information to the press?...News flash, I always knew that that was an inside job. I was just pointing fingers at the wrong people."

Soledad laughed. "No. No, that is not it at all. It was never about the money. Although the financial gain was an added bonus, it was never about the money."

"Then what was this all for then?"

"Justice."

"Justice?"

"Yes, justice. And it wasn't all that difficult to obtain because you are one despised woman, Alexandre Denton-Hall."

Alexandre shrugged. "Well, that goes without saying."

"Touché." After a brief silence, she asked, "Shall we get going?"

Alexandre shook her head, knowing that her chances of survival would greatly plummet if she left the premises with her. "I'm not leaving here with you."

Soledad smiled as she recalled a benefit of being a courthouse employee—a badge that allowed her to bypass the stringent security checks. After she placed her foot on the desk, Soledad removed the small firearm that she daily concealed at her ankle.

"My friend here begs to differ," Soledad taunted, brandishing the weapon in her left hand.

Alexandre nervously swallowed the knot in her throat and surmised, "So, you're going to kill me."

"No, the initial plan was to first destroy your life as you did mine, starting with your career by way of a forced resignation after a series of missing and dead children as well as a harsh public outcry. And then…an unsuspecting suicide."

As she spoke, Alexandre mediated on the various unresolved events that had occurred within the last year. Many of them coincided with the timeframe of Soledad's hiring—which coincidentally paralleled Cynthia's date of hire.

Lowering her lids over her eyes, Alexandre began to immediately regret her misfire in Cynthia's direction. She noted that, upon her survival of this incident, their reconciliation would be among her priorities.

When she opened her eyes, Alexandre questioned, "…You murdered those children?"

"No, I executed justice," Soledad corrected in a simple answer and then continued, "my job as a security officer is to ensure safety. I did that by making right of the wrongs you discounted—to leave them unchecked would cause pandemonium."

Alexandre huffed at her asinine logic. "No, what was right was already achieved by *me* in accordance to the law. Therefore, what *you* committed was not justice, but revenge."

"STOP talking!" Soledad exclaimed, exhausted by the chatter that she believed to be a poor de-escalation of the matter. She took a deep breath to allow her temperament, as well as her intonation, to level.

"Now," Soledad calmly began again. "The way I see it, you can leave with me and we can do this in your car or some remote area after you have written a crafty note. Or, we can do this here. However, I prefer not to do this at the workplace; it's far too messy and traumatic for our colleagues."

Alexandre scoffed as she shook her head in incredulity and recited again, "You are insane."

Soledad thought for a moment and then shifted her head from side-to-side in disagreement. "No, I'm not…Now that I have had an opportunity to really think about it, I'm not insane at all. I'm just a mother."

Soledad placed Alexandre's keys in the pocket of her smock. Afterwards, she motioned to the door with her firearm as she stepped from behind the desk. "Let's go. We'll take the service elevator down to the basement garage."

Once she turned on her heels, Alexandre felt the hard metal press into her spine. With her brain racing quicker than her heart, she contemplated a way out of her plight. A weapon now threatening her life, Alexandre now knew that her chances of survival would not plummet, but be fully eliminated if she left the courthouse with her nemesis.

Feeling her daughter kick towards the rapid drumming in her chest, Alexandre dropped her hands to her womb and quick-wittedly feigned agony to a sharp pain. She bellowed as she folded over, holding tighter her large protrusion. When Soledad moved to assist her, Alexandre, first, knocked the firearm free of her grip, then, forcefully shunted her into the desk. Several contents crashed to the floor as each woman wrestled with the strength of the other. Their arms and legs flailed and their bodies shifted until they finally reached the edge of the desk.

Soledad groaned in pain when her back hit the hard floor first, Alexandre landing on top of her second. As the room rotated, Soledad gasped for the faintest of air that her lungs would allow with the extra weight resting on them.

"Get off me," she panted, shoving Alexandre's abdominal bulge.

Alexandre slowly rose to her knees, feeling, now, true discomfort in her womb. She released a low cry when the mere discomfort became intense pain that increased as it crept from the right side of her body to the left.

Grunting and panting her misery, Alexandre muttered, "Some…Something…Something is wrong with the baby."

Soledad loosened the button of the leather sheath at her side and removed her hunting knife. With heartening satisfaction, she boasted, "At least now you will know the hardship of losing a child before you leave this earth."

Alexandre's adrenaline prompted her to ignore her pain and lunge for the firearm that was across her chambers. Once the cold metal was in her hands, she swiftly turned on her back and aimlessly pulled the trigger. Though the shot pierced Soledad's upper thigh, she merely gripped the wound and continued towards Alexandre. She abruptly raised the knife high in the air and-

Quickly aligning her sights, just as Jacob had taught her, Alexandre pulled the trigger two more times. This time, each bullet penetrated her assailant's chest.

Soledad dropped the knife while she fell to her knees. She touched her chest and peered at the blood on her hands. "Y-you sh-

shot m-me." She chuckled in disbelief and repeated, "Y-you—you really sh-shot m-me."

Alexandre gradually rose to her feet, nervously gripping the gun with both hands. "I can be an advocate of capital punishment when it suits the crime," she remarked, finally entertaining and disabusing the accusation that she was soft on crime.

Soledad chuckled once again and then groaned her pain.

Walking to retrieve her cell phone from the place where it had landed on the floor during their struggle, Alexandre breathed through the pains in her womb as she called for assistance.

"9-1-1. What's your emergency?"

"This is Judge Alexandre Denton-Hall," she panted, slowly walking to stand behind a visitor's chair. "I have just been attacked in my chambers at the Mecklenburg Courthouse. Please...please send the police and an ambulance." She looked down at Soledad's near-to-lifeless body and added, "and the coroner."

The acute pain in her abdomen caused Alexandre to drop her phone, and grip the swell of her belly with one hand and the back of the chair with the other. She cried out in excruciating pain. Although she could hear the emergency operator calling out to her, requesting she stay on the line, and assuring that help was on the way, Alexandre could not respond. The pain was overwhelming, rendering her breathless and speechless.

Soledad coughed as she struggled to speak, "All...all I ever wanted...was a life for a life...and, and the life...the life that I wanted yours...But, I-I can be content with...with the loss of your baby f-for the loss of my...my son."

Breathing through her angst, Alexandre asked, "All—all... this for...for your dis—distorted view of...jus-justice?"

Soledad coughed once more as she shook her head. In the final moment of her last breaths, she had nothing more to lose in disclosing the truth. "No...revenge," she admitted at last.

"R-revenge?" Alexandre repeated despite knowing this to be true already. Her education taught her that justice would have been an appeal that would have sought harsher punishment. However, it was her experience that taught her that revenge was the untamed beast that sought to appease its insatiable appetite by its own hands.

"All—all this for revenge?" Alexandre repeated once more, delirious from the pain that started in her womb, but slowly enveloped her whole body. As a result, she began to feel feverish.

When Soledad spoke nothing in response, Alexandre breathlessly panted and then asked, "Was…was this revenge really worth your life?"

Soledad feebly grinned. "O-of c-course—course it was…Revenge is…revenge is sweeter than life."

Alexandre shook her head as she thought of Soledad's remaining children who would survive her death. By the devasting loss of their beloved mother, they will soon possess an increased likelihood of delinquent behavior. These behaviors would eventually bring them before judgment and continually perpetuate until a lifetime of imprisonment or death. Summating all the losses that accompanied revenge, Alexandre concluded that there was nothing sweet about it.

"…If you think that," Alexandre murmured to her, "then you truly are a fool."

She watched Soledad close her eyes and exhale her last breath. Accompanying another sharp wave of pains was the rivulet of warm fluid that trickled down her inner thigh. At the sight of blood on the wood floor, tears flooded Alexandre's eyes. Her maternal intuition unveiled that she was miscarrying her fetus.

She unhurriedly plodded to retrieve her cell phone, terminated the call with the emergency operator, and called the person she knew that would help her through the disappointing loss of her little girl.

"Hi, I'm—I'm Jacob Hall," he greeted after rushing to the hospital's reception desk. Jaamyas was not too far behind them. "My wife called a little over an hour ago and told me to meet her here. She said it was an emergency."

"What's the name?" The male receptionist inquired, peering at the computer screen as he typed on his keyboard.

"Jacob Hall," Jacob repeated in vexation.

The receptionist looked away from the monitor and clarified, "Your wife's name, sir."

"I'm sorry. Alex—Alexandre Denton-Hall."

Jacob anxiously tapped his fingertips on the counter as he awaited a response.

"Are you sure that's the-"

"Try Denton! Try Hall! Try any damn combination—just tell me where my fucking wife is!"

"Sir, please, calm yourself. I cannot help you if you do not calm dow-"

Agitated by the receptionist's lack of urgency, Jacob hollered, "Do not tell me to calm down! My wife is-"

"Delivery room two," announced a nurse approaching the desk. "Denton-Hall?"

Jacob turned in her direction and nodded. "Yes."

"Delivery room two, but hurry. She came in as an ambulatory emergency."

"Is Mom going to be okay?" Jaamyas anxiously inquired in fear.

Jacob pivoted to him and firmly held his shoulders with each of his hands. "She is going to be just fine, Jay, but I need you to be strong and to pray. Okay?"

Jaamyas nodded and recited, "Okay."

"Wait for me in the waiting area and look out for your grandparents—they should be here momentarily." With that, Jacob turned on his heels and dashed to delivery room two.

"Who are you?" The nurse questioned, stopping him at the door as he attempted to enter the room without invitation or permission.

"I'm Jacob Hall, the father—her husband."

The nurse nodded toward the bed. "You're her husband?"

"Yes, she called me about an hour ago saying to meet her here, and that she was in labor." He hastily retrieved his wallet and furnished his identification.

The nurse quickly ushered him into the room and immediately pulled him to the side. As she assisted him into a surgical gown, she apprised, "Both mother and baby are in distress. Mother's blood pressure is dropping and baby's heart rate is increasing." She extended to him a mask, cap, and shoe covers. "She is approximately in her 30th week of gestation and is now fully dilated. So, a c-section at this point is far too risky for the both of them."

After donning the garments she offered him, Jacob thoroughly washed his hands. "Okay. What are our other options?"

"There is only one. She has to push…In order for mother and child to get through this," she peered deep into his eyes and spoke with conviction, "you have to encourage her to push."

Jacob nodded, understanding the seriousness of the matter that she urgently, but calmly, conveyed.

Following his walk to the bedside, he took Alexandre's cold hand into his hand and whispered in her ear, "Alex."

"Jacob," she muttered.

"Yeah, it's me. I'm here."

"I'm so tired…"

"I know you are…You're doing great, though."

"Mr. Hall," the physician called out to him from the opposite end of the bed. "We really need her to start pushing."

Jacob nodded. "Come on, baby, you can do this…On the next contraction, push."

Alexandre pushed through the sharp pangs of anguish until the brief surge of energy left her and she collapsed back into the pillows. She released a somber cry, fretting that, "…Some…something is wrong… Something…something is wrong with the baby…"

The physician glanced at the monitor and confirmed Alexandre's worries. Only her dropping vitals vexed him as well. "We need her to keep pushing," he commanded with anxious frustration.

"Alexandre, please," Jacob pleaded. "Please try again."

She met his eyes and breathlessly spoke, "…J-just…just save the baby."

Though the tears fell from his eyes, he maintained his strength so that she would not give up hope. "No, you can do this...Alex, look at me. Look at me, Alex," he requested when she closed her eyes. He gently tapped her face. "Hey, look at me." When she opened her eyes again, he encouraged, "You can do this, Alexandre." He touched her dry cold lips with his warm moist ones and beseeched, "Please, don't give up...You can do this." As a last attempt to encourage her, he revealed, "Jay is waiting for you."

"...Jaamyas."

Jacob nodded. "Yes, he is in the waiting room with your parents, waiting for you and his little sister."

"We need her to push and keep pushing, or we are going to lose them both."

"Alex, please...please," Jacob implored.

Alexandre held his hand tightly has she pushed mightily through her next contraction. When her energy passed, she collapsed into the pillows. Though her body quivered from the cold temperature in the room, she appreciated the damp, cool cloth the nurse pressed on her feverish head.

"That was a good one," the physician praised. He checked the monitor, rubbed his brow with the back of his gloved hand in distress, and exhaled with nervousness. "Okay, two more like that and you will have brought your daughter into the world."

Alexandre muscled through the last two of her laborious exertions. When she heard the screams of her new daughter, she fell back into the bed and cried. She felt Jacob press his head against hers and cry as well.

"You did it...Thank God you did it." He kissed her forehead, her nose, and then her lips. "I love you so much, Alex...I'm so very proud of you."

Jacob released her hand to cut the umbilical cord and then returned to her side.

"Is...is s-she okay?" Alexandre feebly asked.

He pushed the wet hairs from her face and kissed her forehead another time. "She's fine. They are cleaning her and will bring her right to you."

She trembled from the coolness in the room. "It's...it's so cold in here."

He chuckled at what he believed to be her wit. "I will check in a bit to see how soon before they move you to another room."

Alexandre merely nodded as she fought to control her chattering teeth and quivering lips. The room grew increasingly cold.

"...Jacob...," she muttered, feeling her heartbeat slow and the life within her gradually drift into an abyss.

He kissed the back of her hand and responded, "Yes, baby."

"...Please...," she spoke lowly with the remaining energy she possessed. "...Please, take care of our children..."

Alexandre lowered her lids over her eyes and exhaled slowly.

"...Alex..." Jacob gently tapped her face.

There was no response.

"Alex...Alex. ALEX." In panic, he shook her lifeless body. "ALEX!"

"Doctor, we're losing her!" The nurse exclaimed. "We're losing her!"

As Alexandre's faint heartbeat flatlined, Jacob was shuffled out of the way so that life-saving protocol could commence. "ALEX...ALEX," he cried out over their wailing daughter.

"Mr. Hall, please," a nurse spoke, gently backing him to the door. "We need you to step out of the room so that we can save your wife."

Jacob shoved her hand from his torso, stared deep into her eyes, and vehemently warned, "I'm not going anywhere."

She nervously swallowed the bulge in her throat. "Fine...But, please just stand here—out of the way."

He nodded in concurrence and anxiously observed for several minutes as they vigorously delivered chest compressions, shocks of the defibrillator, and artificial respiration, to no avail.

Despite the penetrating tone of the monitor, wails of the newborn infant, and frantic commotion of the medical practitioners, Jacob heard the physician breathlessly concede, "We have to call it."

Everyone slowed their life-saving efforts to a halt as it was finally announced, "Time of death, 3:16."

About The Author

LaKeisha LaKay is a behavioral and social scientist who has studied in the fields of criminal justice, criminology, sociology, and law. She has spent a number of years examining human behavior, societal issues, and political policies.

Passionate about community, women, and youth, LaKeisha LaKay often spends time volunteering for causes in these realms. Her other interests include spending time with family and friends, foreign travel, reading, playing the piano, and a spectrum of arts and crafts.

LaKeisha LaKay is a former "army brat" who is the eldest of five children. Several years of constant movement and time spent with her childhood (and lifelong) playmates inevitably fuels her imagination. They also drive the vivid delivery of the stories she writes.

LaKeisha LaKay was born in Texas, raised many years in Germany, and lived in several states in America. However, she currently resides in Virginia.

Other works by the author include *The Devil Is In The Details* in which the 2022 New York Book Festival Honorable Mention award and 2022 Eric Hoffer Finalist award have been bestowed.

Share Your Thoughts

Did you enjoy the book? If so, please share your thoughts by writing a review on Good Reads, Amazon, book retail websites, or social media.

You can also connect with the author directly via:

- lakeishalakay@gmail.com

- https://www.amazon.com/author/lakeishalakay

- https://www.facebook.com/lakeisha.l.jones.3

www.ingramcontent.com/pod-product-compliance
Lightning Source LLC
Chambersburg PA
CBHW020639020726
47494CB00001B/257